Silver Threads fall . . .
    and the beautiful, shimmering parasites bring
    black ruin and destruction to Pern.

This is why the great, sensitive dragons of Pern
    hurl themselves through the skies, flaming
    gouts of scorching fire to destroy Thread
    before it can reach the ground.

This is why Pern desperately needs her dragons,
    and her dragonriders—and why no rider
    can afford to fight with another.

For when dragon and rider are one, anger between
    riders can cause desperate agony to the
    great beasts—and a real rift could be
    the deathknell of Pern . . .

Also by Anne McCaffrey
available now from Ballantine Books:

DRAGONFLIGHT

THE SHIP WHO SANG

DECISION AT DOONA

RESTOREE

DRAGONQUEST

Volume 2 of
"The Dragonriders of Pern"

Anne McCaffrey

BALLANTINE BOOKS • NEW YORK

A Del Rey Book
Published by Ballantine Books

Copyright © 1971 by Anne McCaffrey

ISBN 0-345-27063-0-175

Manufactured in the United States of America

First Edition: May 1971
Seventh Printing: January 1977

First Canadian Printing: May 1971

Cover art by Gino D'Achille

CONTENTS

CRAFTMASTERS

Robinton, Masterharper—Fort Hold
  journeymen and apprentices:
  Sebell, Talmor, Brudegan, Tagetarl

Fandarel, Mastersmith—Telgar Hold
  Terry, Craftmaster
  Wansor, Craftmaster

Zurg, Masterweaver—South Boll Hold

Nicat, Masterminer—Crom Hold

Belesden, Mastertanner—Igen Hold

Idarolan, Masterfisher—Tillek Hold

Sograny, Masterherdsman—Keroon Hold

Andemon, Masterfarmer—Nerat Hold

WEYRS

BENDEN WEYR
F'lar, Weyrleader—bronze Mnementh
Lessa, Weyrwoman—Ramoth, queen
F'nor, Wing-second—Canth, brown
N'ton, (craftbred) bronze Lioth
Felessan, born of Lessa, F'lar's son
Manora, head woman of the Lower Caverns
Celina, second queen rider

FORT WEYR (oldest Weyr on Pern)
T'ron, Weyrleader—bronze Fidranth
Mardra, Weyrwoman—Loranth, queen
P'zar, Wing-second—bronze Roth
B'naj—Beth, green
T'reb—Seventh, brown

ISTA WEYR
D'ram, Weyrleader—bronze
Fanna, Weyrwoman—Mirath, queen

TELGAR WEYR
R'mart, Weyrleader—bronze Branth
Bedella, Weyrwoman
M'rek, Wing-second—bronze Gyarmath

IGEN WEYR
G'narish, Weyrleader
Nadira, Weyrwoman

HIGH REACHES WEYR
T'kul, Weyrleader—bronze Salth
Merika, Weyrwoman
Pilgra, second queen rider, Segrith

SOUTHERN WEYR
T'bor, Weyrleader—bronze Orth
Kylara, Weyrwoman—Prideth, queen
Vanira, second queen rider
Brekke, youngest queen rider—Wirenth
Mirrim, Brekke's fosterling

HOLDS

weyrbound to Benden Weyr:
Benden Hold—Lord Holder Raid
Bitra Hold—Lord Holder Sifer
Lemos Hold—Lord Holder Asgenar
Famira, his wife, half-sister to Larad, Lord Holder of Telgar
Bendarek, Crafthall Mastersmith

weyrbound to Fort Weyr:
Fort Hold (oldest Hold on Pern) —Lord Holder Groghe
Ruatha Hold—Lord Holder Jaxom (a minor, in the care of Lord Warder Lytol)
South Boll Hold—Lord Holder Sangel

weyrbound to Ista Weyr:
Ista Hold—Lord Holder Warbret
Igen Hold—Lord Holder Laudey
Nerat Hold—Lord Holder Vincet

weyrbound to Telgar Weyr:
Telgar Hold—Lord Holder Larad
Crom Hold—Lord Holder Nessel

weyrbound to Igen Weyr:
Keroon Hold—Lord Holder Corman
parts of upper Igen Hold
Southern Telgar Hold

weyrbound to High Reaches Weyr:
Nabol Hold, Lord Holder Meron
High Reaches Hold—Lord Holder Bargen
Tillek Hold—Lord Holder Oterel

Pern

LEMOS BITRA

BENDEN

KEROON

IGEN

NERAT

N
W E
S

☐ Plains
▨ Plateau and Tablelands
⌒ Hill lands
⋀ Mountains
〜 Rivers
◠ Lakes
★ Weyrs
● Holds

PRELUDE

Rukbat, in the Sagittarian Sector, was a golden G-type star. It had five planets, two asteroid belts, and a stray planet it had attracted and held in recent millennia. When men first settled on Rukbat's third world and called it Pern, they had taken little notice of the stranger planet, swinging around its adopted primary in a wildly erratic elliptical orbit. For two generations, the colonists gave the bright red star little thought—until the desperate path of the wanderer brought it close to its stepsister at perihelion.

When such aspects were harmonious and not distorted by conjunctions with other planets in the system, the indigenous life of the wanderer sought to bridge the space gap to the more temperate and hospitable planet.

The initial losses the colonists suffered were staggering, and it was during the subsequent long struggle to survive and combat this menace dropping through Pern's skies like silver threads that Pern's tenuous contact with the mother planet was broken.

To control the incursions of the dreadful Threads (for the Pernese had cannibalized their transport ships early on and abandoned such technological sophistication as was irrelevant to this pastoral planet), the resourceful men embarked on a long-term plan. The first phase involved breeding a highly specialized variety of a life-form indigenous to their new world. Men and women with high empathy ratings and some innate telepathic ability were trained to use and preserve these unusual animals. The "dragons" (named for the mythical Terran beast they resembled) had two extremely useful characteristics: they could get from one place to another instantly and, after chewing a phosphine-bearing rock, they could emit a flaming gas. As the dragons could "fly," they'd be able to char Thread mid-air, yet escape its worse ravages themselves. It took generations to develop to the full the use of this first phase. The second phase of the proposed defense against the spore incursions would take longer to mature. For Thread, a space-traveling mycorrhizoid spore, devoured organic matter with mindless voracity and, once grounded, burrowed and proliferated with terrifying speed.

The originators of the two-stage defense program did not compensate sufficiently for chance nor for the psychological effect of visible extermination of this avid foe. For it was psychologically reassuring and deeply satisfying to the endangered Pernese to see the menace charred to impotence in mid-air. Also, the southern continent, where the second phase was initiated, proved untenable and the entire colony was moved to the northern continent to seek refuge from the Threads in the natural caves of the northern mountain ranges. The significance of the southern hemisphere lost meaning in the immediate struggle to establish new settlements in the north. Recollections of Earth receded further from Pernese history with each successive generation until memory of their origins degenerated past legend or myth and into oblivion.

The original Fort constructed in the eastern face of the great West Mountain range soon grew too small to hold the colonists. Another settlement was started slightly to the north, by a great lake conveniently nestled near a cave-filled cliff. Ruatha Hold, too, became overcrowded in a few generations.

Since the Red Star rose in the East, it was decided to start a holding in the eastern mountains, provided suitable accomodations could be found. Suitable accommodations now meant caves, for only solid rock and metal (of which Pern was in distressingly light supply) were impervious to the burning score of Thread.

The winged, tailed, fiery-breathed dragons had now been

bred to a size which required more space than the cliffside Holds could provide. The ancient cave-pocked cones of extinct volcanoes, one high above the first Fort, the other in the Benden mountains, proved to be adequate, needing only a few improvements to be made habitable. However, such projects took the last of the fuel for the great stonecutters (which had been programmed for only diffident mining operations, not wholesale cliff excavations), and subsequent holds and weyrs were hand-hewn.

The dragons and the riders in their high places and the people in their caves went about their separate tasks and each developed habits that became custom, which solidified into tradition as incontrovertible as law.

Then came an interval—of two hundred Turns of the planet Pern around its primary—when the Red Star was at the other end of its erratic orbit, a frozen, lonely captive. No Thread fell on Pern's soil. The inhabitants began to enjoy life as they had thought to find it when they first landed on the lovely planet. They erased the depredations of Thread and grew crops, planted orchards, thought of reforestry for the slopes denuded by Thread. They could even forget that they had been in grave danger of extinction. Then the Threads returned for another orbit around the lush planet—fifty years of danger from the skies—and the Pernese again thanked their ancestors, now many generations removed, for providing the dragons who seared the dropping Thread mid-air with their fiery breath.

Dragonkind, too, had prospered during that interval; had settled in four other locations, following the master plan of interim defense. Men managed to forget completely that there had been a secondary measure against Thread.

By the third Pass of the Red Star, a complicated sociopolitical-economic structure had been developed to deal with this recurrent evil. The six Weyrs, as the old volcanic habitations of the dragonfolk were called, pledged themselves to protect all Pern, each Weyr having a geographical section of the northern continent literally under its wings. The rest of the population would tithe to support the Weyrs since these fighters, these dragonmen, did not have any arable land in their volcanic homes, nor could they take time away from the nurture of dragonkind to learn other trades during peacetime, nor time away from protecting the planet during Passes.

Settlements, called Holds, developed wherever natural caves were found; some, of course, more extensive or strategically placed than others. It took a strong man to hold frantic, terrified people in control during Thread attacks; it took wise administration to conserve victuals when nothing could safely be grown, and extraordinary measures to control population and keep it useful and healthy until such time as the menace had passed. Men with special skills in metalworking, animal breeding, farming, fishing, mining (such as there was), weaving, formed Crafthalls in each large Hold and looked to one Mastercrafthall where the precepts of their craft were taught, and craft skills preserved and guarded from one generation to another. So that one Lord Holder could not deny the products of the Crafthall situated in his Hold to others of the planet, the Crafts were decreed independent of a Hold affiliation, each Craftmaster of a hall owing allegiance to the Master of that particular craft (an elected office based on proficiency and administrative ability). The Mastercraftsman was responsible for the output of his halls, the distribution, fair and unprejudiced, of all craft products on a planetary rather than parochial basis.

Certain rights and privileges accrued to the different leaders of Holds and Masters of Crafts, and naturally, to the dragonriders to whom all Pern looked for protection during Threadfalls.

The Red Star would swing inexorably close to Pern, but it would also Pass again, and life could settle into a less frenzied pattern. Occasionally, the conjunction of Rukbat's natural five satellites would prevent the Red Star from passing close enough to Pern to drop its fearful spores. Sometimes, though, as siblings will, Pern's sister planets seemed to draw the Red Star closer still and Thread rained relentlessly on the unfortunate victim. Fear creates fanatics and the Pernese were no exception. Only the dragonmen could save Pern, and their position in the structure of the planet became inviolable.

Mankind has a history of forgetting the unpleasant, the undesirable. By ignoring its existence, it can make the source of past Terror disappear. And the Red Star did not pass close enough to Pern to drop its Threads. The people prospered and multiplied, spreading out across the rich land, carving more holds out of solid rock, and so busy with their pursuits, that they did not realize that there were only a few dragons in the skies, and only one Weyr of dragonriders left on Pern. The Red Star wasn't due back for a long, long while. Why worry about such distant possibilities? In five generations or so, the descendants of the heroic dragonmen fell into disfavor. The legends of past braveries and the very reason for their existence fell into disrepute.

When, in the course of natural forces, the Red Star began to spin closer to Pern, winking with a baleful red eye on its intended, ancient victim, one man, F'lar, rider of the bronze dragon, Mnementh, believed that the ancient tales had truth in them. His half-brother, F'nor, rider of brown Canth, listened to his arguments and found belief in them more exciting than the dull ways of the lone Weyr of Pern. When the last golden egg of a dying queen dragon lay hardening on the Benden Weyr Hatching Ground, F'lar and F'nor seized this opportunity to gain control of the Weyr. Searching through Ruatha Hold for a strong woman to ride the soon-to-be hatched young queen, F'lar and F'nor discovered Lessa, the only surviving member of the proud Bloodline of Ruatha Hold. She Impressed young Ramoth, the new queen, and became Weyrwoman of Benden Weyr. When F'lar's bronze Mnementh flew the young queen in her first mating, F'lar became Weyrleader of Pern's remaining dragonmen. The three riders, F'lar, Lessa and F'nor forced the Lord Holders and Craftsmen to recognize their imminent danger and prepare the almost defenseless planet against Thread. But it was distressingly obvious that the scant two hundred dragons of Benden Weyr could not defend the sprawling settlements. Six full Weyrs had been needed in the olden days when the settled land had been much smaller. In learning to direct her queen dragon *between* one place and another, Lessa discovered that dragons could teleport *between* time as well. Risking her life as well as Pern's only queen dragon, Lessa and Ramoth went back in time, four hundred Turns, before the mysterious disappearance of the other five Weyrs, just after the last Pass of the Red Star had been completed.

The five Weyrs, seeing only the decline of their prestige and bored with inactivity after a lifetime of exciting combat, agreed to help Lessa's Weyr and came forward to her Turn.

Seven Turns have now passed since that triumphant journey forward, and the initial gratitude of the Holds and Crafts to the rescuing Oldtime Weyrs has faded and soured. And the Oldtimers themselves do not like the Pern in which they are now living. Four hundred Turns brought too many subtle changes, and dissensions mount.

CHAPTER I

Morning at Mastercrafthall, Fort Hold
Several Afternoons Later at Benden Weyr
Midmorning (Telgar Time) at
Mastersmithcrafthall, Telgar Hold

How to begin? mused Robinton, the Masterharper of Pern.
He frowned thoughtfully down at the smoothed, moist sand
in the shallow trays of his workdesk. His long face settled
into deep-grooved lines and creases, and his eyes, usually
snapping blue with inner amusement, were gray-shadowed
with unusual gravity.

He fancied the sand begged to be violated with words
and notes while he, Pern's repository and glib dispenser of
any ballad, saga or ditty, was inarticulate. Yet he had to
construct a ballad for the upcoming wedding of Lord Asgenar of Lemos Hold to the half-sister of Lord Larad of Telgar Hold. Because of recent reports of unrest from his

1

network of drummers and Harper journeymen, Robinton had decided to remind the guests on this auspicious occasion— for every Lord Holder and Craftmaster would be invited—of the debt they owed the dragonmen of Pern. As the subject of his ballad, he had decided to tell of the fantastic ride, *between* time itself, of Lessa, Weyrwoman of Benden Weyr on her great golden queen, Ramoth. The Lords and Craftsmen of Pern had been glad enough then for the arrival of dragonriders from the five ancient Weyrs from four hundred Turns in the past.

Yet how to reduce those fascinating, frantic days, those braveries, to a rhyme? Even the most stirring chords could not recapture the beat of the blood, the catch of breath, the chill of fear and the hopeless surge of hope of that first morning after Thread had fallen over Nerat Hold; when F'lar had rallied all the frightened Lords and Craftmasters at Benden Weyr and enlisted their enthusiastic aid.

It had not been just a sudden resurgence of forgotten loyalties that had prompted the Lords, but the all too real sense of disaster as they envisioned their prosperous acres blackened with the Thread they had dismissed as myth, of the thought of burrows of the lightning propagating parasites, of themselves walled up in the cliff-Holds behind thick metal doors and shutters. They'd been ready to promise F'lar their souls that day if he could protect them from Thread. And it was Lessa who had bought them that protection, almost with her life.

Robinton looked up from the sandtrays, his expression suddenly bleak.

"The sand of memory dries quickly," he said softly, looking out across the settled valley toward the precipice that housed Fort Hold. There was one watchman on the fire ridges. There ought to be six, but it was planting time; Lord Holder Groghe of Fort Hold had everyone who could walk upright in the fields, even the gangs of children who were supposed to weed spring grass from stone interstices and pull moss from the walls. Last spring, Lord Groghe would not have neglected that duty no matter how many dragonlengths of land he wanted to put under seed.

Lord Groghe was undoubtedly out in the fields right now, prowling from one tract of land to another on one of those long-legged running beasts which the Masterherdsman Sograny was developing. Groghe of Fort Hold was indefatigable, his slightly protruberant blue eyes never missing an unpruned tree or a badly harrowed row. He was a burly man, with grizzled hair which he wore tied in a neat band. His complexion was florid, with a temper to match. But, if he pushed his holders, he pushed himself as well, demanding nothing of his people, his children nor his fosterlings that he was not able to do himself. If he was conservative in his thinking, it was because he knew his own limitations and felt secure in that knowledge.

Robinton pulled at his lower lip, wondering if Lord Groghe was an exception in his disregard for this traditional Hold duty of removing all greenery near habitations. Or was this Lord Groghe's answer to Fort Weyr's growing agitation over the immense forest lands of Fort Hold which the dragonriders ought to protect? The Weyrleader of Fort Weyr, T'ron, and his Weyrwoman, Mardra, had become less scrupulous about checking to see that no Thread burrows had escaped their wing riders to fall on the lush forests. Yet Lord Groghe had been scrupulous in the matter of ground crews and flamethrowing equipment when Thread fell over his forests. He had a stable of runners spread out through the Hold in an efficient network so that if dragonriders were competent in flight, there was adequate ground coverage for any Thread that might elude the flaming breath of the airborne beasts.

But Robinton had heard ugly rumors of late, and not just from Fort Hold. Since he eventually heard every derogatory whisper and accusation uttered in Pern, he had learned to separate fact from spite, calumny from crime. Not basically an alarmist, because he'd found much sifted itself out in the course of time, Robinton was beginning to feel the stirrings of alarm in his soul.

The Masterharper slumped in his chair, staring out on the bright day, the fresh new green of the fields, the yellow blossoms on the fruit trees, the neat stone Holds that lined the road up to the main Hold, the cluster of artisans' cotholds below the wide ramp up to the Great Outer Court of Fort Hold.

And if his suspicions were valid, what could he do? Write a scolding song? A satire? Robinton snorted. Lord Groghe was too literal a man to interpret satire and too righteous to take a scold. Furthermore, and Robinton pushed himself upright on his elbows, if Lord Groghe was neglectful, it was in protest at Weyr neglect of far greater magnitude. Robinton shuddered to think of Thread burrowing in the great stands of softwoods to the south.

He ought to sing his remonstrances to Mardra and T'ron as Weyrleaders—but that, too, would be vain effort. Mardra had soured lately. She ought to have sense enough to retire gracefully to a chair and let men seek her favors if T'ron no longer attracted her. To hear the Hold girls talk, T'ron was lusty enough. In fact, T'ron had better restrain himself. Lord Groghe didn't take kindly to too many of his chattels bearing dragonseed.

Another impasse, thought Robinton with a wry smile. Hold customs differed so from Weyr morals. Maybe a word to F'lar of Benden Weyr? Useless, again. In the first place there was really nothing the bronze rider could do. Weyrs were autonomous and not only could T'ron take umbrage for any advice F'lar might see fit to offer, but Robinton was sure that F'lar might tend to take the Lord Holders' side.

This was not the first time in recent months that Robinton regretted that F'lar of Benden Weyr had been so eager to relinquish his leadership after Lessa had gone back *between* to bring the five lost Weyrs forward in time. For a brief few months then, seven Turns ago, Pern had been united under F'lar and Lessa against the ancient menace of Thread. Every Holder, Craftmaster, landsman, crafter, all had been of one mind. That unity had dissipated as the Oldtime Weyrleaders had reasserted their traditional domination over the Holds bound to their Weyr for protection, and a grateful Pern had ceded them those rights. But in four hundred Turns the interpretation of that old hegemony had altered, with neither party sure of the translation.

Perhaps now was the time to remind Lord Holders of those perilous days seven Turns ago when all their hopes hung on fragile dragon wings and the dedication of a scant two hundred men.

Well, the Harper has a duty, too, by the Egg, Robinton thought, needlessly smoothing the wet sand. And the obligation to broadcast it.

In twelve days, Larad, Lord of Telgar, was giving his half-sister, Famira, to Asgenar, Lord of Lemos Hold. The Masterharper had been enjoined to appear with appropriate new songs to enliven the festivities. F'lar and Lessa were invited as Lemos Hold was weyrbound to Benden Weyr. There'd be other notables among Weyr, Lord and Craft to signalize so auspicious an occasion.

"And among my jolly songs, I'll have stronger meat."

Chuckling to himself at the prospect, Robinton picked up his stylus.

"I must have a tender but intricate theme for Lessa. She's legend already." Unconsciously the Harper smiled as he pictured the dainty, child-sized Weyrwoman, with her white skin, her cloud of dark hair, the flash of her gray eyes, heard the acerbity of her clever tongue. No man of Pern failed of respect for her, or braved her displeasure, with the exception of F'lar.

Now a well-stated martial theme would do for Benden's Weyrleader, with his keen amber eyes, his unconscious superiority, the intense energy of his lean fighter's frame. Could he, Robinton, rouse F'lar from his detachment? Or was he perhaps unnecessarily worried about these minor irritations between Lord Holder and Weyrleader? But without the dragonriders of Pern, the land would be sucked dry of any sustenance by Thread, even if every man, woman and child of the planet were armed with flame throwers. One burrow, well established, could race across plain and forest as fast as a dragon could fly it, consuming everything that grew or lived, save solid rock, water or metal. Robinton shook his head, annoyed with his own fancies. As if dragonmen would ever desert Pern and their ancient obligation.

Now—a solid beat on the biggest drum for Fandarel, the Mastersmith, with his endless curiosity, the great hands with their delicate skill, the ranging mind in its eternal quest for efficiency. Somehow one expected such an immense man to be as slow of wit as he was deliberate of physical movement.

A sad note, well sustained, for Lytol who had once ridden a Benden dragon and lost his Larth in an accident in the Spring Games—had it been fourteen or fifteen Turns ago? Lytol had left the Weyr—to be among dragonfolk only exacerbated his tremendous loss—and taken to the craft of weaving. He'd been Crafthall Master in the High Reaches Hold when F'lar had discovered Lessa on Search. F'lar had appointed Lytol to be Lord Warder of Ruatha Hold when Lessa had abdicated her claim to the Hold to young Jaxom.

And how did a man signify the dragons of Pern? No theme was grand enough for those huge, winged beasts, as gentle as they were great, Impressed at Hatching by the men who rode them, flaming against Thread, who tended them, loved them, who were linked, mind to mind, in an unbreakable bond that transcended speech! (What was that really like? Robinton wondered, remembering that his youthful ambition had been to be a dragonman.) The dragons of Pern who could transfer themselves in some mysterious fashion *between* one place and another in the blink of an eye. *Between* even one Time and another!

The Harper's sigh came from his soul but his hand moved to the sand and pressed out the first note, wrote the first word, wondering if he would find some answer himself in the song.

He had barely filled the completed score with clay to preserve the text, when he heard the first throb of the drum. He strode quickly to the small outer court of the Crafthall, bending his head to catch the summons; it was his sequence all right, in urgent tempo. He concentrated so closely on the drumroll that he did not realize that every other sound common to the Harper's Hall had ceased.

"Thread?" His throat dried instantly. Robinton didn't need to consult the timetable to realize that the Threads were falling on the shores of Tillek Hold prematurely.

Across the valley on Fort Hold's ramparts, the single watchman made his monotonous round, oblivious to disaster.

There was a soft spring warmth to the afternoon air as F'nor and his big, brown Canth emerged from their weyr in Benden Weyr. F'nor yawned slightly and stretched until he heard his spine crack. He'd been on the western coast all the previous day, Searching for likely lads—and girls, since there was a golden egg hardening on the Benden Weyr Hatching Grounds—for the next Impression. Benden Weyr certainly produced more dragons, and more queens, than the five Oldtimers' Weyrs, F'nor thought.

"Hungry?" he asked courteously of his dragon, glancing down the Weyr Bowl to the Feeding Grounds. No dragons were dining and the herdbeasts stood in their fenced pasture, legs spraddled, heads level with their bony knees as they drowsed in the sunlight.

Sleepy, said Canth, although he had slept as long and deeply as his rider. The brown dragon proceeded to settle himself on the sun-warmed ledge, sighing as he sank down.

"Slothful wretch," F'nor said, grinning affectionately at his beast.

The sun was full on the other side of the enormous mountain cup that formed the dragonman's habitation on the eastern coast of Pern. The cliffside was patterned with the black mouths of the individual dragon weyrs, starred where sun flashed off mica in the rocks. The waters of the Weyr's spring-fed lake glistened around the two green dragons bathing as their riders lounged on the grass verge. Beyond, in front of the weyrling barracks, young riders formed a semicircle around the Weyrlingmaster.

F'nor's grin broadened. He stretched his lean body indolently, remembering his own weary hours in such a semicircle, twenty odd Turns ago. The rote lessons which he had echoed as a weyrling had far more significance to this present group of dragonriders. In his Turn, the Silver Thread of those teaching songs had not dropped from the Red Star for over four hundred Turns, to sear the flesh of man and beast and devour anything living which grew on Pern. Of all the dragonmen in Pern's lone Weyr, only F'nor's half-brother, F'lar, bronze Mnementh's rider, had believed that there might be truth in those old legends. Now Thread was an inescapable fact, falling to Pern from the skies with diurnal regularity. Once more, its destruction was a way of life for dragonriders. The lessons these lads learned would save their skins, their lives and, more important, their dragons.

The weyrlings are promising, Canth remarked as he locked his wings to his back and curled his tail against his hind legs. He settled his great head to his forelegs, the many-faceted eye nearest F'nor gleaming softly on his rider.

Responding to the tacit plea, F'nor scratched the eye ridge until Canth began to hum softly with pleasure.

"Lazybones!"

When I work, I work, Canth replied. *Without my help, how would you know which holdbred lad would make a good dragonrider? And do I not find girls who make good queen riders, too?*

F'nor laughed indulgently, but it was true that Canth's ability to spot likely candidates for fighting dragons and breeding queens was much vaunted by Benden Weyr dragonmen.

Then F'nor frowned, remembering the odd hostility of the small holders and crafters he'd encountered in Southern Boll's Holds and Crafts. Yes, the people had been hostile until—until he'd identified himself as a Benden Weyr dragonrider. He'd have thought it'd be the other way round. Southern Boll was weyrbound to Fort Weyr. Traditionally—and F'nor grinned wryly since the Fort Weyrleader, T'ron, was so adamant in upholding all that was traditional, customary . . . and static —traditionally, the Weyr which protected a territory had first claim on any possible riders. But the five Oldtime Weyrs rarely sought beyond their own Lower Caverns for candidates. Of course, thought F'nor, the Oldtime queens didn't produce large clutches like the modern queens, nor many golden queen eggs. Come to think on it, only three queens had been Hatched in the Oldtime Weyrs in the seven Turns since Lessa brought them forward.

Well, let the Oldtimers stick to their ways if that made them feel superior. But F'nor agreed with F'lar. It was only common sense to give your dragonets as wide a choice as possible. Though the women in the Lower Caverns of Benden Weyr were certainly agreeable, there simply weren't enough weyrborn lads to match up the quantity of dragons hatched.

Now, if one of the other Weyrs, maybe G'narish of Igen Weyr or R'mart of Telgar Weyr, would throw open their junior queens' mating flights, the Oldtimers might notice an improvement in size of clutch and the dragons that hatched. A man was a fool to breed only to his own Bloodlines all the time.

The afternoon breeze shifted and brought with it the pungent fumes of numbweed a-boil. F'nor groaned. He'd forgotten that the women were making numbweed for salve that was the universal remedy for the burn of Thread and other painful afflictions. That had been one main reason for going on Search yesterday. The odor of numbweed was pervasive. Yesterday's breakfast had tasted medicinal instead of cereal. Since the preparation of numbweed salve was a tedious as well as smelly process, most dragonmen made themselves scarce during its manufacture. F'nor glanced across the Weyr Bowl to the queen's weyr. Ramoth, of course, was in the Hatching Ground, hovering over her latest clutch of eggs, but bronze Mnementh was absent from his accustomed perch on the ledge. F'lar and he were off somewhere, no doubt escaping the smell of numbweed as well as Lessa's uncertain temper. She conscientiously took part in even the most onerous duties of Weyrwoman, but that didn't mean she had to like them.

Numbweed stink notwithstanding, F'nor was hungry. He hadn't eaten since late afternoon yesterday, and, since there was a good six hours' time difference between Southern Boll on the western coast and Benden Weyr in the east, he'd missed the dinner hour at Benden Weyr completely.

With a parting scratch, F'nor told Canth that he'd get some food, and started down the stone ramp from his ledge. One of the privileges of being Wing-second was choice of quarters. Since Ramoth as senior queen would permit only two junior queens in Benden Weyr, there were two unoccupied Weyrwoman quarters. F'nor had appropriated one and did not need to disturb Canth when he wished to descend to a lower level.

As he approached the entrance of the Lower Caverns, the aroma of boiling numbweed made his eyes smart. He'd grab some *klah*, bread and fruit and go listen to the Weyrlingmaster. They were upwind. As Wing-second, F'nor liked to take every opportunity to measure up the new riders, particularly those who were not weyrbred. Life in a Weyr required certain adjustments for the craft and holdbred. The freedom and privileges sometimes went to a boy's head, particularly after he was able to take his dragon *between*—anywhere on Pern —in the space it takes to count to three. Again, F'nor agreed with F'lar's preference in presenting older lads at Impression though the Oldtimers deplored that practice at Benden Weyr, too. But, by the Shell, a lad in his late teens recognized the responsibility of his position (even if he were holdbred) as a dragonrider. He was more emotionally mature and, while there was no lessening of the impact of Impression with his dragon, he could absorb and understand the implications of a lifelong link, of an in-the-soul contact, the total empathy between himself and his dragon. An older boy didn't get carried away. He knew enough to compensate until his dragonet's instinctive sensibility unfolded. A baby dragon had precious little sense and, if some silly weyrling let his beast eat too much, the whole Weyr suffered through its torment. Even an older beast lived for the here and now, with little thought for the future and not all that much recollection—except on the instinctive level—for the past. That was just as well, F'nor

9

thought. For dragons bore the brunt of Thread-score. Perhaps if their memories were more acute or associative, they'd refuse to fight.

F'nor took a deep breath and, blinking furiously against the fumes, entered the huge kitchen Cavern. It was seething with activity. Half the female population of the Weyr must be involved in this operation, F'nor thought, for great cauldrons monopolized all the large hearths set in the outside wall of the Cavern. Women were seated at the broad tables, washing and cutting the roots from which the salve was extracted. Some were ladling the boiling product into great earthenware pots. Those who stirred the concoction with long-handled paddles wore masks over nose and mouth and bent frequently to blot eyes watering from the acrid fumes. Older children were fetching and carrying, fuelrock from the store caves for the fires, pots to the cooling caves. Everyone was busy.

Fortunately the nighthearth, nearest the entrance, was operating for normal use, the huge *klah* pot and stew kettle swinging from their hooks, keeping warm over the coals. Just as F'nor had filled his cup, he heard his name called. Glancing around, he saw his blood mother, Manora, beckon to him. Her usually serene face wore a look of puzzled concern.

Obediently F'nor crossed to the hearth where she, Lessa, and another young woman who looked familiar though F'nor couldn't place her, were examining a small kettle.

"My duty to you, Lessa, Manora—" and he paused, groping for the third name.

"You ought to remember Brekke, F'nor," Lessa said, raising her eyebrows at his lapse.

"How can you expect anyone to see in a place dense with fumes?" F'nor demanded, making much of blotting his eyes on his sleeve. "I haven't seen much of you, Brekke, since the day Canth and I brought you from your crafthold to Impress young Wirenth."

"F'nor, you're as bad as F'lar," Lessa exclaimed, somewhat testily. "You never forget a dragon's name, but his rider's?"

"How fares Wirenth, Brekke?" F'nor asked, ignoring Lessa's interruption.

The girl looked startled but managed a hesitant smile, then pointedly looked towards Manora, trying to turn attention from herself. She was a shade too thin for F'nor's tastes, not much taller than Lessa whose diminutive size in no way lessened the authority and respect she commanded. There was however, a sweetness about Brekke's solemn face, unexpectedly framed with dark curly hair, that F'nor did find appealing. And he liked her self-effacing modesty. He was wondering how she got along with Kylara, the tempestuous and irresponsible senior Weyrwoman at Southern Weyr, when Lessa tapped the empty pot before her.

"Look at this, F'nor. The lining has cracked and the entire kettle of numbweed salve is discolored."

F'nor whistled appreciatively.

"Would you know what it is the Smith uses to coat the metal?" Manora asked. "I wouldn't dare use tainted salve, and yet I hate to discard so much if there's no reason."

F'nor tipped the pot to the light. The dull tan lining was seamed by fine cracks along one side.

"See what it does to the salve?" and Lessa thrust a small bowl at him.

The anesthetic ointment, normally a creamy, pale yellow, had turned a reddish tan. Rather a threatening color, F'nor thought. He smelled it, dipped his finger in and felt the skin immediately deaden.

"It works," he said with a shrug.

"Yes, but what would happen to an open Thread score with that foreign substance cooked into the salve?" asked Manora.

"Good point. What does F'lar say?"

"Oh, him." Lessa screwed her fine delicate features into a grimace. "He's off to Lemos Hold to see how that woodcraftsman of Lord Asgenar's is doing with the wood pulp leaves."

F'nor grinned. "Never around when you want him, huh, Lessa?"

She opened her mouth for a stinging reply, her gray eyes snapping, and then realized that F'nor was teasing.

"You're as bad as he is," she said, grinning up at the tall Wing-second who resembled her Weyrmate so closely. Yet the two men, though the stamp of their mutual sire was apparent in the thick shocks of black hair, the strong features, the lean rangy bodies (F'nor had a squarer, broader frame with not enough flesh on his bones so that he appeared unfinished), the two men were different in temperament and personality. F'nor was less introspective and more easygoing than his half brother, F'lar, the elder by three Turns. The Weyrwoman sometimes found herself treating F'nor as if he were an extension of his half brother and, perhaps for this reason, could joke and tease with him. She was not on easy terms with many people.

F'nor returned her smile and gave her a mocking little bow for the compliment.

"Well, I've no objections to running your errand to the Mastersmithhall. I'm supposed to be Searching and I can Search in Telgar Hold as well as anywhere else. R'mart's nowhere near as sticky as some of the other Oldtime Weyrleaders." He took the pot off the hook, peering into it once more, than glanced around the busy room, shaking his head. "I'll take your pot to Fandarel but it looks to me as though you've already got enough numbweed to coat every dragon in all six—excuse me—seven Weyrs." He grinned at Brekke for the girl seemed curiously ill at ease. Lessa could be snap-tempered when she was preoccupied and Ramoth was fussing over her latest clutch like a novice—which would tend to make Lessa more irritable. Strange for a junior Weyrwoman from Southern Weyr to be involved in any brewing at Benden.

"A Weyr can't have too much numbweed," Manora said briskly.

"That isn't the only pot that's showing cracks, either," Lessa cut in, testily. "And if we've got to gather more numbweed to make up what we've lost . . ."

"There's the second crop at the Southern Weyr," Brekke suggested, then looked flustered for speaking up.

But the look Lessa turned on Brekke was grateful. "I've no intention of shorting you, Brekke, when Southern Weyr does the nursing of every fool who can't dodge Thread."

"I'll take the pot. I'll take the pot," F'nor cried with humorous assurance. "But first, I've got to have more in me than a cup of *klah*."

Lessa blinked at him, her glance going to the entrance and the late afternoon sun slanting in on the floor.

"It's only just past noon in Telgar Hold," he said, patiently. "Yesterday I was all day Searching at Southern Boll so I'm hours behind myself." He stifled a yawn.

"I'd forgotten. Any luck?"

"Canth didn't twitch an ear. Now let me eat and get away from the stink. Don't know how you stand it."

Lessa snorted. "Because I can't stand the groans when you riders don't have numbweed."

F'nor grinned down at his Weyrwoman, aware that Brekke's eyes were wide in amazement at their good-natured banter. He was sincerely fond of Lessa as a person, not just as Weyrwoman of Benden's senior queen. He heartily approved of F'lar's permanent attachment of Lessa, not that there seemed much chance that Ramoth would ever permit any dragon but Mnementh to fly her. As Lessa was a superb Weyrwoman for Benden Weyr, so F'lar was the logical bronze rider. They were well matched as Weyrwoman and Weyrleader, and Benden Weyr—and Pern—profited. So did the three Holds bound to Benden for protection. Then F'nor remembered the hostility of the people at Southern Boll yesterday until they learned that he was a Benden rider. He started to mention this to Lessa when Manora broke his train of thought.

"I am very disturbed by this discoloration, F'nor," she said. "Here. Show Mastersmith Fandarel these," and she put two small pots into the larger vessel. "He can see exactly the change that occurs. Brekke, would you be kind enough to serve F'nor?"

"No need," F'nor said hastily and backed away, pot swinging from his hand. He used to be annoyed that Manora, who was only his mother, could never rid herself of the notion that he was incapable of doing for himself. She was certainly quick enough to make her fosterlings fend for themselves, as his foster mother had made him.

"Don't drop the pot when you go *between*, F'nor," was her parting admonition.

F'nor chuckled to himself. Once a mother, always a mother, he guessed, for Lessa was as broody about Felessan, the only child she'd borne. Just as well the Weyrs practiced fostering. Felessan—as likely a lad to Impress a bronze dragon as F'nor had seen in all his Turns at Searching—got along far better with his placid foster mother than he would have with Lessa had she had the rearing of him.

As he ladled out a bowl of stew, F'nor wondered at the perversity of women. Girls were constantly pleading to come to Benden Weyr. They'd not be expected to bear child after child till they were worn-out and old. Women in the Weyrs remained active and appealing. Manora had seen twice the Turns that, for instance, Lord Sifer of Bitra's latest wife had, yet Manora looked younger. Well, a rider preferred to seek his own loves, not have them foisted on him. There were enough spare women in the Lower Caverns right now.

The *klah* might as well be medicine. He couldn't drink it. He quickly ate the stew, trying not to taste his food. Perhaps he could pick something up at Smithcrafthall at Telgar Hold.

"Canth! Manora's got an errand for us," he warned the brown dragon as he strode from the Lower Cavern. He wondered how the women stood the smell.

Canth did, too, for the fumes had kept him from napping on the warm ledge. He was just as glad of an excuse to get away from Benden Weyr.

F'nor broke out into the early morning sunshine above Telgar Hold, then directed brown Canth up the long valley to the sprawling complex of buildings on the left of the Falls.

Sun flashed off the water wheels which were turned endlessly by the powerful waters of the three-pronged Falls and operated the forges of the Smithy. Judging by the thin black smoke from the stone buildings, the smelting and refining smithies were going at full capacity.

As Canth swooped lower, F'nor could see the distant clouds of dust that meant another ore train coming from the last portage of Telgar's major river. Fandarel's notion of putting wheels on the barges had halved the time it took to get raw ore downriver and across land from the deep mines of Crom and Telgar to the crafthalls throughout Pern.

Canth gave a bugle cry of greeting which was instantly answered by the two dragons, green and brown, perched on a small ledge above the main Crafthall.

Beth and Seventh from Fort Weyr, Canth told his rider, but the names were not familiar to F'nor.

Time was when a man knew every dragon and rider in Pern.

"Are you joining them?" he asked the big brown.

They are together, Canth replied so pragmatically that F'nor chuckled to himself.

The green Beth, then, had agreed to brown Seventh's advances. Looking at her brilliant color, F'nor thought their riders shouldn't have brought that pair away from their home Weyr at this phase. As F'nor watched, the brown dragon extended his wing and covered the green possessively.

F'nor stroked Canth's downy neck at the first ridge but the

14

dragon didn't seem to need any consolation. He'd no lack of partners after all, thought F'nor with little conceit. Greens would prefer a brown who was as big as most bronzes on Pern.

Canth landed and F'nor jumped off quickly. The dust made by his dragon's wings set up twin whirls, through which F'nor had to walk. In the open sheds which F'nor passed on his way to the Crafthall, men were busy at a number of tasks, most of them familiar to the brown rider. But at one shed he stopped, trying to fathom why the sweating men were winding a coil of metal through a plate, until he realized that the material was extruded as a fine wire. He was about to ask questions when he saw the sullen, closed expressions of the crafters. He nodded pleasantly and continued on his way, uneasy at the indifference—no, the distaste—exhibited at his presence. He was beginning to wish that he hadn't agreed to do Manora's errand.

But Smithcraftmaster Fandarel was the obvious authority on metal and could tell why the big kettle had suddenly discolored the vital anesthesic salve. F'nor swung the kettle to make sure the two sample pots were within, and grinned at the self-conscious gesture; for an instant he had a resurgence of his boyhood apprehension of losing something entrusted to him.

The entrance to the main Smithcrafthall was imposing: four landbeasts could be driven abreast through that massive portal and not scrape their sides. Did Pern breed Smithcraft-masters in proportion to that door? F'nor wondered as its maw swallowed him, for the immense metal wings stood wide. What had been the original Smithy was now converted to the artificers' use. At lathes and benches, men were polishing, engraving, adding the final touches to otherwise completed work. Sunlight streamed in from the windows set high in the building's wall, the eastern shutters were burnished with the morning sun which reflected also from the samples of weaponry and metalwork in the open shelves in the center of the big Hall.

At first, F'nor thought it was his entrance which had halted all activity, but then he made out two dragonriders who were menacing Terry. Surprised as he was to feel the tension in the Hall, F'nor was more disturbed that Terry was its brunt, for the man was Fandarel's second and his major innovator. Without a thought, F'nor strode across the floor, his bootheels striking sparks from the flagstone.

"And a good day to you, Terry, and you, sirs," F'nor said, saluting the two riders with airy amiability. "F'nor, Canth's rider, of Benden."

"B'naj, Seventh's rider of Fort," said the taller, grayer of the two riders. He obviously resented the interruption and kept slapping an elaborately jeweled belt knife into the palm of his hand.

"T'reb, Beth's rider, also of Fort. And if Canth's a bronze, warn him off Beth."

"Canth's no poacher," F'nor replied, grinning outwardly but marking T'reb for a rider whose green's *amours* affected his own temper.

"One never knows just what is taught at Benden Weyr," T'reb said with thinly veiled contempt.

"Manners, among other things, when addressing Wing-seconds," F'nor replied, still pleasant. But T'reb gave him a sharp look, aware of a subtle difference in his manner. "Good Master Terry, may I have a word with Fandarel?"

"He's in his study . . ."

"And you told us he was not about," T'reb interrupted, grabbing Terry by the front of his heavy wher-hide apron.

F'nor reacted instantly. His brown hand snapped about T'reb's wrist, his fingers digging into the tendons so painfully that the green rider's hand was temporarily numbed.

Released, Terry stood back, his eyes blazing, his jaw set.

"Fort Weyr manners leave much to be desired," F'nor said, his teeth showing in a smile as hard as the grip with which he held T'reb. But now the other Fort Weyr rider intervened.

"T'reb! F'nor!" B'naj thrust the two apart. "His green's proddy, F'nor. He can't help it."

"Then he should stay weyrbound."

"Benden doesn't advise Fort," T'reb cried, trying to step past his Weyrmate, his hand on his belt knife.

F'nor stepped back, forcing himself to cool down. The whole episode was ridiculous. Dragonriders did not quarrel in public. No one should use a Craftmaster's second in such a fashion. Outside, dragons bellowed.

Ignoring T'reb, F'nor said to B'naj, "You'd better get out of here. She's too close to mating."

But the truculent T'reb would not be silenced.

"Don't tell me how to manage my dragon, you . . ."

The insult was lost in a second volley from the dragons to which Canth now added his warble.

"Don't be a fool, T'reb," B'naj said. "Come! Now!"

"I wouldn't be here if you hadn't wanted that knife. Get it and come."

The knife B'naj had been handling lay on the floor by Terry's foot. The Craftsman retrieved it in such a way that F'nor suddenly realized why there had been such tension in the Hall. The dragonriders had been about to confiscate the knife, an action his entrance had forestalled. He'd heard too much lately of such extortions.

"You'd better go," he told the dragonriders, stepping in front of Terry.

"We came for the knife. We'll leave with it," T'reb shouted and, feinting with unexpected speed, ducked past F'nor, grabbing the knife from Terry's hand, slicing the smith's thumb as he drew the blade.

Again F'nor caught T'reb's hand and twisted it, forcing him to drop the knife.

T'reb gave a gurgling cry of rage and, before F'nor could duck or B'naj could intervene, the infuriated green rider had plunged his own belt knife into F'nor's shoulder, viciously slicing downward until the point hit the shoulder bone.

F'nor staggered back, aware of nauseating pain, aware of Canth's scream of protest, the green's wild bawl and the brown's trumpeting.

"Get him out of here," F'nor gasped to B'naj, as Terry reached out to steady him.

"Get out!" the Smith repeated in a harsh voice. He signaled urgently to the other craftsmen who now moved decisively toward the dragonmen. But B'naj yanked T'reb savagely out of the Hall.

F'nor resisted as Terry tried to conduct him to the nearest bench. It was bad enough that dragonrider should attack dragonrider, but F'nor was even more shocked that a rider should ignore his beast for the sake of a coveted bauble.

There was real urgency in the green's shrill ululation now. F'nor willed T'reb and B'naj on their beasts and away. A shadow fell across the great portal of the Smithhall. It was Canth, crooning anxiously. The green's voice was suddenly still.

"Are they gone?" he asked the dragon.

Well gone, Canth replied, craning his neck to catch sight of his rider. *You hurt.*

"I'm all right. I'm all right," F'nor lied, relaxing into Terry's urgent grip. In a blackening daze, he felt himself lifted, then the hard surface of bench under his back before the dizzying shock and pain overwhelmed him. His last conscious thought was that Manora would be annoyed that he had not seen Fandarel first.

CHAPTER II

Evening (Fort Weyr Time).
Meeting of the Weyrleaders at Fort Weyr

When Mnementh burst out of *between* above Fort Weyr, he entered so high above the Weyr mountain that it was a barely discernible black point in the darkening land below. F'lar's exclamation of surprise was cut off by the thin cold air that burned his lungs.

You must be calm and cool, Mnementh said, doubling his rider's astonishment. *You must command at this meeting.* And the bronze dragon began a long spiral glide down to the Weyr.

F'lar knew that no admonitions could change Mnementh's mind when he used that firm tone. He wondered at the great beast's unexpected initiative. But the bronze dragon was right.

F'lar could accomplish little if he stormed in on T'ron and the other Weyrleaders, bent on extracting justice for his wounded Wing-second. Or if F'lar was still seething from the subtle insult implicit in the timing of this meeting. As Weyr-leader of the offending rider, T'ron had delayed answering F'lar's courteously phrased request for a meeting of all Weyr-leaders to discuss the untoward incident at the Craftmaster-hall. When T'ron's reply finally arrived, it set the meeting for the first watch, Fort Weyr time; or high night, Benden time, a most inconsiderate hour for F'lar and certainly inconvenient for the other easterly Weyrs, Igen, Ista and even Telgar. D'ram of Ista Weyr and R'mart of Telgar, and probably G'narish of Igen would have something sharp to say to T'ron about such timing, though their lag was not as great as Benden Weyr's.

So T'ron wanted F'lar off balance and irritated. Therefore, F'lar would appear all amiability. He'd apologize to D'ram, R'mart and G'narish for inconveniencing them, while making certain that they knew T'ron was responsible.

The main issue, to F'lar's now calm mind, was not the attack on F'nor. The real issue was the abrogation of two of the strongest Weyr restrictions; restrictions that ought to be so ingrained in any dragonrider that their fracture was impossible.

It was an absolute that a dragonrider did not take a green dragon or a queen from her Weyr when she was due to rise for mating. It made no difference whatsoever that a green dragon was sterile because she chewed firestone. Her lust could affect even the most insensitive commoners with sexual cravings. A mating female dragon broadcast her emotions on a wide band. Some green-brown pairings were as loud as bronze-gold. Herdbeasts within range stampeded wildly and fowls, wherries and whers went into witless hyster-ics. Humans were susceptible, too, and innocent Hold young-sters often responded with embarrassing consequences. That particular aspect of dragon matings didn't bother weyrfolk who had long since disregarded sexual inhibitions. No, you did not take a dragon out of her Weyr in that state.

It was irrelevant to F'lar's thinking that the second viola-tion stemmed from the first. From the moment riders could take their dragons *between*, they were abjured to avoid situa-tions that might lead to a duel, particularly since dueling was an accepted custom among Craft and Hold. Any differ-ences between riders were settled in unarmed bouts, closely refereed within the Weyr. Dragons suicided when their riders died. And occasionally a beast panicked if his rider was badly hurt or remained unconscious for long. A berserk dragon was almost impossible to manage and a dragon's death severely upset his entire Weyr. So armed dueling, which might injure or kill a rider, was the most absolute proscription.

Today, a Fort Weyr rider had deliberately—judging from the testimony F'lar had from Terry and the other smith-crafters present—abrogated these two basic restrictions. F'lar experienced no satisfaction that the offending rider came from Fort Weyr even if T'ron, the major critic of Benden Weyr's relaxed attitudes toward some traditions, was in a very embarassing position. F'lar might argue that his innovations breached no fundamental Weyr precepts, but the five Old-time Weyrs categorically dismissed every suggestion originating from Benden Weyr. And T'ron bleated the most about the deplorable manners of modern Holders and Crafters, so different—so less subservient, F'lar amended—to the acquies-cence of Holders and Crafters in their distant past Turn.

It would be interesting, F'lar mused, to see how T'ron the Traditionalist explained away the actions of his riders, now guilty of far worse offenses against Weyr traditions than anything F'lar had suggested.

Common sense had dictated F'lar's policy—eight Turns ago—of throwing open Impressions to likely lads from Holds and Crafts; there hadn't been enough boys of the right age in Benden Weyr to match the number of dragon eggs. If the Oldtimers would throw open the mating flights of their junior queens to bronzes from other Weyrs, they'd soon have clutch-es as large as the ones at Benden, and undoubtedly queen eggs, too. However, F'lar could appreciate how the Oldtimers felt. The bronze dragons at Benden and Southern Weyr were larger than most Oldtimer bronzes. Consequently, they'd fly the queens. But, by the Shell, F'lar hadn't suggested that the senior queens be flown openly. He did not intend to challenge the Oldtimer Weyrleaders with modern bronzes. He did feel that they'd profit by new blood among their beasts. Wasn't an improvement in dragonkind anywhere of benefit to all the Weyrs?

And it was practical diplomacy to invite Holders and Craft-ers to Impressions. There wasn't a man alive in Pern who hadn't secretly cherished the notion that he might be able to Impress a dragon. That he could be linked for life to the love and sustaining admiration of these gentle great beasts. That he could transverse Pern in a twinkling, astride a dragon. That he would never suffer the loneliness that was the condition of most men—a dragonrider always had his dragon. So, whether the commoners had a relative on the Hatching Ground hoping to attach a dragonet or not, the spectators enjoyed the vicarious thrill of being present, at witnessing this "mysterious rite." He'd observed that they were also subtly reassured that such dazzling fortune was available to some lucky souls not bred in the Weyrs. And those bound to a Weyr should, F'lar felt, get to know the riders since those riders were responsible for their lives and livelihoods.

To have assigned messenger dragons to every major Hold and Craft had been a very practical measure, too, when Benden had been Pern's only dragonweyr. The northern continent was broad. It took days to get messages from one coast to the other. The Harpercraft's system of drums was a poor second when a dragon could transport himself, his rider and an ungarbled message instantly anywhere on the planet.

F'lar, too, was exceedingly aware of the dangers of isolation. In the days before the first Thread had again fallen on Pern—could it be only seven Turns ago?—Benden Weyr had been vitiated by its isolation, and the entire planet all but lost. Where F'lar earnestly felt that dragonmen should make themselves accessible and friendly, the Oldtimers were obsessed by a need for privacy. Which only fertilized the ground for such incidents as had just occurred. T'reb on a disturbed green had swooped down on the Smithmastercrafthall and demanded—not requested—that a craftsman give up an artifact, which had been made by commission for a powerful Lord Holder.

With thoughts that were more disillusioned than vengeful, F'lar realized that Mnementh was gliding fast toward Fort Weyr's jagged rim. The Star Stones and the watchrider were silhouetted against the dying sunset. Beyond them were the forms of three other bronzes, one a good half-tail larger than the others. That would be Orth, so T'bor was already arrived from Southern Weyr. But only three bronzes? Who was yet to come to the meeting?

Salth from High Reaches and Branth with R'mart of Telgar Weyr are absent, Mnementh informed his rider.

High Reaches and Telgar Weyrs missing? Well, T'kul of

High Reaches was likely late on purpose. Odd though; that caustic Oldtimer ought to enjoy tonight. He'd have a chance to snipe at both F'lar and T'bor and he'd thoroughly enjoy T'ron's discomfiture. F'lar had never felt any friendliness for or from the dour, dark-complected High Reaches Weyrleader. He wondered if that was why Mnementh never used T'kul's name. Dragons ignored human names when they didn't like the bearer. But for a dragon not to name a Weyrleader was most unusual.

F'lar hoped that R'mart of Telgar would come. Of the Oldtimers, R'mart and G'narish of Igen were the youngest, the least set in their ways. Though they tended to side with their contemporaries in most affairs against the two modern Weyrleaders, F'lar and T'bor, F'lar had noticed lately that those two were sympathetic to some of his suggestions. Could he work on that to his advantage today—tonight? He wished that Lessa could have come with him for she was able to use deft mental pressures against dissenters and could often get the other dragons to answer her. She had to be careful, for dragonriders were apt to suspect they were being manipulated.

Mnementh was now within the Bowl of Fort Weyr itself and veering toward the ledge of the senior queen's weyr. T'ron's Fidranth was not there, guarding his queen Weyrmate as Mnementh would have been. Or perhaps Mardra, the senior Weyrwoman, was gone. She was as quick to find exception and slights as T'ron, though once she hadn't been so touchy. In those first days after the Weyrs had come up, she and Lessa had been exceedingly close. But Mardra's friendship had gradually turned into an active hatred. Mardra was a handsome woman, with a full, strong figure, and while she was nowhere near as promiscuous with her favors as Kylara of Southern Weyr, she was much sought after by bronze riders. By nature she was intensely possessive and not, F'lar realized, particularly intelligent. Lessa, dainty, oddly beautiful, already a Weyr legend for that spectacular ride *between* time, had unconsciously attracted attention from Mardra. Mardra evidently didn't consider the fact that Lessa made no attempt to entice any favorite from Mardra, did not, indeed, dally with any man (for which F'lar was immensely pleased). Add to that the ridiculous matter of their mutual Ruathan origin—Mardra conceived a hatred for Lessa. She seemed to feel that Lessa, the only survivor of that Bloodline, had had no right to renounce her claim on Ruatha Hold to young Lord Jaxom. Not that a Weyrwoman could take Hold or would want to. The bases for Mardra's hatred of Lessa were spurious. Lessa had no control over her beauty and had had no real choice about taking Hold at Ruatha.

So it was as well the Weyrwomen had not been included in this meeting. Put Mardra in the same room with Lessa and there'd be problems. Add Kylara of the Southern Weyr who was apt to make trouble for the pure joy of getting attention by disrupting others, and nothing would be accomplished. Nadira of Igen Weyr liked Lessa but in a passive way. Bedella of Telgar Weyr was stupid and Fanna of Ista, taciturn. Merika of the High Reaches was as much a sour sort as her Weyrleader T'kul.

This was a matter for men to settle.

F'lar thanked Mnementh as he slid down the warm shoulder to the ledge, stumbling as his bootheels caught on the ridges of claw scars on the edge. T'ron might have put out a basket of glows, F'lar thought irritably, and then caught himself. Another trick to put everyone in as unreceptive a mood as possible.

Loranth, senior queen dragon of Fort Weyr, solemnly regarded F'lar as he entered the main room of the Weyr. He gave her a cordial greeting, suppressing his relief that there was no sign of Mardra. If Loranth was solemn, Mardra would have been downright unpleasant. Undoubtedly the Fort Weyrwoman was sulking beyond the curtain between weyr and sleeping room. Maybe this awkward time had been her idea. It was after western dinner hours and too late for more than wine for those from later time zones. She thus avoided the necessity of playing hostess.

Lessa would never resort to such mean-spirited strategies. F'lar knew how often the impulsive Lessa had bitten back quick answers when Mardra had patronized her. In fact, Lessa's forbearance with the haughty Fort Weyrwoman was miraculous, considering Lessa's temper. F'lar supposed that his Weyrmate felt responsible for uprooting the Oldtimers. But the final decision to go forward in time had been theirs.

Well, if Lessa could endure Mardra's condescension out of gratitude, F'lar could try to put up with T'ron. The man did know how to fight Thread effectively and F'lar had learned a great deal from him at first. So, in a determinedly pleasant frame of mind, F'lar walked down the short passage to the Fort Weyr Council Room.

T'ron, seated in the big stone chair at the head of the Table, acknowledged F'lar's entry with a stiff nod. The light of the glows on the wall cast unflattering shadows on the Oldtimer's heavy, lined face. It struck F'lar forcibly that the man had *never* known anything but fighting Thread. He must have been born when the Red Star began that last fifty-Turn long Pass around Pern, and he'd fought Thread until the Star had finished its circuit. Then followed Lessa forward. A man could get mighty tired of fighting Thread in just seven short Turns. F'lar halted that line of thought.

D'ram of Ista Weyr and G'narish of Igen also contented themselves with nods. T'bor, however, gave F'lar a hearty greeting, his eyes glinting with emotion.

"Good evening, gentleman," F'lar said to all. "I apologize for taking you from your own affairs or rest with this request for an emergency meeting of all Weyrleaders, but it could not wait until the regular Solstice Gathering."

"I'll conduct the meetings at Fort Weyr, Benden," T'ron said in a cold harsh voice. "I'll wait for T'kul and R'mart before I have any discussion of your—your complaint."

"Agreed."

T'ron stared at F'lar as if that hadn't been the answer he'd anticipated and had gathered himself for an argument that hadn't materialized. F'lar nodded to T'bor as he took the seat beside him.

"I'll say this now, Benden," T'ron continued. "The next time you elect to drag us all out of our Weyrs suddenly, you apply to me first. Fort's the oldest Weyr on Pern. Don't just irresponsibly send messengers out to everyone."

"I don't see that F'lar acted irresponsibly," G'narish said, evidently surprised by T'ron's attitude. G'narish was a stocky young man, some Turns F'lar's junior and the youngest of the Weyrleaders to come forward in time. "Any Weyrleader can call a joint meeting if circumstances warrant it. And these do!" G'narish emphasized this with a curt nod, adding when he saw the Fort Weyrleader scowling at him, "Well, they do."

"Your rider was the aggressor, T'ron," D'ram said in a stern voice. He was a rangy man, getting stringy with age, but his astonishing shock of red hair was only lightly grizzled at the temples. "F'lar's within his rights."

"You had the choice of time and place, T'ron," F'lar pointed out, all deference.

T'ron's scowl deepened.

"Wish Telgar'd get here," he said in a low, irritated tone.

"Have some wine, F'lar?" T'bor suggested, an almost malicious smile playing on his lips for T'ron ought to have offered immediately. "Of course, it's not Benden Hold wine, but not bad. Not bad."

F'lar gave T'bor a long warning look as he took the proffered cup. But the Southern Weyrleader was watching to see how T'ron reacted. Benden Hold did not tithe of its famous wines as generously to the other Weyrs as it did to the one which protected its lands.

"When are we going to taste some of those Southern Weyr wines you've been bragging about, T'bor?" G'narish asked, instinctively trying to ease the growing tensions.

"Of course, we're entering our fall season now," T'bor said, making it seem that Fort was to blame for the chill outside—and inside—the Weyr. "However, we expect to start pressing soon. We'll distribute what we can spare to you northerners."

"What do you mean? What you can spare?" T'ron asked, staring hard at T'bor.

"Well, Southern plays nurse to every wounded dragonrider. We need sufficient on hand to drown their sorrows adequately. Southern Weyr supports itself, you must remember."

F'lar stepped on T'bor's booted foot as he turned to D'ram and inquired of the Istan Weyrleader how the last Laying had gone.

"Very well, thanks," D'ram replied pleasantly, but F'lar knew the older man did not like the mood that was developing. "Fanna's Mirath laid twenty-five and I'll warrant we've half a dozen bronzes in the clutch."

"Ista's bronzes are the fastest on Pern," F'lar said gravely. When he heard T'bor stirring restlessly beside him, he reached swiftly to Mnementh with a silent *Ask Orth to please tell T'bor to speak with great thought for the consequences. D'ram and G'narish must not be atagonized.* Out loud he said, "A weyr can never have too many good bronzes. If only to keep the queens happy." He leaned back, watching T'bor out of the corner of his eye to catch his reaction when the dragons completed the message relay. T'bor gave a sudden slight jerk, then shrugged, his glance shifting from D'ram to T'ron and back to F'lar. He looked more rebellious than cooperative. F'lar turned back to D'ram. "If you need some likely prospects for any green dragons, there's a boy . . ."

"D'ram follows tradition, Benden," T'ron cut in. "Weyrbred is best for dragonkind. Particularly for greens."

"Oh?" T'bor glared with malicious intent at T'ron.

D'ram cleared his throat hastily and said in a too loud voice, "As it happens, we've a good group of likely boys in our Lower Caverns. The last Impression at G'narish's Weyr left him with a few he has offered to place at Ista Weyr. So I thank you kindly, F'lar. Generous indeed when you've eggs hardening at Benden too. And a queen, I hear?"

D'ram exhibited no trace of envy for another queen egg at Benden Weyr. And Fanna's Mirath hadn't produced a single golden egg since she'd come time *between*.

"We all know Benden's generosity," T'ron said in a sneering tone, his eyes flicking around the room, everywhere but at F'lar. "He extends help everywhere. And interferes when it isn't needed."

"I don't call what happened at the Smithhall interference," D'ram said, his face assuming grave lines.

"I thought we were going to wait for T'kul and R'mart," G'narish said, glancing anxiously up the passageway.

So, F'lar mused, D'ram and G'narish are upset by today's events.

"T'kul's better known for the meetings he misses than the ones he attends," T'bor remarked.

"R'mart always comes," G'narish said.

"Well, they're neither of them here. And I'm not waiting on their pleasure any longer," T'ron announced, rising.

"Then you'd better call in B'naj and T'reb," D'ram suggested with a heavy sigh.

"They're in no condition to attend a meeting." T'ron seemed surprised at D'ram's request. "Their dragons only returned from flight at sunset."

D'ram stared at T'ron. "Then why did you call the meeting for tonight?"

"At F'lar's insistence."

T'bor rose to protest before F'lar could stop him, but D'ram waved him to be seated and sternly reminded T'ron that the Fort Weyrleader had set the time, not F'lar of Benden.

"Look, we're here now," T'bor said, banging his fist on the table irritably. "Let's get on with it. It's full night in southern Weyr. I'd like . . ."

"I conduct the Fort Weyr meetings, Southern," T'ron said in a loud, firm voice, although the effort of keeping his temper told in the flush of his face and the brightness of his eyes.

"Then conduct it," T'bor replied. "Tell us why a green rider took his dragon out of your Weyr when she was close to heat."

"T'reb was not aware she was that close . . ."

"Nonsense," T'bor cut in, glaring at T'ron. "You keep telling us how much of a traditionalist you are, and how well trained your riders are. Then don't tell me a rider as old as T'reb can't estimate his beast's condition."

F'lar began to think he didn't need an ally like T'bor.

"A green changes color rather noticeably," G'narish said, with some reluctance, F'lar noted. "Usually a full day before she wants to fly."

"Not in the spring," T'ron pointed out quickly. "Not when she's off her feed from Threadscore. It can happen very quickly. Which it did." T'ron spoke loudly, as if the volume of his explanation would bear more weight than its logic.

"That is possible," D'ram admitted slowly, nodding his head up and down before he turned to see what F'lar thought.

"I accept that possibility," F'lar replied, keeping his voice even. He saw T'bor open his mouth to protest and kicked the man under the table. "However, according to the testimony of Craftmaster Terry, my rider urged T'reb repeatedly to take his dragon away. T'reb persisted in his attempt to—to acquire the belt knife."

"And you accept the word of a commoner against a rider?" T'ron leaped on F'lar's statement with a great show of surprised indignation and incredulity.

"What would a Craftmaster," and F'lar emphasized the title, "gain by bringing false witness?"

"Those smithcrafters are the most notorious misers of Pern," T'ron replied as if this were a personal insult. "The worst of all the crafts when it comes to parting with an honest tithe."

"A jeweled belt knife is not a tithe item."

"What difference does that make, Benden?" T'ron demanded.

28

F'lar stared back at the Fort Weyrleader. So T'ron was trying to set the blame on Terry! Then he knew that his rider had been at fault. Why couldn't he just admit it and discipline the rider? F'lar only wanted to see that there'd be no repetitions of such an incident.

"The difference is that that knife had been crafted for Lord Larad of Telgar as a gift to Lord Asgenar of Lemos Hold for his wedding six days from now. The blade was not Terry's to give or withhold. It already belonged to a Lord Holder. Therefore, the rider was . . ."

"Naturally you'd take the part of your rider, Benden," T'ron cut in with a slight, unpleasant smile on his face. "But for a rider, a Weyrleader, to take the part of a Lord Holder against dragonfolk—" and T'ron turned to D'ram and G'narish with a helpless shrug of dismay.

"If R'mart were here, you'd be—" T'bor began.

D'ram gestured at him to be quiet. "We're not discussing possession but what seems to be a grave breach of Weyr discipline," he said in a voice that overwhelmed T'bor's protest. "However, F'lar, you do admit that a green, off her feed from Threadscore, can suddenly go into heat without warning?"

F'lar could feel T'bor urging him to deny that possibility. He knew that he had made a mistake in pointing out that the knife had been commissioned for a Lord Holder. Or in taking the part of a Holder not bound to Benden Weyr. If only R'mart had been here to speak in Lord Larad's behalf. As it was, F'lar had prejudiced his case. The incident had disturbed D'ram so much that the man was deliberately closing his eyes to fact and seeking any extenuating circumstance he could. If F'lar forced him to see the event clearly, would he prove anything to a man unwilling to believe that dragonriders could be guilty of error? Would he get D'ram to admit that Craft and Hold had privileges, too?

He took a slow deep breath to control the frustrated anger he felt. "I have to concede that it is possible a green can go into heat without warning under those conditions." Beside him, T'bor cursed under his breath. "But for exactly that reason, T'reb ought to have known to keep his green in the Weyr."

"But T'reb's a Fort Weyr rider," T'bor began heatedly, jumping to his feet. "And I've been told often enough that . . ."

"You're out of order, Southern," T'ron said in a loud voice, glaring at F'lar, not T'bor. "Can't *you* control your riders, F'lar?"

"That is quite enough, T'ron," D'ram cried, on his feet.

As the two Oldtimers locked glances, F'lar murmured urgently to T'bor, "Can't you see he's trying to anger us? Don't lose control!"

"We're trying to settle the incident, T'ron," D'ram continued forcefully, "not complicate it with irrelevant personalities. Since you are involved in this business, perhaps I'd better conduct the meeting. With your permission, of course, Fort."

To F'lar's mind, that was a tacit admission that D'ram realized, however he might try to evade it, how serious the incident was. The Istan Weyrleader turned to F'lar, his brown eyes dark with concern. F'lar entertained a half hope that D'ram might have seen through T'ron's obstructiveness, but the Oldtimer's next words disabused him. "I do not agree with you, F'lar, that the Crafter acted in good part. No, let me finish. We came to the aid of your troubled time, expecting to be recompensed and supported in proper fashion, but the manner and the amount of tithing rendered the Weyrs from Hold and Craft has left much to be desired. Pern is much more productive than it was four Hundred Turns ago and yet that wealth has not been reflected in the tithes. There is four times the population of our Time and much, much more cultivated land. A heavy responsibility for the Weyrs. And—" he cut himself off with a rueful laugh. "I'm digressing, too. Suffice it to say that once it was obvious a dragonrider found the knife to his liking, Terry should have gifted it him. As craftsmen used to, without any question or hesitation.

"Then," and D'ram's face brightened slightly, "T'reb and B'naj would have left before the green went into full heat, your F'nor would not have become involved in a disgraceful public brawl. Yes, it is all too plain," and D'ram straightened his shoulders from the burden of decision, "that the first error of judgment was on the part of the craftsman." He looked at each man, as if none of them had control over what a craftsman might do. T'bor refused to meet his eyes and ground a bootheel noisily into the stone floor.

D'ram took another deep breath. Was he, F'lar wondered bitterly, having trouble disgesting that verdict?

"We cannot, of course, permit a repetition of a green in

mating heat outside her weyr. Or dragonriders in an armed duel . . ."

"There wasn't any duel!" The words seemed to explode from T'bor. "T'reb *attacked* F'nor without warning and sliced him up. F'nor never even drew his knife. That's no duel. That's an unwarranted attack . . ."

"A man whose green is in heat is unaccountable for his actions," T'ron said, loud enough to drown T'bor out.

"A green who never should have been out of her weyr in the first place no matter how you dance around the truth, T'ron," T'bor said, savage with frustration. "The first error in judgment was T'reb's. Not Terry's."

"Silence!" D'ram's bellow silenced him and Loranth answered irritably from her weyr.

"That does it," T'ron exclaimed, rising. "I'm not having my senior queen upset. You've had your meeting, Benden, and your—your grievance has been aired. This meeting is adjourned."

"Adjourned?" G'narish echoed him in surprise. "But— but nothing's been done." The Igen Weyrleader looked from D'ram to T'ron puzzled, worried. "And F'lar's rider was wounded. If the attack was . . ."

"How badly wounded is the man?" D'ram asked, turning quickly to F'lar.

"Now you ask!" cried T'bor.

"Fortunately," and F'lar held T'bor's angry eyes in a stern, warning glance before turning to D'ram to answer, "the wound is not serious. He will not lose the use of the arm."

G'narish sucked his breath in with a whistle. "I thought he'd only been scratched. I think we . . ."

"When a rider's dragon is lustful—" D'ram began, but broke off when he caught sight of the naked fury on T'bor's face, the set look on F'lar's. "A dragonrider can never forget his purpose, his responsibility, to his dragon or to his Weyr. This can't happen again. You'll speak to T'reb, of course, T'ron?"

T'ron's eyes widened slightly at D'ram's question.

"Speak to him? You may be sure he'll hear from me about this. And B'naj, too."

"Good," said D'ram, with the air of a man who has solved a difficult problem equitably. He nodded toward the others. "It would be wise if we Weyrleaders caution all our riders against the possibility of a repetition. Put them all on their guard. Agreed?" He continued nodding, as if to spare the others the effort. "It is hard enough to work with some of these arrogant Holders and Crafters without giving them any occasion to fault us." D'ram sighed deeply and scratched his head. "I never have understood how commoners can forget how much they owe dragonriders!"

"In four hundred Turns, a man can learn many new things," F'lar replied. "Coming, T'bor?" and his tone was just short of command. "My greetings to your Weyrwomen, riders. Good night."

He strode from the Council Room, T'bor pounding right behind him, swearing savagely until they got to the outer passageway to the Weyr ledge.

"That old fool was in the wrong, F'lar, and you know it!"

"Obviously."

"Then why didn't you . . ."

"Rub his nose in it?" F'lar finished, halting in mid-stride and turning to T'bor in the dark of the passageway.

"Dragonriders don't fight. Particularly Weyrleaders."

T'bor let out a violent exclamation of utter disgust.

"How could you let a chance like that go by? When I think of the times he's criticized you—us—" T'bor broke off. "Never understand how commoners can forget all they owe dragonriders?" and T'bor mimicked D'ram's pompous intonation, "If they really want to know . . ."

F'lar gripped T'bor by the shoulder, appreciating the younger man's sentiments all too deeply.

"How can you tell a man what he doesn't want to hear? We couldn't even get them to admit that T'reb was in the wrong. T'reb, not Terry, and not F'nor. But I don't think there'll be another lapse like today's and that's what I really worried about."

"What?" T'bor stared at F'lar in puzzled confusion.

"That such an incident *could* occur worries me far more than who was in the wrong and for what reason."

"I can't follow that logic any more than I can follow T'ron's."

"It's simple. Dragonmen don't fight. Weyrleaders can't. T'ron was hoping I'd be mad enough to lose control. I think he was hoping I'd attack him."

"You can't be serious!" T'bor was plainly shaken.

"Remember, T'ron considers himself the senior Weyrleader on Pern and therefore infallible."

T'bor made a rude noise. Despite himself, F'lar grinned.

"True," he continued, "but I've never had a reason to challenge him. And don't forget, the Oldtimers taught us a great deal about Thread fighting we certainly didn't know."

"Why, our dragons can fight circles around the Oldtimers."

"That's not the point, T'bor. You and I, the modern Weyrs, have certain obvious advantages over the Oldtimers—size of dragons, number of queens—that I'm not interested in mentioning because it only makes for bad feeling. Nevertheless, we can't fight Thread without the Oldtimers. We need the Oldtimers more than they need us." F'lar gave T'bor a wry, bitter grin. "D'ram was partly right. A dragonman can never forget his purpose, his responsibility. When D'ram said 'to his dragon, to his Weyr', he's wrong. Our initial and ultimate responsibility is to Pern, to the people we were established to protect."

They had proceeded to the ledge and could see their dragons dropping off the height to meet them. Full dark had descended over Fort Weyr now, emphasizing the weariness that engulfed F'lar.

"If the Oldtimers have become introverted, we, Benden and Southern, cannot. We understand our Turn, our people. And somehow we've got to make the Oldtimers understand them, too."

"Yes, but T'ron was in the wrong!"

"Would we have been more right to make him *say* it?"

T'bor bit back an angry response and F'lar hoped that the man's rebellion was dissipating. There was good heart and mind in the Southern Weyrleader. He was a fine dragonrider, a superb fighter, and his Wings followed him without hesitation. He was not as strong out of the skies, however, but with subtle guidance had built Southern Weyr into a productive, self-supporting establishment. He instinctively looked to F'lar and Benden Weyr for direction and companionship. Part of that, F'lar was sure, was because of the difficult and disturbing temperament of the Southern Weyrwoman, Kylara.

Sometimes F'lar regretted that T'bor proved to be the only bronze rider who could cope with that female. He wondered what subtle deep tie existed between the two riders, because T'bor's Orth consistently outflew every bronze to mate with

Prideth, Kylara's queen, though it was common knowledge that Kylara took many men to her bed.

T'bor might be short-tempered and not the most diplomatic adherent, but he was loyal and F'lar was grateful to him. If he'd only held his temper tonight . . .

"Well, you usually know what you're doing, F'lar," the Southern Weyrleader admitted reluctantly, "but I don't understand the Oldtimers and lately I'm not sure I care."

Mnementh hovered by the ledge, one leg extended. Beyond him, the two men could hear Orth's wings beating the night air as he held his position.

"Tell F'nor to take it easy and get well. I know he's in good hands down at Southern," F'lar said as he scrambled up Mnementh's shoulder and urged him out of Orth's way.

"We'll have him well in next to no time. You need him," replied T'bor.

Yes, thought F'lar as Mnementh soared up out of the Fort Weyr Bowl, I need him. I could have used his wits beside me tonight. I could have used his thinking on T'ron's invidious attempts to switch blame.

Well, if it had been another rider, wounded under the same circumstances, he couldn't have brought F'nor anyhow. And T'bor with his short temper would still have been present, and played right into T'ron's hands. He couldn't honestly blame T'bor. He'd felt the same burning desire to *make* the Oldtimers see the facts in realistic perspective. But—you can't take a dragon to a place you've never seen. And T'bor's outbursts had not helped. Strange, T'bor hadn't been so touchy as a weyrling nor when he was a Benden Weyr Wing-second. Being weyrmate to Kylara had changed him but that woman was enough to unsettle; to unsettle D'ram.

F'lar entertained the wild mental image of the blonde sensual Kylara seducing the sturdy Oldtimer. Not that she'd even glanced at the Istan Weyrleader. And she certainly wouldn't have stayed with him. F'lar was glad that they'd eased her out of Benden Weyr. Hadn't she been found on the same Search as Lessa? Where'd she come from? Oh, yes, Telgar Hold. Come to think of it, she was the present Lord's full-blooded sister. Just as well Kylara was in Weyrlife. With her proclivity, she'd have had her throat sliced long ago in a Hold or a Crafthall.

Mnementh transferred them *between* and the cold of that

awful nothingness made his bones ache. Then they emerged over the Benden Weyr Star Stones and answered the watch-rider's query.

Lessa wasn't going to like his report of the meeting, F'lar thought. If only D'ram, usually an honest thinker, had seen past the obvious. He had a feeling that maybe G'narish had.

Yes, G'narish had been troubled. Maybe the next time the Weyrleaders met to confer, G'narish might side with the modern riders.

Only, F'lar hoped, there wouldn't be another occasion for this evening's grievance.

CHAPTER III

Morning Over Lemos Hold

Ramoth, Bendeu's golden queen, was in the Hatching Ground when she got the green's frantic summons from Lemos Hold.

Threads at Lemos. Thread falls at Lemos! Ramoth told every dragon and rider, her full-throated brassy bugle reverberating through the Bowl.

Men scrambled frantically from couch and bathing pool, upset tables and dropped tools before the first echo had rolled away. F'lar, idly watching the weyrlings drill, was dressed for fighting since the Weyr had expected to be at Lemos Hold late that day. Mnementh, his magnificent bronze, sunning himself on a ledge, swooped down at such a rate that he gouged a narrow trench in the sand of the floor with his left wingtip. F'lar was atop his neck and they were circling to the Eye Rock before Ramoth had had time to stamp out of the Hatching Cavern.

Thread at Lemos northeast, Mnementh reported, picking up the information from his mate Ramoth as she projected

herself toward her weyr ledge for Lessa. Dragons were now
streaming from every weyr opening, their riders struggling
into fighting gear or securing bulging firesacks.

F'lar didn't waste time wondering why Thread was falling hours ahead of schedule or northeast instead of southwest. He checked to see if there were enough riders assembled and aloft to make up a full low altitude wing. He
hesitated long enough to have Mnementh order every weyrling to proceed immediately to Lemos to help fly ground
crews to the area and then told his dragon to take the
wing *between.*

Thread was indeed falling, a great sheet plummeting down
toward the delicate new leafing hardwoods that were Lord
Asgenar's prime forestry project. Screaming, flaming, dragons broke out of *between,* skimming the spring forest to get
quick bearings before they soared up to meet the attack.

Incredibly, F'lar believed they had actually managed to
beat Thread to the forest. That green's rider would have
his choice of anything in F'lar's power to give. The thought
of Thread in those hardwood stands chilled the Weyrleader
more thoroughly than an hour *between.*

A dragon screamed directly above F'lar. Even as he
glanced upward to identify the wounded beast, both dragon
and rider had gone *between* where the awful cold would
shatter and break the entangling Threads before they could
eat into membrane and flesh.

A casualty minutes into an attack? Even an attack that
was so unpredictably early? F'lar winced.

Virianth, R'nor's brown, Mnementh informed his rider as
he soared in search of a target. He craned his sinuous neck
around in a wide sweep, eyeing the forest lest Thread had
actually started burrowing. Then, with a warning to his rider,
he folded his wings and dove toward an especially thick
patch, braking his descent with neck-snapping speed. As
Mnementh belched fire, F'lar watched, grinning with intense
satisfaction as the Thread curled into black dust and floated
harmlessly to the forests below.

Virianth caught his wingtip, Mnementh said as he beat
upward again. *He'll return. We need him. This Thread falls
wrong.*

"Wrong and early," F'lar said, gritting his teeth against
the fierce wind of their ascent. If he hadn't been in the custom

of sending a messenger on to the Hold where Thread was
due ...

Mnementh gave him just enough warning to secure his
hold as the great bronze veered suddenly toward a dense
clump. The stench of the fiery breath all but choked F'lar.
He flung up an arm to protect his face from the hot charred
flecks of Thread. Then Mnementh was turning his head for
another block of firestone before swooping again at dizzying speed after more Thread.

There was no further time for speculation; only action
and reaction. Dive. Flame. Firestone for Mnementh to chew.
Call a weyrling for another sack. Catch it deftly mid-air.
Fly above the fighting wings to check the pattern of flying
dragons. Gouts of flame blossoming across the sky. Sun
glinting off green, blue, brown, bronze backs as dragons
veered, soared, dove, flaming after Thread. He'd spot a beast
going *between*, tense until he reappeared or Mnementh reported their retreat. Part of his mind kept track of the casualties, another traced the wing line, correcting it when the
riders started to overlap or flew too wide a pattern. He
was aware, too, of the golden triangle of the queens' wing,
far below, catching what Thread escaped from the upper
levels.

By the time Thread had ceased to fall and the dragons
began to spiral down to aid the Lemos Hold ground crews,
F'lar almost resented Mnementh's summary.

*Nine minor brushes, four just wingtips; two bad lacings,
Sorenth and Relth, and two face-burned riders.*

Wingtip injuries were just plain bad judgment. Riders cutting it too fine. They weren't riding competitions, they were
fighting! F'lar ground his teeth ...

Sorenth says they came out of between *into a patch that
should not have been there. The Threads are not falling
right*, the bronze said. *That is what happened to Relth and
T'gor.*

That didn't assuage F'lar's frustration for he knew T'gor
and R'mel as good riders.

How could Thread fall northeast in the morning when it
wasn't supposed to drop until evening and in the southwest?
he wondered, savage with frustrated worry.

Automatically, F'lar started to ask Mnementh to have
Canth fly close in. But then he remembered that F'nor was

wounded and half a planet away in Southern Weyr. F'lar swore long and imaginatively, wishing T'reb of Fort Weyr immured *between* with Weyrleader T'ron fast beside him. Why did F'nor have to be absent at a time like this? It still rankled F'lar deeply that Fort's Weyrleader had tried to shift the blame of the fight from his very guilty rider to Terry. Of all the specious, contrived, ridiculous contentions for T'ron to stand by!

Lamanth is flying well, the bronze dragon remarked, cutting into his rider's thoughts.

F'lar was so surprised at the unexpected diversion that he glanced down to see the young queen.

"We're lucky to have so many to fly today," F'lar said, amused despite his other concerns by the bronze's fatuous tone. Lamanth was the queen from Mnementh's second mating with Ramoth.

Ramoth flies well too, for one so soon from the Hatching Ground. Thirty-eight eggs and another queen, Mnementh added with no modesty.

"We're going to have to do something about that third queen."

Mnementh rumbled about that. Ramoth disliked sharing the bronze dragons of her Weyr with too many queens, in spite of the fact that she would mate only with Mnementh. Many queens were the mark of virility in a bronze and it was natural for Mnementh to want to flaunt his prowess. Benden Weyr had to maintain more than one golden queen to placate the rest of the bronzes and to improve the breed in general, but three?

After the meeting the other night at Fort Weyr, F'lar hesitated to suggest to any of the other Weyrleaders that he'd be glad of a home for the new queen: They'd probably contrive it to be bad management of Ramoth or coddling of Lessa. Still, Benden queens were bigger than Oldtimer queens, just as modern bronzes were bigger, too. Maybe R'mart at Telgar Weyr wouldn't take offense. Or G'narish? F'lar couldn't think how many queens G'narish had at Igen Weyr. He grinned to himself, thinking of the expression of T'ron's face when he heard Benden was giving away a queen dragon.

"Benden's known for its generosity, but what's behind such a maneuver?" T'ron would say. "It's not traditional."

But it was. There were precedents. F'lar would far rather cope with T'ron's snide remarks than Ramoth's temper. He glanced down, sighting the gleaming triangle of the queens' wing, with Ramoth easily sweeping along, the younger beasts working hard to keep up with her.

Threads dropping out of pattern! F'lar gritted his teeth. Worse, out of a pattern which he'd so painstakingly researched from hundreds of disintegrating Record skins in his efforts seven Turns ago to prepare his ill-protected planet. Patterns, F'lar thought bitterly, which the Oldtimers had enthusiastically acclaimed and *used*—though that was scarcely traditional. Just useful.

Now how could Thread, which had no mind, no intelligence at all, deviate from patterns it had followed to the split second for over seven Turns? How could it change time and place overnight? The last Fall in Benden's Weyr jurisdiction had been on time and over upper Benden Hold as expected.

Could he possibly have misread the timetables? F'lar thought back, but the carefully drawn maps were clear in his mind and, if he *had* made an error, Lessa would have caught it.

He'd check, double check, as soon as he returned to the Weyr. In the meantime, he'd better make sure they had cleared the Fall from Edge to Edge. He directed Mnementh to find Asgenar, Lord Holder of Lemos.

Mnementh obediently turned out of the leisurely glide and dropped swiftly. F'lar could thank good fortune that it was Lord Asgenar of Lemos to whom he must explain, rather than Lord Sifer of Bitra Hold or Lord Raid of Benden Hold. The former would rant against the injustice and the latter would contrive to make a premature arrival of Thread a personal insult to him by dragonmen. Sometimes the Lords Raid and Sifer tried F'lar's patience. True, those three Holds, Benden, Bitra and Lemos, had conscientiously tithed to support Benden Weyr when it was the sole dragonweyr of Pern. But Lord Raid and Lord Sifer had an unpleasant habit of reminding Benden Weyr riders of their loyalty at every opportunity. Gratitude is an ill-fitting tunic that can chafe and smell if worn too long.

Lord Asgenar of Lemos Hold, on the other hand, was young and had been confirmed in his honors by the Lord Holders' Conclave only five Turns ago. His attitude toward the Weyr which protected his Holdlands from Thread was refreshingly untainted by invidious reminders of past services.

Mnementh glided toward the expanse of the Great Lake which separated Lemos Hold from upper Telgar Hold. The Threads' advance edge had just missed the verdant softwoods that surrounded the northern shores. Mnementh circled down, causing F'lar to lean into the great neck, grasping the fighting straps firmly. Despite his weariness and worry, he felt the sharp surge of elation which always gripped him when he flew the huge bronze dragon; that curious merging of himself with the beast, against air and wind, so that he was not only F'lar, Weyrleader of Benden, but somehow Mnementh, immensely powerful, magnificently free.

On a rise overlooking the broad meadow that swept down to the Great Lake, F'lar spotted the green dragon. Lemos' Lord Holder, Asgenar, would be near her. F'lar smiled sardonically at the sight. Let the Oldtimers disapprove, let them mutter uneasily when F'lar put non-weyrfolk on dragonback, but if F'lar had not, Thread would have fallen unseen over those hardwoods.

Trees! Another bone of contention between Weyr and Hold, with F'lar staunchly upholding the Lords' position. Four hundred Turns ago, such timber stands had not existed, were not permitted to grow. Too much living green to protect. Well, the Oldtimers were eager enough to own products of wood, overloading Fandarel's woodcraftsman, Bendarek, with their demands. On the other hand, they wouldn't permit the formation of a new Crafthall under Bendarek. Probably because, F'lar thought bitterly, Bendarek wanted to stay near the hardwoods of Lemos, and that would give Benden Weyr a Crafthall in its jurisdiction. By the Egg, the Oldtimers were almost more trouble than they were worth!

Mnementh landed with sweeping backstrokes that flattened the thick meadow grass. F'lar slid down the bronze's neck to join Lord Asgenar while Mnementh trumpeted approval to the green dragon and F'rad, his rider.

F'rad wants to warn you that Asgenar . . .

"Not much gets through Benden's wings," Asgenar was saying by way of greeting so that Mnementh didn't finish his thought. The young man was wiping soot and sweat from his face for he was one Lord who directed his ground crews personally instead of staying comfortably in his main Hold. "Even if Threads have begun to deviate. How do you account for all these recent variations?"

"Variations?" F'lar repeated the word, feeling stupid because he somehow realized that Asgenar was not referring just to this day's unusual occurrence.

"Yes! And here we thought your timetables were the last word. To be relied on forever, especially since they were checked and approved by the Oldtimers." Asgenar gave F'lar a sly look. "Oh, I'm not faulting you, F'lar. You've always been open in our dealings. I count myself lucky to be weyrbound to you. A man knows where he stands with Benden Weyr. My brother-in-law elect, Lord Larad, has had problems with T'kul of the High Reaches Weyr, you know. And since those premature falls at Tillek and Upper Crom, he's got a thorough watch system set up." Asgenar paused, suddenly aware of F'lar's tense silence. "I do not presume to criticize weyrfolk, F'lar," he said in a more formal tone, "but rumor can outfly a dragon and naturally I heard about the others. I can appreciate the Weyrs not wishing to alarm commoners but—well—a little forewarning would be only courteous."

"There was no way of predicting today's fall," F'lar said slowly, but his mind was turning so rapidly that he felt sick. Why had nothing been said to him? R'mart of Telgar Weyr hadn't been at the meeting about T'reb's transgressions. Could R'mart have been busy fighting Thread at that time? As for T'kul of the High Reaches Weyr imparting any information, particularly news that might show him in a bad light, that one wouldn't give coordinates to save a rider's life.

No, they'd have had good reason not to mention premature falls to F'lar that night. If T'kul had confided in anyone. But why hadn't R'mart let them know?

"But Benden Weyr's not caught sleeping. Once is all we'd need in those forests, huh, F'lar?" Asgenar was saying, his eyes scanning the spongewoods possessively.

"Yes. All we'd need. What's the report from the leading Edge of this Fall? Have you runners in yet?"

"Your queens' wing reported it safe two hours past." Asgenar grinned and rocked back and forth on his heels, his confidence not a bit jarred by today's unpredicted event. F'lar envied him.

Again the bronze rider thanked good fortune that he had Lord Asgenar to deal with this morning instead of punctilious Raid or suspicious Lord Sifer. He devoutly hoped that the young Lord Holder would not find his trust misplaced. But the question haunted him: how could Threads change so?

Both Weyrleader and Lord Holder froze as they watched a blue dragon hover attentively above a stand of trees to the northeast. When the beast flew on, Asgenar turned to F'lar with troubled eyes.

"Do you think these odd falls will mean that those forests must be razed?"

"You know my views on wood, Asgenar. It's too valuable a commodity, too versatile, to sacrifice needlessly."

"But it takes every dragon to protect . . ."

"Are you for or against?" F'lar asked with mild amusement. He gripped Asgenar's shoulder. "Instruct your foresters to keep constant watch. Their vigilance is essential."

"Then you don't know the pattern in the Thread shifts?"

F'lar shook his head slowly, unwilling to perjure himself to this man. "I'll leave the long-eyed F'rad with you."

A wide smile broke the thin troubled face of the Lord Holder.

"I couldn't ask, but it's a relief. I shan't abuse the privilege."

F'lar glanced at him sharply. "Why should you?"

Asgenar gave him a wry smile. "That's what the Old-timers carp about, isn't it? And instant transportation to any place on Pern is a temptation."

F'lar laughed, remembering that Asgenar, Lord of Lemos, was to take Famira, the youngest sister of Larad, Lord of Telgar Hold, to wife. While the Telgar lands marched the boundaries of Lemos, the Holds were separated by deep forest and several ranges of steep rocky mountains.

Three dragons appeared and circled above them, wing-riders reporting on the ground activities. Nine infestations had been sighted and controlled with minimum loss of property. Sweepriders had reported that the mid-Fall area was clear. F'lar dismissed them. A runner came loping up the meadow to his Lord Holder, carefully keeping several dragonlengths between himself and the two beasts. For all that every Pernese knew the dragons would harm no human, many would never lose their fearfulness. Dragons were confused by this distrust so that F'lar strolled casually to his bronze and scratched the left eye ridge affectionately until Mnementh allowed one lid to droop in pleasure over the gleaming opalescent eye.

The runner had come from afar, managing to gasp out his reassuring message before he collapsed on the ground, his chest heaving with the effort to fill his starved lungs. Asgenar stripped off his tunic and covered the man to prevent his chilling and made the runner drink from his own flask.

"The two infestations on the south slope are char!" Asgenar reported to the Weyrleader as he rejoined him. "That means the hardwood stands are safe." Asgenar's relief was so great that he took a swig on the bottle himself. Then hastily offered it to the dragonrider. When F'lar politely refused, he went on, "We may have another hard winter and my people will need that wood. Cromcoal costs!"

F'lar nodded. Free provision of fuelwood meant a tremendous saving to the average holder, though not every Lord saw it in this aspect. Lord Meron of Nabol Hold, for instance, refused to let his commoners chop fuelwood, forcing them to pay the high rates for Cromcoal, increasing his profit at their expense.

"That runner came from the south slope? He's fast."

"My forest men are the best in all Pern. Meron of Nabol has twice tried to lure that man from me."

"And?"

Lord Asgenar chuckled. "Who trusts Meron? My man had heard tales of how that Lord treats his people." He seemed about to add another thought but cleared his throat instead, glancing nervously away as if catching a glimpse of something in the woods.

"What all Pern needs is an efficient means of communication," remarked the dragonman, his eyes on the gasping runner.

"Efficient?" and Asgenar laughed aloud. "Is all Pern infected with Fandarel's disease?"

"Pern benefits by such an illness." F'lar must contact the Mastersmith the moment he got back to the Weyr. Pern needed the genius of the giant Fandarel now more than ever.

"Yes, but will we recover from the feverish urge for perfection?" Asgenar's smile faded as he added, in a deceptively casual fashion, "Have you heard whether a decision has been reached about Bendarek's guild?"

"None yet."

"*I* do not insist that a Craftmaster's Hall be sited in Lemos—" Asgenar began, urgent and serious.

F'lar held up his hand. "Nor I, though I have trouble convincing others of my sincerity. Lemos Hold has the biggest stands of wood, Bendarek needs to be near his best source of supply, and he comes of Lemos!"

"Every single objection raised has been ridiculous," Asgenar replied, his gray eyes sparkling with anger. "You know as well as I that a Craftmaster owes no allegiance to a Lord Holder. Bendarek's as unprejudiced as Fandarel as far as loyalty to anything but his craft is concerned. All the man thinks of is wood and pulp and those new leaves or sheets or what-you-ma-callums he's mucking about with."

"I know. I know, Asgenar. Larad of Telgar Hold and Corman of Keroon Hold side with you or so they've assured me."

"When the Lord Holders meet in Conclave at Telgar Hold, I'm going to speak out. Lord Raid and Sifer will back me, if only because we're weyrbound."

"It isn't the Lords or Weyrleaders who must make this decision," F'lar reminded the resolute young Lord. "It's the other Craftmasters. That's been my thought since Fandarel first proposed a new craft designation."

"Then what's holding matters up? All the Mastercraftsmen will be at the wedding at Telgar Hold. Let's settle it once and for all and let Bendarek alone." Asgenar threw his arms wide with frustration. "We need Bendarek settled, we need what he's been producing and he can't keep his mind on important work with all this shifting and shouting."

"Any proposal that smacks of change right now," (especially now, F'lar added to himself, thinking of this Threadfall,) "is going to alarm certain Weyrleaders and Lord Holders. Sometimes I think that only the Crafts constantly look for change, are interested and flexible enough to judge what is improvement or progressive. The Lord Holders and the—" F'lar broke off.

Fortunately another runner was approaching from the north, his legs pumping strongly. He came straight past the green dragon, right up to his Lord.

"Sir, the northern section is clear. Three burrows have been burned out. All is secure."

"Good man. Well run."

The man, flushed with praise and effort, saluted the Weyrleader and his Lord. Then, breathing deeply but without labor, he strode over to the prone messenger and began massaging his legs.

Asgenar smiled at F'lar. "There's no point in our rehearsing arguments. We are basically in agreement. If we could just make those others see!"

Mnementh rumbled that the wings were reporting an all-clear. He so pointedly extended his foreleg that Asgenar laughed.

"That does it," he said. "Any idea how soon before we have another Fall?"

F'lar shook his head. "F'rad is here. You ought to have seven days free. You'll hear from me as soon as we've definite news."

"You'll be at Telgar in six days, won't you?"

"Or Lessa will have my ears!"

"My regards to your lady."

Mnementh bore him upward in an elliptical course that allowed them to make one final check of the forest lands. Wisps of smoke curled to the north and farther to the east, but Mnementh seemed unconcerned. F'lar told him to go *between*. The utter cold of that dimension painfully irritated the Thread scores on his face. Then they were above Benden Weyr. Mnementh trumpeted his return and hung, all but motionless, until he heard the booming response of Ramoth. At that instant, Lessa appeared on the ledge of the weyr, her slight stature diminished still further by distance. As Mnementh glided in, she descended the long flight of stairs in much the same headlong fashion for which they criticized their weyrling son, Felessan.

Reprimands were not likely to break Lessa of that habit either, thought F'lar. Then he noticed what Lessa had in her hands and rounded angrily on Mnementh. "I'm barely touched and you babble on me like a weyrling!"

Mnementh was not the least bit abashed as he backwinged to land lightly by the Feeding Ground. *Thread hurts.*

"I don't want Lessa upset over nothing!"

I don't want Ramoth angry over anything!

F'lar slid from the bronze's neck, concealing the twinges he felt as the gritty wind from the Feeding Grounds aggravated the cold-seared lacerations. This was one of those times when the double bond between riders and dragons became a serious disadvantage. Particularly when Mnementh took the initiative, not generally a draconic characteristic.

Mnementh gave an awkward half-jump upward, clearing the way for Lessa. She hadn't changed from wher-hide riding clothes and looked younger than any Weyrwoman ought as she ran towards them, her plaited hair bouncing behind her. Although neither motherhood nor seven Turns of security had added flesh to her small-boned body, there was a subtle roundness to breast and hip, and that certain look in her great gray eyes that F'lar knew was for him alone.

"And you complain about the timing of other riders," she said, gasping, as she came to an abrupt stop at his side. Before he could protest the insignificance of his injuries, she was smearing numbweed on the burns. "I'll have to wash them once the feeling's gone. Can't you duck ash yet? Virianth will be all right but Sorenth and Relth took awful lacings. I do wish that glass craftsman of Fandarel's—Wansor's his name, isn't it?—would complete those eyeguards he's been blathering about. Manora thinks she can save P'ratan's good looks but we'll have to wait and see about his eye." She paused to take a deep breath. "Which is just as well because if he doesn't stop raiding Holds for new lovers, we won't be able to foster all the babies. Those holdbred girls are convinced its evil to abort." She stopped short, set her lips in the thin line which F'lar had finally catalogued as Lessa veering away from a painful subject.

"Lessa! No, don't look away." He forced her head up so she had to meet his eyes. She who couldn't conceive must find it hard, too, to help terminate unwanted pregnancies. Would she never stop yearning for another child? How could she forget she had nearly died with Felessan? He'd been relieved that she had never quickened again. The thought of losing Lessa was not even to be thought. "Riding *between* so much makes it impossible for a Weyrwoman to carry to term."

"It doesn't seem to affect Kylara," Lessa said with bitter resentment. She had turned away, watching Mnementh rend a fat buck with such an intense expression in her eyes that F'lar had no difficulty guessing that she'd prefer Kylara thus rendered.

"That one!" F'lar said with a sharp laugh. "Dear heart, if you must model yourself after Kylara to bear children as Weyrwoman, I prefer you barren!"

"We've more important things to discuss than her," Lessa said, turning to him in a complete change of mood. "What did Lord Asgenar say about the Threadfall? I'd have joined you in the meadow, but Ramoth's got the notion she can't leave her clutch without someone spying on them. Oh, I sent messengers out to the other Weyrs to tell them what's happened here. They ought to know and be on their guard."

"It would've been courteous of them to have apprised us first," F'lar said so angrily that Lessa glanced up at him, startled. He told her then what the Lemos Lord Holder had said on the mountain meadow.

"And Asgenar assumed that we all knew? That it was simply a matter of changing the timetables?" Shock faded from her face and her eyes narrowed, flashing with indignation. "I would I had never gone back to get those Oldtimers. You'd have figured out a way for *us* to cope."

"You give me entirely too much credit, love." He hugged her for her loyalty. "However, the Oldtimers are here and we've got to deal with them."

"Indeed we will. We'll bring them up to date if . . ."

"Lessa," and F'lar gave her a little shake, his pessimism dispersed by the vehemence of her response and the transparency of her rapid calculations on how to bring about such changes. "You can't change a watch-wher into a dragon, my love . . ."

Who'd want to? demanded Mnementh from the Feeding Ground, his appetite sated.

The bronze dragon's tart observation elicited a giggle from Lessa. F'lar hugged her gratefully.

"Well, it's nothing we can't cope with," she said firmly, allowing him to tuck her under his shoulder as they walked back to the weyr. "And it's nothing I don't expect from that T'kul of the ever-so-superior High Reaches. But R'mart of Telgar Weyr?"

"How long have the messengers been gone?"

Lessa frowned up at the bright midmorning sky. "Only

just. I wanted to get any last details from the sweepriders."

"I'm as hungry as Mnementh. Feed me, woman."

The bronze dragon had glided up to the ledge to settle in his accustomed spot just as a commotion started in the tunnel. He extended his wings to flight position, neck craned toward the one land entrance to the dragonweyr.

"It's the wine train from Benden, silly," Lessa told him, chuckling as Mnementh gave voice to a loud brassy grumble and began to arrange himself again, completely disinterested in wine trains. "Now don't tell Robinton the new wine's in, F'lar. It has to settle first, you know."

"And why would I be telling Robinton anything?" F'lar demanded, wondering how Lessa knew that he had only just started to think of the Masterharper himself.

"There has never been a crisis before us when you haven't sent for the Masterharper and the Mastersmith." She sighed deeply. "If we only had such cooperation from our own kind." Her body went rigid under his arm. "Here comes Fidranth and he says that T'ron's very agitated."

"T'ron's agitated?" F'lar's anger welled up instantly.

"That's what I said," Lessa replied, freeing herself and taking the steps two at a time. "I'll order you food." She halted abruptly, turning to say over her shoulder, "Keep your temper. I suspect T'kul never told anyone. He's never forgiven T'ron for talking him into coming forward, you know."

F'lar waited beside Mnementh as Fidranth circled smartly into the weyr. From the Hatching Cavern came Ramoth's crotchety challenge. Mnementh answered her soothingly that the intruder was only Fidranth and no threat. At least not to her *clutch*. Then the bronze rolled one scintillating eye toward his rider. The exchange, so like one between himself and Lessa, drained anger from F'lar. Which was as well, for T'ron's opening remarks were scarcely diplomatic.

"I found it! I found what you forgot to incorporate in those so-called infallible timetables of yours!"

"You've found what, T'ron?" F'lar asked, tightly controlling his temper. If T'ron had found anything that would be of help, he could not antagonize the man.

Mnementh had courteously stepped aside to permit Fidranth landing room, but with two huge bronze bodies there was so little space that T'ron slid in front of the Benden

Weyrleader, waving a portion of a Record hide right under his nose.

"Here's proof your timetables didn't include every scrap of information from *our* Records!"

"You've never questioned them before, T'ron," F'lar reminded the exercised man, speaking evenly.

"Don't hedge with me, F'lar. You just sent a messenger with word that Thread was falling out of pattern."

"And I'd have appreciated knowing that Thread had fallen out of pattern over Tillek and High Crom in the past few days!"

The look of shock and horror on T'ron's face was too genuine to be faked.

"You'd do better to listen to what commoners say, T'ron, instead of immuring yourself in the Weyr," F'lar told him. "Asgenar knew of it yet neither T'kul nor R'mar thought to tell the other Weyrs, so we could prepare and keep watch. Just luck I had F'rad . . ."

"You've not been housing dragonmen in the Holds again?"

"I always send a messenger on ahead the day of a Fall. If I didn't follow the practice, Asgenar's forest lands would be gone by now."

F'lar regretted that heated reference. It would give T'ron the wedge he needed for another of his diatribes about overforestration. To divert him, F'lar reached for the piece of Record, but T'ron twitched it out of his grasp.

"You'll have to take my word for it . . ."

"Have I ever questioned your word, T'ron?" Those words, too, were out before F'lar could censor them. He could and did keep his face expressionless, hoping T'ron would not read in it an additional allusion to that meeting. "I can see that the Record's badly eroded, but if you've deciphered it and it bears on this morning's unpredicted shift, we'll all be in your debt."

"F'lar?" Lessa's voice rang down the corridor. "Where are your manners? The *klah's* cooling and it is predawn T'ron's time."

"I'd appreciate a cup," T'ron admitted, as obviously relieved as F'lar by the interruption.

"I apologize for rousing you . . ."

"I need none, not with this news."

Unaccountably F'lar was relieved to realize that T'ron had

obviously not known of Threadfall. He had come charging in here, delighted at an opportunity to put F'lar and Benden in the wrong. He'd not have been so quick—witness his evasiveness and contradictions over the belt-knife fight—if he'd known.

When the two men entered the queen's weyr, Lessa was gowned, her hair loosely held by an intricate net, and seated gracefully at the table. Just as if she hadn't ridden hard all morning and been suited five minutes before.

So Lessa was all set to charm T'ron again, huh? Despite the unsettling events, F'lar was amused. Still, he wasn't certain that this ploy would lessen T'ron's antagonism. He didn't know what truth there was in a rumor that T'ron and Mardra were not on very good terms for a Weyrwoman and Weyrleader.

"Where's Ramoth?" T'ron asked, as he passed the queen's empty weyr.

"On the Hatching Ground, of course, slobbering over her latest clutch." Lessa replied with just the right amount of indifference.

But T'ron frowned, undoubtedly reminded that there was another queen egg on Benden's warm sands and that the Oldtimers' queens laid few gold eggs.

"I do apologize for starting your day so early," she went on, deftly serving him a neatly sectioned fruit and fixing *klah* to his taste. "But we need your advice and help."

T'ron grunted his thanks, carefully placing the Record hide side down on the table.

"Threadfall could come when it would if we didn't have all those blasted forests to care for," T'ron said, glaring at F'lar through the steam of the *klah* as he lifted his mug.

"What? And do without wood?" Lessa complained, rubbing her hands on the carved chair which Bendarek had made with his consummate artistry. "Those stone chairs may fit you and Mardra," she said in a sweet insinuating voice, "but I had a cold rear end all the time."

T'ron snorted with amusement, his eyes wandering over the dainty Weyrwoman in such a way that Lessa leaned forward abruptly and tapped the Record.

"I ought not to take your valuable time with chatter. Have you discovered something here which we missed?"

F'lar ground his teeth. He hadn't overlooked a single

legible word in those moldy Records, so how could she imply negligence so casually?

He forgave her when T'ron responded by flipping over the hide. "The skin is badly preserved, of course," and he made it sound as if Benden's wardship were at fault, not the depredations of four hundred Turns of abandonment, "but when you sent that weyrling with this news, I happened to remember seeing a reference to a Pass where all previous Records were no help. One reason *we* never bothered with timetable nonsense."

F'lar was about to demand why none of the Oldtimers had seen fit to mention that minor fact, when he caught Lessa's stern look. He held his peace.

"See, this phrase here is partly missing, but if you put 'unpredictable shifts' here, it makes sense."

Lessa, her gray eyes wide with an expression of unfeigned awe (her dissembling nearly choked F'lar), looked up from the Record at T'ron.

"He's right, F'lar. That would make sense. See—" and she deftly slipped the Record from T'ron's reluctant fingers and passed it to F'lar. He took it from her.

"You're right, T'ron. Very right. This is one of the older skins which I had to abandon, unable to decipher them."

"Of course, it was much more readable when I first studied it four hundred Turns back, before it got so faded." T'ron's smug manner was hard to take, but he could be managed better so than when he was defensive and suspicious.

"But that doesn't tell us how the shift changes, or how long it lasted," F'lar said.

"There must be other clues, T'ron," Lessa suggested, bending seductively toward the Fort Weyrleader when he began to bristle at F'lar's words. "Why would Thread fall out of a pattern they've followed to the second for seven mortal Turns this Pass? You yourself told me that you followed a certain rhythm in your Time. Did it vary much then?"

T'ron frowned down at the blurred lines. "No," he admitted slowly, and then brought his fist down on the offending scrap. "Why have we lost so many techniques? Why have these Records failed us just when we need them most?"

Mnementh began to bugle from the ledge, with Fidranth adding his note.

Lessa "listened," head cocked.

"D'ram and G'narish," she said. "I don't think we need expect T'kul, but R'mart is not an arrogant man."

D'ram of Ista and G'narish of Igen Weyrs entered together. Both men were agitated, sparing no time for amenities.

"What's this about premature Threadfall?" D'ram demanded. "Where are T'kul and R'mart? You did send for them, didn't you? Were your wings badly torn up? How much Thread burrowed?"

"None. We arrived at first Fall. And my wings sustained few casualties, but I appreciate your concern, D'ram. We've sent for the others."

Though Mnementh had given no warning, someone was running down the corridor to the Weyr. Everyone turned, anticipating one of the missing Weyrleaders, but it was a weyrling messenger who came racing in.

"My duty, sirs," the boy gasped out, "but R'mart's badly hurt and there're so many wounded men and dragons at Telgar Weyr, it's an awful sight. And half the Holds of High Crom are said to be charred."

The Weyrleaders were all on their feet.

"I must send some help—" Lessa began, to be halted by the frown on T'ron's face and D'ram's odd expression. She gave a small impatient snort. "You heard the boy, wounded men and dragons, a Weyr demoralized. Help in time of disaster is *not* interference. That ancient lay about Weyr autonomy can be carried to ridiculous lengths and this is one of them. Not to help Telgar Weyr, indeed!"

"She's right, you know," G'narish said, and F'lar knew the man was one step closer to gaining a modern perspective.

Lessa left the chamber, muttering something about personally flying to Telgar Weyr. The weyrling followed her, dismissed by F'lar's nod.

"T'ron found a reference to unpredictable shifts in this old Record Skin," F'lar said, seizing control. "D'ram, do you have any recollections from your studies of Istan Records four hundred Turns ago?"

"I wish I did," the Istan leader said slowly, then looked toward G'narish who was shaking his head. "Before I came here, I ordered immediate sweepwatches within my Weyr's bounds and I suggest we all do the same."

"What we need is a Pern-wide guard," F'lar began, carefully choosing his words.

But T'ron wasn't deceived and banged the table so hard that he set the crockery jumping. "Just waiting for the chance to lodge dragons in Holds and Crafthalls again, huh, F'lar? Dragonfolk stick together . . ."

"The way T'kul and R'mart are doing by not warning the rest of us?" asked D'ram in such an acid tone that T'ron subsided.

"Actually, why should dragonfolk weary themselves when there is so much more manpower available in the Holds now?" asked G'narish in a surprised way. He smiled slightly with nervousness when he saw the others staring at him. "I mean, the individual Holds could easily supply the watchers we'll need."

"And they've the means, too," F'lar agreed, ignoring T'ron's surprised exclamation. "It's not so very long ago that there were signal fires on every ridge and hill, across the plains, in case Fax began another of his acquisitive marches. In fact, I shouldn't be surprised if most of those beacon fireguards are still in place."

He was faintly amused by the expressions on the three faces. The Oldtimers never had recovered from the utter sacrilege of a Lord attempting to hold more than one territory. F'lar had no doubt this prompted such conservatives as T'kul and T'ron to impress on the commoners at every opportunity just how dependent they were on dragonfolk; and why they tried to limit and curtail contemporary freedoms and licenses. "Let the Holders light fires when Thread masses on the horizon—a few strategically placed riders could oversee great areas. Use the weyrlings; that'd keep them out of mischief and give 'em good practice. Once we know how the Thread falls now, we'll be able to judge the changes." F'lar forced himself to relax, smiling. "I don't think this is as serious a matter as it first appears. Particularly if shifts have occurred before. Of course, if we could find some reference to how long the shift lasted, if Thread went back to the original pattern, it'd help."

"It would have helped if T'kul had sent word as you did," D'ram muttered.

"Well, we all know how T'kul is," F'lar said tolerantly. "He'd no right to withhold such vital information from us," T'ron said, again pounding the table. "Weyrs should stick together."

"The Lord Holders aren't going to like this," G'narish remarked, no doubt thinking of Lord Corman of Keroon, the most difficult one of the Holders bound to his Weyr.

"Oh," F'lar replied with more diffidence than he felt, "if we tell them we've expected such a shift at about this time in the Pass . . ."

"But—but the timetables they have? They're not fools," T'ron sputtered.

We're the dragonfolk, T'ron. What they can't understand, they don't need to know—or worry about," F'lar replied firmly. "It's not their business to demand explanations of us, after all. And they'll get none."

"That's a change of tune, isn't it, F'lar?" asked D'ram.

"I never explained myself to them, if you'll think back, D'ram. I told them what had to be done and they did it."

"They were scared stupid seven Turns ago," G'narish remarked. "Scared enough to welcome us with wide-open arms and goods."

"If they want to protect all those forests and croplands, they'll do as we suggest or start charring their profits."

"Let Lord Oterel of Tillek or that idiot Lord Sangel of Boll start disputing my orders and I'll fire their forests myself," said T'ron, rising.

"Then we're agreed," said F'lar quickly, before the hypocrisy he was practicing overcame him with disgust. "We mount watches, aided by the Holders, and we keep track of the new shift. We'll soon know how to judge it."

"What of T'kul?" G'narish asked.

D'ram looked squarely at T'ron. "We'll explain the situation to him."

"He respects you two," F'lar agreed. "It might be wiser, though, not to suggest we knew about . . ."

"We can handle T'kul, without your advice, F'lar," D'ram cut him off abruptly, and F'lar knew that the momentary harmony between them was at an end. The Oldtimers were closing ranks against the crime of their contemporary, just as they had at that abortive meeting a few nights ago. He could console himself with the fact that they hadn't been able to escape all the implications of this incident.

Lessa came back into the weyr just then, her face flushed,

her eyes exceedingly bright. Even D'ram bowed low to her in making his farewells.

"Don't leave, D'ram, T'ron. I've good word from Telgar Weyr," she cried, but catching F'lar's glance, did not try to keep them when they demurred.

"R'mart's all right?" G'narish asked, trying to smooth over the awkwardness.

Lessa recovered herself with a smile for the Igen leader.

"Oh that messenger—he's only a boy—he exaggerated. Ramoth bespoke Solth the senior queen at Telgar Weyr. R'mart is badly scored, yes. Bedella evidently overdosed him with numbweed powder. *She* hadn't the wit to send word to anyone. And the Wing-second assumed that we'd all been informed because he'd heard R'mart telling Bedella to send messengers, never dreaming she hadn't. When R'mart passed out, she forgot everything." Lessa's shrug indicated her low opinion of Bedella. "The Wing-second says he'd be grateful for your advice."

"H'ages is Wing-second at Telgar Weyr," G'narish said. "A sound enough rider but he's got no initiative. Say, you're Thread-bared yourself, F'lar."

"It's nothing."

"It's bleeding," Lessa contradicted. "And you haven't eaten a thing."

"I'll stop at Telgar Weyr, F'lar, and talk to H'ages," G'narish said.

"I'd like to come with you, G'narish, if you've no objections . . ."

"I've objections," Lessa put in. "G'narish's capable of ascertaining the extent of the Fall there and can relay the information to us. I'll see him to the ledge while *you* start *eating*." Lessa was so didactic that G'narish chuckled. She tucked her arm in his and started toward the corridor. "I've not made my duty to Gyarmath," she said, smiling sweetly up at G'narish, "and he's a favorite of mine, you know."

She was flirting so outrageously that F'lar wondered that Ramoth wasn't roaring protest. As if Gyarmath could ever catch Ramoth in flight! Then he heard Mnementh's rumble of humor and was reassured.

Eat, his bronze advised him. *Let Lessa flatter G'narish. Gyarmath doesn't mind. Nor Ramoth. Nor I.*

"What I do for my Weyr," said Lessa with an exaggerated sigh as she returned a few moments later.

F'lar gave her a cynical look. "G'narish is more of a modern mind than he knows."

"Then we'll have to make him conscious of it," Lessa said firmly.

"Just so long as it is 'we' who make him," F'lar replied with mock severity, catching her hand and pulling her to him.

She made a token resistance, as she always did, scowling ferociously at him and then relaxed against his shoulder all at once. "Signal fires and sweepriding are not enough, F'lar," she said thoughtfully. "Although I do believe we've worried too much about the change in Threadfall."

"That nonsense was to fool G'narish and the others, but I thought you'd . . ."

"But don't you see that you were right?"

F'lar gave her a long incredulous look.

"By the Egg, Weyrleader, you astonish me. Why can't there be deviations? Because you, F'lar, compiled those Records and to spite the Oldtimers they must remain infallible? Great golden eggs, man, there were such things as Intervals when no Threads fell—as we both know. Why not a change of pace in Threadfall itself during a Pass?"

"But why? Give me one good reason why."

"Give me one good reason why not! The same thing that affects the Red Star so that it doesn't always pass close enough to cast Thread on us can pull it enough off course to change Fall! The Red Star is not the only one to rise and set with the seasons. There could be another heavenly body affecting not only us but the Red Star."

"Where?"

Lessa shrugged impatiently. "How do I know? I'm not long in the eye like F'rad. But we can try to find out. Or have seven full Turns of certainty and schedule dulled your wits?"

"Now, see here, Lessa . . ."

Suddenly she pressed herself close to him, full of contrition for her sharp tongue. He held her close, all too aware that she was right. And yet . . . There had been that long and lonely wait until he and Mnementh could come into their own. The terrible dichotomy of confidence in his own prophecy that Thread would fall and fear that nothing would rescue the Dragonriders from their lethargy. Then the crushing realization that those all too few dragonmen were all that could save an entire world from destruction; the three days of torture between the initial fall over the impending one at Nerat Hold and Telgar Hold with Lessa who-knew-where. Did he not have a right to relax his vigilance? Some freedom from the weight of responsibility?

"I've no right to say such things to you," Lessa was whispering in soft remorse.

"Why not? It's true enough."

"I ought never to diminish you, and all you've done, to placate a trio of narrow-minded, parochial, conservative . . ."

He stopped her words with a kiss, a teasing kiss that abruptly became passionate. Then he winced as her hands, curving sensuously around his neck, rubbed against the Thread-bared skin.

"Oh, I'm so sorry. Here, let me—" and Lessa's apology trailed off as she swiveled her body around to reach for the numbweed jar.

"I forgive you, dear heart, for all your daily machinations," F'lar assured her sententiously. "It's easier to flatter a man than fight him. I wish I had F'nor here right now!"

"I still haven't forgiven that old fool T'ron," Lessa said, her eyes narrowing, her lips pursed. "Oh, *why* didn't F'nor just let T'reb have the knife?"

"F'nor acted with integrity," F'lar said with stiff disapproval.

"He could've ducked quicker then. And you're no better." Her touch was gentle but the burns stung.

"Hmmm. What I have ducked is my responsibility to *our* Pern in bringing the Oldtimers forward. We've let ourselves get bogged down on small issues, like whose was the blame in that asinine fight at the Mastersmith's Hall. The real problem is to reconcile the old with the new. And we may just be able to make this new crisis work there to our advantage, Lessa."

She heard the ring in his voice and smiled back at him approvingly.

"When we cut through traditions before the Oldtimers came forward, we also discovered how hollow and restrictive some of them were; such as this business of minimal contact between Hold, Craft and Weyr. Oh, true, if we wish to bespeak another Weyr, we can go there in a few seconds on a dragon, but it takes Holder or Crafter days to get from one place to another. They had a taste of convenience seven Turns ago. I should never have acquiesced and let the Oldtimers talk me out of continuing a dragon in Hold and Craft. Those signal fires won't work, and neither will sweepriders. You're absolutely right about that, Lessa. Now if Fandarel can think up some alternative method of . . . What's the matter? Why are you smiling like that?"

"I knew it. I knew you'd want to see the Smith and the Harper so I sent for them, but they won't be here until you've eaten and rested." She tested the fresh numbweed to see if it had hardened.

"And of course you've eaten and rested, too?"

She got off his lap in one fluid movement, her eyes almost black. *"I'll* have sense enough to go to bed when I'm tired. *You'll* keep on talking with Fandarel and Robinton long after you've chewed your business to death. And you'll drink —as if you haven't learned yet that only a dragon could out-drink that Harper and that Smith—" She broke off again, her scowl turning into a thoughtful frown. "Come to think of it, we'd do well to invite Lytol, if he'd come. I'd like to know exactly what the Lord Holders' reactions are. But first, you eat!"

F'lar laughingly obeyed, wondering how he could suddenly feel so optimistic when it was now obvious that the problems of Pern were coming home to roost on his weyr ledge again.

CHAPTER IV

Midday at Southern Weyr

Kylara whirled in front of the mirror, turning her head to watch her slender image, observing the swing and fall of the heavy fabric of the deep red dress.

"I knew it. I told him that hem was uneven," she said, coming to a dead stop, facing her reflection, suddenly aware of her own engaging scowl. She practiced the expression, found one attitude that displeased her and carefully schooled herself against an inadvertent re-use.

"A frown is a mighty weapon, dear," her foster mother had told her again and again, "but do cultivate a pretty one. Think what would happen if your face *froze* that way."

Her posing diverted her until she twisted, trying to assess her profile, and again caught sight of the swirl of the guilty hem.

"Rannelly!" she called, impatient when the old woman did not answer instantly. "Rannelly!"

"Coming, poppet. Old bones don't move as fast. Been

setting your gowns to air. There do be such sweetness from that blooming tree. Aye, the wonder of it, a fellis tree grown to such a size." Rannelly carried on a continuous monologue once summoned, as if the sound of her name turned on her mind. Kylara was certain that it did, for her old nurse voiced, like a dull echo, only what she heard and saw.

"Those tailors are no better than they should be, and sloppy about finishing details," Rannelly muttered on, when Kylara sharply interrupted her maundering with the problem. She exhaled on the note of a bass drone as she knelt and flipped up the offending skirt. "Aye and just see these stitches. Taken in haste they were, with too much thread on the needle . . ."

"That man promised me the gown in three days and was seaming it when I arrived. But I need it."

Rannelly's hands stopped; she stared up at her charge. "You weren't ever away from the Weyr without saying a word. . . ."

"I go where I please," Kylara said, stamping her foot. "I'm no babe to be checking my movements with you. I'm the Weyrwoman here at Southern. I ride the queen. No one can do anything to me. Don't forget that."

"There's none as forgets my poppet's . . ."

"Not that this is a proper Weyr, at all . . ."

" . . . And that's an insult to my nursling, it is, to be in . . ."

"Not that *they* care, but they'll see they can't treat a Telgar of the Blood with such lack of courtesy . . ."

" . . . And who's been discourteous to my little . . ."

"Fix that hem, Rannelly, and don't be all week about it. I must look my best when I go home," Kylara said, turning her upper torso this way and that, studying the fall of her thick, wavy blonde hair. "Only good thing about this horrible, horrible place. The sun does keep my hair bright."

"Like a fall of sunbeams, my sweetling, and me brushing it to bring out the shine. Morning and night I brushes it. Never miss. Except when you're away. *He* was looking for you earlier . . ."

"Never mind *him*. Fix that hem."

"Oh, aye, that I can do for you. Slip it off. There now. Ooooh, my precious, my poppet. Whoever treated you so! Did *he* make such marks on . . ."

"Be quiet!" Kylara stepped quickly from the collapsed

dress at her feet, all too aware of the livid bruises that
stood out on her fair skin. One more reason to wear the
new gown. She shrugged into the loose linen robe she had
discarded earlier. While sleeveless, its folds almost covered
the big bruise on her right arm. She could always blame
that on a natural accident. Not that she cared a whistle
what T'bor thought but it made for less recrimination. And
he never knew what he did when he was well wined-up.

"No good will come of it," Rannelly was moaning as she
gathered up the red gown and began to shuffle across to
her cubby. "You're weyrfolk now. No good comes of weyrfolk mixing with Holders. Stick to your own. You're some-
body here . . ."

"Shut up, you old fool. The whole point of being Weyrwoman is I can do what *I* please. I'm not my mother. I don't
need your advice."

"Aye, and I know it," the old nurse said with such sharp
bitterness that Kylara stared after her.

There, she'd frowned unattractively. She must remember
not to screw her brows that way; it made wrinkles. Kylara
ran her hands down her sides, testing the smooth curves
sensuously, drawing one hand across her flat belly. Flat even
after five brats. Well, there'd be no more. She had the way
of it now. Just a few moments longer *between* at the proper
time and . . .

She pirouetted, laughing, throwing her arms up to the
ceiling in a tendon-snapping stretch and hissing as the bruised
deltoid muscle pained her.

Meron need not . . . She smiled languorously. Meron
did need to, because *she* needed it.

He is not a dragonrider, said Prideth, rousing from sleep.
There was no censure in the golden dragon's tone; it was
a statement of fact. Mainly the fact that Prideth was bored
with excursions which landed her in Holds rather than Weyrs.
When Kylara's fancy took them visiting other dragons,
Prideth was more than agreeable. But a Hold, with only the
terrified incoherencies of a watch-wher for company was another matter.

"No, he's *not* a dragonrider," Kylara agreed emphatically,
a smile of remembered pleasure touching her full red lips.
It gave her a soft, mysterious, alluring look, she thought,

bending to the mirror. But the surface was mottled and the close inspection made her skin appear diseased.

I itch, Prideth said, and Kylara could hear the dragon moving. The ground under her feet echoed the effect.

Kylara laughed indulgently and, with a final swirl and a grimace at the imperfect mirror, she went out to ease Prideth. If only she could find a real man who could understand and adore her the way the dragon did. If, for instance, F'lar . . .

Mnementh is Ramoth's, Prideth told her rider as she entered the clearing which served as gold queen's Weyr in Southern. The dragon had rubbed the dirt off the bedrock just beneath the surface. The southern sun baked the slab so that it gave off comfortable heat right through the coolest night. All around, the great fellis trees drooped, the pink clustered blossoms scenting the air.

"Mnementh could be yours, silly one," she told her beast, scrubbing the itchy spot with the long-handled brush.

No. I do not contend with Ramoth.

"You would quick enough if you were in mating heat," Kylara replied, wishing she had the nerve to attempt such a coup. "It's not as if there was anything immoral about mating with your father or clutching your mother . . ."

Kylara thought of her own mother, a woman too early used and cast aside by Lord Telgar, for younger, more vital bedmates. Why, if she hadn't been found on Search, she might have had to marry that dolt what-ever-his-name-had-been. She'd never have been a Weyrwoman and had Prideth to love her. She scrubbed fiercely at the spot until Prideth, sighing in an excess of relief, blew three clusters of blooms off their twigs.

You are my mother, Prideth said, turning great opalescent eyes on her rider, her tone suffused with love, admiration, affection, awe and joy.

Despite her annoying reflections, Kylara smiled tenderly at her dragon. She couldn't stay angry with the beast, not when Prideth gazed at her that way. Not when Prideth loved her, Kylara, to the exclusion of all other considerations. Gratefully the Weyrwoman rubbed the sensitive ridge of Prideth's right eye socket until the protecting lids closed one by one in contentment. The girl leaned against the wedge-shaped head, at peace momentarily with herself, with the world, the balm of Prideth's love assuaging her discontent.

Then she heard T'bor's voice in the distance, ordering the weyrlings about, and she pushed away from Prideth. Why did it have to be T'bor? He was so ineffectual. He never came near making her feel the way Meron did, except of course when Orth was flying Prideth and then, then it was bearable. But Meron, without a dragon, was almost enough. Meron was just ruthless and ambitious enough so that together they could probably control all Pern . . .

"Good day, Kylara."

Kylara ignored the greeting. T'bor's forcedly cheerful tone told her that he was determined not to quarrel with her over whatever it was he had on his mind this time. She wondered what attraction he had ever held for her, though he was tall and not ill-favored; few dragonriders were. The thin lines of Thread scars more often gave them a rakish rather than repulsive appearance. T'bor was not scarred but a frown of apprehension and a nervous darting of his eyes marred the effect of his good looks.

"Good day, Prideth," he added.

I like him, Prideth told her rider. *And he is really devoted to you. You are not kind to him.*

"Kindness gets you nowhere," Kylara snapped back at her beast. She turned with indolent reluctance to the Weyrleader. "What's on your mind?"

T'bor flushed as he always did when he heard that note in Kylara's voice. She meant to unsettle him.

"I need to know how many weyrs are free. Telgar Weyr is asking."

"Ask Brekke. How should I know?"

T'bor's flush deepened and he set his jaw. "It is customary for the Weyrwoman to direct her own staff . . ."

"Custom be Thread-bared! She knows. I don't. And I don't see why Southern should be constantly host to every idiot rider who can't dodge Thread."

"You know perfectly well, Kylara, why Southern Weyr . . ."

"We haven't had a single casualty of any kind in seven Turns of Thread."

"We don't get the heavy, constant Threadfall that the northern continent does, and now I understand . . ."

"Well, I don't understand why their wounded must be a constant drain on our resources . . ."

"Kylara. Don't argue with every word I say."

Smiling, Kylara turned from him, pleased that she had pushed him so close to breaking his childish resolve.

"Find out from Brekke. *She* enjoys filling in for me." She glanced over her shoulder to see if he understood exactly what she meant. She was certain that Brekke shared his bed when Kylara was otherwise occupied. The more fool Brekke, who, as Kylara well knew, was pining after F'nor. She and T'bor must have interesting fantasies, each imagining the other the true object of their unrequited loves.

"Brekke is twice the woman and far more fit to be Weyrwoman than you!" T'bor said in a tight, controlled voice.

"You'll pay for that, you scum, you snivelling boy-lover," Kylara screamed at him, enraged by the unexpectedness of his retaliation. Then she burst out laughing at the thought of Brekke as the Weyrwoman, or Brekke as passionate and adept a lover as she knew herself to be. Brekke the Bony, with no more roundness at the breast than a boy. Why, even Lessa looked more feminine.

Thought of Lessa sobered Kylara abruptly. She tried again to convince herself that Lessa would be no threat, no obstacle in her plan. Lessa was too subservient to F'lar now, aching to be pregnant again, playing the dutiful Weyrwoman, too content to see what could happen under her nose. Lessa was a fool. She could have ruled all Pern if she had half-tried. She'd had the chance and lost it. The stupidity of going back to bring up the Oldtimers when she could have had absolute dominion over the entire planet as Weyrwoman to Pern's only queen! Well, Kylara had no intention of remaining in the Southern Weyr, meekly tending the world's wounded weyrmen and cultivating acres and acres of food for everyone else but herself. Each egg hatched a different way, but a crack at the right time speeded things up.

And Kylara was all ready to crack a few eggs, *her* way. Noble Larad, Lord of Telgar Hold, might not have remembered to invite her, his only full-blood sister, to the wedding, but surely there was no reason why she should remain distant when her own half sister was marrying the Lord Holder of Lemos.

Brekke was changing the dressing on his arm when F'nor heard T'bor calling her. She tensed at the sound of his voice, an expression of compassion and worry momentarily clouding her face.

"I'm in F'nor's weyr," she said, turning her head toward the open door and raising her light voice.

"Don't know why we insist on calling a hold made of wood a weyr," said F'nor, wondering at Brekke's reaction. She was such a serious child, too old for her years. Perhaps being junior Weyrwoman to Kylara had aged her prematurely. He had finally got her to accept his teasing. Or was she humoring him, F'nor wondered, during the painful process of having the deep knife wound tended.

She gave him a little smile. "A weyr is where a dragon is, no matter how it's constructed."

T'bor entered at that moment, ducking his head, though the door was plenty high enough to accommodate his inches.

"How's the arm, F'nor?"

"Improving under Brekke's expert care. There's a rumor," F'nor said, grinning slyly up at Brekke, "that men sent to Southern heal quicker."

"If that's why there are always so many coming back, I'll give her other duties." T'bor sounded so bitter that F'nor stared at him. "Brekke, how many more wounded can we accommodate?"

"Only four, but Varena at West can handle at least twenty."

From her expression, F'nor could tell she hoped there weren't that many wounded.

"R'mart asks to send ten, only one badly injured," T'bor said, but he was still resentful.

"He'd best stay here then."

F'nor started to say that he felt Brekke was spreading herself too thin as it was. It was obvious to him that, though she had few of the privileges, she had assumed all the responsibilities that Kylara ought to handle, while that one did much as she pleased. Including complaining that Brekke was shirking or stinting this or that. Brekke's queen, Wirenth, was still young enough to need a lot of care; Brekke fostered young Mirrim though she had had no children herself and none of the Southern riders seemed to share her bed. Yet Brekke also took it upon herself to nurse the most seriously wounded dragonriders. Not that F'nor wasn't grateful to her.

She seemed to have an extra sense that told her when numbweed needed renewing, or when fever was high and made you fretful. Her hands were miracles of gentleness, cool, but she could be ruthless, too, in disciplining her patients to health.

"I appreciate your help, Brekke," T'bor said. "I really do."

"I wonder if other arrangements ought to be made," F'nor suggested tentatively.

"What do you mean?"

Oh-ho, thought F'nor, the man's touchy. "For hundreds of Turns, dragonriders managed to get well in their own Weyrs. Why should the Southern ones be burdened with wounded useless men, constantly dumped on them to recuperate?"

"Benden sends very few," Brekke said quietly.

"I don't mean just Benden. Half the men here right now are from Fort Weyr. They could as well bask on the beaches of Southern Boll . . ."

"T'ron's no leader—" T'bor said in a disparaging tone.

"So Mardra would like us to believe," Brekke interrupted with such uncharacteristic asperity that T'bor stared at her in surprise.

You don't miss much, do you, little lady?" said F'nor with a whoop of laughter. "That's what Lessa said and I agree."

Brekke flushed.

"What do you mean, Brekke?" asked T'bor.

"Just that five of the men most seriously wounded *were flying in Mardra's wing!*"

"Her wing?" F'nor glanced sharply at T'bor, wondering if this was news to him, too.

"Hadn't you heard?" Brekke asked, almost bitterly. "Ever since D'nek was Threaded, she's been flying . . ."

"A queen eating firestone? Is that why Loranth hasn't risen to mate?"

"I didn't say Loranth ate firestone," Brekke contradicted. "Mardra's got some sense left. A sterile queen's no better than a green. And Mardra'd not be senior *or* Weyrwoman. No, she uses a fire thrower."

"On an upper level?" F'nor was stunned. And T'ron had the nerve to prate how Fort Weyr kept tradition?

"That's why so many men are injured in her wing; the dragons fly close to protect their queen. A flame thrower throws 'down' but not out, or wide enough to catch airborne Thread at the speed dragons fly."

"That is without doubt . . . ouch!" F'nor winced at the pain of an injudicious movement of his arm. "That's the most ridiculous thing I've ever heard. Does F'lar know?"

T'bor shrugged. "If he did, what could he do?"

Brekke pushed F'nor back onto the stool to reset the bandage he had disarranged.

"What'll happen next?" he demanded of no one.

"You sound like an Oldtimer," T'bor remarked with a harsh laugh. "Bemoaning the loss of order, the permissiveness of—of times which are so chaotic . . ."

"Change is not chaos."

T'bor laughed sourly. "Depends on your point of view."

"What's your point of view, T'bor?"

The Weyrleader regarded the brown rider so long and hard, his face settling into such bitter lines, that he appeared Turns older than he was.

"I told you what happened at that farce of a Weyrleaders' meeting the other night, with T'ron insisting it was Terry's fault." T'bor jammed one fist into the palm of his other hand, his lips twitching with a bitter distaste at the memory. "The Weyr above all, even common sense. Stick to your own, the hindmost falls *between.* Well, I'll keep my own counsel. And I'll make my weyrfolk behave. All of them. Even Kylara if I have to . . ."

"Shells, what's Kylara up to now?"

T'bor gave F'nor a thoughtful stare. Then, with a shrug he said, "Kylara means to go to Telgar Hold four days hence. Southern Weyr hasn't been invited. I take no offense. Southern Weyr has no obligation to Telgar Hold and the wedding is Holder business. But she means to make trouble there, I'm sure. I know the signs. Also she's been seeing the Lord Holder of Nabol."

"Meron?" F'nor was unimpressed with him as a source of trouble. "Meron, Lord of Nabol, was outmaneuvered and completely discredited at that abortive battle at the Benden Weyr Pass, eight Turns ago. No Lord Holder would ally himself with Nabol again. Not even Lord Nessel of Crom who never was very bright. How he got confirmed as Lord of Crom by the Conclave, I'll never understand."

"It's not Meron we have to guard against. It's Kylara. Anything she touches gets—distorted."

F'nor knew what T'bor meant. "If she were going to, say, Lord Groghe's Fort Hold, I'd not be concerned. He thinks she should be strangled. But don't forget that she's full blood sister to Larad of Telgar Hold. Besides, Larad can manage her. And Lessa and F'lar will be there. She's not likely to tangle with Lessa. So what can she do? Change the pattern of Thread?"

F'nor heard Brekke's sharp intake of breath, saw T'bor's sudden twitch of surprise.

"She didn't change Thread patterns. No one knows why that happened," T'bor said gloomily.

"How *what* happened?" F'nor stood, pushing aside Brekke's hands.

"You heard that Thread is dropping out of pattern?"

"No, I didn't hear," and F'nor looked from T'bor to Brekke who managed to be very busy with her medicaments.

"There wasn't anything you could do about it, F'nor," she said calmly, "and as you were still feverish when the news came . . ."

T'bor snorted, his eyes glittering as if he enjoyed F'nor's discomposure. "Not that F'lar's precious Thread patterns ever included us here in the Southern continent. Who cares what happens in this part of the world?" With that, T'bor strode out of the Weyr. When F'nor would have followed, Brekke grabbed his arm.

"No, F'nor, don't press him. Please?"

He looked down at Brekke's worried face, saw the deep concern in her expressive eyes. Was that the way of it? Brekke fond of T'bor? A shame she had to waste affection on someone so totally committed to a clutching female like Kylara.

"Now, be kind enough to give me the news about that change in Thread pattern. My arm was wounded, not my head."

Without acknowledging his rebuke, she told him what had occurred at Benden Weyr when Thread had fallen hours too soon over Lemos Hold's wide forests. F'nor was disturbed to learn that R'mart of Telgar Weyr had been badly scored.

He was not surprised that T'kul of High Reaches Weyr hadn't even bothered to inform his contemporaries of the unexpected falls over his weyrbound territories. But he had to agree that he would have worried had he known. He was worried now but it sounded as if F'lar was coping with his usual ingenuity. At least the Oldtimers had been roused. Took Thread to do it.

"I don't understand T'bor's remark about our not caring what happens in this part of the world . . ."

Brekke put her hand on his arm appealingly. "It's not easy to live with Kylara, particularly when it amounts to exile."

"Don't I just know it!" F'nor had had his run-ins with Kylara when she was still at Benden Weyr and, like many other riders, had been relieved when she'd been made Weyrwoman at Southern. The only problem with convalescing here in Southern, however, was her proximity. For F'nor's peace, her interest in Meron of Nabol couldn't have been more fortunate.

"You can see how much T'bor has made out of Southern Weyr in the Turns he's been Weyrleader here," Brekke went on.

F'nor nodded, honestly impressed. "Did he ever complete the exploration of the southern continent?" He couldn't recall any report on the matter coming in to Benden Weyr.

"I don't think so. The deserts to the west are terrible. One or two riders got curious but the winds turned them back. And eastward, there's just ocean. It probably extends right around to the desert. This is the bottom of the earth, you know."

F'nor flexed his bandaged arm.

"Now you listen to me, Wing-second F'nor of Benden," Brekke said sharply, interpreting that gesture accurately. "You're in no condition to go charging back to duty or to go exploring. You haven't the stamina of a fledgling and you certainly can't go *between*. Intense cold is the worst thing for a half-healed wound. Why do you think you were flown here straight?"

"Why, Brekke, I didn't know you cared," F'nor said, rather pleased at her vehement reaction.

She gave him such a piercingly candid look that his smile

faded. As if she regretted that all too intimate glance, she gave him a half-playful push toward the door.

"Get out. Take your poor lonely dragon and lie on the beach in the sun. Rest. Can't you hear Canth calling you?"

She slipped by him, out the door, and was across the clearing before he realized that *he* hadn't heard Canth.

"Brekke?"

She turned, hesitantly, at the edge of the woods.

"Can you hear other dragons?"

"Yes." She whirled and was gone.

"Of all the—" F'nor was astounded. "Why didn't you tell me?" he demanded of Canth as he strode into the sun-baked wallow behind the weyr and stood glaring at his brown dragon.

You never asked, Canth replied. *I like Brekke.*

"You're impossible," F'nor said, exasperated, and looked back in the direction Brekke had gone. "Brekke?" And he stared hard at Canth, somewhat disgusted by his obtuseness. Dragons as a rule did not name people. They tended to project a vision of the person referred to by pronoun, rarely by name. That Canth, who was of another Weyr, should speak of Brekke so familiarly was a double surprise. He must tell that to F'lar.

I want to get wet. Canth sounded so wistful that F'nor laughed aloud.

"You swim. I'll watch."

Gently Canth nudged F'nor on the good shoulder. *You are nearly well. Good. We'll soon be able to go back to the Weyr we belong to.*

"Don't tell me that you knew about the Thread pattern changing."

Of course, Canth replied.

"Why, you, wher-faced, wherry-necked . . ."

Sometimes a dragon knows what's best for his rider. You have to be well to fight Thread. I want to swim. And there was no arguing with Canth further, F'nor knew. Aware he'd been manipulated, F'nor also had no redress with Canth so he put the matter aside. Once he was well, his arm completely healed, however . . .

Although they had to fly straight toward the beaches, an irritatingly lengthy process for someone used to instantaneous transport from one place to another, F'nor elected to go a good distance west, along the coastline, until he found a secluded cove with a deep bay, suitable to dragon bathing.

A high dune of sand, probably pushed up from winter storms, protected the beach from the south. Far, far away, purple on the horizon, he could just make out the headland that marked Southern Weyr.

Canth landed him somewhat above the high-water mark in the cove, on the clean fine sand, and then, taking a flying leap, dove into the brilliantly blue water. F'nor watched, amused, as Canth cavorted—an unlikely fish—erupting out of the sea, reversing himself just above the surface and then diving deeply. When the dragon considered himself sufficiently watered, he floundered out, flapping his wings mightily until the breeze brought the shower up the beach to F'nor who protested.

Canth then irrigated himself so thoroughly with sand that F'nor was half-minded to send him back to rinse, but Canth protested, the sand felt so good and warm against his hide. F'nor relented and, when the dragon had finally made his wallow, couched himself on a convenient curl of tail. The sun soon lulled them into drowsy inertia.

F'nor, Canth's gentle summons penetrated the brown rider's delicious somnolence, *do not move.*

That was sufficient to dispel drowsy complacence, yet the dragon's tone was amused, not alarmed.

Open one eye carefully, Canth advised.

Resentful but obedient, F'nor opened one eye. It was all he could do to remain limp. Returning his gaze was a golden dragon, small enough to perch on his bare forearm. The tiny eyes, like winking green-fired jewels, regarded him with wary curiosity. Suddenly the miniature wings, no bigger than the span of F'nor's fingers, unfurled into gilt transparencies, aglitter in the sunlight.

"Don't go," F'nor said, instinctively using a mere mental whisper. Was he dreaming? He couldn't believe his eyes.

The wings hesitated a beat. The tiny dragon tilted its head.

Don't go, little one, Canth added with equal delicacy. *We are of the same blood.*

The minute beast registered an incredulity and indecision which were transmitted to man and dragon. The wings remained up but the tautness which preceded flight relaxed. Curiosity replaced indecision. Incredulity grew stronger. The little dragon paced the length of F'nor's arm to gaze steadfastly into his eyes until F'nor felt his eye muscles strain to keep from crossing.

Doubt and wonder reached F'nor, and then he understood the tiny one's problem.

"I'm not of your blood. The monster above us is," F'nor communicated softly. "You are of *his* blood."

Again the tiny head cocked. The eyes glistened actively as they whirled with surprise and increased doubt.

To Canth, F'nor remarked that perspective was impossible for the little dragon, one hundredth his size.

Move back then, Canth suggested. *Little sister, go with the man.*

The little dragon flew up on blurringly active wings, hovering as F'nor slowly rose. He walked several lengths from Canth's recumbent hulk, the little dragon following. When F'nor turned and slowly pointed back to the brown, the little beast circled, took one look and abruptly disappeared.

"Come back," F'nor cried. Maybe he *was* dreaming.

Canth rumbled with amusement. *How would you like to see a man as large to you as I am to her?*

"Canth, do you realize that *that was a fire lizard?*"
Certainly.

"I actually had a fire lizard on my arm! Do you realize how many times people have tried to catch one of those creatures?" F'nor stopped, savoring the experience. He was probably the first man to get that close to a fire lizard. And the dainty little beauty had registered emotion, understood simple directions and then—gone *between*.

Yes, she went between, Canth confirmed, unmoved.

"Why, you big lump of sand, do you realize what that means? Those legends *are* true. You were bred from something as small as her!"

I don't remember, Canth replied, but something in his tone made F'nor realize that the big beast's draconic complacency was a little shaken.

F'nor grinned and stroked Canth's muzzle affectionately. "How could you, big one? When we—men—have lost so much knowledge and we can record what we know."

There are other ways of remembering important matters, Canth replied.

"Just imagine being able to breed tiny fire lizards into a creature the size of you!" He was awed, knowing how long it had taken to breed faster landbeasts.

Canth rumbled restlessly. *I am useful. She is not.*

"I'd wager she'd improve rapidly with a little help." The prospect fascinated F'nor. "Would you mind?"

Why?

F'nor leaned against the great wedge-shaped head, looping his arm under the jaw, as far as he could reach, feeling extremely fond and proud of his dragon.

"No, that was a stupid question for me to ask you, Canth, wasn't it?"

Yes.

"I wonder how long it would take me to train her."

To do what?

"Nothing you can't do better, of course. No, now wait a minute. If, by chance, I could train her to take messages . . . You said she went *between?* I wonder if she could be taught to go *between,* alone, and come back. Ah, but will she come back here to us now?" At this juncture, F'nor's enthusiasm for the project was deflated by harsh reality.

She comes, Canth said very softly.

"Where?"

Above your head.

Very slowly, F'nor raised one arm, hand outstretched, palm down.

"Little beauty, come where we can admire you. We mean you no harm." F'nor saturated his mental tone with all the reassuring persuasiveness at his command.

A shimmer of gold flickered at the corner of his eye. Then the little lizard hovered at F'nor's eye level, just beyond his reach. He ignored Canth's amusement that the tiny one was susceptible to flattery.

She is hungry, the big dragon said.

Very slowly F'nor reached into his pouch and drew out a meatroll. He broke off a piece, bent slowly to lay it on the rock at his feet, then backed away.

"That is food for you, little one."

The lizard continued to hover, then darted down and, grabbing the meat in her tiny claws, disappeared again.

F'nor squatted down to wait.

In a second, the dragonette returned, ravenous hunger foremost in her delicate thoughts along with a wistful plea. As F'nor broke off another portion, he tried to dampen his elation. If hunger could be the leash . . . Patiently he fed her tiny bits, each time placing the food nearer to him until he got her to take the final morsel from his fingers. As she cocked her head at him, not quite sated, though she had eaten enough to satisfy a grown man, he ventured to stroke an eye ridge with a gentle fingertip.

The inner lids of the tiny opalescent eyes closed one by one as she abandoned herself to the caress.

She is a hatchling. You have Impressed her, Canth told him very softly.

"A hatchling?"

She is the little sister of my blood after all and so must come from an egg, Canth replied reasonably.

"There are others?"

Of course. Down on the beach.

F'nor, careful not to disturb the little lizard, turned his head over his shoulder. He had been so engrossed in the one at hand, he hadn't even heard above the surf sounds the pitiful squawks which were issuing from the litter of shining wings and bodies. There seemed to be hundreds of them on the beach, above the high-tide mark, about twenty dragon lenths from him.

Don't move, Canth cautioned him. *You'll lose her.*

"But if they're hatching . . . they can be Impressed . . . Canth, rouse the Weyr! Speak to Prideth. Speak to Wirenth. Tell them to come. Tell them to bring food. Tell them to hurry. Quickly or it'll be too late."

He stared hard at the purple blotch on the horizon that was the Weyr, as if he himself could somehow bridge the gap with his thoughts. But the frenzy on the beach was attracting attention from another source. Wild wherries, the carrion eaters of Pern, instinctively flocked to the shore, their wings making an ominous line of v's in the southern sky. The vanguard was already beating to a height, preparing to dive at the unprotected weak fledglings. Every nerve in F'nor's body yearned to go to their rescue, but Canth repeated his warning. F'nor would jeopardize his fragile rapport with the little queen if he moved. Or, F'nor realized, if he communicated his agitation to her. He closed his eyes. He couldn't watch.

The first shriek of pain vibrated through his body as well as the little lizard's. She darted into the folds of his arm sling, trembling against his ribs. Despite himself, F'nor opened his eyes. But the wherries had not stooped yet, though they circled lower and lower with rapacious speed. The fledglings were voraciously attacking each other. He shuddered and the little queen rattled her pinions, uttering a delicate fluting sound of distress.

"You're safe with me. Far safer with me. Nothing can harm you with me," F'nor told her repeatedly, and Canth crooned reassurance in harmony with that litany.

The strident shriek of the wherries as they plunged suddenly changed to their piercing wail of terror. F'nor glanced up, away from the carnage on the beach, to see a green dragon in the sky, belching flame, scattering the avian hunters. The green hovered, several lengths above the beach, her head extended downward. She was riderless.

Just then, F'nor saw three figures, charging, sliding, slipping down the high sand dune, heading as straight as possible toward the many-winged mass of cannibals. Although they looked as if they'd carom right into the middle, they somehow managed to stop.

Brekke said she has alerted as many as she could, Canth told him.

"Brekke? Why'd you call her? She's got enough to do."

She is the best one, Canth replied, ignoring F'nor's reprimand.

"Are they too late?" F'nor glanced anxiously at the sky and at the dune, willing more men to arrive.

Brekke was wading toward the struggling hatchlings now, her hands extended. The other two were following her example. Who had she brought? Why hadn't she got more riders? They'd know instantly how to approach the beasts.

Two more dragons appeared in the sky, circled and landed with dizzying speed right on the beach, their riders racing in to help. The skyborne green flamed off the insistent wherries, bugling to her fellows to help her.

Brekke has one. And the girl. So does the boy but the beast is hurt. Brekke says that many are dead.

Why, wondered F'nor suddenly, if he had only just seen

the truth of the legend of fire lizards, did he ache for their deaths? Surely the creatures had been hatching on lonely beaches for centuries, been eaten by wherries and their own peers, unseen and unmourned.

The strong survive, said Canth, undismayed.

They saved seven, two badly hurt. The young girl, Mirrim, Brekke's fosterling, attached three; two greens and a brown, seriously injured by gouges on his soft belly. Brekke had a bronze with no mark on him, the green's rider had a bronze, and the other two riders had blues, one with a wrenched wing which Brekke feared might never heal properly for flight.

"Seven out of over fifty," said Brekke sadly after they had disposed of the broken bodies with agenothree. A precaution which Brekke suggested as a frustration for the carrion eaters and to prevent other fire lizards from avoiding the beach as dangerous to their kind. "I wonder how many would have survived if you hadn't called us."

"She was already far from the others when she discovered us," F'nor remarked. "Probably the first to hatch, or on top of the others."

Brekke'd had the wit to bring a full haunch of buck, though the Weyr might eat light that evening. So they had gorged the hatchlings into such a somnolent state that they could be carried, unresisting, back to the Weyr, or to Brekke's Infirmary.

"You're to fly home straight," Brekke told F'nor, in much the way a woman spoke to a rebellious weyrling.

"Yes, ma'am," F'nor replied, with mock humility, and then smiled because Brekke took him so seriously.

The little queen nestled in his arm sling as contentedly as if she'd found a weyr of her own. "A weyr is where a dragon is no matter how it's constructed," he murmured to himself as Canth winged steadily eastward.

When F'nor reached Southern, it was obvious the news had raced through the Weyr. There was such an aura of excitement that F'nor began to worry that it might frighten the tiny creatures *between.*

No dragon can fly when he is belly-bloated, Canth said. *Even a fire lizard.* And took himself off to his sun-warmed wallow, no longer interested.

"You don't suppose he's jealous, do you?" F'nor asked

Brekke when he found her in her Infirmary, splinting the little blue's wrenched wing.

"Wirenth was interested, too, until the lizards fell asleep," Brekke told him, a twinkle in her green eyes as she looked up at him briefly. "And you know how touchy Wirenth is right now. Mercy, F'nor, what is there for a dragon to be jealous of? These are toys, dolls as far as the big ones are concerned. At best, children to be protected and taught like any fosterling."

F'nor glanced over at Mirrim, Brekke's foster child. The two green lizards perched asleep on her shoulders. The injured brown, swathed from neck to tail in bandage, was cradled in her lap. Mirrim was sitting with the erect stiffness of someone who dares not move a muscle. And she was smiling with an incredulous joy.

"Mirrim is very young for this," he said, shaking his head.

"On the contrary, she's as old as most weyrlings at their first Impression. And she's more mature in some ways than half a dozen grown women I know with several babes of their own."

"Oh-ho. The female of the species in staunch defense . . ."

"It's no teasing matter, F'nor," Brekke replied with a sharpness that put F'nor in mind of Lessa. "Mirrim will do very well. She takes every responsibility to heart." The glance Brekke shot her fosterling was anxious as well as tender.

"I still say she's young . . ."

"Is age a prerequisite for a loving heart? Does maturity always bring compassion? Why are some weyrbred boys left standing on the sand and others, never thought to have a chance, walk off with the bronzes? Mirrim Impressed three, and the rest of us, though we tried, with the creatures dying at our feet, only managed to attach one."

"And why am I never told what occurs in my own Weyr?" Kylara demanded in a loud voice. She stood on the threshold of the Infirmary, her face suffused with an angry flush, her eyes bright and hard.

"As soon as I finished this splinting, I was coming to tell you," Brekke replied calmly, but F'nor saw her shoulders stiffen.

Kylara advanced on the girl, with such overt menace that F'nor stepped around Brekke, wondering to himself as he

79

did so whether Kylara was armed with more than a bad temper.

"Events moved rather fast, Kylara," he said, smiling pleasantly. "We were fortunate to save as many of the lizards as we did. Too bad you didn't hear Canth broadcast the news. You might have Impressed one yourself."

Kylara halted, the full skirts of her robe swirling around her feet. She glared at him, twitching the sleeve of her dress but not before he saw the black bruise on her arm. Unable to attack Brekke, she turned, spotting Mirrim. She swept up to the girl, staring down in such a way that the child looked appealingly toward Brekke. At this point, the tension in the room roused the lizards. The two greens hissed at Kylara but it was the crystal bugle of the bronze on G'sel's shoulder that diverted the Weyrwoman's attention.

"I'll have the bronze! Of course. The bronze'll do fine," she exclaimed. There was something so repellent about the glitter in her eyes and the nasty edge to her laugh that F'nor felt the hair rise on the back of his neck.

"A bronze dragon on my shoulder will be most effective, I think," Kylara went on, reaching for G'sel's bronze lizard.

G'sel put up a warning hand.

"I said they were Impressed, Kylara," F'nor warned her, quickly signaling the rider to refuse. G'sel was only a green rider and new to this Weyr at that; he was no match for Kylara, particularly not in this mood. "Touch him at your own risk."

"Impressed, you say?" Kylara hesitated, turning to sneer at F'nor. "Why, they're nothing but fire lizards."

"And from what creature on Pern do you think dragons were bred?"

"Not that old nursery nonsense. How could you possibly make a fighting dragon from a fire lizard?" She reached again for the little bronze. It spread its wings, flapping them agitatedly.

"If it bites you, don't blame G'sel," F'nor told her in a pleasant drawl though it cost him much to keep his temper. It was too bad you couldn't beat a Weyrwoman with impunity. Her dragon wouldn't permit it but a sound thrashing was what Kylara badly needed.

"You can't be certain they're that much like dragons,"

Kylara protested, glancing suspiciously around at the others. "No one's ever caught one and you just found them."

"We're not certain of anything about them," F'nor replied, beginning to enjoy himself. It was a pleasure to see Kylara frustrated by a lizard. "However, look at the similarities. My little queen . . ."

"*You?* Impressed a queen?" Kylara's face turned livid as F'nor casually drew aside a fold of his sling to expose the sleeping gold lizard.

"She went *between* when she was frightened. She communicated that fright, plus curiosity, and she evidently received our reassurances. At least she came back. Canth said she'd just hatched. I fed her and she's still with me. We managed to save only these seven because they got Impressed. The others turned cannibal. Now, how long these will be dependent on us for food and companionship is pure conjecture. But the dragons admit a blood relationship and they have ways of knowing beyond ours."

"Just how did you Impress them?" Kylara demanded, her intentions transparent. "No one's ever caught one before."

If it got her out of the Weyr and kept her on sandy beaches and off Brekke's back, F'nor was quite agreeable to telling her.

"You Impress them by being there when they hatch, same as with dragons. After that, I assume the ones which survive stay wild. As to why no one ever caught any before, that's simple; the fire lizards hear them coming and disappear *between*." And, my dear, may it be a warm night *between* before you catch one.

Kylara stared hard at Mirrim and so resentfully at G'sel that the young rider began to fidget and the little bronze rustled his wings nervously.

"Well, I want it clearly understood that this is a working Weyr. We've no time for pets who serve no purpose. I'll deal severely with anyone shirking their duties or—" She broke off.

"No shirking or tramping the beaches until you've had a chance to get one first, huh, Kylara?" asked F'nor, still grinning pleasantly.

"I've better things to do," She spat the words at him and then, skirts kicking out before her, swept out of the room.

"Maybe we ought to warn the lizards," F'nor said in a facetious way, trying to dispel the tension in the Infirmary.

"There's no protection against someone like Kylara," Brekke said, motioning the rider to take his bandaged blue. "One learns to live with her."

G'sel gave an odd gargle and rose, almost unsettling his lizard.

"How can you say that, Brekke, when she's so mean and nasty to you?" Mirrim cried, and subsided at a stern look from her foster mother.

"Make no judgments where you have no compassion," Brekke replied. "And I, too, will not tolerate any shirking of duties to care for these pretties. I don't know why we saved them!"

"Make no judgments where you have no compassion," F'nor retorted.

"*They* needed us," Mirrim said so emphatically that even she was surprised at her temerity, and immediately became absorbed in her brown.

"Yes, they did," F'nor agreed, aware of the little queen's golden body nestled trustingly against his ribs. She had twined her tail as far as it would reach around his waist. "And true weyrmen one and all, we responded to the cry for succor."

"Mirrim Impressed three and she's no weyrman," Brekke said in a dry, didactic correction. "And if they are Impressionable by non-riders, they might well be worth every effort to save."

"How's that?"

Brekke frowned a little at F'nor as if she didn't credit his obtuseness.

"Look at the facts, F'nor. I don't know of a commoner alive who hasn't entertained the notion of catching a fire lizard, simply because they resemble small dragons—no, don't interrupt me. You know perfectly well that it's just in these last eight Turns that commoners were permitted on the Ground as candidates at Impression. Why, I remember my brothers plotting night after night in the hope of catching a fire lizard, a personal dragon of their own. I don't think it ever occurred to anyone, really, that there might be some truth in that old myth that dragons—weyrdragons—were

bred from lizards. It was just that fire lizards were not pro-
scribed to commoners, and dragons were. Out of our reach."
Her eyes softened with affection as she stroked the tiny
sleeping bronze in the crook of her arm. "Odd to realize
that generations of commoners were on the right track and
never knew it. These creatures have the same talent dragons
have for capturing our feelings. I oughtn't to take on another responsibility but nothing would make me relinquish
my bronze now he's made himself mine." Her lips curved
in a very tender smile. Then, as if aware she was display-
ing too much of her inner feelings, she said very briskly,
"It'd be a very good thing for people—for commoners—
to have a small taste of dragon."

"Brekke, you can't mean you think that a fire lizard's loving company would mellow someone like Vincet of Nerat
or Meron of Nabol toward dragonriders?" Out of respect for
her, F'nor did not laugh aloud. Brekke was a sackful of
unexpected reactions.

She gave him such a stern look that he began to regret
his words.

"If you'll pardon me, F'nor," G'sel spoke up, "I think
Brekke's got a good thought there. I'm holdbred myself.
You're weyrbred. You can't imagine how I used to feel
about dragonriders. I honestly didn't know myself—until I
Impressed Roth." His face lit with a startling joy at the
memory. He paused, unabashed, to savor the moment anew.
"It'd be worth a try. Even if the fire lizards are dumb,
it'd make a difference. *They* wouldn't understand how much
more it is with a dragon. Look, F'nor, here's this perfectly
charming creature, perched on my shoulder, adoring me. He
was all ready to bite the Weyrwoman to stay with me. You
heard how angry he was. You don't know how—spectacular
—it'd make a commoner feel."

F'nor looked around, at Brekke, at Mirrim, who did not
evade his eyes this time, at the other riders.

"Are you all holdbred? I hadn't realized. Somehow, once
a man becomes a rider, you forget he ever had another
affiliation."

"I was craftbred," Brekke said, "but G'sel's remarks are
as valid for the Craft as the Hold."

"Perhaps we ought to get T'bor to issue an order that

lizard-watching has now become a Weyr duty," F'nor suggested, grinning slyly at Brekke.

"That'll show Kylara," someone murmured very softly from Mirrim's direction.

CHAPTER V

Midmorning at Ruatha Hold
Early Evening at Benden Weyr

Jaxom's pleasure in riding a dragon, in being summoned to Benden Weyr, was severely dim.nished by his guardian's glowering disapproval. Jaxom had yet to learn that most of Lord Warder Lytol's irritation was for a far larger concern than his ward's mischievous habit of getting lost in the unused and dangerous corridors of Ruatha Hold. As it was, Jaxom was quite downcast. He didn't *mean* to irritate Lytol, but he never seemed able to *please* him, no matter how hard he tried. There was such an unconscionable number of things that he, Jaxom, Lord of Ruatha Hold, must know, must do, must understand, that his head swam until he had to run away, to be by himself, to think. And the only empty places to think in in Ruatha, where no one ever went or would bother you, were in the back portions of the hollowed-out cliff that was Ruatha Hold. And while he could, just possibly, get lost or trapped behind a rockfall (there hadn't been a cave-in at Ruatha in the memory of living man or the Hold Records as far back as they were still legible), Jaxom hadn't got into trouble or danger. He knew his way around perfectly. Who could tell? His investigations might someday save Ruatha Hold from another invader like Fax, his father. Here Jaxom's thoughts faltered. A father he had never seen, a mother who died bearing him, had made him Lord of Ruatha, though his mother had been of Crom Hold and Fax his father, of the High Reaches. It was Lessa, who was now Weyrwoman at Benden, who had been the last of Ruathan Blood. These were contradictions he didn't understand and must.

He had changed his clothes now, from the dirty everyday ones to his finest tunic and trousers, with a wher-hide over-tunic and knee boots. Not that even they could stop the horrible cold of *between*. Jaxom shuddered with delighted terror. It was like being suspended nowhere, until your throat closed and your bowels knotted and you were scared silly that you'd never again see the light of day, or even night's darkness, depending on local time of day where you were supposed to emerge. He was very jealous of Felessan, de-spite the fact that it was by no means sure his friend would be a dragonrider. But Felessan *lived* at Benden Weyr, and he had a mother and a father, and dragonriders all around him, and . . .

"Lord Jaxom!" Lytol's call from the Great Courtyard broke through the boy's reverie and he ran, suddenly afraid that they'd leave without him.

It was only a green, Jaxom thought with some disappoint-ment. You'd think they'd send a brown at the very least, for Lytol, Warder of Ruatha Hold, one time dragonrider himself. Then Jaxom was overwhelmed by contrition. Ly-tol's dragon had been a brown and it was well known that half a man's soul left him when his dragon died and he remained among the living.

The green's rider grinned a welcome as Jaxom scrambled up the extended leg.

"Good morning, Jeralte," he said, slightly startled because he'd played in the Lower Caves with the young man only two Turns back. Now he was a full-fledged rider.

"J'ralt, please, Lord Jaxom," Lytol corrected his ward.

"That's all right, Jaxom," J'ralt said and looped the riding belt deftly around Jáxom's waist.

Jaxom wanted to sink; to be corrected by Lytol in front of Jer—J'ralt, and not to remember to use the honorific contraction! He didn't enjoy the thrill of rising, a-dragonback, over the great towers of Ruatha Hold, of watching the valley, spread out like a wall hanging under the dragon's sinuous green neck. But as they circled, Jaxom had to balance himself against the dragon's unexpectedly soft hide, and the warmth of that contact seemed to ease his inner misery. Then he saw the line of weeders in the fields and knew that they must be looking up at the dragon. Did those bullying Hold boys know that he, Jaxom, Lord of Ruatha, was a-dragonback? Jaxom was himself again.

To be a dragonman was surely the most wonderful thing in the world. Jaxom felt a sudden wave of overwhelming pity for Lytol who had had this joy and—lost it, and now must suffer agonies to ride another's beast. Jaxom looked at the rigid back in front of him, for he was sandwiched between the two men, and wished that he might comfort his Warder. Lytol was always fair, and if he expected Jaxom to be perfect, it was because Jaxom must be perfect to be the Lord of Ruatha Hold. Which was no little honor, even if it wasn't being a dragonrider.

Jaxom's reflections were brought to an abrupt stop as the dragon took them *between*.

You count to three slowly, Jaxom told his frantic mind as he lost all sense of sight and sound, of contact, even of the soft dragon hide beneath his hands. He tried to count and couldn't. His mind seemed to freeze, but just as he was about to shriek, they burst out into the late afternoon, over Benden Weyr. Never had the Bowl seemed so welcome, with its high walls softened and colored by the lambent sun. The black maws of the individual weyrs, set in the face of the inner wall, were voiceless mouths, greeting him all astonished.

As they circled down, Jaxom spotted bronze Mnementh, surely the hugest dragon ever hatched, lounging on the ledge to the queen's weyr. *She'd* be in the Hatching Ground, Jaxom knew, for the new clutch was still hardening on the warm sands. There'd be another Impression soon. And there was a golden queen egg in the new clutch. Jaxom had heard that another Ruathan girl had been one of those chosen on

Search. Another Ruathan Weyrwoman, he was positive. His Hold had bred up more Weyrwomen . . . Mardra, of course, was nowhere near as important as Lessa or Moreta, but she had come from Ruatha. She'd some real funny notions about the Hold. She always annoyed Lytol. Jaxom knew that, because the twitch in his Warder's cheek would start jumping. It didn't when Lessa visited. Except that lately Lessa had stopped coming to Ruatha Hold.

The young Lord of Ruatha spotted Lessa now, as they circled again to bring the queen's weyr in flight line. She and F'lar were on the ledge. The green called, answered by Mnementh's bass roar. A muffled bellow reverberated through the Weyr. Ramoth, the queen, took notice of their arrival.

Jaxom felt much better, particularly when he also caught sight of a small figure, racing across the Bowl floor to the stairs up to the queen's weyr. Felessan. His friend. He hadn't seen him in months. Jaxom didn't want the flight to end but he couldn't wait to see Felessan.

Jaxom was nervously conscious of Lytol's critical eyes as he made his duty to the Weyrwoman and the Weyrleader. He'd rehearsed words and bow often enough. He ought to have it down heart-perfect, yet he heard himself stammering out the traditional words and felt the fool.

"You came, you came. I told Gandidan you'd come," cried Felessan, dashing up the steps, two at a time. He nearly knocked Jaxom down with his antics. Felessan was three Turns his junior but he was of the dragonfolk, and even if Lessa and F'lar had turned their son over to a foster mother, he ought to have more manners. Maybe what Mardra was always carping about was true. The new weyrmen had no manners.

In that instant, as if the younger boy sensed his friend's disapproval, he drew himself up and, still all smiles, bowed with commendable grace to Lytol.

"Good afternoon to you, Lord Warder Lytol. And thank you for bringing Lord Jaxom. May we be excused?"

Before any adult could answer, Felessan had Jaxom by the hand and was leading him down the steps.

"Stay out of trouble, Lord Jaxom," Lytol called after them.

"There's little trouble they can get into here," Lessa laughed.

"I had the entire Hold mustered this morning, only to

find him in the bowels of the Hold itself, where a rock-fall . . ."

Now why did Lytol have to tell Lessa? Jaxom groaned to himself, with a flash of his previous discontent.

"Did you find anything?" Felessan demanded as soon as they were out of earshot.

"Find anything?"

"Yes, in the bowels of the Hold." Felessan's eyes widened and his voice took on Lytol's inflections.

Jaxom kicked at a rock, pleased by the trajectory and the distance it flew. "Oh, empty rooms, full of dust and rubbish. An old tunnel that led nowhere but an old slide. Nothing great."

"C'mon, Jax."

Felessan's sly tone made Jaxom look at him closely.

"Where?"

"I'll show you."

The weyrboy led Jaxom into the Lower Cavern, the main chamber with a vaulting roof where the Weyr met for sociability and evening meals. There was a smell of warm bread and simmering meats. Dinner preparations were well along, tables set and women and girls bustling about, making pleasant chatter. As Felessan veered past a preparation table, he snatched up a handful of raw roots.

"Don't you dare spoil your dinner, you young wher-whelp," cried one of the women, swinging at the retreating pair with her ladle. "And a good day to you, Lord Jaxom," she added.

The attitude of the weyrfolk toward himself and Felessan never failed to puzzle Jaxom. Why, Felessan was just as important as a Lord Holder, but he wasn't always being watched, as if he might break apart or melt.

"You're so lucky," Jaxom sighed as he accepted his share of Felessan's loot.

"Why?" the younger boy asked, surprised.

"You're—you just are, that's all."

Felessan shrugged, chomping complacently on the sweet root. He led Jaxom out of the Main Cavern and into the inner one, which was actually not much smaller, though the ceiling was lower. A wide, banistered ledge circled the Cavern a half-dragonlength above the floor, giving access to the individual sleeping rooms that ringed the height. The main floor was devoted to other homey tasks. No one was at the looms now, of course, with dinner being prepared, nor was anyone bathing at the large pool to one side of the Cavern, but a group of boys Felessan's age were gathered by the miggsy circle. One boy made a loud, meant-to-be-overheard remark which was fortunately lost in the obedient loud cackles of laughter from the others.

"C'mon, Jaxom. Before one of those baby boys wants to tag along," Felessan said.

"Where are we going?"

Felessan shushed him peremptorily, looking quickly over his shoulder to see if they were being observed. He walked very fast, making Jaxom lengthen his stride to keep up.

"Hey, I don't want to get in trouble here, too," he said when he realized they were heading still farther into the caves. It was one thing, according to Jaxom's lexicon, to be adventurous in one's own Hold, but quite another to invade the sanctity of another's, much less a Weyr! That was close to blasphemy, or so he'd been taught by his ex-dragonrider guardian. And while he could weather Lytol's wrath, he never, never, never wanted to anger Lessa . . . or—his mind whispered the name—*F'lar!*

"Trouble? We won't get caught. Everybody's too busy this near dinner, I'd've had to help if you hadn't come," and the boy grinned smugly. "C'mon!"

They had arrived at a fork in the passageway, one leading left, deeper into the Weyr, the other bending right. This one was ill-lit and Jaxom faltered. You didn't waste glows on unused corridors.

"What's the matter?" Felessan asked, frowning back at his reluctant guest. "You're not afraid, are you?"

"Afraid?" Jaxom quickly stepped to Felessan's side. "It's not a question of fear."

"C'mon then. And be quiet."

"Why?" Jaxom had already lowered his voice.

"You'll see. Only be quiet now, huh? And take this."

From a hidey-hole, Felessan handed Jaxom a half-shielded basket with one feebly gleaming glow. He had another for himself. Whatever objections Jaxom might have had were stilled by the challenge in the younger boy's eyes. He turned haughtily and led the way down the shadowy corridor. He was somewhat reassured by the footprints in the dust, all leading the same way. But this hall was not frequented by adults. All the footprints were smallish, not a bootheel among 'em. Where did it lead?

They passed locked, covered doorways, long unused and scary in the flickering light of the dim glows. Why couldn't Felessan have stolen some new ones while he was about it? These wouldn't last too long. Jaxom earnestly wanted to know how far they were going. He had no liking for a trip through back halls and dangerous corridors without full illumination to aid his vision and reduce his imagination. But he couldn't ask. What could there possibly be this far back in the Weyr? A huge rectangle of absolute black rose on his left and he swallowed against terror, as Felessan marched purposefully past it, his weak glow back-lighting the threatening maw into another innocently empty corridor junction.

"Hurry up," Felessan said, sharply.

"Why?" Jaxom was pleased with the steady, casual tone he managed.

"Because *she* always goes to the lake about this time of day and it's the only chance you'll ever get."

"Chance to what? Who's she?"

"Ramoth, thickwit," Felessan stopped so quickly that Jaxom bumped into him and the glow in his basket began to flicker.

"Ramoth?"

"Sure. Or are you afraid to sneak a look at her eggs?"

"At her eggs? Honest?" Breathless terror battled with insatiable curiosity and the knowledge that this would really put him one up on the Hold boys.

"Honest! Now, c'mon!"

The other corridors they passed held no unknown evils for Jaxom now, with such a promised end to this dark trek. And Felessan did seem to know where he was going. Their passage churned up the dust, further dimming the glows, but ahead was a sliver of light.

"There's where we're heading."

"Have you ever seen an Impression, Felessan?"

"Sure. A whole gang of us watched the last one and ooh, that was the most scary-velous time. It was just great. First the eggs wobbled back and forth, see, and then these great cracks appeared. Zigzaggy ones down the eggs, longwise," Felessan excitedly illustrated the point with his glow basket. "Then, all of a sudden," and his voice dropped to a more dramatic pitch, "one enormous, dragon-sized split and the head—comes through. You know what color the first one was?"

"Don't you know that from the color of the shell?"

"No, except for the queen. They're biggest and they gleam kinda. You'll see."

Jaxom gulped but nothing could have kept him from continuing now. None of the Hold boys or even the other young lordlings had seen eggs, or an Impression. Maybe he could lie a little . . .

"Hey, keep off my heels," Felessan commanded.

The sliver of light ahead widened, touching the smooth wall opposite with a comforting rectangle. As they got closer and their glows augmented the outside light, Jaxom could make out the end of the corridor just beyond the fissure of the slot. The jumble of rock gave evidence of an ancient slide. But sure enough, they could really spy on the mottled eggs as they lay maturing on the mist-heated sands. Occasionally an egg rocked slightly as Jaxom watched, fascinated.

"Where's the queen egg?" he asked in a reverent undertone.

"You don't need to whisper. See? Ground's empty. Ramoth's gone to the lake."

"Where's the queen egg?" Jaxom repeated and was disgusted when his voice broke.

"It's kinda to that side, out of sight."

Jaxom craned his neck up and down, trying to get a glimpse of the golden egg.

"You really want to see it?"

"Sure. Talina's been taken on Search from my Hold and she'll be a Weyrwoman. Ruathan girls always become Weyrwomen."

Felessan gave him a long stare, then shrugged. He twisted sideways and inserted his body into the slit, easing his way past the rocks.

"C'mon," he urged his friend in a hoarse whisper.

Jaxom eyed the slit dubiously. He was heavier as well as taller than Felessan. He presented the side of his body to the slit and took a deep breath. His left leg and arm got through fine but his chest was caught against the rocks. Helpfully, Felessan grabbed his left arm and yanked. Jaxom manfully suppressed a yelp as knee and chest were scraped skin deep by rock.

"Eggshells, I'm sorry, Jaxom."

"I didn't tell you to *pull!*" Then he added as he saw Felessan's contrite expression, "I'm all right, I guess."

Felessan pulled his tunic up to dab at the young Lord's bloody bare chest. The rock had torn through fabric. Jaxom slapped his hand away. It smarted enough as it was. Then he saw the great golden egg, reposing by itself, a little apart from the motley group.

"It's—it's—so glisteny," he murmured, swallowing against awe and reverence, and a growing sense of sacrilege. Only the weyrbred had the right to see the Eggs.

Felessan was casting a judicious eye over the gold egg.

"And big, too. Bigger'n the last queen egg at Fort. Their stock is falling off noticeably," he remarked with critical detachment.

"Not to hear Mardra talk. She says it's obvious Benden stock is in trouble; the dragons are too large to maneuver properly."

"N'ton says Mardra's a pain in the ass, the way she treats T'ron."

Jaxom didn't like the trend of the conversation now. After all, Ruatha Hold was weyrbound to Fort Weyr and while he didn't much like Mardra, he ought not listen to such talk.

"Well, this one's not so big. Looks like a wherry egg. It's half the size of even the smallest one of the others," and he touched the smooth shell of an egg that lay almost against the rock wall, apart from the others.

"Hey, don't touch it!" Felessan protested, visibly startled.

"Why not? Can't hurt it, can I? Hard as leather," and Jaxom rapped it gently with his knuckles and then spread his hand flat on the curve. "It's warm."

Felessan pulled him away from the egg.

"You don't touch eggs. Not ever. Not until it's your turn. And you're not weyrbred."

Jaxom looked disdainfully at him. "You're scared to." And he caressed the egg again to prove that he was not.

"I am *not* scared. But you *don't* touch eggs," and Felessan slapped at Jaxom's impious hand. "Not unless you're a candidate. And you're not. And neither am I, yet."

"No, I'm a Lord Holder," and Jaxom drew himself up

proudly. He couldn't resist the urge to pat the small egg once more because, while it was all right to be a Lord Holder, he was more than a little jealous of Felessan, and fleetingly wished that he, too, could look forward to being a dragonrider one day. And that egg looked lonely, small and unwanted, so far from the others.

"You're being a Lord Holder wouldn't matter a grain of sand in Igen if Ramoth came back and caught us here," Felessan reminded him and jerked Jaxom firmly toward the slit.

A sudden rumble at the far end of the Hatching Ground startled them. One look at the shadow on the sand by the great entrance was enough. Felessan, being more agile and faster, got to the exit first and squeezed through. This time Jaxom did not object at all as Felessan frantically yanked him past the rock. They didn't even stop to see if it really was Ramoth, returning. They grabbed the glow baskets and ran.

When the light from the slit was lost in the curve of the corridor, Jaxom stopped running. His chest hurt from his exertions as well as from his rough passage through the fissure.

"C'mon," Felessan urged him, halting several paces further.

"I can't. My chest . . ."

"Is it bad?" Felessan held his glow up; blood traced smeared patterns on Jaxom's pale skin. "That looks bad. We'd better get you to Manora quick."

"I . . . got . . . to . . . catch . . . my . . . breath."

In rhythm with his labored exhalations, his glow sputtered and darkened completely.

"We'll have to walk slow then," Felessan said, his voice now shakier with anxiety than from running.

Jaxom got to his feet, determined not to show the panic he was beginning to feel; a cold pressure gripped his belly, his chest was hot and painful, while sweat was starting to creep down his forehead. The salty drops fell on his chest and he swore one of the wardguard's favorites.

"Let's walk fast," he said and, holding onto the now useless glow basket, suited action to words.

By common consent they kept to the outer edge of the corridor, where the now dimly seen footsteps gave them courage.

"It's not much further, is it?" Jaxom asked as the second glow flickered ominously.

"Ah—no. It better not be."

"What's the matter?"

"Ah—we've just run out of footprints."

They hadn't retraced their steps very far before they ran out of glow, too.

"Now what do we do, Jaxom?"

"Well, in Ruatha," Jaxom said, taking a deep breath, a precaution against his voice breaking on him, "when they miss me, they send out search parties."

"In that case, you'll be missed as soon as Lytol wants to go home, won't you? He never stays here long."

"Not if Lytol gets asked to dinner and he will, if dinner is as close as you said it was." Jaxom couldn't suppress his bitterness at this whole ill-advised exploration. "Haven't you any idea where we are?"

"No," Felessan had to admit, sounding suddenly out of his depth. "I always followed the footprints, just like I did now. There were footprints. You saw them."

Jaxom didn't care to agree for that would mean he was in part to blame for their predicament.

"Those other corridors we passed on the way to the hole, where do they go?" he finally asked.

"I don't know. There's an awful lot of the Weyr that's empty. I've—I've never gone any farther than the slit."

"What about the others? How far in have they gone?"

"Gandidan's always talking about how far he's gone but —but—I don't remember what he said."

"For the Egg's sake, don't blubber."

"I'm not blubbering. I'm just hungry!"

"Hungry? That's it. Can you smell dinner? Seemed to me we could smell it an awful long ways down the corridor."

They sniffed at the air in all directions. It was musty but not with stew. Sometimes, Jaxom remembered, you *could* smell fresher air and find your own way back. He put out a hand to touch the wall; the smooth, cold stone was somehow comforting. In *between*, you couldn't feel anything, though this corridor was just as dark. His chest hurt and throbbed, in a steady accompaniment to his blood.

With a sigh, he backed up against the smooth wall and, sliding down it, settled to the ground with a bump.

"Jaxom?"

"I'm all right. I'm just tired."

"Me, too," and with a sigh of relief, Felessan sat down, his shoulder touching Jaxom's. The contact reassured them both.

"I wonder what it was like," Jaxom mused at length.

"Wonder what what was like?" asked Felessan in some surprise.

"When the Weyrs and the Holds were full. When these corridors were lighted and used."

"They've never *been* used."

"Nonsense. No one wastes time carving out corridors that'll lead nowhere. And Lytol said there are over five hundred weyrs in Benden and only half-used . . ."

"We have four hundred and twelve fighting dragons at Benden now."

"Sure, but ten Turns ago there weren't two hundred, so why so many weyrs if they weren't all used once? And why are there miles and miles of halls and unused rooms in Ruatha Hold if they weren't used once . . ."

"So?"

"I mean, where did all the people go? And *how* did they carve out whole mountains in the first place?"

. Clearly the matter had never troubled Felessan.

"And did you ever notice? Some of the walls are smooth as . . ."

Jaxom stopped, stunned by a dawning realization. Almost fearfully he turned and ran his hand down the wall behind him. It *was* smooth. He gulped and his chest hurt more than the throb of the scratches. "Felessan . . . ?"

"What—what's the matter?"

"This wall is smooth."

"So what?"

"But it's smooth. It's not rough!"

"Say what you mean." Felessan sounded almost angry.

"It's smooth. It's an old wall."

"So?"

"We're in the old part of Benden." Jaxom got to his feet, running a hand over the wall, walking a few paces.

"Hey!" Jaxom could hear Felessan scrambling to his feet. "Don't leave me. Jaxom! I can't see you."

Jaxom stretched his hand back, touched fabric, and jerked Felessan to his side.

"Now hang on. If this is an old corridor, sooner or later it'll run out. Into a dead end, *or* into the main section. It's got to."

"But how do you know you're going in the right direction?"

"I don't, but it's better than sitting on my rump getting hungrier." With one hand on the wall, the other clinging to Felessan's belt, Jaxom moved on.

They couldn't have walked more than twenty paces before Jaxom's fingers stumbled over the crack. An even crack, running perpendicular to the floor.

"Hey, warn a guy!" cried Felessan, who had bumped into him.

"I found something."

"What?"

"A crack up and down, evenly." Excitedly Jaxom stretched both arms out, trying to find the other side of what might even be a doorway.

At shoulder height, just beyond the second cut, he found a square plate and, in examining it, pressed. With a rumbling groan, the wall under his other hand began to slide back and light came up on the other side.

The boys had only a few seconds to stare at the brightly lit wonders on the other side of the threshold before the inert gas with which the room had been flooded rushed out to overcome them. But the light remained a beacon to guide the searchers.

"I had the entire Hold mustered this morning, only to find him in the bowels of the Hold itself where a rockfall had barred his way," Lytol said to Lessa as he watched the boys running toward the Lower Cavern.

"You've forgotten your own boyhood then," F'lar laughed, gesturing courteously for Lytol to proceed him to the weyr. "Or didn't you explore the back corridors as a weyrling?"

Lytol scowled and then gave a snort, but he didn't smile. "It was one thing for me. I wasn't heir to the Hold."

"But, Lytol, heir to the Hold or not," Lessa said, taking the man's arm, "Jaxom's a boy, like any other. No, now please,

I am not criticizing. He's a fine lad, well grown. You may be proud of him."

"Carries himself like a Lord, too," F'lar ventured to say.

"I do my best."

"And your best is very well indeed," Lessa said enthusiastically. "Why, he's grown so since the last time I saw him!"

But the tic started in Lytol's cheek and Lessa fumed, wondering what Mardra had been complaining about in the boy lately. That woman had better stop interfering . . . Lessa caught herself, grimly reminded that she could be accused of interfering right now, having invited Jaxom here on a visit. When Mardra heard that Lytol had been to Benden Weyr . . .

"I'm glad *you* think so," Lytol replied, confirming Lessa's suspicions.

Harper Robinton rose to greet Lytol, and the Mastersmith Fandarel's face broke into the almost feral expression that passed as his smile. While F'lar seated them, Lessa poured wine.

"The new train is in, Robinton, but not settled enough to serve," she said, grinning down at him. It was a private joke that Robinton visited Benden more for the wine than for companionship or business. "You'll have to make do with last year's tithe."

"Benden wine is always acceptable to me," Robinton replied suavely, using the compliment as an excuse to take a sip.

"I appreciate your coming, gentlemen," F'lar began, taking charge of the meeting. "And I apologize for taking you from your business at such short notice, but I . . ."

"Always glad to come to Benden," Robinton murmured, his eyes twinkling as he tipped his cup again.

"I have news for you so I was glad of this opportunity," Fandarel rumbled.

"And I," Lytol said in a dark voice, the tic moving agitatedly.

"My news is very serious and I need to know your reactions. There has been premature Threadfall . . ." F'lar began.

"Thread*falls*," Robinton corrected him with no vestige of his previous levity. "The drumroll brought me the news from Tillek and Crom Holds."

"I wish I'd as reliable messengers," F'lar said bitterly,

gritting his teeth. "Didn't you question the Weyrs' silence, Robinton?" He had counted the Harper his friend.

"My Craft is weyrbound to Fort, my dear F'lar," the Craftmaster replied, an odd smile on his lips, "although Weyrleader T'ron does not appear to follow custom in keeping the Master Harper advised of auspicious events. I had no immediate, or privy way to bespeak Benden Weyr."

F'lar took a deep breath; Robinton confirmed the fact that T'ron had not known. "T'kul saw fit not to inform the other Weyrleaders of the unscheduled Fall in Tillek Hold."

"That doesn't surprise me," the Harper murmured cynically.

"We learned only today that R'mar was so badly injured in the Fall at Crom Hold that he couldn't dispatch any messengers."

"You mean, that numbwitted Weyrwoman Bedella forgot to," Lessa interjected.

F'lar nodded and went on. "The first Benden knew of this was when Thread fell in Lemos northeast, midmorning, when the table indicated southwest and evening. Because I always send a rider on ahead to act as messenger for any last moment problems, we were able to reach Lemos before the leading Edge."

Robinton whistled with appreciation.

"You mean, the timetables are wrong?" Lytol exclaimed. All the color had drained from his swarthy face at the news. "I thought that rumor had to be false."

F'lar shook his head grimly; he'd been watching for Lytol's reaction to this news.

"They're not accurate any more; they don't apply to this shift," he said. "Lessa reminded me, as I do you, that there have been deviations in the Red Star's passage that cause long intervals. We must assume that something can cause a change in the rhythm of the Fall as well. As soon as we can gauge a pattern again, we'll correct the tables or make new ones."

Lytol stared at him uncomprehendingly. "But how long will it take you? With three Falls, you ought to have some idea now. I've acres of new plantings, forests. How can I protect them when I can't be sure where Thread will fall?" He controlled himself with an effort. "I apologize but this is —this is terrible news. I don't know how the other Lord

Holders will receive it on top of everything else." He took a quick drink of wine.

"What do you mean, on top of everything else?" F'lar asked, startled.

"Why, the way the Weyrs are behaving. That disaster in Esvay valley in Nabol, those plantations of Lord Sangel's."

"Tell me about the Esvay Valley and Lord Sangel."

"You hadn't heard that either?" Robinton asked in real surprise. "Don't the Weyrs talk to one another?" And he glanced from F'lar to Lessa.

"The Weyrs are autonomous," F'lar replied. "We don't interfere . . ."

"You mean, the Oldtimers keep exchanges with us contemporary radicals to a bare minimum," Lessa finished, her eyes flashing indignantly. "Don't scowl at me, F'lar. You know it's true. Though I'm sure D'ram and T'ron were as shocked as we were that T'kul would keep premature Threadfall a secret. Now, what happened at Esvay Vale and in Lord Sangel's Southern Boll?"

It was Robinton who answered her in an expressionless voice. "Several weeks back, T'kul refused to help Meron of Nabol clear some furrows from wooded slopes above the Esvay valley. Said it was the job of the ground crews and Meron's men were lazy and inefficient. The whole valley had to be fired in order to stop the burrows' spreading. Lytol sent help; he knows. I went to see some of the families. They're holdless now and very bitter about dragonmen.

"A few weeks later, Weyrleader T'ron left Southern Boll Hold without clearing with Lord Sangel's groundchief. They had to burn down three adult plantations. When Lord Sangel protested to T'ron, he was told that the wings had reported the Fall under control.

"On another level but disturbing in the over-all picture, I've heard of any number of girls, snatched on the pretext of Search . . ."

"Girls beg to come to the Weyr," Lessa put in tartly.

"To Benden Weyr, probably," Robinton agreed. "But my harpers tell me of unwilling girls, forced from their babes and husbands, ending as drudges to Weyrladies. There is deep hatred building, Lady Lessa. There has always been resentment, envy, because weyrlife is different and the ease with which dragonriders can move across the continent while lesser folk struggle, the special privileges riders enjoy—" The Harper waved his hands. "The Oldtimers really believe in special privilege, and that exacerbates the dangers inherent in such outdated attitudes. As for matters in the Crafthalls, the belt knife incident at Fandarel's is a very minor item in the list of depredations. The crafts generously tithe of their products, but Weaver Zurg and Tanner Belesden are bitterly disillusioned now by the stiff rate of additional levies."

"Is that why they were so cool to me when I asked for gown material?" Lessa asked. "But Zurg himself helped me choose."

"I fancy that no one at Benden Weyr abuses privilege," Robinton replied. "No one at *Benden* Weyr. After all," and he grinned toothily, managing to resemble T'ron as he did so, "Benden is the backsliding Weyr which has forgotten true custom and usage, become lax in their dealings. Why, they permit Holds bound to Benden Weyr to retain dignity, possession and forest. They encourage the Crafts to proliferate, hatching bastard breeds of who-knows-what. But Benden Weyr," and Robinton was himself again, and angry, "is respected throughout Pern."

"As a dragonrider, I ought to take offense," F'lar said, so disturbed by this indictment that he spoke lightly.

"As Benden's Weyrleader, you ought to take charge," Robinton retorted, his voice ringing. "When Benden stood alone, seven Turns ago, you said that the Lord Holders and Craftsmen were too parochial in their views to deal effectively with the real problem. They at least learned something from their mistakes. The Oldtimers are not only incurably parochial, but worse—adamantly inflexible. They will not, they cannot adapt to our Turn. Everything we accomplished in the four hundred Turns that separate our thinking is wrong and must be set aside, set back for *their* ways, their standards. Pern has grown—is growing and changing. They have not. And they are alienating the Lord Holders and Craftsmen so completely that I am sincerely concerned—no, I'm scared—about the reaction to this new crisis."

"They'll change their minds when Thread falls unexpectedly," Lessa said.

"Who will change? The Weyrleaders? The Holders? Don't count on it, Lady Lessa."

"I have to agree with Robinton," Lytol said in a tired

voice. "There's been precious little cooperation from the Weyrs. They're overbearing, wrongheaded and demanding. I find that I, Lytol, ex-dragonrider, resent any more demands on me as Lytol, Lord Warder. And now it appears they are incapable even of doing their job. What, for instance, can be done right in the present crisis? Are they willing to do *any*thing?"

"There'll be cooperation from the Weyrs, I can guarantee it," F'lar told Lytol. He must rouse the man from his dejection. "The Oldtimers were shaken men this morning. Ruatha Hold's weyrbound to Fort and T'ron's setting up sweepriders. You're to man the watch fires on the heights and light them when Thread mass is sighted. You'll get prompt action the instant a watch fire is seen."

"I'm to rely on shaken men and fires on the heights?" Lytol demanded, eyes wide with disbelief.

"Fire is not efficient," Fandarel intoned. "Rain puts it out. Fog hides it."

"I'll gladly assign my drummers to you if you think they'd be of help," Robinton put in.

"F'lar," Lytol said urgently, "I know Benden Weyr sends messengers ahead to Holds under Threadfall. Won't the other Weyrleaders agree *now* to assign riders to the Holds? Just until we know about the shifts and learn to anticipate them? I don't like most of the Fort Weyr riders, but at least I'd feel secure knowing there was instant communication with the Weyr."

"As I was saying," Fandarel boomed in such a portentous voice that they all turned to him a little startled, "there has been a regrettable lack of efficient communication on this planet which I believe my craft can effectually end. That is the news I brought."

"What?" Lytol was on his feet.

"Why didn't you speak up sooner, you great lout?" demanded the Harper.

"How long would it take to equip all major Holds and Weyrs?" F'lar's question drowned the others.

Fandarel looked squarely at the Weyrleader before he answered what had been almost a plea.

"More time, unfortunately, than we apparently have as margin in this emergency. My halls have been overbusy turning out flame throwers. There's been no time to devote to my little toys."

"How long?"

"The instruments which send and receive distance writing are easy to assemble, but wire must be laid between them. That process is time-consuming."

"Man-consuming, too, I warrant," Lytol added and sat down, deflated.

"No more than watch fires," Fandarel told him placidly. "*If* each Lord and Weyr could be made to cooperate and work together. We did once before," and the Smith paused to look pointedly at F'lar, "when Benden called."

Lytol's face brightened and he grabbed F'lar urgently by the arm.

"The Lord Holders would listen to you, F'lar of Benden, because they trust you!"

"F'lar couldn't approach other Lords, not without antagonizing the Weyrleaders," Lessa objected, but she too was alert with hope.

"What the other Weyrleaders don't know—" Robinton suggested slyly, warming to the strategy. "Come, come, F'lar. This is not the time to stick at principles—at least ones which have proved untenable. Look beyond affiliations, man. You did before and we won. Consider Pern, all Pern, not one Weyr," and he pointed a long callused finger at F'lar; "one Hold," and he swiveled it to Lytol; "or one Craft," and he cocked it at Fandarel. "When we five combined our wits seven Turns ago, we got ourselves out of a very difficult position."

"And I set the stage for this one," Lessa said with a bitter laugh.

Before F'lar could speak, Robinton was waggling his finger at her. "Silly people waste time assigning or assuming guilt, Lessa. You went back and you brought the Oldtimers forforward. *To save Pern*. Now we have a different problem. You're not silly. You and F'lar, and all of us, must find other solutions. Now we've that so conveniently scheduled wedding at Telgar Hold. There'll be a bevy of Lords and Craftmasters doing honor to Lemos and Telgar. We are all invited. Let us make very good use of that social occasion, my Lady Lessa, my lord F'lar, and bend them all to Benden's way of thinking. Let Benden Weyr be a model—and all the other Holds and Crafts will follow those weyrbound to Benden . . ."

He leaned back suddenly, smiling with great anticipation.

F'lar said quietly, "Disaffection is apparently universal. We are going to need more than words and example to change minds."

"The Crafts will back you, Weyrleader, to the last Hall," Fandarel said. "You champion Bendarek. F'nor defended Terry, and against dragonmen because they were in the wrong. F'nor is all right, is he not?" The Smith turned questioningly to Lessa.

"He'll be back in a week or so."

"We need him now," Robinton said. "He'd be useful at Telgar Hold, the commoners account him a hero. What do you say, F'lar? We're yours to command again."

They all turned to him, Lessa slipping a hand to his knee, her eyes eager. This was what she wanted, all right; for him to assume the responsibility. It was what he knew he had to do, finishing the task he had relinquished, hopefully, to those he thought better qualified than he to protect Pern.

"About that distance-writer of yours, Fandarel, could you rig one to Telgar Hold in time for the marriage?" F'lar asked.

Robinton let out a whoop that reverberated through the chamber, causing Ramoth to grumble from the Hatching Ground. The Smith showed all his stained tusks and clenched his huge fists on the table as if choking any opposition a-borning. The tic in Lytol's cheek gave a spasmodic leap and stopped.

"Marvelous idea," Robinton cried. "Hope's a great encourager. Give the Lords a reliable means of keeping in touch and you've undone much of the Weyrs' isolation policies."

"Can you do it, Fandarel?" F'lar asked the Smith.

"To Telgar I could lay wire. Yes. It could be done."

"How is this distance writing done? I don't understand."

Fandarel inclined his head toward the Masterharper. "Thanks to Robinton, we have a code that permits us to send long and complicated messages. One must train a man to understand it, to send and receive it. If you could spare an hour of your time . . ."

"I can spare you as much time as you need, Fandarel," F'lar assured him.

"Let's go tomorrow. There's nothing could fall here tomorrow," Lessa urged, excited.

"Good. I shall arrange a demonstration. I shall put more people to work on the wire."

"I shall speak to Lord Sangel of Southern Boll and Lord Groghe of Fort Hold," Lytol said. "Discreetly, of course, but they know Ruatha is not favored by the Weyr." He got to his feet. "I have been a dragonrider, and a craftsman, and now I am a Holder. But Thread makes no distinction. It sears wherever, whatever it touches."

"Yes, we must remind everyone of that," Robinton said with an ominous grin.

"I shall, of course, agree to whatever T'ron orders me to do, now I have hopes of a surer deliverance." Lytol bowed to Lessa. "My duty to you, my lady. I'll collect Lord Jaxom and beg the favor of a return flight . . ."

"You've missed your lunch, stay for our dinner."

Lytol shook his head regretfully. "There'll be much to set in motion."

"In the interests of conserving dragon strength, I'll ride with Lytol and Jaxom," Robinton said, swallowing the rest of his wine after a rueful toast to such haste. "That will leave you two beasts to share the burden of Fandarel."

Fandarel stood up, a tolerantly smiling giant, his massive bulk dwarfing the Harper, who was by no measure a short man. "I sympathize with dragons, forced to endure the envy of frail, small creatures."

None of them left, however, because neither Jaxom nor Felessan could be located. One of Manora's women remembered seeing them pilfering vegetables and thought they'd gone to join the boys playing miggsy. On questioning, one of the children, Gandidan, admitted seeing them go toward the back corridors.

"Gandidan," Manora said sternly, "have you been teasing Felessan about the peekhole again?" The child hung his head and suddenly the others couldn't look at anyone. "Hmmm," and she turned to the anxious parents. "I've been missing used glows again, F'lar, so I imagine there've been some trips to look at the eggs."

"What?" Lessa exclaimed, as startled as the boys who had turned to guilty statues.

Before she could berate them, F'lar laughed aloud. "That's where they are, then."

"Where?"

The boys huddled together, terrified by the coldness in her voice, even if it was directed toward the Weyrleader.

"In the corridor behind the Hatching Ground. Oh, don't fuss, Lessa. That's all part of growing up in the Weyr, isn't it, Lytol? I did it when I was Felessan's age."

"You've been aware of these excursions, Manora?" Lessa demanded imperiously, ignoring F'lar.

"Certainly, Weyrwoman," Manora replied unintimidated. "And kept track to be sure they all returned. How long ago did they set out, Gandidan? Did they play with you for a time?"

"No wonder Ramoth's been so upset; I kept thinking she was only being broody. How could you allow such activities to continue?"

"Come now, Lessa," F'lar said soothingly. "It's a matter of adolescent pride," and F'lar dropped his voice to a whisper and widened his eyes dramatically, "not to shrink from the challenge of dark, dusty corridors; dim, flickering glows. Will the glows last long enough to get us to the peekhole and back? Or will we be lost forever in the blackness of the Weyr?"

The Harper was grinning, the boys stunned and open-mouthed. Lytol was not amused, however.

"How long ago, Gandidan?" Manora repeated, tipping the boy's face up. When he seemed unable to speak, she glanced at the scared expressions of the others. "I think we'd better look. It's easy to take the wrong turning if you have inadequate glows. And they did."

There was no lack of searchers, and F'lar quickly split them up into sections to explore each corridor segment. Sounds echoed through halls undisturbed for hundreds of Turns. But it was not long before F'lar and Lytol led their group to the guiding light. Once they saw the figures lying in the patch of light, F'lar sent for the others.

"What's the matter with them?" Lytol demanded, supporting his ward against him, and anxiously feeling for his pulse. "Blood?" He held up stained fingers, his face bleak, cheek a-twitch.

So, thought F'lar, Lytol's heart had unfrozen a little. Lessa was wrong to think Lytol too numb to care for the boy. Jaxom was a sensitive boy and children needed affection, but there are many ways of loving.

F'lar gestured for more glows. He turned back the dusty linen of the boy's shirt, baring the horizontal scratches.

"Doesn't look to me like more than scrapes. Probably stumbled against the wall in the dark. Who's got some numb-weed on him? Don't look like that, Lytol. The pulse is strong."

"But he's not asleep. He doesn't wake." Lytol shook the limp figure, at first gently, then more insistently.

"There isn't a mark on Felessan," the Weyrleader said, turning his son in his arms.

Manora and Lessa came running then, kicking up dust in spite of F'lar's urgent caution. But Manora reassured them that the boys were all right and briskly delegated two men to carry them back to the Weyr proper. Then she turned to the curious crowd that had assembled in the corridor.

"The emergency is over. Everyone back. Dinner's ready, my lady, my lords. Pick up your feet, Silon. No need to stir up more dust." She glanced at the Weyrleader and the Mastersmith. As one, the two men approached the mysterious doorway, Lessa and Lytol joining them.

Her crisp instructions cleared the corridor quickly until there were only the five remaining.

"The light is *not* made by glows," announced the Mastersmith as he peered cautiously into the bright room. "And from the smoothness of the walls, this is part of the original Weyr." He scowled at F'lar. "Were you aware such rooms existed?" It was almost an accusation.

"There were rumors, of course," F'lar said, stepping inside, "but I don't think I ever got very far down any of the unused corridors when I was a weyrling. Did you, Lytol?"

The Lord Warder snorted irritably but now that he knew Jaxom was all right, he could not resist looking in.

"Perhaps you should give him leave to prowl in Ruatha if he can find treasure rooms like this one," Robinton suggested slyly. "And what under the sun could this represent? Lessa, you're our expert on wall hangings, what do you say?"

He pointed to a drawing, composed of weird interconnecting varicolored rods and balls which spread in several ladder-like columns from floor to ceiling.

"I wouldn't call it artistic, but the colors are pretty," she said, peering closely at the wall. She touched a portion with a finger. "Why, the color is baked on the wall. And look here! Someone didn't like it although I don't think their correction helps. It's more a scribble than a design. And it's not even in the same type of coloring."

Fandarel scrutinized the drawing, his nose an inch from the wall. "Odd. Very odd." Then he moved off to other wonders, his huge hands reverently caressing the metallic counters, the hanging shelves. His expression was so rapt that Lessa suppressed a giggle. "Simply amazing. I believe that this countertop was extruded in a single sheet." He clucked to himself. "If it has been done, it can be done. I must think about it."

F'lar was more interested in the scribble-design. There was something tantalizingly familiar about it.

"Lessa, I'd swear I've seen just such a nonsense before."

"But we've never been here. No one has."

"I've got it. It's like the pattern on that metal plate F'nor found at Fort Weyr. The one that mentioned fire lizards. See, this word," his finger traced lines that would read "eureka" to older eyes, "is the same. I'd swear it. And it was obviously added after the rest of this picture."

"If you want to call it a picture," Lessa said dubiously. "But I do think you're right. Only why would they circle this part of the ladder—and that one over there—with a scribble?"

"There are so many, many puzzles in this room," Fandarel intoned. He'd opened a cabinet door, struggling briefly with the magnetic catch, then opened and closed it several times, smiling absently in delight for such efficiency. Only then did he notice the strange object on the deep shelf.

He exhaled in wonder as he took the ungainly affair down.

"Have a care. It may waddle away," Robinton said, grinning at the Smith's performance.

Though the device was as long as a man's arm, the Smith's great hands seemed to envelop it as his fingers explored its exterior. "And they could roll metal without seam. Hmmm. It's coated," and he glanced up at F'lar, "with the same substance used in the big kettles. Coated for protection? With what?" He looked at it, peered at the top. "Ah, glass. Fine glass. Something to look through?" He fiddled with the easily swiveled coated glass that was fitted under a small ledge at the base of the instrument. He placed his eye at the opening on the top of the tube. "Nothing to see but through." He straightened, his brows deeply furrowed. A rumbling sound issued from him as if the gears of his thinking were shifting audibly. "There is a very badly eroded diagram which Wansor showed me not long ago. A device," and his fingers rested lightly on the wheels placed alongside the barrel, "which magnifies objects hundreds of times their proper size. But it takes so long to make lenses, polish mirrors. Hmmm." He bent again and with extremely careful fingers played with the knobs at the side of the tube. He glanced quickly at the mirror, wiped it with one stained finger and looked at it once with his own eye, then again through the tube. "Fascinating. I can see every imperfection in the glass." He was completely unconscious of the fact that everyone else was watching him, fascinated by his behavior. He pulled a coarse short hair from his head and held it under the end of the barrel, above the mirror, right across a small aperture. Another careful adjustment and he gave a bellow of joy. "Look. Look. It is only my hair. But look at the size of it now. See dust like stones, see the scales, see the broken end."

Exuberantly, he pulled Lessa into position, all but holding her head down to the eyepiece. "If you can't see clearly, move this knob until you can."

Lessa complied, but with a startled exclamation, jumped back. Robinton stepped up before F'lar could.

"But that's fantastic," the Harper muttered, playing with the knobs and quickly taking a comparative look at the actual hair.

"May I?" asked F'lar so pointedly that Robinton grinned an apology for his monopoly.

Taking his place, F'lar in turn had to check the specimen to believe in what he saw through the instrument. The strand of hair became a coarse rope, motes of dust sparkling in the light along it, fine lines making visible segmentation points.

When he lifted his head, he turned toward Fandarel, speaking softly because he almost dared not utter this fragile hope aloud.

"If there are ways of making tiny things this large, are

there ways of bringing distant objects near enough to observe closely?"

He heard Lessa's breath catch, was aware that Robinton was holding his, but F'lar begged the Smith with his eyes to give him the answer he wanted to hear.

"I believe there ought to be," Fandarel said after what seemed to be hours of reflection.

"F'lar?"

He looked down at Lessa's white face, her startled eyes black with awe and fear, her hands half-raised in frightened protest.

"You can't *go* to the Red Star!" Her voice was barely audible.

He captured her hands, cold and tense, and though he drew her to him reassuringly, he spoke more to the others.

"Our problem, gentleman, has always been to get rid of Thread. Why not at its source? A dragon can go anywhere if he's got a picture of where he's going!"

When Jaxom woke, he was instantly aware that he was not in the Hold. He opened his eyes bravely, scared though he was, expecting darkness. Instead, above him was a curving roof of stone, its expanse sparkling from the full basket of glows in its center. He gave an inarticulate gasp of relief.

"Are you all right, lad? Does your chest hurt?" Manora was bending over him.

"You found us? Is Felessan all right?"

"Right as rain, and eating his dinner. Now, does your chest hurt?"

"My chest?" His heart seemed to stop when he remembered how he got that injury. But Manora was watching him. He felt cautiously. "No, thank-you-for-inquiring."

His stomach further embarrassed him with its grinding noises.

"I think you need some dinner, too."

"Then Lytol's not angry with me? Or the Weyrleader?" he dared to ask.

Manora gave him a fond smile, smoothing down his tousled hair.

"Not to worry, Lord Jaxom," she said kindly. "A stern word or two perhaps. Lord Lytol was beside himself with worry."

Jaxom had the most incredible vision of two Lytols side by side, cheeks a-twitch in unison.

"However, I wouldn't advise any more unauthorized expeditions anywhere." She gave a little laugh. "That is now the special pastime of the adults."

Jaxom was too busy worrying if she *knew* about the slit, if she knew the weyrboys had been peeking through. If she knew *he* had. He endured a little death, waiting to hear her say Felessan had confessed to their crime, then realized she had said they weren't to be more than scolded. You could always trust Manora. And if she knew and wasn't angry . . . But if she didn't know and he asked, she might be angry . . .

"You found those rooms, Lord Jaxom. I'd rest on my honors, now, were I you."

"Rooms?"

She smiled at him and held out her hand. "I thought you were hungry."

Her hand was cool and soft as she led him onto the balcony which circled the sleeping level. It must be late, Jaxom thought, as they passed the tightly drawn curtains of the sleeping rooms. The central fire was banked. A few women were grouped by one of the worktables, sewing. They glanced up as Manora and Jaxom passed, and smiled.

"You said 'rooms?' " Jaxom asked with polite insistence.

"Beyond the room you opened were two others and the ruins of a stairway leading up."

Jaxom whistled. "What was in the rooms?"

Manora laughed softly. "I never saw the Mastersmith so excited. They found some odd-shaped instruments and bits and pieces of glass I can't make out at all."

"An Oldtimer room?" Jaxom was awed at the scope of his discovery. And he'd had only the shortest look.

"Oldtimers?" Manora's frown was so slight that Jaxom decided he'd imagined it. Manora never frowned. "Ancient timers, I'd say."

As they entered the Main Cavern, Jaxom realized that their passage interrupted the lively conversations of the dragonmen and women seated around the big dining area. Accustomed as he was to such scrutiny, Jaxom straightened his shoulders and walked with measured stride. He turned his head slowly, giving a grave nod and smile to the riders he knew and those of the women he recognized. He ignored a sprinkle of laughter, being used to that, too, but a Lord of the Hold must act with the dignity appropriate to his rank, even if he were not quite Turned twelve and in the presence of his superiors.

It was full dark, but around the great inner face of the Bowl, he could see the lambent circles of dragon eyes on the weyr ledges. He could hear the muted rush of air as several stirred and stretched their enormous pinions. He looked up toward the Star Rocks, black knobs against the lighter sky, and saw the giant silhouette of the watch dragon. Far down the Bowl, he could even hear the restless tramping of the penned herdbeasts. In the lake in the center, the stars were mirrored.

Quickening his step now, he urged Manora faster. Dignity could be forgotten in the darkness and he was desperately hungry.

Mnementh gave a welcoming rumble on the queen's weyr ledge, and Jaxom, greatly daring, glanced up at the near eye which closed one lid at him slightly in startling imitation of a human wink.

Do dragons have a sense of humor? he wondered. The watch-wher certainly didn't and he was the same breed.

The relationship is very distant.

"I beg your pardon?" Jaxom said, startled, glancing up at Manora.

"For what, young Lord?"

"Didn't you say something?"

"No."

Jaxom glanced back at the bulky shadow of the dragon, but Mnementh's head was turned. Then he could smell roasted meats and walked faster.

As they rounded the bend, Jaxom saw the golden body of the recumbent queen and was suddenly guilt-struck and fearful. But she was fast asleep, smiling with an innocent serenity remarkably like his foster mother's newest babe. He looked away lest his gaze rouse her, and saw the faces of all those adults at the table. It was almost too much for him. F'lar, Lessa, Lytol and Felessan he'd expected, but there was the Mastersmith and the Masterharper, too.

Only drill helped him respond courteously to the greetings of the celebrities. He wasn't aware when Manora and Lessa came to his assistance.

"Not a word until the child has had something to eat, Lytol," the Weyrwoman said firmly, her hands pressing him gently to the empty seat beside Felessan. The boy paused between spoonfuls to look up with a complex series of facial contortions supposed to convey a message that escaped Jaxom. "Jaxom missed lunch at the Hold and is several hours hungrier in consequence. He is well, Manora?"

"He took no more harm than Felessan."

"He looked a little glassy-eyed as you crossed the weyr." Lessa bent to peer at Jaxom who politely looked at her, chewing with sudden self-consciousness. "How do you feel?"

Jaxom emptied his mouth hurriedly, trying to swallow a half-chewed lump of vegetable. Felessan tendered a cup of water and Lessa deftly swatted him between the shoulder blades as he started to choke.

"I feel fine," he managed to say. "I feel fine, thank you." He waited, unable to resist looking at his plate and was relieved when the Weyrleader laughingly reminded Lessa that she was the one who said the boy should eat before anything else.

The Mastersmith tapped his stained, branchlike finger on the faded Record skin which draped the table, except where the boys were sitting. Fandarel had one arm wrapped possessively around something in his lap, but Jaxom couldn't see what it was.

"If I judge this accurately, there should be several levels of rooms in this section, both beyond the one the boys found and above."

Jaxom goggled at the map and caught Felessan's eye. He was excited, too, but he kept on eating. Jaxom spooned up another huge mouthful—it tasted so good—but he did wish that the skin were not upside down to him.

"I'd swear there were no upper weyr entrances on that side of the Bowl," F'lar muttered, shaking his head.

"There was access to the Bowl on the ground level," Fandarel said, his forefinger covering what he ought to be showing. "We found it, sealed up. Possibly because of that rockfall."

Jaxom looked anxiously at Felessan who became engrossed in his plate. When Felessan made those faces, had he meant he hadn't told them? Or he had? Jaxom wished he knew.

"That seam was barely discernible," the Masterharper said. "The sealing substance was more effective than any mortar I've ever seen; transparent, smooth and strong."

"One could not chip it," rumbled Fandarel, shaking his head.

"Why would they seal off an exit to the Bowl?" Lessa asked.

"Because they weren't using that section of the Weyr," F'lar suggested. "Certainly no one has used those corridors for the Egg knows how many Turns. There weren't even footprints in the dust of most of them we searched."

Waiting for the adult wrath that must surely descend on him now, Jaxom kept his eyes on his plate. He couldn't bear Lessa's recriminations. He dreaded the look in Lytol's eyes when he learned of his ward's blasphemous act. How could he have been so deaf to all Lytol's patient teachings?

"We found enough of interest in the dusty, moldy old Records that had been ignored as useless," F'lar's voice went on.

Jaxom hazarded a glance and saw the Weyrleader tousle Felessan's hair; watched as the man actually grinned at him, Jaxom. Jaxom was almost sick with relief. None of the adults knew what he and Felessan had done in the Hatching Grounds.

"These boys have already led us to exquisite treasures, eh, Fandarel?"

"Let us hope that they are not the only legacies left in forgotten rooms," the Mastersmith said in his deep rumble of a voice. Absently he stroked the smooth metal of the magnifying device cradled in the crook of his arm.

CHAPTER VI

Midmorning at Southern Weyr
Early Morning at Nabol Hold:
Next Day

Hot, sandy and sticky with sweat and salt, triumph overrode all minor irritations as Kylara stared down at the clutch she had unearthed.

"They can have their seven," she muttered, staring in the general direction of northeast and the Weyr. "I've got an entire nest. And another gold."

Exultation welled out of her in a raucous laugh. Just wait until Meron of Nabol saw these beauties! There was no doubt in her mind that the Holder hated dragonmen because he envied them their beasts. He'd often carped that Impressions ought not to be monopolized by one inbred sodality. Well, let's see if mighty Meron could Impress a fire lizard. She wasn't sure which would please her more: if he could or if he couldn't. Either way'd work for her. But if he could

Impress a fire lizard, a bronze, say, and she had a queen on her wrist, and the two mated . . . It might not be as spectacular as with the larger beasts, but then, given Meron's natural endowment . . . Kylara smiled in sensuous anticipation.

"You'd better be worth this," she told the eggs.

She put the thirty-four hardened eggs into several thicknesses of the firestone bagging she'd brought along. She wrapped that bundle in wher-hides and then in her thick wool cloak. She'd been Weyrwoman long enough to realize that a suddenly cooled egg would never hatch. And these were mighty close to cracking shell.

So much the better.

Prideth had been tolerant of her rider's preoccupation with fire-lizard eggs. She had obediently landed in a hundred coves along the western coast, waiting, not unhappily in the hot sun, while Kylara quartered the burning sands, looking for any trace of fire-lizard buryings. But Prideth grumbled anxiously when Kylara gave her the coordinates for Nabol Hold, not Southern Weyr.

It was just first light, Nabol time, when Kylara's arrival sent the watch-wher screaming into its lair. The watchguard knew the Southern Weyrwoman too well to protest her entry and some poor wit was dispatched to wake his Lord. Kylara blithely disregarded Meron's angry frown when he appeared on the stairs of the Inner Hold.

"I've fire-lizard eggs for you, Lord Meron of Nabol," she cried, gesturing to the lumpy bundle she'd had a man bring in. "I want tubs of warm sand or we'll lose them."

"Tubs of warm sand?" Meron repeated with overt irritation.

So, he'd someone else in his bed, had he? Kylara thought, of half a mind to take her treasure and disappear.

"Yes, you fool. I've a clutch of fire-lizard eggs about to hatch. The chance of your lifetime. You there," and Kylara pointed imperiously at Meron's holdkeeper who'd come shuffling in, half-dressed. "Pour boiling water over all the cleansing sand you've got and bring it here instantly."

Kylara, born to a high degree in one Hold, knew exactly the tone to take with lesser beings, and was, in fact, so much the female counterpart of her own irascible Lord that the woman scurried to her bidding without waiting for Meron's consent.

"Fire-lizard eggs? What on earth are you babbling about, woman?"

"They're Impressionable. Catch their minds at their hatching, just like dragons, feed 'em into stupidity and they're yours, for life." Kylara was carefully laying the eggs down on the warm stones of the great fireplace. "And I've got them here just in time," she said in triumph. "Assemble your men, quickly. We'll want to Impress as many as possible."

"I'm trying," Meron said through gritted teeth as he watched her performance with some skepticism and much malice, "to apprehend exactly how this will benefit anyone."

"Use your wits, man," Kylara replied, oblivious to the Lord Holder's sour reaction to her imperiousness. "Fire lizards are the ancestors of dragons and *they have all their abilities.*"

It took only a moment longer for Meron to grasp the significance. Even as he shouted orders for his men to be roused, he was beside Kylara, helping her to lay the eggs out before the fire.

"They go *between*? They communicate with their owners?"

"Yes. Yes."

"That's a gold egg," Meron cried, reaching for it, his small eyes glittering with cupidity.

She slapped his hand away, her eyes flashing. "Gold is for me. Bronze for you. I'm fairly sure that that second one—no, that one—is a bronze."

The hot sands were brought and shoveled onto the hearth stones. Meron's men came clattering down the steps from the Inner Hold, dressed for Threadfall. Peremptorily Kylara ordered them to put aside their paraphernalia and began to lecture them on how to Impress a fire lizard.

"No one can catch a fire lizard," someone muttered, well back in the ranks.

"I have but I doubt *you* will, whoever you are," Kylara snapped.

There was something, she decided, in what the Oldtimers said: Holders were getting far too arrogant and aggressive. No one would have dared speak up in her father's Hold when he was giving instructions. No one in the Weyrs interrupted a Weyrwoman.

"You'll have to be quick," she said. "They hatch ravenous and eat anything in reach. They turn cannibal if you don't stop them."

"I want to hold mine til it hatches," Meron told Kylara in an undertone. He'd been stroking the three eggs whose mottled shells he fancied contained bronzes.

"Hands aren't warm enough," Kylara replied in a loud, flat voice. "We'll need red meat, plenty of it. Fresh-slaughtered is the best."

The platter which was subsequenlty brought in was contemptuously dismissed as inadequate. Two additional loads were prepared, still steamy from the body heat of the slaughtered animals. The smell of the bloody raw meat was another odor to mingle with the sweat of men, the overheated, crowded hall and the general tension.

"I'm thirsty, Meron. I require bread and fruit and some chilled wine," Kylara said.

She ate daintily when the food was brought, eyeing Lord Meron's sloppy table habits with veiled amusement. Someone passed bread and sourwine to the men, who had to eat standing about the room. Time passed slowly.

"I thought you said they were about to hatch," Meron said in an aggrieved voice. He was as restless as his men and beginning to have second thoughts about this ridiculous project of Kylara's.

Kylara awarded him a slightly contemptuous smile. "They are, I assure you. You Holders ought to learn patience. It's needed in dealing with dragonkind. You can't beat dragons, you know, or fire lizards, as you do a landbeast. But it'll be worth it."

"You're sure?" Meron's eyes glittered with unconcealed irritation.

"Think of the effect on dragonmen when you arrive at Telgar Hold in a few days with a fire lizard clinging to your arm."

The slight smile on Meron's face told Kylara that her suggestion appealed to him. Yes, Meron could be patient if it gave him any advantage over dragonmen.

"It will be at my beck and call?" Meron asked, his gaze avidly caressing his trio.

Kylara didn't hesitate to reassure him, though she wasn't at all sure a fire lizard would be faithful, or intelligent. Still, Meron didn't require intelligence, just obedience. Or compliance. And if the fire lizards did not live up to his expectation, she could always say the lack was in him.

"With such messengers, I'd have the advantage," Meron said so softly that she barely caught the words.

"More than mere advantage, Lord Meron," she said, her voice an insinuating purr. "Control."

"Yes, to have solid, dependable communications would mean I'd have control. I could tell that wherry-blooded High Reaches Weyrleader T'kul to . . ."

One of the eggs rocked on its long axis and Meron started from his chair. Hoarsely he ordered his men to come closer, swearing as they halted at the normal distance from him.

"Tell them again, Weyrwoman, tell them exactly how they are to capture these fire lizards."

It never troubled Kylara that even after nine Turns in a Weyr and seven Turns as a Weyrwoman herself, she could not have given the criteria by which one candidate was accepted by a dragon and another, discernibly as worthy, was rejected by an entire Hatching. Nor why the queens invariably chose women raised outside the Weyr. (For instance, at the time that boy-thing Brekke had Impressed Wirenth, there had been three other girls, any of whom Kylara would have thought considerably more interesting to a dragonette queen. But Wirenth had made a skyline directly to the craftbred girl. The three rejected candidates had remained at Southern Weyr—any girl in her right mind would—and one of them, Varena, had been presented at the next queen Impression and taken. One simply couldn't judge.) Generally speaking, weyrbred lads were always acceptable at one Hatching or another, for a weyrboy could attend Hatchings until he was in his twentieth Turn. No one was ever required to leave his Weyr, but those few who did not become riders usually left, finding places in one of the crafts.

Now, of course, with Benden and Southern Weyrs producing more dragons' eggs than the weyrwomen bore babies, it was necessary to range Pern to find enough candidates to stand on the Hatching Grounds. Evidently a commoner simply couldn't realize that the dragons, usually the browns or bronzes, did the choosing, not their riders.

There seemed to be no accounting for draconic tastes. A well-favored commoner might find himself passed over for the skinny, the unattractive.

Kylara looked around the hall, at the variety of anxious expressions on the rough men assembled. It could be hoped that fire lizards weren't as discriminating as dragons for there wasn't much to offer them in this motley group. Then Kylara remembered that that brat of Brekke's had Impressed three. In that case, anything on two legs in this room would stand a chance. It had been handed them, their one big opportunity to prove that dragonkind did not need special qualities for Impression, that common Pernese of Holds and Crafts need only be exposed to dragons to have the same chance as the elite of the Weyrs.

"You don't *capture* them," Kylara corrected Meron with a malicious smile. Let these Holders see that there is far more to being chosen by a dragon than physical presence at the moment of Hatching. "You lure them to you with thoughts of affection. A dragon cannot be possessed."

"We have fire lizards here, not dragons."

"They are the same for our purposes," Kylara said sharply. "Now heed me or you'll lose the lot of them." She wondered why she'd bothered to sweat and toil and bring him a gift, an opportunity which he was obviously unable to accept or appreciate. And yet, if she had a gold and he a bronze, when they mated it *ought* to be worth her troubles. "Shut out any thought of fear or profit," she told the listening circle. "The first puts a dragon off, the second he can't understand. As soon as one will approach you, feed it. Keep feeding it. Get it on your hand, if possible, and move to a quiet corner and keep feeding it. Think how much you love it, want it to stay with you, how happy its presence makes you. Think of nothing else or the fire lizard will go *between*. There's just the short time between its hatching and its first big meal in which to make Impression. You succeed or you don't. It's up to you."

"You heard what she said. Now do it. Do it right. The man who fails—" Meron's voice trailed off threateningly.

Kylara laughed, breaking the ominous silence that followed. She laughed at the black look on Meron's face, laughed until the Lord Holder, angered beyond caution, shook her arm roughly, pointing to the eggs which were now indulging in wild maneuvers as their occupants tried to break out.

"Stop that cackling, Weyrwoman. It'll prejudice the hatchlings."

"Laughter is better than threats, Lord Meron. Even you can't order the preference of dragonkind. And tell me, good Lord Meron, will you be subject to the same dire unspeakable punishment if *you* fail?"

Meron grabbed her arm in a painful grip, his eyes riveted on the cracks now showing in one of his chosen eggs. He snapped his fingers for meat. Blood oozed from the raw handful as he knelt by the eggs, his body bowed tautly in his effort to effect an Impression.

Trying to show no concern, Kylara rose languidly from her chair. She strolled to the table and picked over the meaty gobbets until she had a satisfactory heap on the trencher. She signaled the tense guardsmen to supply themselves as she moved sedately back to the hearth.

She could not suppress her own excitement and heard Prideth warbling from the heights above the Hold. Ever since Kylara had seen the tiny fledglings F'nor and Brekke had Impressed, she had craved one of these dainty creatures. She would never understand that her imperious nature had subconsciously fought against the emotional symbiosis of her dragon queen. Instinctively Kylara had known that only as a Weyrwoman, a queen's rider, could she achieve the unparalleled power, privilege and unchallenged freedom as a woman on Pern. Skilled at ignoring what she didn't wish to admit, Kylara never realized that Prideth was the only living creature who could dominate her and whose good opinion she had to have. In the fire lizard, Kylara saw a miniature dragon which she could control—easily control—and physically dominate in a way she could not dominate Prideth.

And in presenting these fire-lizard eggs to a Holder, particularly the most despised Holder of all, Meron of Nabol, Kylara struck back at all the ignominies and imagined slights she had endured at the hands of both dragonmen and Pernese. The most recent insult—that the dishfaced fosterling of Brekke's had Impressed three, rejecting Kylara—would be completely avenged.

Well, Kylara would not be rejected here. She knew the way of it and, whatever else, she would be a winner.

The golden egg rocked violently, and a massive crack split it lengthwise. A tiny golden beak appeared.

"Feed her. Don't waste time," Meron whispered to her hoarsely.

"Don't tell me how to hatch eggs, you fool. Tend to your own."

The head had emerged, the body struggled to right itself, claws scrabbling against the wet shell. Kylara concentrated on thoughts of welcoming affection, of joy and admiration, ignoring the cries and exhortations around her.

The little queen, no bigger than her hand, staggered free of its casing and instantly looked around for something to eat. Kylara laid a glob of meat in its path and the beast swooped on it. Kylara placed a second a few inches from the first, leading the fire lizard toward her. Squawking ferociously, the fire lizard pounced, her steps less awkward, the wings spread and drying rapidly. Hunger, hunger, hunger was the pulse of the creature's thoughts and Kylara, reassured by receipt of this broadcast, intensified her thoughts of love and welcome.

She had the fire-lizard queen on her hand by the fifth lure. She rose carefully to her feet, popping food into the wide maw every time it opened, and moved away from the hearth and the chaos there.

For it was chaos, with the overanxious men making every mistake in the Record, despite her advice. Meron's three eggs cracked almost at once. Two hatchlings immediately set upon each other while Meron was awkwardly trying to imitate Kylara's actions. In his greed, he'd probably lose all three, she thought with malicious pleasure. Then she saw that there were other bronzes emerging. Well, all was not lost when her queen needed to mate.

Two men had managed to coax fire lizards to their hands and had followed Kylara's example by removing themselves from the confused cannibalism on the hearth.

"How much do we feed them, Weyrwoman?" one asked her, his eyes shining with incredulous joy and astonishment.

"Let them eat themselves insensible. They'll sleep and they'll stay by you. As soon as they wake, feed them again. And if they complain about itchy skin, bathe and rub them with oil. A patchy skin breaks *between* and the awful cold can kill even a fire lizard or dragon." How often she'd told that to weyrlings when she'd had to lecture them as Weyr-woman. Well, Brekke did that now, thank the First Egg.

"But what happens if they go *between?* How do we keep them?"

"You can't *keep* a dragon. He *stays* with you. You don't chain a dragon like a watch-wher, you know."

She became bored with her role as instructor and re-plenished her supply of meat. Then, disgustedly observing the waste of creatures dying on the hearth, she mounted the steps to the Inner Hold. She'd wait in Meron's chambers—there'd better be no one else there now—to see if he had, after all, managed to Impress a fire lizard.

Prideth told her that she wasn't happy that she had trans-ported the clutch to death on a cold, alien hearth.

"They lost more than this at Southern, silly one," Kylara told her dragon. "This time we've a pretty darling of our own."

Prideth grumbled on the fire ridge, but not about the liz-ard so Kylara paid her no heed.

CHAPTER VII

Midmorning at Benden Weyr

Early Morning at the Mastersmith's
Crafthall in Telgar Hold

F'lar received F'nor's message, five leaves of notes, just as he was about to set out to the Smithcrafthall to see Fandarel's distance-writing mechanism. Lessa was already aloft and waiting.

"F'nor said it was urgent. It's about the—" G'nag said.

"I'll read it as soon as I can," F'lar interrupted him. The man would talk your ear off. "My thanks and my apologies."

"But, F'lar . . ." The rest of the man's sentence was lost as Mnementh's claws rattled against the stone of the ledge and the bronze dragon began to beat his way up.

It didn't help F'lar's temper to realize that Mnementh was making a gentle ascent. Lessa had been so right when she had teased him about staying up drinking and talking with Robinton. The man was a sieve for wine. Around midnight Fandarel had left, taking his treasure of a contraption. Lessa had wagered that he'd never go to bed, and likely no one in his Hall would either. After extracting a promise from F'lar that he'd get some rest soon, too, she'd retired.

He had meant to, but Robinton knew so much about the different Holds, which minor Holders were important in swaying their Lords' mind—essential information if F'lar was going to effect a revolution.

Reverence for the older rider was part of weyrlife, and respect for the able Threadfighter. Seven Turns back, when F'lar had realized humbly how inadequate was Pern's one Weyr, Benden, and how ill-prepared for actual Threadfighting conditions, he had ascribed many virtues to the Oldtimers which were difficult—now—for him arbitrarily to sweep away. He—and all Benden's dragonriders—had learned the root of Threadfighting from the Oldtimers. Had learned the many tricks of dodging Thread, gauging the varieties of Fall, of conserving the strength of beast and rider, of turning the mind from the horrors of a full scoring or a phosphine emission too close. What F'lar didn't realize was how his Weyr and the Southerners had improved on the teaching; improved and surpassed, as they could on the larger, stronger, more intelligent contemporary dragons. F'lar had been able, in the name of gratitude and loyalty to his peers, to ignore, forget, rationalize the Oldtimers' shortcomings. He could do so no longer as the weight of their insecurity and insularity forced him to re-evaluate the results of their actions. In spite of this disillusionment, some part of F'lar, that inner soul of a man which requires a hero, a model against which to measure his own accomplishments, wanted to unite all the dragonmen; to sweep away the Oldtimers' intractable resistance to change, their tenacious hold on the outmoded.

Such a feat rivaled his other goal—and yet, the distance separating Pern and the Red Star was only a different sort of step *between*. And one man had to take if he was ever to free himself of the yoke of Thread.

The cool air—the sun was not full on the Bowl yet—reminded him of his face scores but it felt good against his aching forehead. As he bent forward to brace himself against Mnementh's neck, the leaves of the message pressed into his ribs. Well, he'd find out what Kylara was doing later.

He glanced below, squeezing his lids shut briefly as the

dizzying speed affected his unfocusing eyes. Yes, N'ton was already directing a crew of men and dragons in the removal of the sealed entrance. With more light and fresher air flooding the abandoned corridors, exploration could go on effectively. They'd keep Ramoth out of the way so she'd not complain that men were coming too close to her maturing clutch.

She knows, Mnementh informed his rider.

"And?"

She is curious.

They were now poised above the Star Rocks, above and beyond the watchrider, who saluted them. F'lar frowned at the Finger Rock. Now, if a man had a proper lens, fitted into the Eye Rock, would he be able to see the Red Star? No, because at this time of year you did not see the Red Star at that angle. Well . . .

F'lar glanced down at the panorama, the immense cup of rock at the top of the mountain, the tail-like road starting at a mysterious point on the right face, leading down to the lake on the plateau below the Weyr. The water glittered like a gigantic dragon eye. He worried briefly about haring off on this project with Thread falling so erratically. He had set up sweep patrols and sent the diplomatic N'ton (again he regretted F'nor's absence) to explain the necessary new measures to those Holds for which Benden Weyr was responsible. Raid had sent a stiff reply in acknowledgment, Sifer a contentious rebuke, although that old fool would come round after a night's thought on the alternatives.

Ramoth dipped her wings suddenly and disappeared from sight. Mnementh followed. A cold instant later they were wheeling above Telgar's chain of brilliant stair lakes, startlingly blue in the early morning sun. Ramoth was gliding downward, framed briefly against the water, sunlight unnecessarily gilding her bright body.

She's almost twice the size of any other queen, F'lar thought with a surge of admiration for the magnificent dragon.

A good rider makes a good beast, Mnementh remarked voluntarily.

Ramoth coyly swooped into a high banking turn before matching her speed with her Weyrmate's. The two flew, wingtip to wingtip, up the lake valleys to the Smithcraft. Behind them the terrain dropped slowly seaward, the river which was fed by the lakes running through wide farm and pasturelands, converging with the Great Dunto River which finally emptied into the sea.

As they landed before the Crafthall, Terry came running out of one of the smaller buildings set back in a grove of stunted fellis trees. He urgently waved them his way. The Craft was getting an early start today, sounds of industry issued from every building. Their riders aground, the dragons said they were going to swim, and took off again. As F'lar joined Lessa, she was grinning, her gray eyes dancing.

"Swimming, indeed!" was her comment and she caught her arm around his waist.

"So I must suffer uncomforted?" But he put an arm around her shoulders and matched his long stride to hers as they crossed the distance to Terry.

"You are indeed well come," Terry said, bowing continuously and grinning from ear to ear.

"Fandarel's already developed a long-distance glass?" asked F'lar.

"Not quite yet," and the Craft-second's merry eyes danced in his tired face, "but not for want of trying all night."

Lessa laughed sympathetically but Terry quickly demured.

"I don't mind, really. It's fascinating what the fine-viewer can make visible. Wansor is jubilant and depressed by turns. He's been raving all night to the point of tears for his own inadequacy."

They were almost at the door of the small hall when Terry turned, his face solemn.

"I wanted to tell you how terribly I feel about F'nor. If I'd only given them that rackety knife in the first place, but it had been commissioned as a wedding gift for Lord Asgenar from Lord Larad and I simply . . ."

"You had every right to prevent its appropriation," F'lar replied, gripping the Craft-second's shoulder for emphasis.

"Still, if I had relinquished it . . ."

"If the skies fell, we'd not be bothered by Thread," Lessa said so tartly that Terry was obliged to desist from his apologies.

The Hall, though apparently two-storied to judge by the windows, was in fact a vast single room. There was a small forge at one of the two hearths that were centered in each end. The black stone walls, smoothed and apparently seamless, were covered with diagrams and numbers. A long table dominated the center of the room, its wide ends deep sand trays, the rest a conglomerate of Record skins, leaves of paper and a variety of bizarre equipment. The Smith was standing to one side of the door, spread-legged, fists jammed against the wide waist belt, chin jutting out, a deep frown scoring his brow. His bellicose mood was directed toward a sketch on the black stone before him.

"It *must* be a question of the visual angle, Wansor," he muttered in an aggrieved tone, as if the sketch were defying his will. "Wansor?"

"Wansor is as good as *between*, Craftmaster," Terry said gently, gesturing toward the sleeping body all but invisible under skins on the outsized couch in one corner.

F'lar had always wondered where Fandarel slept, since the main Hall had long ago been given over to working space. No ordinary craftcot would be spacious enough to house the Craftmaster. Now he remembered seeing couches like this in most of the major buildings. Undoubtedly Fandarel slept anywhere and anytime he could no longer stay awake. The Smith thrived on what could burn out another man.

The Smith glanced crossly at the sleeper, grunted with resignation and only then noticed Lessa and F'lar. He smiled down at the Weyrwoman with real pleasure.

"You come early, and I'd hoped to have some progress to report on a distance-viewer," he said, gesturing toward the sketch. Lessa and F'lar obediently inspected the series of lines and ovals, innocently white on the black wall. "It is regrettable that the construction of perfect equipment is dependent on the frailty of men's minds and bodies. I apologize . . ."

"Why? It is barely morning," F'lar replied with a droll expression. "I will give you until nightfall before I accuse you of inefficiency."

Terry tried to smother a laugh; what came out was a slightly hysterical giggle.

They were all somewhat startled to hear the booming gargle that was Fandarel's laugh. He nearly knocked F'lar down with a jovial slap on the shoulder blades as he whooped with mirth.

"You give me . . . until nightfall . . . before . . . inefficiency . . ." the Smith gasped between howls.

"The man's gone mad. We've put too much of a strain on him," F'lar told the others.

"Nonsense," Lessa replied, looking at the convulsed Smith with small sympathy. "He hasn't slept and if I know his single-mindedness, he hasn't eaten. Has he, Terry?"

Terry plainly had to search his mind for an answer.

"Rouse your cooks, then. Even *he*," and Lessa jerked her thumb at the exasperating Smith, "ought to stoke that hulk of his with food once a week."

Her insinuation that the Smith was a dragon was not lost on Terry who this time began to laugh uncontrollably.

"I'll rouse them myself. You're all next to useless, you men," she complained and started for the door.

Terry intercepted her, masterfully suppressing his laughter, and reached for a button in the base of a square box on the wall. In a loud voice he bespoke a meal for the Smith and four others.

"What's that?" F'lar asked, fascinated. It didn't look capable of sending a message all the way to Telgar.

"Oh, a loudspeaker. Very efficient," Terry said with a wry grin, "if you can't bellow like the Craftmaster. We have them in every hall. Saves a lot of running around."

"One day I will fix it so that we can channel the message to the one area we want to speak to." The Smith added, wiping his eyes, "Ah, but a man can sleep anytime. A laugh restores the soul."

"Is that the distance-writer you're going to demonstrate for us?" asked the Weyrleader, frankly skeptical.

"No, no, no," Fandarel reassured him, dismissing the accomplishment almost irritably and striding to a complex arrangement of wires and ceramic pots. "This is my distance-writer!"

It was difficult for Lessa and F'lar to see anything to be proud of in that mystifying jumble.

"The wallbox looks more efficient," F'lar said at length, bending to test the mixture in a pot with a finger.

The Smith struck his hand away.

"That would burn your skin as quick as pure agenothree," he exclaimed. "Based on that solution, too. Now, observe. These tubs contain blocks of metal, one each of zinc and copper, in a watered solution of sulfuric acid which makes the metal dissolve in such a way that a chemical reaction occurs. This gives us a form of activity I have called chemical reaction energy. The c.r. produced can be controlled at this point," and he ran a finger down the metal arm which was poised over an expanse of thin grayish material, attached at both ends to rollers. The Smith turned a knob. The pots began to bubble gently. He tapped the arm and a series of red marks of different lengths began to appear on the material which wound slowly forward. "See, this is a message. The Harper adapted and expanded his drum code, a different sequence and length of lines for every sound. A little practice and you can read them as easily as written words."

"I do not see the advantage of writing a message here," and F'lar pointed to the roll, "when you say . . ."

The Smith beamed expansively. "Ah, but as I write with this needle, another needle at the Masterminer's in Crom or at the Crafthall at Igen repeats the line simultaneously."

"That would be faster than dragon flight," Lessa whispered, awed. "What do these lines say? Where did they go?" She inadvertently touched the material with her finger, snatching it back for a quick examination. There was no mark on her finger but a blotch of red appeared on the paper.

The Smith chuckled raspingly.

"No harm in that stuff. It merely reacts to the acidity of your skin."

F'lar laughed. "Proof of your disposition, my dear!"

"Put *your* finger there and see what occurs," Lessa ordered with a flash of her eyes.

"It would be the same," the Smith remarked didactically. "The roll is made of a natural substance, litmus, found in Igen, Keroon and Tillek. We have always used it to check the acidity of the earth or solutions. As the chemical reaction energy is acid, naturally the litmus changes color when the needle touches its surface, thus making the message for us to read."

"Didn't you say something about having to lay wire? Explain."

The Smith lifted a coil of fine wire which was hooked into the contraption. It ran out the window to a stone post. Now F'lar and Lessa noticed that posts were laid in a line marching toward the distant mountains, and, one assumed, the Masterminer in Crom Hold.

"This connects the c.r. distance-writer here with the one at Crom. That other goes to Igen. I can send messages to either Crom or Igen, or both, by adjusting this dial."

"To which did you send that?" Lessa asked, pointing to the lines.

"Neither, my lady, for the c.r. was not being broadcast. I had the dial set to receive messages, not send. It is very efficient, you see."

At this point, two women, dressed in the heavy wher-hide garb of smithcrafters, entered the room, laden with trays of steaming food. One was evidently solely for the Smith's consumption, for the woman jerked her head at him as she placed the heavy platter on a rest evidently designed to receive it and not disturb work in the sand tray beneath. She bobbed to Lessa as she crossed in front of her, gesturing peremptorily to her companion to wait as she cleared space on the table. She did this by sweeping things out of her way with complete disregard for what might be disarranged or broken. She gave the bared surface a cursory swipe with a towel, signaled the other to put the tray down, then the two of them swept out before Lessa, stunned by such perfunctory service, could utter a sound.

"I see you've got your women trained, Fandarel," F'lar said mildly, catching and holding Lessa's indignant eyes. "No talking, no fluttering, no importunate demands for attention."

Terry chuckled as he freed one chair of its pile of abandoned clothing and gestured Lessa to sit. F'lar righted one overturned stool that would serve him while Terry hooked a foot round a second that had got kicked under the long table, seating himself with a fluid movement that proved he had long familiarity with such makeshift repasts.

Now that he had food before him, the Smith was eating with single-minded intensity.

"Then it is the wire-laying process that holds you up," F'lar said, accepting the *klah* Lessa poured for him and Terry. "How long did it take you to extend it from here to Crom Hold, for instance?"

"We did not stick to the work," Terry replied for his Craftmaster whose mouth was too full for speech. "The posts were set up first by apprentices from both halls and those Holders willing to take a few hours from their own tasks. It was difficult to find the proper wire, and it takes time to extrude perfect lengths."

"Did you speak to Lord Larad? Wouldn't he volunteer men?"

Terry made a face. "Lord Holder Larad is more interested in how many flame throwers we can make him, or how many crops he can plant for food."

Lessa had taken a sip of the *klah* and barely managed to swallow the acid stuff. The bread was lumpy and half-baked, the sausage within composed of huge, inedible chunks, yet both Terry and Fandarel ate with great appetite. Indifferent service was one matter; but decent food quite another.

"If this is the food he barters you for flame throwers, I'd refuse," she exclaimed. "Why, even the fruit is rotten."

"Lessa!"

"I wonder you can achieve as much as you do if you have to survive on this," she went on, ignoring F'lar's reprimand. "What's your wife's name?"

"Lessa," F'lar repeated, more urgently.

"No wife," the Smith mumbled, but the rest of his sentence came out more as breadcrumbs than words and he was reduced to shaking his head from side to side.

"Well, even a headwoman ought to be able to manage better than this."

Terry cleared his mouth enough to explain. "Our headwoman is a good enough cook but she's so much better at bringing up faded ink on the skins we've been studying that she's been doing that instead."

"Surely one of the other wives . . ."

Terry made a grimace. "We've been so pressed for help, with all these additional projects," and he waved at the distance-writer, "that anyone who can has turned crafter—" He broke off, seeing the consternation on Lessa's face.

"Well, I've women sitting around the Lower Cavern doing make-work. I'll have Kenalas and those two cronies of hers here to help as soon as a green can bring 'em. And," Lessa added emphatically, pointing a stern finger at the Smith, "they'll have strict orders to do nothing in the *craft*, no matter what!"

Terry looked frankly relieved and pushed aside the meatroll he had been gobbling down, as if he had only now discovered how it revolted him.

"In the meantime," Lessa went on with an indignation that was ludicrous to F'lar. He knew who managed Benden Weyr's domestic affairs. *"I'm* making a decent brew of *klah.* How you could have choked down such bitter dregs as this is beyond my comprehension!" She swept out the door, pot in hand, her angry monologue drifting back to amused listeners.

"Well, she's right," F'lar said, laughing. "This is worse than the worst the Weyr ever got."

"To tell the truth, I never really noticed before," Terry replied, staring at his plate quizzically.

"That's obvious."

"It keeps me going," the Smith said placidly, swallowing a half-cup of *klah* to clear his mouth.

"Seriously, are you that short of men that you have to draft your women, too?"

"Not short of men, exactly, but of people who have the dexterity, the interest some of our projects require," Terry spoke up, in quick defense of his Craftmaster.

"I mean no criticism, Master Terry," F'lar said, hastily.

"We've done a good deal of reviewing of the old Records, too," Terry went on, a little defensively still. He flipped the pile of skins that had been spilled down the center of the table. "We've got answers to problems we didn't know existed and haven't encountered yet."

"And no answers to the troubles which beset us," Fandarel added, gesturing skyward with his thumb.

"We've had to take time to copy these Records," Terry continued solemnly, "because they are all but illegible now . . ."

"I contend that we lost more than was saved and useful. Some skins were worn out with handling and their message obliterated."

The two smiths seemed to be exchanging portions of a well-rehearsed complaint.

"Did it never occur to you to ask the Masterharper for help in transcribing your Records?" asked F'lar.

Fandarel and Terry exchanged startled glances.

"I can see it didn't. It's not the Weyrs alone who are autonomous. Don't you Craftmasters speak to each other?" F'lar's grin was echoed by the big Smith, recalling Robinton's words of the previous evening. "However, the Harperhall is usually overflowing with apprentices, set to copying whatever Robinton can find for them. They could as well take that burden from you."

"Aye, that would be a great help," Terry agreed, seeing that the Smith did not object.

"You sound doubtful—or hesitant? Are any Crafts secret?"

"Oh, no. Neither the Craftmaster nor I hold with cabalistic, inviolable sanctities, passed at deathbed from father to son . . ."

The Smith snorted with such powerful scorn that a skin on the top of the pile slithered to the floor. "No sons!"

"That's all very well when one can count on dying in bed and at a given time, but I—and the Craftmaster—would like to see all knowledge available to all who need it," Terry said.

F'lar gazed with increased respect at the stoop-shouldered Craft-second. He'd known that Fandarel relied heavily on Terry's executive ability and tactfulness. The man could always be counted on to fill in the gaps in Fandarel's terse explanations or instructions, but it was obvious now that Terry had a mind of his own, whether it concurred with his Craftmaster's or not.

"Knowledge has less danger of being lost, then," Terry went on less passionately but just as fervently. "We knew so much more once. And all we have are tantalizing bits and fragments that do almost more harm than good because they only get in the way of independent development."

"We will contrive," Fandarel said, his ineffable optimism complementing Terry's volatility.

"Do you have men enough, and wire enough, to install one of those things at Telgar Hold in two days?" asked F'lar, feeling a change of subject might help.

"We could take men off flame throwers and hardware. And I can call in the apprentices from the Smithhalls at Igen, Telgar and Lemos," the Smith said and then glanced slyly at F'lar. "They'd come faster dragonback!"

"You'll have them," F'lar promised.

Terry's face lit up with relief. "You don't know what a difference it is to work with Benden Weyr. You *see* so clearly what needs to be done, without any hedging and hemming."

"You've had problems with R'mart?" asked F'lar with quick concern.

"It's not that, Weyrleader," Terry said, leaning forward earnestly. "You still care what happens, what's happening."

"I'm not sure I understand."

The Smith rumbled something but there seemed to be no interrupting Terry.

"I see it this way, and I've seen riders from every Weyr by now. The Oldtimers have been fighting Thread since their birth. That's all they're known. They're tired and not just from skipping forward in time four hundred Turns. They're heart-tired, bone-tired. They've had too much rising to alarms, seen too many friends and dragons die, Thread-scored. They rest on custom, because that's safest and takes the least energy. And they feel entitled to anything they want. Their minds may be numb with too much time *between*, though they think fast enough to talk you out of anything. As far as they're concerned, there's always been Thread. There's nothing else to look forward to. They don't remember, they can't really conceive of a time, *of four hundred* Turns without *Thread*. We can. Our fathers could and their fathers. We live at a different rhythm because Hold and Craft alike threw off that ancient fear and grew in other ways, in other paths, which we can't give up now. We exist only because the Oldtimers lived in their Time *and* in ours. And fought in both Times. We can see a way out, a life without Thread. They knew only one thing and they've taught us that. How to fight Thread. They simply can't see that *we*, that anyone, could take it just one step further and destroy Thread forever."

F'lar returned Terry's earnest stare.

"I hadn't seen the Oldtimers in just that light," he said slowly.

"Terry's absolutely right, F'lar," said Lessa. She'd evidently paused on the threshold, but moved now briskly into the room, filling the Smith's empty mug from the pitcher of *klah* she'd brewed. "And it's a judgment we ought to consider in our dealings with them." She smiled warmly at Terry as she filled his cup. "You're as eloquent as the Harper. Are you sure you're a smith?"

"That is *klah!*" announced Fandarel, having drunk it all.

"Are you sure you're a Weyrwoman?" retorted F'lar, extending his cup with a sly smile. To Terry he said, "I wonder none of us realized it before, particularly in view of recent events. A man can't fight day after day, Turn after Turn—though the Weyrs were eager to come forward—" He looked questioningly at Lessa.

"Ah, but that was something new, exciting," she replied. "And it was new here, too, for the Oldtimers. What isn't new is that they have another forty-some Turns to fight Thread in our time. Some of them have had fifteen and twenty Turns of fighting Thread. We have barely seven."

The Smith put both hands on the table and pushed himself to his feet.

"Talk makes no miracles. To effect an end to Thread we must get the dragons to the source. Terry, pour a cup of that excellent *klah* for Wansor and let us attack the problem with good heart."

As F'lar rose with Lessa, F'nor's message rustled at his belt.

"Let me take a look at F'nor's message, Lessa, before we go."

He opened the closely written pages, his eye catching the repetition of "fire lizard" before his mind grasped the sense of what he was reading.

"Impressing? A fire lizard?" he exclaimed, holding the letter so that Lessa could verify it.

"No one's ever managed to catch a fire lizard," Fandarel said.

"F'nor has," F'lar told him, "and Brekke, and Mirrim. Who's Mirrim?"

"Brekke's fosterling," the Weyrwoman replied absently, her eyes scanning the message as rapidly as possible. "One of L'trel's by some woman or other of his. No, Kylara wouldn't have liked that!"

F'lar shushed her, passing the sheets over to Fandarel who was curious now.

"Are fire lizards related to dragons?" asked the Craft-second.

"Judging by what F'nor says, more than we realized." F'lar handed Terry the last page, looking up at Fandarel. "What do you think?"

The Smith began to realign his features into a frown but stopped, grinning broadly instead.

"Ask the Masterherder. *He* breeds animals. I breed machines."

He saluted Lessa with his mug and strode to the wall he had been comtemplating when they entered, immediately lost in thought.

"A good point," F'lar said with a laugh to his remaining audience.

"F'lar? Remember that flawed piece of metal, with that garble of words? The one with the scribble like last night's. It mentioned fire lizards, too. That was one of the few words that made sense."

"So?"

"I wish we hadn't given that plate back to Fort Weyr. It was more important than we realized."

"There may be more at Fort Weyr that's important," F'lar said, gloomily. "It was the first Weyr. Who knows what we might find if we could search there!"

Lessa made a face, thinking of Mardra and T'ron.

"T'ron's not hard to manage," she mused.

"Lessa, no nonsense now."

"If fire lizards are so much like dragons, could they be trained to go *between*, as dragons can, and be messengers?" asked Terry.

"How long would that take?" asked the Smith, less unaware of his surroundings than he looked. "How much time *have* we got this Turn?"

CHAPTER VIII

Midmorning at Southern Weyr

"No, Rannelly, I've not seen Kylara all morning," Brekke told the old woman patiently, for the fourth time that morning.

"And you've not taken a good look at your own poor queen, either, I'll warrant, fooling around with these—these nuisancy flitterbys," Rannelly retorted, grumbling as she limped out of the Weyrhall.

Brekke had finally found time to see to Mirrim's wounded brown. He was so stuffed with juicy tidbits from the hand of his overzealous nurse that he barely opened one lid when Brekke inspected him. Numbweed worked as well on lizard as dragon and human.

"He's doing just fine, dear," Brekke told the anxious girl, the greens fluttering on the child's shoulders in response to her exaggerated sigh of relief. "Now, don't overfeed them. They'll split their hides."

"Do you think they'll stay?"

"With such care as you lavish on them, sweeting, they're

not likely to leave. But you have chores which I cannot in conscience permit you to shirk . . ."

"All because of Kylara . . ."

"Mirrim!"

Ashamed, the girl hung her head, but she deeply resented the fact that Kylara gave all the orders and did no work, leaving her tasks to fall to Brekke. It wasn't fair. Mirrim was very very glad that the little lizards had preferred her to that woman.

"What did old Rannelly mean about your queen? You take good care of Wirenth. She lacks for nothing," said Mirrim.

"Ssssh. I'll go see. I left her sleeping."

"Rannelly's as bad as Kylara. She thinks she's so wise and knows everything . . ."

Brekke was about to scold her fosterling when she heard F'nor calling her.

"The green riders are bringing back some of the meat hung in the salt caves," she said, issuing quick instructions instead. "None of that is to go to the lizards, Mirrim. Now, mind. The boys can trap wild wherries. Their meat is as good, if not better. We've no idea what effect too much red-blood meat will have on lizards." With that caution to inhibit Mirrim's impulsive generosity, Brekke went out to meet F'nor.

"There's been no rider in from Benden?" he asked her, easing the arm sling across his shoulder.

"You'd've heard instantly," she assured him, deftly adjusting the cloth at his neck. "In fact," she added in mild rebuke, "there are no riders in the Weyr at all today."

F'nor chuckled. "And not much to show for their absence, either. There isn't a beach along the coastline that doesn't have a dragon couchant, with rider a-coil, feigning sleep."

Brekke put her hand to her mouth. It wouldn't do for Mirrim to hear her giggling like a weyrling.

"Oh, you laugh?"

"Aye, and they've made a note of both occasions that I did," she said with due solemnity, but her eyes danced. Then she noticed that the sling was missing its usual occupant. "Where's . . ."

"Grall is curled between Canth's eyes, so stuffed she'd likely not move if we went *between*. Which I've half a mind

140

to do. If you hadn't told me I could trust G'nag, I'd swear he'd not delivered my letter to F'lar, or else he's lost it."

"You are not going *between* with that wound, F'nor. And if G'nag said he delivered the letter, he did. Perhaps something has come up."

"More important than Impressing fire lizards?"

"There could be something. Threads are falling out of phase—" Brekke broke off, she oughtn't to have reminded F'nor of that, judging by the bleak expression on his face. "Maybe not, but they've got to get the Lord Holders to supply watchers and fires and it may be F'lar is occupied with that. It certainly isn't *your* fault you're not there to help. Those odious Fort riders have no self-control. Imagine taking a green out of her Weyr close to mating—" Brekke stopped again, snapping her mouth closed. "But Rannelly said 'my queen,' not 'her' queen."

The girl turned so white that F'nor thrust his good hand under her elbow to steady her.

"What's the matter? Kylara hasn't ducked Prideth out of here when she's due to mate? Where is Kylara, by the way?"

"I don't know. I must check Wirenth. Oh, no, she couldn't be!"

F'nor followed the girl's swift steps through the great hanging trees that arched over the Southern Weyr's sprawling compound.

"Wirenth's scarcely hatched," he called after her and then remembered that Wirenth was actually a long time out of her shell. It was just that he tended to think of Brekke as the most recent of the Southern Weyrwomen. Brekke looked so young, much too young . . .

She is the same age as Lessa was when Mnementh first flew Ramoth, Canth informed him.

"Is Wirenth ready to rise?" F'nor asked his brown, stopping dead in his tracks.

Soon. Soon. Bronzes will know.

F'nor ticked over in his mind the bronze complement of Southern. The tally didn't please him. Not that the bronzes were few in number, a discourtesy to a new queen, but that their riders had always contended for Kylara, whether Prideth's mating was at stake or not. No matter whose bronze flew Wirenth, the rider would have Brekke and the thought of anyone who had vyed for Kylara's bed favor making love to Brekke irritated the brown rider.

Canth's as big or bigger than any bronze here, he thought resentfully. He had never entertained such an invidious comparison before and ruthlessly put it out of his mind.

Now, if N'ton, a clean-cut lad and a top wingrider just happened to be in Southern? Or B'dor of Ista Weyr. F'nor had ridden with the Istan when his Weyr and Benden joined forces over Nerat and Keroon. Nicely conformed bronzes, both of them, and while F'nor favored N'ton more, if B'dor's beast flew Wirenth, she and Brekke would have the option of removing to Ista Weyr. They'd only three queens there, and Nadira was a far better Weyrwoman than Kylara, despite her coming from the Oldtime.

Pleased with this solution, though he hadn't a notion how to accomplish it, F'nor continued along the path to Wirenth's sun-baked clearing.

He paused at the edge, affected by the sight of Brekke, totally involved with her queen. The girl stood at Wirenth's head, her body gracefully inclined against the dragon, as she tenderly scratched the near eye ridge. Wirenth was somnolent, one lid turning back enough to prove she was aware of the attention, her wedge-shaped head resting on one foreleg, her hindquarters neatly tucked under and framed by her long, graceful tail. In the sun she gleamed with an orange-yellow of excellent health—a color which would very shortly turn a deeper-burnished gold. All too shortly, F'nor realized, for Wirenth had lost every trace of the fatty softness of adolescence; her hide was sleek and smooth, not a blemish to suggest imperfect care. She was an extremely well-proportioned dragon; not one bit too leggy, short-tailed or wherry-necked. Despite her size, for she was easily the length of Prideth, she had a more lithesome appearance. She was one of the best bred from Ramoth and Mnementh.

F'nor frowned slightly at Brekke, subtly changed in her dragon's presence. She seemed more feminine—and desirable. Sensing him, Brekke turned, and the languid look of adoration for her queen made her radiant face almost embarrassing to F'nor.

He hastily cleared his throat. "She'll rise soon, you realize," he said, more gruffly than he intended.

"Yes, I think she will, my beauty. I wonder how that will

affect him," Brekke asked, her expression altering. She stepped to one side and pointed to the tiny bronze tucked between Wirenth's jaw and forearm.

"Can't tell, can we?" F'nor replied and, with another series of throat-clearings, covered his savagery at the thought of Brekke mating any of the bronze riders at Southern.

"You're not sickening with something, are you?" she asked with concern and was abruptly transformed back into the Brekke he knew best.

"No. Who's going to be the lucky rider?" he heard himself asking. It was a civil enough question. He was, after all, F'lar's Wing-second and had a right to be curious about such matters. "You can ask for an open flight, you know," he added defensively.

She turned pale and leaned back against Wirenth. As if for comfort.

As if for comfort, F'nor repeated the observation to himself, and remembered, with no relief, the way Brekke had looked at T'bor the day before. "It doesn't matter if the rider's already attached, you know, not in a first mating." He blurted it out, then realized like the greenest dolt that that was stupid. Brekke'd know exactly what Kylara's reaction would be if T'bor's Orth flew Wirenth. She'd know she would have no peace at all. He groaned at his ineptitude.

"Your arm is hurting?" she asked, solicitous.

"No. Not my arm," and he stepped forward, gripping her shoulder with his good hand. "Look, it'd be better if you called for an open flight. There are plenty of good bronzes. N'ton of Benden Weyr, B'dor of Ista Weyr. Both are fine men with good beasts. Then you could leave Southern . . ."

Brekke's eyes were closed and she seemed to go limp in his grasp.

"No! No!" The denial was so soft he barely heard it. "I belong here. Not—Benden."

"N'ton could transfer."

A shudder went through Brekke's body and her eyes flew open. She slipped away from his grip.

"No, N'ton—shouldn't come to Southern," she said in a flat voice.

"He's got no use for Kylara, you know," F'nor continued, determined to reassure her. "She doesn't succeed with every man, you know. And you're a very sweet person, you know."

With a shift of mood as sudden as any of Lessa's, Brekke smiled up at him.

"That's nice to know."

And somehow F'nor had to laugh with her, at his own blundering interference, at the notion of him, a brown rider, giving advice to someone like Brekke, who had more sense in her smallest finger than he.

Well, he was going to get a message to N'ton and B'dor anyhow. Ramoth would help him.

"Have you named your lizard?" he asked.

"Berd. Wirenth and I decided. She likes him," Brekke replied, smiling tenderly on the sleeping pair. "Although it's very confusing. Why do I have a bronze, you a queen and Mirrim *three?*"

F'nor shrugged and grinned at her. "Why not? Of course, once we tell them that's not how it's done, they may conform to time-honored couplings."

"What I meant was, if the fire lizards—who seem to be miniature dragons—can be Impressed by anyone who approaches them at the crucial moment, then fighting dragons —not just queens who don't chew firestone anyhow—could be Impressed by women, too."

"Fighting Thread is hard work. Leave it to men."

"You think managing a Weyr isn't hard work?" Brekke kept her voice even but her eyes darkened angrily. "Or plowing fields and hollowing cliffs for Holds? And . . ."

F'nor whistled. "Why, Brekke, such revolutionary thoughts from a craftbred girl? Where women know there's only one place for them . . . Oh, you've got Mirrim in mind as a rider?"

"Yes. She'd be as good or better than some of the male weyrlings I know," and there was such asperity in Brekke's voice that F'nor wondered just which boys she found so lacking. "Her ability to Impress three fire lizards indicates . . ."

"Hey—backwing a bit, girl. We've enough trouble with the Oldtimers as it is without trying to get them to accept a girl riding a fighting dragon! C'mon, Brekke. I know your fondness for the child and she seems a good intelligent girl, but you must be realistic."

"I am," Brekke replied, so emphatically that F'nor looked at her in surprise. "Some riders should have been crafters or farmers—or—nothing, but they were acceptable to dragons on Hatching. Others are real riders, heart and soul and mind. Dragons are the beginning and end of their ambition. Mirrim . . ."

A dragon broke into the air above the Weyr, trumpeting.

"F'lar!" With such a wingspan, it could be no other.

F'nor broke into a run, motioning Brekke to follow him to the Weyr landing field.

"No. You go. Wirenth's waking. I'll wait."

F'nor was relieved that she preferred to stay. He didn't want her to come out with that drastic theory in front of F'lar, particularly when he wanted his half-brother to shift N'ton and B'dor here for her sake. Anything to spare Brekke the kind of scene Kylara would throw if T'bor's Orth flew Wirenth.

"Where is everyone?" was F'lar's curt greeting as his brother joined him. "Where's Kylara? Mnementh can't find Prideth. She's not to be haring off on her own."

"Everyone's out trying to trap fire lizards."

"With Thread falling out of pattern? Of all the stupidities . . . This continent is by no means immune! Where in the image of all shells is T'bor? That'd be all we need—Threads ravaging the southern continent!"

The outburst was so uncharacteristic that F'nor stared at the Weyrleader. F'lar passed his hand over his eyes, rubbing his temples. The cold of *between* had started his headache again. The talk at the Crafthall had been unsettling. He gripped his half-brother's arm in apology.

"That was inexcusable of me, F'nor. I beg your pardon."

"Accepted, of course. That's Orth wheeling in right now."

F'nor decided to wait before asking F'lar what was really bothering him. He could just imagine what Raid of Benden Hold or Sifer of Bitra Hold had had to say about new levies of manpower. Probably felt that the change of Threadfall was a personal insult, dreamed up by Benden Weyr to annoy the faithful Holds of Pern.

T'bor landed and strode toward the waiting men.

Perhaps Brekke was not so far off in her heretical doctrine, F'nor thought. T'bor had made Southern Weyr self-sufficient and productive, no small task. He'd obviously have made a good Holder.

"Orth said you were here, F'lar. What brings you to

Southern? You heard our news about the fire lizards?" T'bor called, brushing the sand from his clothes as he walked.

"Yes, I did," replied F'lar in so formal a tone that T'bor's welcoming smile faded. "And I thought you'd heard ours, that Thread is dropping out of pattern."

"There's a rider along every inch of coastline, F'lar, so don't accuse me of negligence," T'bor said, his smile returning. "Dragons don't need to be a-wing to spot Thread. Shells, man, you can hear it hissing across the water."

"I assume you were looking for fire lizard eggs?" F'lar sounded testy and not completely reassured by T'bor's report. "Have you found any?"

T'bor shook his head. "There's evidence, far to the west, of another clutch, but there isn't a sign of shell or corpse. The wherries can make fast work of anything edible."

"Were I you, T'bor, I'd not release an entire Weyr to search for lizard eggs. There's no guarantee Thread will move in on this continent from the ocean."

"But it always has. What little we get."

"Thread fell ten hours before schedule across Lemos north when it should have fallen on Lemos south and Telgar southeast," F'lar told him in a hard voice. "I have since heard that Thread fell, unchecked," and he paused to let that sink in to T'bor's mind, "in Telgar Hold and Crom Hold, both times out of phase with the tables though we do not yet know the time differential. We can't rely on any previous performance."

"I'll mount guards immediately and send the wings to sweep as far south as we've penetrated," T'bor said briskly and, shrugging into his riding jacket, trotted back to Orth. They were aloft in one great leap.

"Orth looks well," F'lar said and then eyed his half-brother closely before he smiled, jabbing a fist affectionately at F'nor's good shoulder. "You do, too. How's the arm healing?"

"I'm at Southern," F'nor replied in oblique explanation. "Are Threadfalls really that erratic?"

"I don't know," F'lar said with an irritable shrug. "Tell me about these fire lizards if you please. Are they worth the time of every able-bodied rider in this Weyr? Where's yours? I'd like to see it for myself before I go back to Benden." He glanced northeast, frowning.

"Shells, can't I leave Benden Weyr for a week without everything falling apart?" F'nor demanded so vehemently that F'lar stared at him in momentary surprise before he chuckled and seemed to relax. "That's better," F'nor said, echoing the grin. "Come. There are a couple of the lizards in the Weyrhall and I need some *klah*. I was out hunting clutches all morning myself, you know. Or would you prefer to sample some of Southern's wine?"

"Ha!" F'lar made the exclamation a challenge.

When they entered the Weyrhall, Mirrim was there alone, stirring the stew in the big kettles. The two greens were watching her from the long, wide mantel. She gave the appearance of having an odd deformity of chest until F'nor realized that she had rigged a sling around her shoulders in which the wounded brown was supended, his little eyes pinpoints of light. At the sound of their boots on the paving, she swung round, her eyes wide with an apprehension which turned to surprise as she glanced from F'nor to F'lar. Her mouth made an "o" of astonishment as she recognized the Benden Weyrleader by his resemblance to F'nor.

"And you're the—the young lady who Impressed three?" F'lar asked, crossing the big room to her.

Mirrim bobbed a series of nervous curtsies, causing the brown to squawk in protest to such bouncing.

"May I see him?" F'lar asked and deftly stroked a tiny eye ridge. "He's a real beauty! Canth in miniature," and F'lar glanced slyly at his half-brother to see if the jibe registered. "Will he recover from his wounds—ah . . ."

"Mirrim is her name," F'nor prompted in a bland tone that implied his brother's memory was failing him.

"Oh, no, Weyrleader—he's healing nicely," the girl said with another bob.

"Full stomach, I see," F'lar commented approvingly. He glanced at the pair huddled together on the mantel and crooned soft encouragement. They began to preen, stretching fragile, translucent green wings, arching their backs and emitting an echoing hum in pleasure. "You'll have your hands full with this trio."

"I'll manage them, sir. I promise. And I won't forget my duties, either," she said breathlessly, her eyes still wide. With a gasp, she turned to give a splashing stir to the contents of the nearest pot, then whirled back again before the men could turn. "Brekke's not here. Would you like some *klah*? Or the stew? Or some . . ."

"We'll serve ourselves," F'nor assured her, picking up two mugs.

"Oh, I ought to do that, sir . . ."

"You ought to watch your kettles, Mirrim. We'll manage," F'lar told her kindly, mentally contrasting the state of domestic affairs at the Crafthall to the order and the cooking of good rich food at this hall.

He motioned the brown rider to take the table furthest from the kitchen hearth.

"Can you hear anything from the lizards?" he asked in a low voice.

"From hers, you mean? No, but I can easily see what they must be thinking from their reactions. Why?"

"Idle question. But she's not from a Search, is she?"

"No, of course not. She's Brekke's fosterling."

"Hmmm. Then she's not exactly proof, is she?"

"Proof of what, F'lar? I've suffered no head injury but I can't follow your thought."

F'lar gave his brother an absent smile and then exhaled wearily.

"We're going to have trouble with the Lord Holders; they're disillusioned and dissatisfied with the Oldtime Weyrs and are going to balk at any more expeditious measures against Thread."

"Raid and Sifer give you a hard time?"

"I wish it were only that, F'nor. They'd come round." F'lar gave his half-brother a terse account of what he'd learned from Lytol, Robinton and Fandarel the day before.

"Brekke was right when she said something really important had come up," F'nor said afterward. "But . . ."

"Yes, that news's a hard roll to eat, all right, but our ever efficient Craftsmith's got what might be an answer, not only to the watch on Thread but to establishing decent communications with every Hold and Hall on Pern. Especially since we can't get the Oldtimers to assign riders outside the Weyrs. I saw a demonstration of the device today and we're going to rig one for the Lord Holders at Telgar's wedding . . ."

"And the Threads will wait for that?"

F'lar snorted. "They may be the lesser evil, frankly. The

Threads prove to be more flexible in their ways than the Oldtimers and less trouble than the Lord Holders."

"One of the basic troubles between Lord Holders and Weyrmen are dragons, F'lar, and those fire lizards might just ease matters."

"That's what I was thinking earlier, considering that young Mirrim had Impressed three. That's really astonishing, even if she is weyrbred."

"Brekke would like to see her Impress a fighting dragon," F'nor said in a casual way, watching his half-brother's face closely.

F'lar gave him a startled stare and then threw back his head and laughed.

"Can you . . . imagine . . . T'ron's reaction?" . . . he managed to say.

"Well enough to spare myself your version, but the fire lizard may do the trick! *And,* have the added talent of keeping Hold in contact with Weyr *if* these creatures prove amenable to training."

"If—if! Just how similar to dragons are fire lizards?"

F'nor shrugged. "As I told you, they are Impressionable—if rather undiscriminating," he pointed to Mirrim at the Hearth and then grinned maliciously, "although they detested Kylara on sight. They're slaves to their stomachs, though after Hatching that's very definitely draconic. They respond to affection and flattery. The dragons themselves admit the relationship, seem totally free of jealousy of the creatures. I can detect basic emotions in the thoughts of mine and they generally inspire affection in those who handle them."

"And they can go *between?*"

"Grall—my little queen—did. About chewing firestone I couldn't hazard a guess. We'll have to wait and see."

"And we don't have time," F'lar said, clenching his fists, his eyes restless with the current of his thoughts.

"*If* we could find a hardened clutch, all set to Hatch, in time for that wedding—*that,* combined with Fandarel's gadget—" F'nor let his sentence trail off.

F'lar got up in a single decisive movement. "I'd like to see your queen. You named her Grall?"

"You're solid dragonman, F'lar," F'nor chuckled, remembering what Brekke had said. "You had no trouble remembering the lizard's name but the girl's—? Never mind, F'lar. Grall's with Canth."

"Any chance you could call her—here?"

F'nor considered the intriguing possibility but shook his head.

"She's asleep, full up to the jawline."

She was and daintily curled in the hollow by Canth's left ear. Her belly was distended from the morning's meal and F'nor dabbed it with sweet oil. She condescended to lift two lids but her eye was so dull she did not take notice of the additional visitor, nor Mnementh peering down at her. He thought her a very interesting creature.

"Charming. Lessa'll want one, I'm sure," F'lar murmured, a delighted half-smile on his face as he jumped down from Canth's forearm on which he'd stood to observe her. "Hope she grows a little. Canth could yawn and inadvertently inhale her."

Never, and the brown's comment did not need to be passed to the bronze rider.

"If we'd only an estimate of how long it would take to train them, if they are trainable. But time's as inflexible as an Oldtimer." F'lar looked his half-brother squarely in the eye, no longer hiding the deep worry that gnawed at him.

"Not entirely, F'lar," the brown rider said, returning his gaze steadily. "As you said, the greater evil is the sickness in our own . . ."

A dragon's brassy scream, the klaxon of Thread attack, stopped F'nor midsentence. The brown rider had swung toward his dragon, instinctively reacting to the alert, when F'lar caught him by the arm.

"You can't fight thread with an unhealed wound, man. Where do they keep firestone here?"

Whatever criticism F'lar might have had of T'bor's permissiveness at Southern, he could not fault the instant response of the Weyr's fighting complement. Dragons swarmed in the skies before the alert had faded. Dragons swooped to weyrs while riders fetched fighting gear and firestone. The Weyr's women and children were at the supply shed, stuffing sacks. A message had been sent to the seahold where fishermen from Tillek and Ista had established a settlement. They acted as ground crew. By the time F'lar was equipped and aloft, T'bor was issuing the coordinates.

Thread was falling in the west, at the edge of the desert where the terrain was swampy, where sharp broad-edged grasses were interspersed with dwarfed spongewoods and low berry bushes. For Thread, the muddy swamp was superb burrowing ground, with sufficient organisms on which to feed as the burrow proliferated and spread.

The wings, fully manned and in good order, went *between* at T'bor's command. And, in a breath, the dragons hung again in sultry air and began to flame at the thick patches of Thread.

T'bor had signaled a low altitude entry, of which F'lar approved. But the wing movement was upward, seeking Thread at ever higher levels as they eliminated the immediate airborne danger. Weyrfolk and convalescents swelled the sea-hold group as ground crew but F'lar thought they'd need low ground support here. There were only three fighting queens, *and where was Kylara?*

F'lar directed Mnementh to fly a skim pattern just as the ground crews arrived, piling off the transport dragons, and flaming any patch of grass that seemed to move. They kept shouting to know where the leading Edge of the Fall was and F'lar directed Mnementh east by north. Mnementh complied, but abruptly turned due north, his head barely skimming the vegetation. He backwinged so abruptly that he nearly offset his rider. He hovered, peering so intently at the ground, that F'lar leaned over the great neck to see what attracted him. Dragons could adjust the focus of their eyes to either great distances or close inspection.

Something moved—away, the dragon said.

The gusts of his backwinging flattened grasses. Then F'lar saw the pin-sized, black-rimmed punctures of Thread on the leaves of the berry bushes. He stared hard, trying to discern the telltale evidence of burrows, the upheaval of soil, the consumption of the lush swamp greenery. The bush, the grass, the soil stood still.

"What moved?"

Something bright. It's gone.

Mnementh landed, his feet sinking into the oozing terrain. F'lar jumped off and peered closely at the bush. Had the holes been made by droplets of hot Thread during a previous Fall? No. The leaves would long since have dropped off. He examined every nearby hummock of grass. Not a sign of

burrows. Yet Thread had fallen—and it had to be *this* Fall—
had pierced leaves, grass and tree over a widespread area—
and vanished without a trace. No, that was impossible!
Gingerly, for viable Thread could eat through wher-hide
gloves, F'lar dug around the berry bush. Mnementh helpfully
scooped out a deep trench nearby. The displaced soil teamed
with grub life, writhing in among the thick tough grass roots.
The unexpectedly gray, gnarly taproots of the bush were
thick with the black earth but not a sign of Thread.

Mystified, F'lar raised his eyes in answer to a summons
from the hovering weyrlings.

They wish to know if this is the Edge of Threadfall,
Mnementh reported to his rider.

"It must be further south," F'lar replied and waved the
weyrlings in that direction. He stood looking down at the
overturned earth, at the grubs burrowing frantically away
from sunlight. He picked up a stout barkless branch and
jabbed the earth of the trench Mnementh had made, prod-
ding for the cavities that meant Thread infestations. "It has
to be further south. I don't understand this." He ripped a
handful of the leaves from a berry bush and sifted them
through his gloves. "If this happened some time ago, rain
would have washed the char from the punctures. The damaged leaves would have dropped."

He began to work his way south, and slightly east, trying
to ascertain exactly where Thread had started. Foliage on
every side gave evidence of its passage but he found no burrows.

When he located drowned Thread in the brackish water
of a swamp pool, he had to consider that as the leading
Edge. But he wasn't satisfied and bogged himself down in
syrtis muds investigating, so that Mnementh had to pull him
free.

So intent was he on the anomalies of this Fall, that he did
not notice the passage of time. He was somewhat startled,
then, to have T'bor appear overhead, announcing the end
of Fall. And both men were alarmed when the ground-crew
chief, a young fisherman from Ista named Toric, verified
that the Fall had lasted a scant two hours since discovery.

"A short Fall, I know, but there's nothing above, and
Toric here says the ground crews are mopping up the few

patches that got through," T'bor said, rather pleased with the efficient performance of his Weyr.

Every instinct told F'lar that something was wrong. Could Thread have changed its habits that drastically? He had no precedent. It always fell in four-hour spans—yet clearly the sky was bare.

"I need your counsel, T'bor," he said and there was that edge of concern in his voice that brought the other to his side instantly.

F'lar scooped up a handful of the brackish water, showing him the filaments of drowned Thread.

"Ever notice this before?"

"Yes, indeed," T'bor replied in a hearty voice, obviously relieved. "Happens all the time here. Not many fish to eat Thread in these foot-sized pools."

"Then there's something in the swamp waters that does for them?"

"What do you mean?"

Wordlessly, F'lar tipped back the scarred foliage nearest him. He warily turned down the broad saw-edged swamp grasses. Catching T'bor's stunned eyes, he gestured back the way he had come, where ground crews moved without one belch of flame from their throwers.

"You mean, it's like that? How far back?"

"To Threadfall Edge, an hour's fast walk," F'lar replied grimly. "Or rather, that's where I assume Thread Edge is."

"I've seen bushes and grasses marked like that in these swampy deltas closer to the Weyr," T'bor admitted slowly, his face blanched under the tan, "but I thought it was char. We mark so few infestations—and there've been no burrows."

T'bor was shaken.

Orth says there have been no infestations, Mnementh reported quietly and Orth briefly turned glowing eyes toward the Benden Weyrleader.

"And Thread was always short-timed?" F'lar wanted to know.

Orth says this is the first, but then the alarm came late. T'bor turned haunted eyes to F'lar.

"It wasn't a short Fall, then," he said, half-hoping to be contradicted.

Just then Canth veered in to land. F'lar suppressed a reprimand when he saw the flame thrower on his half-brother's back.

"That was the most unusual Fall I've ever attended," F'nor cried as he saluted the two bronze riders. "We can't have got it all airborne, but there's not a trace of burrow. And dead Thread in every water pocket. I suppose we should be grateful. But I don't understand it."

"I don't like it, F'lar," T'bor said, shaking his head. "I don't like it. Thread wasn't due here for another few weeks, and then, not in this area."

"Thread apparently is falling when and where it chooses."

"How can Thread choose?" T'bor demanded with the anger of a frightened man. "It's mindless!"

F'lar gazed up at tropical skies so brilliant that the fateful stare of the Red Star, low on the horizon, wasn't visible. "If the Red Star deviates for four hundred Turn Intervals, why not a variation in the way it falls?"

"What do we do then?" asked T'bor, a note of desperation in his voice. "Thread that pierces and doesn't burrow! Thread falling days out of phase and then for only two hours!"

"Put out sweepriders, to begin with, and let me know where and when Thread falls here. As you said, Thread is mindless. Even in these new Shifts, we may find a predictable pattern." F'lar frowned up at the hot sun; he was sweating in the wher-hide fighting clothes more suited to upper levels and cold *between*.

"Fly a sweep with me, F'lar," T'bor suggested anxiously. "F'nor, are you up to it? If we missed even one burrow here . . ."

T'bor had Orth call in every rider, even the weyrlings, told them what to look for, what was feared.

The entire complement of Southern spread out, wingtip to wingtip, flying at minimum altitude, and scanned the swampy region right back to Fall Edge. Not one man or beast could report any unusual disturbance of greenery or ground. The land over which Thread had so recently fallen was now undeniably Threadfree.

The clearance made T'bor even more apprehensive, but another tour seemed pointless. The fighting wings went *between* to the Weyr then, leaving the convalescents to fly straight.

As T'bor and F'lar glided in over the Weyr compound, the roofs of the weyrholds and the bare black soil and rock of the dragonbeds flashed under them like a pattern through the leaves of the giant fellis and spongewood trees. In the main clearing by the Weyrhall, Prideth extended her neck and wings, bugling to her Weyrmates.

"Circle once again, Mnementh," F'lar said to his bronze. First he'd better get over the urge to beat Kylara, and give T'bor the chance to reprimand her privately. He regretted, once more, that he had ever suggested to Lessa that she pressure that female into being a Weyrwoman. It had seemed a logical solution at the time. And he was sincerely sorry for T'bor, although the man did manage to keep her worst depredations under control. But the absence of a queen from a Weyr . . . Well, how could Kylara have known Thread would fall here ahead of schedule? Yet where was she that she couldn't hear that alarm? No dragon slept that deeply.

He circled as the rest of the dragons peeled off to their weyrs and realized that none had had to descend by the Infirmary.

"Fighting Thread with no casualties?"

I like that, Mnementh remarked.

Somehow that aspect of the day's encounter unsettled F'lar the most. Rather than delve into that, F'lar judged it time to land. He didn't relish the thought of confronting Kylara, but he hadn't had the chance to tell T'bor what had been happening north.

"I told you," Kylara was saying in sullen anger, "that I found a clutch and Impressed this queen. When I got back, there wasn't anyone left here who knew where you'd all gone. Prideth has to have coordinates, you know." She turned toward F'lar now, her eyes glittering. "My duty to you, F'lar of Benden," and her voice took on a caressing tone which made T'bor stiffen and clench his teeth. "How kind of you to fight with us when Benden Weyr has troubles of its own."

F'lar ignored the jibe and nodded a curt acknowledgment.

"See my fire lizard. Isn't she magnificent?" She help up her right arm, exhibiting the drowsing golden lizard, the outlines of her latest meal pressing sharp designs against her belly hide.

"Wirenth was here and Brekke. They knew," T'bor told her.

"Her!" Kylara dismissed the weyrwoman with a negligent shrug of contempt. "She gave me some nonsensical coordinates, deep in the western swamp. Threads don't fall . . ."

"They did today," T'bor cried, his face suffused with anger. "Do tell!"

Prideth began to rumble restlessly and Kylara, the hard defiant lines of her face softening, turned to reassure her.

"See, you've made her uneasy and she's so near mating again."

T'bor looked dangerously close to an outburst which, as Weyrleader, he could not risk. Kylara's tactic was so obvious that F'lar wondered how the man could fall for it. Would it improve matters to have T'bor supplanted by one of the other bronze riders here? F'lar considered, as he had before, throwing Prideth's next mating flight into open competition. And yet, he owed T'bor too much for coping with this—this female to insult him by such a measure. On the other hand, maybe one of the more vigorous Oldtime bronzes with a rider just sufficiently detached from Kylara's ploys, and interested enough in retaining a Leadership, might keep her firmly in line.

"T'bor, the map of this continent's in the Weyrhall, isn't it?" F'lar asked, diverting the man. "I'd like to set the coordinates of this Fall in my mind . . ."

"Don't you like my queen?" Kylara asked, stepping forward and raising the lizard right under F'lar's nose.

The little creature, unbalanced by the sudden movement, dug her razor-sharp claws into Kylara's arm, piercing the wher-hide as easily as Thread pierced leaf. With a yelp, Kylara shook her arm, dislodging the fire lizard. In midfall the creature disappeared. Kylara's cry of pain changed to a shriek of anger.

"Look what you've done, you fool. You've lost her."

"Not I, Kylara," F'lar replied in a hard, cold voice. "Take good care you do not push others to their limit!"

"I've limits, too, F'lar of Benden," she screamed as the two men strode quickly toward the Weyrhall. "Don't push me. D'you hear? Don't push *me!*" She kept up her curses until Prideth, now highly agitated, drowned her out with piteous cries.

At first the two Weyrleaders went through the motions of studying the map and trying to figure out where Thread might have fallen elsewhere undetected on the Southern continent. Then Prideth's complaints died away and the clearing was vacant.

"It comes down to manpower again, T'bor," F'lar said. "There ought to be a thorough search of this continent. Oh, I'm aware," and he held up his hand to forestall a defensive rebuttal, "that you simply don't have the personnel to help, even with the influx of holderfolk from the mainland. But Thread can cross mountains," he tapped the southern chain, "and we don't know what's been happening in these uncharted areas. We've assumed that Threadfall occurred only in this coastline portion. Once established though, a single burrow could eat its way across any land mass and—" He made a slashing movement of both hands. "I'd give a lot to know how Thread could fall unnoticed in those swamps for two hours and leave no trace of a burrow!"

T'bor grunted agreement but F'lar sensed that his mind was not on this problem.

"You've had more than your share of grief with that woman, T'bor. Why not throw the next flight open?"

"No!" And Orth echoed that vehement refusal with a roar. F'lar looked at T'bor in amazement.

"No, F'lar. I'll keep her in hand. I'll keep myself in hand, too. But as long as Orth can fly Prideth, Kylara's mine."

F'lar looked quickly away from the torment in the other's face.

"And you'd better know this, too," T'bor continued in a heavy low voice. "She found a full clutch. She took them to a Hold. Prideth told Orth."

"Which Hold?"

T'bor shook his head wearily. "Prideth doesn't like it so she doesn't name it. She doesn't like taking fire lizards away from the weyrs either."

F'lar brushed his forelock back from his eyes in an irritated movement. This was the most unhealthy development. A dragon displeased with her rider? The one restraint they had all counted on was Kylara's bond with Prideth. The woman wouldn't be fool enough, wanton enough, perverted enough to strain that, too, in her egocentric selfishness.

Prideth will not hear me, Mnementh said suddenly. *She will not hear Orth. She is unhappy. That isn't good.*

Threads falling unexpectedly, fire lizards in Holder hands, a dragon displeased with her rider and another anticipating his rider's questions! And F'lar had thought he'd had problems seven Turns ago!

"I can't sort this all out right now, T'bor. Please mount guards and let me know the instant you've any news of any kind. If you do uncover another clutch, I would very much appreciate some of the eggs. Let me know, too, if that little queen returns to Kylara. I grant the creature had reason, but if they frighten *between* so easily, they may be worthless except as pets."

F'lar mounted Mnementh and saluted the Southern Weyrleader, reassured by nothing in this visit. And he'd lost the advantage of surprising the Lord Holders with fire lizards. In fact, Kylara's precipitous donation would undoubtedly cause more trouble. A Weyrwoman meddling in a Hold not bound to her own Weyr? He almost hoped that these creatures would be nothing more than pets and her action could be soft-talked. Still, there was the psychological effect of that miniature dragon, Impressionable by anyone. That would have been a valuable asset in improving Weyr-Hold relations.

As Mnementh climbed higher, to the cooler levels, F'lar worried most about that Threadfall. It had fallen. It had pierced leaf and grass, drowned in the water, and yet left no trace of itself in the rich earth. Igen's sandworms would devour Thread, almost as efficiently as agenothree. But the grub life that had swarmed in the rich black swamp mud bore little resemblance to the segmented, shelled worms.

Unable to leave Southern without a final check, F'lar gave Mnementh the order to transfer to the western swamp. The bronze obediently brought him right to the trench his claw had made. F'lar slid from his shoulder, opening the wher-hide tunic as the humid, sticky, sun-steamed swamp air pressed against him like a thick wet skin. There was a ringing, rasping chorus of tiny sound all around him, splashings and burblings, none of which he'd noted earlier in the day. In fact, the swamp had been remarkably silent, as if hushed by the menace of Thread.

When he turned back the hummock of grass by the roots of the berry bush, the earth was untenanted, the gray roots sleekly damp. Kicking up another section, he did find a small cluster of the larvae, but not in the earlier profusion. He held the muddy ball in his hand, watching the grubs squirm away from light and air. It was then that he saw that the foliage of that bush was no longer Thread-scored. The char had disappeared and a thin film was forming over the hole, as if the bush were mending itself.

Something writhed against the skin of his palm and he hastily dropped the ball of dirt, rubbing his hand against his leg.

He broke off a leaf, the sign of Thread healing in the green foliage.

Could the grubs possibly be the southern continent's equivalent of sandworms?

Abruptly he gave a running jump to Mnementh's shoulder, grabbing the riding straps.

"Mnementh, take me back to the beginning of this Fall. That'd make it six hours back. The sun would be at zenith."

Mnementh didn't grumble but his thoughts were plain: F'lar was tired, F'lar ought to go back to Benden and rest, talk to Lessa. Jumping *between* time was hard on a rider.

Cold *between* enveloped them, and F'lar hastily closed the tunic he'd opened, but not before the cold seemed to eat into his chest bone. He shivered, with more than physical chill, as they burst out over the steamy swamp again. It took more than a few minutes under that blazing sun to counteract the merciless cold. Mnementh glided briefly northward and then hovered, facing due south.

They didn't have long to wait. High above, the ominous grayness that presaged Threadfall darkened the sky. As often as he had watched it, F'lar never rid himself of fear. And it was harder still to watch that distant grayness begin to separate into sheets and patches of silvery Thread. To watch and to permit it to fall unchecked on the swamp below. To watch as it pierced leaf and green, hissing as it penetrated the mud. Even Mnementh stirred restlessly, his wings trembling as he fought every instinct to dive, flaming, at the ancient menace. Yet he, too, watched as the leading Edge advanced southward, across the swamp, a gray rain of destruction.

Without needing a command, Mnementh landed just short of the Edge. And F'lar, fighting an inward revulsion so strong that he was sure he'd vomit, turned back the nearest hummock, smoking with Thread penetration. Grubs, feverishly active, populated the concourse of the roots. As he held the hummock up, bloated grubs dropped to the ground and frantically burrowed into the earth. He dropped that clump, uprooted the nearest bush, baring the gray, twisted rootball. It also teemed with grub life that burrowed away from the sudden exposure to air and light. The leaves of the bush were still smoldering from Thread puncture.

Not quite certain why, F'lar knelt, pulled up another hummock and scooped up a clump of squirming grubs into the fingers of his riding glove. He twisted it tightly shut and secured it under his belt.

Then he mounted Mnementh and gave him the coordinates of the Masterherdsman's Crafthall in Keroon, where the foothills that rose eventually to the massive heights of Benden range gently merged with the wide plains of Keroon Hold.

Masterherdsman Sograny, a tall, bald, leathery man so spare of flesh that his bones seemed held in position by his laced vest, tight hide pants and heavy boots, showed no pleasure in an unexpected visit from Benden's Weyrleader.

F'lar had been met with punctilious courtesy, if some confusion, by crafters. Sograny, it seemed, was supervising the birth of a new mix of herdbeasts, the very swift plains type with the heavy-chested mountain one. A messenger led F'lar to the great barn. Considering the importance of the event, F'lar thought it odd that no one had left his tasks. He was led past neat cots of immaculately cleaned stone, well-tended gardens, past forcing sheds and equipment barns. F'lar thought of the absolute chaos that prevailed at the Smith's, but then remembered what marvels that man accomplished.

"You've a problem for the Masterherdsman, have you, Weyrleader?" Sograny asked, giving F'lar a curt nod, his eyes on the laboring beast in the box stall. "How does that happen?"

The man's attitude was so defensive that F'lar wondered what D'ram of Ista Weyr might have been doing to irritate him.

"Mastersmith Fandarel suggested that you would be able to

advise me, Masterherdsman," F'lar replied, no trace of levity in his manner and no lack of courtesy in his address.

"The Smithcrafter?" Sograny looked at F'lar with narrowed, suspicious eyes. "Why?"

Now what could Fandarel have done to warrant the bad opinion of the Masterherdsman?

"Two anomalies have come to my attention, good Masterherdsman. The first, a clutch of fire-lizard eggs hatched in the vicinity of one of my riders and he was able to Impress the queen . . ."

Sograny's eyes widened with startled disbelief.

"No man can catch a fire lizard!"

"Agreed, but he can Impress one. And certainly did. We believe that the fire lizards are directly related to the dragons."

"That cannot be proved!" Sograny pulled himself straight up, his eyes darting toward his assistants who suddenly found tasks far from F'lar and the Masterherdsman.

"By inference, yes. Because the similar characteristics are obvious. Seven fire lizards were Impressed on the sands of a beach at Southern. One by my Wing-second, F'nor, Canth's rider . . ."

"F'nor? The man who fought those two thieving weyrmen at the Smithcrafthall?"

F'lar swallowed his bile and nodded. That regrettable incident had hatched an unexpected brood of benefits.

"The fire lizards exhibit undeniable draconic traits. Unfortunately, one of them is to stay close to their Impressor or I'd have proof positive."

Sograny only grunted, but he was suddenly receptive.

"I was hoping that you, as Masterherdsman, might know something about the fire lizards. Igen certainly abounds with them . . ."

Sograny was cutting him off with an impatient wave of his hand.

"No time to waste on flitterbys. Useless creatures. No crafter of mine would . . ."

"There is every indication that they may be of tremendous use to us. After all, dragons were bred from fire lizards."

"Impossible!" Sograny stared at him, thin lips firmly denying such an improbability.

"Well, they weren't bred up from watch-whers."

"Man can alter size but only so far. He can, of course, breed the largest to the largest and improve on the original stock," and Sograny gestured toward the long-legged cow. "But to breed a dragon from a fire lizard? Absolutely impossible."

F'lar wasted no further time on that subject but took the glove from his belt and emptied the grubs into the other, gloved palm.

"These, sir. Have you seen such as these . . ."

Sograny's reaction was immediate. With a cry of fear, he grabbed F'lar's hand, tumbling the grubs to the stone of the barn. Yelling for agenothree, he stamped on the squirming grubs as if they were essence of evil.

"How could you—a dragonman—bring such filth into my dwellings?"

"Masterherdsman, control yourself!" F'lar snapped, grabbing the man and shaking him. "They devour Thread. Like sandworms. Like sandworms!"

Sograny was trembling beneath F'lar's hands, staring at him. He shook his skull-like head and the wildness died from his eyes.

"Only flame can devour Thread, dragonman!"

"I told you," F'lar said coldly, "that those grubs devoured Thread!"

Sograny glared at F'lar with considerable animus.

"They are an abomination. You waste my time with such nonsense."

"My deep apologies," F'lar said, with a curt bow. But his irony was wasted on the man. Sograny turned back to his laboring cow as though F'lar had never interrupted him.

F'lar strode off, pulling on his gloves, his forefinger coming into contact with the wet, slippery body of a grub.

"See the Masterherdsman, eh?" he muttered under his breath, waving aside the services of the guide as he left the breeding barn. A bellow from a herdbeast followed him out. "Yes, he breeds animals, but not ideas. Ideas might waste time, be useless."

As he and Mnementh circled upward, F'lar wondered how much trouble D'ram was having with that old fool.

CHAPTER IX

Afternoon at Southern Weyr: Same Day

It was a long flight, the straight way, from the western swamps to Southern Weyr's headland. At first, F'nor rebelled. A short hop *between* would not affect his healing arm, but Canth became unexpectedly stubborn. The big brown soared, caught the prevailing wind and, with great sweeps of his wings, sped through the cooler air, high above the monotonous terrain.

As Canth settled down into long-distance flying, the rhythm began to soothe F'nor. What ought to have been a tedious journey became the blessing of uninterrupted time for reflection. And F'nor had much to think about.

The brown rider had noticed the widespread Thread-scoring. He had turned back bush after bush, heavily pitted by Threadmark, to find no trace of burrow at all in the swamp mud around them. Not once had he used his flame thrower. And the ground crews told him they had so little to do they wondered the Weyr called them at all. Many were from the fishing settlement and they were beginning to resent be-

ing taken from their labors, for they were trying to complete
stone holds against the winter storms. They all preferred
Southern to their old homes, though they did not complain
against Tillek's Lord Oterel, or Lord Warbret of Ista.

It had always amused F'nor that people he had scarcely
met were willing to confide in him, but he had found that
this was often an advantage, despite the hours he'd had to
spend listening to maundering tales. One of the younger men,
the ground-crew chief, Toric, informed him that he'd staked
out a sandy cove near his hold. It was almost inaccessible
from the landside, but he'd seen certain fire-lizard sign. He
was determined to Impress one and positive that he could,
for he'd been lucky with watch-whers. He'd tried to convince
Fort Weyr that he should have a chance at Impressing a
dragon, but he hadn't been given the courtesy of seeing
T'ron. Toric was quite bitter about weyrmen and, knowing
(as everyone seemed to, F'nor had discovered) about the
belt-knife fight, Toric expected F'nor to be disaffected, too.
He was surprised when F'nor brusquely cut off his carping
recital.

It was this curious ambivalence of Holder feeling toward
dragonmen that occupied F'nor's thought. Holders claimed
that weyrfolk held themselves aloof, acted patronizing or
condescending, or plain arrogant in their presence. Yet
there wasn't a man or woman, Holder or Crafter, who
hadn't at one time or another wished he or she had Impressed
a dragon. And in many this turned to bitter envy. Weyrmen
insisted they were superior to commoners even while they
consistently exhibited the same appetites as other men for
material possessions and nubile women. Yet they did indeed
refute the Crafter contention that dragonriding was a skill
no more exacting than any craft on Pern, for in no other
craft did a man risk life as a matter of course. And far
worse, the loss of half his life. Reflexively, F'nor's thought
sheered sharply away from any hint of threat to the great
brown he rode.

The little queen stirred inside the heavy arm sling where
he had been carrying her.

Young Toric, now, would lose some of his bitterness if he
did Impress a fire lizard. He would feel that his claim was
vindicated. And if fire lizards did take to anyone, and could
carry messages back and forth, what a boon that would be. A

lizard for everyone? That would be quite a battle cry. F'nor chortled as he thought of the Oldtimers' reactions to that. Do them good, it would, and he chuckled at the vision of T'ron trying to lure a fire lizard which ignored him to be Impressed by a lowly crafterchild. Something had better pierce the Oldtimers' blind parochiality. Yet even they, at a crucial moment in the sensitive awareness of adolescence, had appealed to dragonkind; they endured cold and possible death to fight an endless and mindless enemy. But there was more to living than that initial achievement and that eternal alert. Adolescence was only a step of life, not a career in itself. When one matured, one knew there was more to living.

Then F'nor remembered that he'd not had the chance to mention Brekke's problem to F'lar. And F'lar would probably have gone back to Benden Weyr by now. F'nor upbraided himself for what was downright interference. Comes from being a wing-second so long, he thought. You can't go around meddling in another's Weyr. T'bor had enough stress. But, by the First Egg, F'nor hated to think of the scenes Kylara would subject Brekke to, if Orth flew Wirenth.

He grew restless with traveling and wasn't even amused when Canth began to croon soothingly. But when the journey was accomplished, and they were circling down into the late afternoon sun over Southern, he felt no fatigue. A few riders were feeding their beasts in the pasture and he inquired if Canth wished to be fed.

Brekke wants to see you, Canth advised F'nor as he landed neatly in his weyr.

"Probably to scold me," F'nor said, slapping Canth's muzzle affectionately. He stood aside watching until the brown settled himself in the warmth of his dusty wallow.

Grall peeked out of the folds of the sling and F'nor transferred her to his shoulder. She squeaked a protest as he strode quickly toward Brekke's weyrhold and dug her claws into the shoulder pad for balance. She was thinking hungry thoughts.

Brekke was feeding her lizard, Berd, when F'nor entered. She smiled as she heard Grall's shrill demand, and pushed the bowl of meat toward F'nor.

"I was worried that you might fly *between*."

"Canth wouldn't let me."

"Canth has sense. How's the arm?"

"Took no hurt. There wasn't much to be done."

"So I hear." Brekke frowned. "Everything's askew. I have the oddest sensation . . ."

"Go on," F'nor urged when she broke off. "What kind of a sensation?" Was Wirenth about to rise? Brekke seemed to remain untouched by so many disturbances, a serene competent personality, tranquilly keeping the Weyr going, healing the wounded. For her to admit to uncertainty was disturbing.

As if she caught his thoughts, she shook her head, her lips set in a fierce line.

"No, it's not personal. It's just that everything is going awry—disorienting, changing . . ."

"Is that all? Didn't I hear you suggesting a minor change or two? Letting a girl Impress a fighting dragon? Handing out fire lizards to placate the common mass?"

"That's change. I'm talking about a disorientation, a violent upheaval . . ."

"And your suggestions don't rank under that heading? Oh, my dear girl," and F'nor suddenly gave her a long, penetrating look. Something in her candid gaze disturbed him deeply.

"Kylara pestering you?"

Brekke's eyes slid from his and she shook her head.

"I told you, Brekke, you can request other bronzes. Someone from another Weyr, N'ton of Benden or B'dor of Ista . . . That would shut Kylara up."

Brekke shook her head violently, but kept her face averted. "Don't keep foisting your friends on me!" Her voice was sharp. "I like Southern. I'm needed here."

"Needed? You're being shamelessly exploited and not just by Southerners!"

She stared at him, as surprised by the impulsive outburst as he was. For one moment he thought he understood why, but her eyes became guarded and F'nor wondered what Brekke could want to hide.

"The need is more apparent than the exploitation. I don't mind hard work," she said in a low voice and popped a piece of meat into the brown's wide-open mouth. "Don't rob me of what fragile contentment I can contrive."

"Contentment?"

"Sssh. You're agitating the lizards."

"They'll survive. They fight. The trouble with you, Brekke,

is that you won't. You deserve so much more than you get. You don't know what a kind, generous, useful—oh, shells!" and F'nor broke off in confusion.

"Useful, worthwhile, wholesome, capable, dependable, the list is categoric, F'nor, I know the entire litany," Brekke said with a funny little catch in her voice. "Rest assured, my friend, I know what I am."

There was such a bitterness in her light words, and such a shadow in her usually candid green eyes that F'nor could not tolerate it. To erase that self-deprecation, to make amends for his own maladroitness, F'nor leaned across the table to kiss her on the lips.

He meant it as no more than a guerdon and was totally unprepared for the reaction in himself, in Brekke. Or for Canth's distant bugle.

His eyes never leaving Brekke's, F'nor rose slowly and circled the table. He slid beside her on the bench, pulling her against him with his good arm. Her head fell back on his shoulder and he bent to the incredible sweetness of her lips. Her body was soft and pliable, her arms went around him, pressing him to her with a total surrender to his virility that he had never before experienced. No matter how eager others had seemed, or gratified, there had never been such a total commitment to him. Such an innocence of . . .

Abruptly F'nor raised his head, looking deep into her eyes.

"You've never slept with T'bor." He stated it as a fact. "You've never slept with any man."

She hid her face in his shoulder, the pliancy of her body gone. He gently forced her head up.

"Why have you deliberately let it be assumed that you and T'bor . . ."

She was shaking her head slightly from side to side, her eyes concealing nothing, her face a mask of sorrow.

"To keep other men from you?" F'nor demanded, giving her a little shake. "Why? Whom are you keeping yourself for?"

He knew the answer before she spoke, knew it when she placed her finger on his lips to silence him. But he couldn't understand her sorrow. He'd been a fool but . . .

"I have loved you since the first day I saw you. You were so kind to us, yanked away from Craft and Hold, dazed because we'd been brought all the way here on Search for

Wirenth. One of us would actually be a Weyrwoman. And you—you were all a dragonman should be, tall and handsome, so kind. I didn't know then—" and Brekke faltered. To F'nor's concern, tears filmed her eyes. "How *could* I know that only bronze dragons fly queens!"

F'nor held the weeping girl to his chest, his lips against her soft hair, her trembling hands folded in his. Yes, there was much about Brekke he could understand now.

"Dear girl," he said when her tears lessened, "is that why you refused N'ton?"

She nodded her head against his shoulder, unwilling to look at him.

"Then you're a silly clunch and deserve all the anguish you've put yourself through," he said, his teasing voice taking the sting from his words. He patted her shoulder and sighed exaggeratedly. "And craftbred as well. Have you taken in nothing you've been told about dragonfolk? Weyrwomen can't be bound by any commoner moralities. A Weyrwoman has to be subservient to her queen's needs, including mating with many riders if her queen is flown by different dragons. Most craft and holdbred girls envy such freedom . . ."

"Of that I'm all too aware," Brekke said and her body seemed to resent his touch.

"Does Wirenth object to me?"

"Oh, no," and Brekke looked startled. "I meant—oh, I don't know what I meant. I love Wirenth, but can't you understand? I'm *not* weyrbred. I don't have that kind of—of—wantonness in my nature. I'm—I'm inhibited. There! I said it. I am inhibited and I'm terrified that I'll inhibit Wirenth. I can't change all of me to conform to Weyr customs. I'm the way I am."

F'nor tried to soothe her. He wasn't sure now how to proceed, for this overwrought girl was a different creature entirely from the calm, serious, reliable Brekke he knew.

"No one wants or expects you to change completely. You wouldn't be our Brekke. But dragons don't criticize. Neither do their riders. Most queens tend to prefer one bronze above the others consistently . . ."

"You still don't understand." The accusation was a hopeless wail. "I never saw any man I wanted to—to have—" The word was an aspirated whisper. "Not that way. Not until I saw you. I don't want any other man to possess me. I'll freeze. I won't be able to draw Wirenth back. And I love her. I love her so and she'll be rising soon and I can't . . . I thought I'd be able to, but I know I'll . . ."

She tried to break away from him, but even with one arm the brown rider was stronger. Trapped, she began to cling to him with the strength of utter despair.

He rocked her gently against him, removing his arm from the sling so he could stroke her hair.

"You won't lose Wirenth. It's different when dragons mate, love. You're the dragon, too, caught up in emotions that have only one resolution." He held her tightly as she seemed to shrink with revulsion from him as well as the imminent event. He thought of the riders here at Southern, of T'bor, and he experienced a disgust of another sort. Those men, conditioned to respond to Kylara's exotic tastes, would brutalize this inexperienced child.

F'nor glanced round at the low couch and rose, Brekke in his arms. He started for the bed, halted, hearing voices beyond the clearing. Anyone might come.

Still holding her, he carried her out of the weyrhold, smothering her protest against his chest as she realized his intention. There was a place behind his weyrhold, beyond Canth's wallow, where the ferns grew sweet and thick, where they would be undisturbed.

He wanted to be gentle but, unaccountably, Brekke fought him. She pleaded with him, crying out wildly that they'd rouse the sleeping Wirenth. He wasn't gentle but he was thorough, and, in the end, Brekke astounded him with a surrender as passionate as if her dragon had been involved.

F'nor raised himself on his elbow, pushing the sweaty, fern-entangled hair from her closed eyes, pleased by the soft serenity of her expression; excessively pleased with himself. A man never really knew how a woman would respond in love. So much hinted at in play never materialized in practice.

But Brekke was as honest in love, as kind and generous, as wholesome as ever; in her innocent wholeheartedness more sensual than the most skilled partner he had ever enjoyed.

Her eyes opened, met his in a wondering stare for a long

moment. With a moan, she turned her head, evading his scrutiny.

"Surely no regrets, Brekke?"

"Oh, F'nor, what will I do when Wirenth rises?"

F'nor began to curse then, steadily, hopelessly, as he cradled her now unresponsive body against him. He cursed the differences between Hold and Weyr, the throbbing wound in his arm that signalized the difference which existed even between dragonmen. He railed at the inescapable realization that what he loved most was insufficient to his need. He hated himself, aware that in his effort to help Brekke, he had compromised her values and was probably destroying her.

Instinctively his confused thoughts reached out to Canth, and he found himself trying to suppress that contact. Canth must never know his rider could fault him for not being a bronze.

I am as large as most bronzes, Canth said with unruffled equanimity. Almost as if he was surprised he had to mention the fact to his rider. *I am strong. Strong enough to outlast any bronze here.*

F'nor's exclamation roused Brekke.

"There's no reason Canth can't fly Wirenth. By the Shell, he could outfly any bronze here. And probably Orth, too, if he puts his mind to it."

"Canth fly Wirenth?"

"Why not?"

"But browns don't fly queens. Bronzes do."

F'nor hugged her fiercely, trying to impart his jubilation, his almost inarticulate joy and relief.

"The only reason browns haven't flown queens is that they're smaller. They don't have the stamina to last in a mating flight. But Canth's big. Canth's the biggest, strongest, fastest brown in Pern. Don't you see, Brekke?"

Her body uncurled. Hope was restoring color to her face, life to her green eyes.

"It's been done?"

F'nor shook his head impatiently. "It's time to discard custom that hampers. Why not this one?"

She permitted him to caress her but there was a shadow lingering in her eyes and a reluctance in her body.

"I want to, oh how I want to, F'nor, but I'm so scared. I'm scared to my bones."

He kissed her deeply, ruthlessly employing subtleties to arouse her. "Please, Brekke?"

"It can't be wrong to be happy, can it, F'nor?" she whispered, a shiver rippling along her body.

He kissed her again, using every trick learned from a hundred casual encounters to wed her to him, body, soul and mind, aware of Canth's enthusiastic endorsement.

Seething with fury, Kylara watched the men walk off and leave her, standing in the clearing. Her conflicting emotions made it impossible for her to retaliate suitably, but she'd make them both regret their words. She'd pay F'lar back for losing the lizard queen. She'd score T'bor for daring to reprimand her, the Weyrwoman of Southern, of the Telgar Bloodline, in the presence of F'lar. Oh, he'd regret that insult. They'd both regret it. She'd show them.

Her arm throbbed from the clawing and she cradled it against her, the pain acerbating her other complaints. Where was some numbweed? Where was that Brekke? Where was everyone else at a time when the Weyr compound should be full of people? Was everyone avoiding her? Where was Brekke?

Feeding the lizard. I'm hungry, too, Prideth said so firmly that Kylara looked around in surprise at her queen.

"Your color isn't good," she said, her stream of mental vituperation deflected by the habit of concern for Prideth's well-being and the instinctive awareness that she must not alienate her dragon.

Well, she didn't want to have to look at Brekke's broad commoner face. She certainly didn't want to see a lizard. Not now. Horrible creatures, no gratitude. No real sensitivity or the thing would have *known* it was only being shown off. Prideth jumped them to the Feeding Ground and landed so smartly that Kylara gave a gasp of pain as her arm was jarred. Tears formed in her eyes. Prideth, too?

But Prideth gave a flying jump to the back of a fat, stupid herdbeast and began to feed with a savagery that fascinated Kylara out of her self-pity. The queen finished the beast with ravenous speed. She was upon a second buck and disemboweling it so voraciously that Kylara could not escape

171

the fact that she had indeed been neglecting Prideth. She felt herself caught up in the hunger and vicariously dissipated her anger by imagining T'bor as the second buck, F'lar as the third, Lessa as the big wherry. By the time Prideth's hunger was sated, Kylara's mind was clear.

She took her queen back to the weyr and spent a long time sanding and brushing her hide until it lost all trace of dullness. Finally Prideth curled in a contented drowse on the sun-warmed rock and Kylara's guilt was absolved.

"Forgive me, Prideth. I didn't mean to neglect you. But they've slighted me so often. And a blow at me is a slam at your prestige, too. Soon they won't dare ignore us. And we won't stay immured in this dreary, underside Weyr. We'll have strong men and the most powerful bronzes begging us for favors. You'll be oiled and fed and scrubbed and scratched and pampered as you ought. You'll see. They'll regret their behavior."

Prideth's eyes were completely lidded now, and her breath came and went with a faint whistle. Kylara glanced at the bulging belly. She'd sleep a long time with that much to content her.

"I ought not to have let her gorge so," Kylara murmured, but there had been something so gratifying in the way Prideth tore into her meat; as if all indignities and affronts and discourtesy had leaked out of Kylara as blood from the slaughtered animals had seeped into the pasture grass.

Her arm began to hurt again. She'd removed the wherhide tunic to groom Prideth, and sand and dust coated the new scabs. Suddenly Kylara felt filthy, disgustingly filthy with sand and dust and sweat. She was aware of fatigue, too. She'd bathe and eat, have Rannelly rub her well with sweet oil and cleansing sand. First, she'd get some numbweed from little nurse-goody Brekke.

She came past the side window of Brekke's weyrhold and heard the murmur of a man's voice and the low delighted laughing response from Brekke. Kylara halted, astonished by the rippling quality of the girl's voice. She peered in, unobserved, because Brekke had eyes only for the dark head bent toward her.

F'nor! And Brekke?

The brown rider raised his hand slowly, stroked back a wayward strand of hair from Brekke's cheek with such loving tenderness that there was no doubt in Kylara's mind that they had only recently been lovers.

Kylara's half-forgotten anger burst into cold heat. Brekke and F'nor! When F'nor had repeatedly turned aside *her* favors? Brekke and F'nor indeed!

Because Kylara moved on, Canth did not tell his rider.

CHAPTER X

Early Morning in Harpercrafthall at Fort Hold
Afternoon at Telgar Hold

Robinton, Masterharper of Pern, adjusted his tunic, the rich green pile of the fabric pleasing to the touch as well as the eye. He turned sideways, to check the fit of the tunic across his shoulders. Masterweaver Zurg had compensated for his tendency to slouch, so the hem did not hike up. The gilded belt and the knife were just the proper dress accouterments.

Robinton grimaced at his reflection. "Belt knives!" He smoothed his hair behind his ears, then stepped back to check the pants. Mastertanner Belesdan had surpassed himself. The fellis dye had turned the soft wher-hide into a deep green the same shade as the tunic. The boots were a shade darker. They fit snug to his calf and foot.

Green! Robinton grinned to himself. Neither Zurg nor Belesdan had been in favor of that shade, though it was easily obtainable. About time we shed another ridiculous superstition, Robinton thought.

He glanced out of his window, checking the sun's position. It was above the Fort range now. That meant midafternoon at Telgar Hold and the guests would be gathering. He'd been promised transport. T'ron of Fort Weyr had grudgingly acceded to that request, though it was a tradition of long standing that the Harper could request aid from any Weyr.

A dragon appeared in the northwest sky.

Robinton grabbed up his overcloak—the dress tunic would never keep out the full cold of *between*—his gloves and felted case that contained the best gitar. He'd hesitated about bringing it. Chad had a fine instrument at Telgar Hold, but fine wood and gut would not be chilled by those cold seconds of *between* as mere flesh would.

When he passed the window, he noticed a second dragon winging down, and was mildly surprised.

By the time he reached the small court of the Harper-crafthall, he gave a snort of amusement. A third dragon had appeared from due east.

Never around when you want 'em, though. Robinton sighed, for it seemed the problems of the day had already begun, instead of waiting dutifully for him (as what trouble does?) at Telgar Hold, where he'd expected it.

Green, blue—and ah-ha—bronze dragon wings in the early morning sun.

"Sebell, Talmor, Brudegan, Tagetarl, into your fine rags. Hurry or I'll skin you and use your lazy innards for strings," Robinton called in a voice that projected into every room facing the Court.

Two heads popped out of an upper window of the apprentice barracks, two more at the journeyman's Hold.

"Aye, sir." "Coming, sir." "In a moment!"

Yes, with four harpers of his own, and the three at Telgar Hold—Sebell played the best bass line, not to mention Chad the Telgar Harper improvising in the treble—they'd have a grand loud group. Robinton tossed his overcloak to his shoulder, forgetting that the pile of the green tunic might crush, and grinned sardonically at the wheeling dragons. He half-expected them all to wink out again at the discovery of this multiplicity.

He should pick the Telgar Weyr blue on the grounds that

he appeared first. However, the green dragon came from Fort Weyr, to whom his Craft was weyrbound. Yet Benden Weyr did the honor of sending a bronze. Perhaps I should take the first to land, though they're all taking their time about it, he thought.

He stepped out of the Court quadrangle to the fields beyond, since it was obvious that's where the beasts were landing.

The bronze landed last, which canceled that method of impartial choice. The three riders met mid-field, some few dragonlengths from the disputed passenger. Each man began arguing his claim at once. When the bronze rider became the target of the other two, Robinton felt obliged to intervene.

"He's weyrbound to Fort Weyr. We have the right," said the green rider indignantly.

"He's guest of Telgar Hold. Lord Holder Larad himself requested . . ."

The bronze rider (Robinton recognized him as N'ton, one of the first non-weyrbred to Impress a dragon at Benden Weyr Turns ago) appeared neither angry nor disconcerted.

"The good Masterharper will know the right of it," and N'ton bowed graciously to Robinton.

The others gave him scarcely a glance but renewed their quarrel.

"Why, there's no problem at all," Robinton said in the firm, decisive tone he rarely employed and which was never contradicted.

The two wranglers fell silent and faced him, the one sullen, the other indignant.

"Still, it does the Craft honor that you vye to serve it," and Robinton accorded the two dissidents an ironic bow. "Fortunately, I have need of three beasts. I've four more harpers to transport to Telgar Hold to grace the happy occasion." He emphasized the adjective, noticing the glares that passed between blue and green riders. Young N'ton, though not weyrbred, had excellent manners.

"I was told to take *you*," the Fort Weyr man said in a sour voice.

"And took such joy of the assignment, it has made my morning merry," Robinton replied crisply. He saw the smug look on the blue rider's face. "And while I appreciate Weyrleader R'mart's thoughtfulness in spite of his recent—ah—

problems at Telgar Hold, I shall ride the Benden Weyr dragon. For they do not grudge the Masterharper the prerogative."

His craftsmen came racing out of the Hall, riding cloaks askew on their shoulders, fitting their instruments in felt wrappings as they came. Robinton gave each a cursory glance as they came to a ragged line in front of him, breathless, flushed and, thank the Shell, happy. He nodded toward Sebell's pants, indicated that Talmor should adjust his twisted belt, approved Brudegan's immaculate appearance, and murmured that Tagetarl was to smooth his wild hair.

"We're ready, sirs," Robinton announced and, giving a curt bow of his head to the other riders, turned on his heel to follow N'ton.

"I've half a mind—" the green rider began.

"Obviously," Robinton cut in, his voice as cold as *between* and as menacing as Thread. "Brudegan, Tagetarl, ride with him. Sebell, Talmor, on the green."

Robinton watched as Brudegan, with no expression on his face, gestured politely to the shorter, green rider to precede them. Of all men on Pern, harpers feared few. Any one deliberately antagonizing them for no cause found himself the butt of a satirical tune which would be played around the land.

There were no further protests. And Robinton was rather pleased to notice that N'ton gave no indication that there'd been any display of ill nature.

Robinton on N'ton's bronze arrived in the air, facing the cliff-palisade that was Telgar Hold. The swift river that had its source in the great striding eastern range of mountains had cut through the softer stone and made a deep incision that gradually widened until a series of high palisades flanked the green, wide Telgar valley. Telgar Hold was situated in one such soaring palisade, at the apex of a slightly triangular section of the cliffs. It faced south, with sides east and west and its hundred or so windows, on five distinct levels, must make pleasant and well-lit rooms. All had the heavy bronze shutters which marked Telgar Hold for a wealthy one.

Today the three cliff faces of Telgar Hold were brilliant with the pennants of every minor Hold which had ever aligned its Blood with theirs. The Great Court was festooned with hundreds of flowering branches and giant fellis blooms, so that the air was heavy with mingled fragrances and appetizing kitchen odors. Guests must have been arriving for hours, to judge by the mass of long-legged runners among the pastured herdbeasts. Every room in old Telgar Hold ought to be filled this night and Robinton was glad that his rank gave him a sure place. A little crowded perhaps because he'd brought four more harpers. They might be superfluous; every harper who could must have wangled his way in here today. Maybe it would be a happy occasion, after all.

I'll concentrate on positive, happy thoughts, Robinton mused to himself, coining Fandarel's phrase. "You'll be staying on, N'ton?"

The young man grinned back at the Harper, but there was a serious shadow in his eyes. "Lioth and I have a sweep to ride, Master Robinton," he said, leaning forward to slap his bronze affectionately on the neck. "But I did want to see Telgar Hold, so when Lord Asgenar asked me to oblige him by bringing you, I was glad of the chance."

"I, too," Robinton said in farewell, as he slid down the dragon's shoulder. "My thanks to you, Lioth, for a smooth journey."

The Harper has only to ask.

Startled, Robinton glanced up at N'ton, but the young man's head was turned toward a party of brightly garbed young women who were walking up from the pasture.

Robinton looked at Lioth, whose opalescent eye gleamed at him an instant. Then the dragon spread his great wings. Hastily Robinton backed away, still not positive he'd heard the dragon. Yet there was no other explanation. Well, this day was certainly unfolding surprises!

"Sir?" inquired Brudegan respectfully.

"Ah, yes, lads." He grinned at them. Talmor had never flown and the boy was a bit glassy in the eye. "Brudegan, you know the hall. Take them to the Harper's room so they'll know their way. And take my instrument, too. I'll not need it until the banquet. Then, lads, you're to mingle, play, talk, listen. You know the ditties I've been rehearsing. Use them. You've heard the drum messages. Utilize them. Brudegan, take Sebell with you, it's his first public performance. No, Sebell, you'd not be with us today if I'd no faith in your abilities. Talmor, watch that temper of yours. Tagetarl, wait until after the banquet to charm the girls. Remember, you'll be a full Harper too soon to jeopardize a good Holding. All of you, mind the distilled wines."

He left them so advised and went up the busy ramp into the Great Court, smiling and bowing to those he knew among the many Holders, Craftsmen and ladies passing to and fro.

Larad, Lord of Telgar Hold, resplendent in dark yellow, and the bridegroom Asgenar, Lord of Lemos, in a brilliant midnight blue, stood by the great metal doors to the Hold's Main Hall. The women of Telgar were in white with the exception of Larad's half-sister, Famira, the bride. Her blond hair streamed to the hem of her traditional wedding dress of graduated shades of red.

Robinton stood for a moment to one side of the gate into the Court, slightly in the shadow of the right-hand tower, scanning the guests already making small groups around the decorated Courtyard. He spotted the Masterherdsman, Sograny, near the stable. The man oughtn't to look as if he smelled something distasteful. Probably not the vicinity, but his neighbors. Sograny disapproved of wasting time. Masterweaver Zurg and his nimble wife moved constantly from group to group. Robinton wondered if they were inspecting fabric and fit. Hard to tell, for Weaver Zurg and spouse nodded and beamed at everyone with good-natured impartiality.

Masterminer Nigot was deep in talk with Mastertanner Belesden and the Masterfarmer Andemon, while their women formed a close conversation knot to one side. Lord Corman of Keroon was apparently lecturing the nine young men ringing him: sons, foster and blood undoubtedly, since most of them bore the old man's nosy signature. They must be recently arrived for, at a signal from him, the boys all smartly turned on their heels and followed their parent, right up to the steps. Lord Raid of Benden was talking to his host and, seeing Corman approach, bowed and stepped away. Lord Sifer of Bitra gestured for Lord Raid to join him and a group of minor Holders conversing near the watchtower steps. Of the other Lord Holders, Groghe of Fort, Sangel of Boll, Meron of Nabol, Nessel of Crom, Robinton saw nothing. Dragons trumpeted on high and a half wing of them began to spiral down to the wide field where Robinton had landed. Bronzes, blues—ah, and five golden queens—came to rest briefly. Discharging their passengers, most of them leaped skyward again, toward the fire ridges above the Hold.

Robinton made his way hastily to his host then, before the newest arrivals swarmed up the ramp to the Great Court.

There was a hearty cheerfulness about Lord Larad's greeting that masked a deep inner anxiety. His eyes, blue and candid, restlessly scanned the Court. The Lord of Telgar was a handsome man though there was scant resemblance between him and his only full sibling, Kylara. Evidently it was Kylara who had inherited their sire's appetites. Just as well.

"Well come, Master Harper, we all look forward to your entertaining songs," Lord Larad said, according the Harper a deep bow.

"We shall play in tune with the times and the occasion, Lord Larad," Robinton replied, grinning broadly at such bluntness. They both heard the ripple of music as the young harpers began to move among the guests.

The whoosh of great wings drew their eyes upward. The dragons flew across the sun, briefly shadowing the Court. All talk died for a moment, then renewed more loudly than before.

Robinton moved on, greeting Lord Larad's first lady and true love, for he had no others besides her. The young Lord of Telgar, at least, was constant.

"Lord Asgenar, my felicitations. Lady Famira, may I wish you all happiness, to have and to hold."

The girl blushed prettily, glancing shyly at Lord Asgenar. Her eyes were as blue as her half-brother's. She had her hand on Asgenar's arm, having known him a long time. Larad and Asgenar had been fosterlings at the Hold of Lord Corman of Keroon, though Larad had been elected earlier to his dignities than Asgenar. There'd be no problem with this wedding, although it remained for the Conclave of Lord Holders to ratify it, since the progeny of this marriage might one day Hold either Telgar or Lemos. A man cast his seed widely if he was a Lord Holder. He had many sons in the hope that one male of his Blood would train up strong enough to be acceptable to the Conclave, when the question of Succession arose. Not that that ancient custom was as scrupulously observed as it had been. The wise Lord extended fosterage to the Blooded children of other Lords, to gain support in Conclave as well as to insure his own progeny being well-fostered.

Robinton stepped quickly among the guests. To hear what he could, enter a conversation with an amusing story, climax another with a deft phrase. He helped himself to a handful of finger-sized meatrolls from the long tables set up near the kitchen entrance. He scooped up a mug of cider. They'd not sit to table until sunset. First the Lord Holders and the major Small Holders would have their Conclave. (He hoped that Chad had found a way for him to "attend" that meeting for he'd a notion that the discussion wouldn't be limited to the Bloodlines of Telgar and Lemos Holds.)

So he wandered, every perception tuned high, every nuance, shrug, laugh, gesture and frown weighed and measured. He observed the groupings, who shifted between the lines of region, craft and rank. When he realized he had seen nothing of the Mastersmith Fandarel or his Craft-second, Terry, or, indeed, any smithcrafters, he began to wonder. Had Fandarel's distance-writer been installed? He took a look down the side of the Hold and could see no posts as had been described to him. He chewed thoughtfully at a rough spot on his lower lip.

Voices and laughter seemed to have a strident edge. From his detached vantage point, he surveyed the Great Court, now so full it appeared as a moving carpet of solid bodies, here and there a tight knot of bent heads. As if—as if everyone were determined to enjoy themselves, frantically grasping pleasure . . .

Dragons trumpeted from the heights. Robinton grinned. They spoke in thirds, he noticed. Now, if a man could direct them—what an accompaniment to his Ballad.

"Good Masterharper, have you seen F'lar or Fandarel?" Lytol had come up to him, the young Lord Jaxom at his elbow.

"Not yet."

Lytol frowned, suggested pointedly that Jaxom look for the young Bloods of Telgar Hold and drew Robinton further from the nearest guests.

"How do you think the Lords will react to Lord Meron of Nabol?"

"React to Meron?" Robinton snorted derisively. "By ignoring him, of course. Not that his opinion would influence the Conclave . . ."

"I don't mean that. I mean his possession of a fire lizard—" Lytol broke off as the Harper stared at him. "You didn't hear? The messenger went through Ruatha Hold yesterday, bound for Fort Hold and your Crafthall."

"He missed me or—was he free with his news?"

"To me, yes. I seem to attract confidences . . ."

"Fire lizard? What about them? I used to spend hours trying to catch one. Never did. In fact I never heard of one being caught. How did Meron manage the trick?"

Lytol grimaced, the tic beginning in his cheek. "They can be Impressed. There always was that nursey tale that fire lizards are the ancestors of dragons."

"And Meron of Nabol Impressed one?"

Lytol gave a mirthless laugh. "Unlikely, I grant you. The fire lizards exhibit a woeful lack of taste. But you can rest assured that Meron of Nabol would not waste time on fire lizards if they weren't of use to him."

Robinton considered this and then shrugged. "I don't think you need be concerned. But how did Nabol get one? How can they be Impressed? I thought that was strictly a draconic trait."

"How Lord Meron of Nabol acquired one is what bothers me the most," Lytol said, glowering. "That Southern Weyrwoman, Kylara, brought him a whole clutch of eggs. Of course, they lost most in the Hatching, but the few that survived are making quite a stir in Nabol Hold. The messenger had seen one, and he was all bright-eyed in the telling. 'A regular dragon in miniature,' he said, and he's all for trying his luck on the sandy beaches in Southern Boll and Fort from the gleam in his eye."

" 'A regular dragon in miniature,' huh?" Robinton began to turn the significance of this around in his mind. He didn't like the angles he saw.

There wasn't a boy alive on Pern that hadn't at one time dreamed of suddenly becoming acceptable to dragonkind, of Impressing. Of having at his beck and call (little dreaming it was more the other way round) an immense creature, capable of going anywhere on Pern in a breath, of defeating all enemies with his flame-ridden breath (also fallacious as dragons never flamed anything but Thread and wouldn't knowingly harm a human). Life at the mountaintop Weyrs assumed a glamor all out of proportion to reality, yet dragonmen were not stooped by the heavy labor of the fields, orchards and craft benches; they were straight and tall, dressed in beautifully tanned wher-hides, and seemed somehow superior. Very few boys could become Lord Holders, unless they were properly Blooded. But there was always that tantalizing possibility that a dragonrider might choose *you* to go to the Weyr for an Impression. So generations of boys had vainly tried to catch a fire lizard, symbolic of that other yearning.

And a "regular miniature dragon" in the possession of a sly-faced underhanded malcontent like Meron of Nabol, who was sour about dragonmen anyway (with some justification in the matter of the Esvay valley against T'kul of the High Reaches Weyr), could be an embarrassment for F'lar at the least, and might disrupt their plans for the day at the worst.

"Well, if Kylara brought the fire-lizard eggs to Nabol Hold, F'lar will know," Robinton told the worried Lord Warder. "They keep pretty close tabs on that woman."

Lytol's glower deepened. "I hope so. Meron of Nabol will certainly let no chance pass to irritate or embarrass F'lar. Have you seen F'lar?"

They both glanced around, hopefully. Then Robinton caught sight of a familiar grizzled head, bobbing toward himself and the Warder.

"Speaking of Benden, here's old Lord Raid charging down on us. I've an idea what he wants and I will *not* sing that ancient lay about the Holders one more time. Excuse me, Lytol."

Robinton slipped into the milling guests, working as rapidly away from the Benden Lord Holder as possible. He happened to dislike Lord Raid's favorite ballad with a passion and, if Raid cornered him, he'd have no choice but to sing it. He felt no compunction about leaving Lytol exposed to Lord Raid's pompous manner. Lytol enjoyed an unusual status with the Lord Holders. They weren't certain how to treat a man who'd been a dragonrider, Weaverhallmaster, and was now Lord Warder of a Ruatha prospering under his guidance. He could deal with Raid.

The Masterharper halted at a point where he could look

up at the cliff, trying to spot Ramoth or Mnementh among the dragons lining the edge.

Fire lizards? How was Meron going to use a fire lizard? Unless it was *because* Kylara, a Weyrwoman, had given *him* one. Yes. That was guaranteed to sow dissension. Undoubtedly every Lord Holder here would want one, so as to be equal to Meron. There couldn't be enough eggs to go around. Meron would capitalize on forgotten yearnings, and chalk up one more irritation against dragonmen.

Robinton found that the meatrolls sat heavily in his stomach. Suddenly Brudegan detached himself from the crowd, bowing with a rueful grin to those he'd been serenading as if he were reluctantly answering his Master's summons.

"The undercurrent is something fierce," the journeyman said, pretending to tune his instrument. "Everyone's so determined to have a good time. Odd, too. It's not what they say, but how they say it that tips you off." The boy flushed as Robinton nodded approvingly. "For instance, they refer to 'that Weyrleader' meaning their own weyrbound leader. 'The Weyrleader' always means F'lar of Benden. 'The Weyrleader' had understood. 'The Weyrleader' had tried. 'She' means Lessa. 'Her' means their own Weyrwoman. Interesting?"

"Fascinating. What's the feeling about Threadfall?"

Brudegan bent his head to the gitar, twanged strings discordantly. He drew his hand across all eight in a dissonant chord that ran a chill down the Masterharper's spine. Then Brudegan turned away with a gay song.

Robinton wished that F'lar and Lessa would arrive. He did see D'ram of Ista Weyr talking earnestly to Igen's Weyrleader, G'narish. He liked that pair best of the Oldtimers, G'narish being young enough to change and D'ram essentially too honest to deny a truth when his nose was in it. Trouble was, he kept his nose inside Ista Weyr too much.

Neither man looked at ease, as much because there was an island of empty space around them—an obvious ostracization with the Court so crowded—as anything else. They greeted Robinton with grave relief.

"Such a happy occasion," he said and, when they reacted with surprise, he hurried on. "Have you heard from F'lar?"

"Should we? There's been more Thread?" G'narish asked, alarmed.

"Not that I know of."

"Have you seen T'ron or T'kul about? We just arrived."

"No, in fact, none of the western people seem to be here except Lord Warder Lytol of Ruatha."

D'ram clenched his teeth with an audible snap.

"R'mart of Telgar can't come," the Oldtimer said. "He took a bad scoring."

"I'd heard it was wicked at Crom Hold," Robinton murmured, sympathetically. "No way to predict it'd fall there at that time, either."

"I see Lord Nessel of Crom and his Holders are here in strength, though," D'ram said, his voice bitter.

"He could scarcely stay away without insulting Lord Larad. How bad were the Telgar Weyr's casualties? And if R'mart's out of action, who's leading?"

D'ram gave the Harper the distinct feeling that he'd asked an impertinent question, but G'narish answered easily.

"The wing-second, M'rek, took over but the Weyr is so badly understrength that D'ram and I talked it over and sent replacements. As it happens, we've enough weyrlings who've just started chewing stone so we're wing-full." G'narish glanced at the older dragonman as if he suddenly realized that he was discussing Weyr affairs with an outsider. He gave a shrug. "It makes more sense with Thread falling out of phase and the Crom Hold demoralized. We used to do it in the Oldtime when a Weyr was understrength. In fact, I flew with Benden one season as a weyrling."

"I'm certain that Crom and Telgar Holds will appreciate your cooperation, Weyrleaders," Robinton said. "Tell me, though, have you had any luck Impressing some fire lizards? Igen and Ista ought to be good hunting grounds."

"Impressing? Fire lizards?" D'ram snorted with as much incredulity as Robinton had expressed earlier.

"That'd be a trick," G'narish laughed. "Look, there's Ramoth and Mnementh now."

There was no mistaking the two beasts who were gliding to the fire heights. It was also unmistakable that the dragons already perched on the pinnacle moved aside to make room for them.

"Now, that's the first time—" G'narish muttered under his breath and stopped, because a sudden lull in the conversation had swept through the assembly, punctuated by audible hushings and scrapings as people turned to the Gate.

Robinton watched, with fond pride, as Lessa and F'lar mounted the steps to their hosts. They were both wearing the soft green of new leaves and the Harper wanted to applaud. However, he restrained himself and, signaling to the dragonmen, began to thread his way toward the new arrivals. Another dragon, closely followed by a bronze, swept in at dangerously low altitude. Gold wingtips showed above the outer wall of the Court and the wind from her backstrokes flung up dust, dirt and the skirts of the ladies nearest the Gate. There was a spate of screams and angry protests from those discommoded which settled into an ominous murmur.

Robinton, his height giving him an advantage, noticed Lord Larad hesitate in the act of bowing to Lessa. He saw Lord Asgenar and the ladies staring intently beyond. Irritated that he was missing something, Robinton pushed urgently on.

He broke through to the corner of the stairs, took the first four in two big strides and halted.

Resplendent in red, her golden hair unbound like a maiden's, Kylara approached the Hall entrance, her smile composed of pure malice, not pleasure. Her right hand rested on the arm of Lord Meron of Nabol Hold, whose red tunic was slightly too orange in cast to blend with hers. Such details Robinton remembered at another time. Now all he saw were the two fire lizards, wings slightly extended for balance; a gold one on Kylara's left arm, a bronze on Meron's. "Regular miniature dragons," beautiful, evoking a feeling of envy and desire in the Harper. He swallowed hastily, firmly suppressing such unbecoming emotions.

The murmur grew as more people became aware of the newest arrivals.

"By the First Shell, they've got fire lizards!" Lord Corman of Keroon Hold bellowed. He stepped out of the crowd into the aisle that had been opened to the Hall entrance, and stalked forward to have a good look.

The golden lizard screamed at his approach, and the little bronze hissed in warning. There was an irritatingly smug smirk on Meron's face.

"Did you know Meron had one?" D'ram demanded in a harsh whisper at the Harper's elbow.

Robinton raised a hand to still further questions.

"And here come Kylara of Southern and Lord Meron of Nabol Hold with living examples of this small token of our best wishes for the happy couple," F'lar's voice rang out.

Utter silence fell as he and Lessa presented felt-wrapped round bundles to Lord Asgenar and his bride, Lady Famira.

"They are just now hard," F'lar said in a loud voice that carried over the murmurings, "and must be kept in heated sands to crack, of course. They come to you through the generosity of one Toric, a seaholder at Southern Weyr, from a clutch he discovered only hours ago. Weyrleader T'bor brought them to me."

Robinton glanced back at Kylara. Her flushed face now matched Meron's tunic while *he* looked ready to kill. Lessa, smiling graciously, turned to Kylara.

"F'lar told me he'd seen your little pet . . ."

"Pet nothing!" Kylara blazed with anger. "She ate Thread yesterday at High Reaches . . ."

What else she'd had to say was lost as her words, "ate Thread," "ate Thread," ricocheted back through the assembly. The raucous screams of the two lizards added cacophony and Kylara and Meron had all they could do to soothe their creatures. To Robinton it was plain that whatever effect Meron of Nabol had planned had been foiled. He was not the only Lord Holder to own "a regular miniature dragon."

Two minor Holders, from Nerat to judge by their devices, bore down on D'ram and G'narish.

"As you love your dragons, pretend you knew about the lizards," Robinton said in an urgent undertone to the two. D'ram started to protest but the anxious Holders closed in with a barrage of eager questions on how to acquire a fire lizard just like Meron's.

Recovering first, G'narish answered with more poise than Robinton thought he'd have. Pressing against the stone wall, the Harper inched his way up the stairs, to push in around the women clustered about Lord Asgenar, his lady Famira and F'lar.

"LORD HOLDERS, OF MAJOR AND MINOR DEGREE, PRESENT YOURSELVES FOR THE CONCLAVE," boomed out the Telgar Hold guard captain. A brass chorus of dragons echoed from the heights, satisfactorily stunning the guests into momentary silence.

The Captain repeated his summons and abjured the crowd to make room.

Lord Asgenar handed Famira his egg, murmuring something in her ear and pointing into the Hall. He stepped aside, gesturing for Lessa and Famira to pass inside. As well they did, for the Holders were now massing up the stairs. Robinton tried to signal F'lar but the dragonman was struggling toward Kylara, against the current. She was arguing heatedly with Meron who gave an angry shrug, left her and began shoving roughly into the Hall, past more polite Holders.

There was another exodus, Robinton noticed, of Craftmasters who congregated near the kitchen.

F'lar needs the Harper.

Robinton glanced around him, wondering who had spoken, amazed that so soft a voice had reached him over the gabbling. He was alerted by a dissonant twang of strings and, turning his head unerringly toward the sound, spotted Brudegan up on the sentry walk with Chad, from the look of him. Had the resident Harper of Telgar Hold found a way to overhear the Conclave?

As Robinton changed his direction for the tower steps, a dragonrider confronted him.

"F'lar wants you, Masterharper."

Robinton hesitated, looking back to the two harpers who were urgently signaling him to hurry.

Lessa listens.

"Did you speak?" Robinton demanded of the rider.

"Yes, sir. F'lar wants you to join him. It's important."

The Harper looked toward the dragons and Mnementh dipped his head up and down. Robinton shook his, trying to cope with another of this day's astonishing shocks. A piercing whistle reached him from above.

He pursed his lips and gave the "go-ahead" sequence, adding in its different tempo the tune for "report later."

Brudegan strummed an "understand" chord with which Chad apparently disagreed. Marks for the journeyman, Robinton thought, and whistled the strident trill for "comply." He wished the harpers had as flexible a code as the one he'd developed for the Smith—and where was he?

That was one man easily spotted in a crowd but, as Robinton followed the dragonrider, he didn't see a smithcrafter anywhere. Of course, the impact of the distance-writer would be anticlimactic to the introduction of the lizards. Robinton felt sorry for the Smith, quietly perfecting an ingenious means of communication only to have it overshadowed by Thread-eating miniature dragons. Creatures who could be Impressed by non-weyrfolk. The average Pernese would be far more struck by a draconic substitute than by any mechanical miracle.

The dragonrider had led him to the watchtower to the right of the Gate. When Robinton looked back over his left shoulder, Brudegan and Chad were no longer visible on the sentry walk.

The lower floor of the tower was a single large room, the stone stairs which rose to the right side of the sentry walk were on the far wall. Sleeping furs were piled in one corner in readiness for such guests as might have to be lodged there that night. Two slit windows, facing each other on the long sides of the room, gave little light. G'narish, the Igen Weyr-leader, was unshielding the glow basket in the ceiling as the Harper entered. Kylara was standing right under it, glaring furiously at T'bor.

"Yes, I went to Nabol. My queen lizard was there. And well I did, for Prideth saw Thread sign across the High Reaches Range!" She had everyone's attention now. Her eyes gleamed, her chin lifted and, Robinton noted, the shrewish rasp left her voice. Kylara was a fine-looking female, but there was a hard ruthlessness about her that repelled him.

"I flew instantly to T'kul." Her face twisted with anger. "He's no dragonman! He refused to believe me. Me! As if *any* Weyrwoman wouldn't know the sign when she sees it. I doubt he's even bothered with sweepriders. He kept harping on the fact that Thread had fallen six days ago at Tillek Hold and couldn't be falling this soon at High Reaches. So I told him about Falls in the western swamp and north Lemos Hold, and he still wouldn't believe me."

"Did the Weyr turn out in time?" F'lar interrupted her coldly.

"Of course," and Kylara drew herself up, her posture tightening the dress against her full-bosomed body. "*I* had Prideth sound the alarm." Her smile was malicious. "T'kul had to act. A queen can't lie. And there isn't a male dragon alive that will disobey one!"

F'lar inhaled sharply, gritting his teeth. T'kul of the High

Reaches was a taciturn, cynical, tired man. However justified Kylara's actions were, her methods lacked diplomacy. And she was contemporary weyrfolk. Oh, well, T'kul was a lost cause anyhow. F'lar glanced obliquely at D'ram and G'narish, to see what effect T'kul's behavior had on them. Surely now ... They looked strained.

"You're a good Weyrwoman, Kylara, and *you* did well. Very well," F'lar said with such conviction that she began to preen and her smile was a smirk of self-satisfaction. Then she stared at him.

"Well, what are you going to do about T'kul? We can't permit him to endanger the world with that Oldtime attitude of his."

F'lar waited, half-hoping that D'ram might speak up. If just one of the Oldtimers ...

"It seems that the dragonriders had better call a conclave, too," he said at length, aware of the tapping of Kylara's foot and the eyes on him. "T'ron of Fort Weyr must hear of this. And perhaps we'd all better go on to Telgar Weyr for R'mart's opinion."

"Opinion?" demanded Kylara, infuriated by this apparent evasion. "You ought to ride out of here now, confront T'kul with flagrant negligence and ..."

"And what, Kylara?" F'lar asked when she broke off.

"And—well—there must be something you can do!"

For a situation that had never before arisen? F'lar looked at D'ram and G'narish.

"You've got to *do* something," she insisted, swinging toward the other men.

"The Weyrs are traditionally autonomous ..."

"A fine excuse to hide behind, D'ram ..."

"There can be no hiding now," D'ram went on, his voice rough, his expression bleak. "Something will have to be done. By *all* of us. When T'ron comes."

More temporizing? F'lar wondered. "Kylara," he said aloud, "you mentioned your lizard eating Thread." There was a lot more to be discussed in this matter than T'kul's incredible behavior. "And may I inquire how you knew your lizard had returned to Nabol?"

"Prideth told me. She Hatched there so she returned to Nabol Hold when you frightened her at Southern."

"You had her at High Reaches Weyr, though?"

191

"No. I told you. I saw Thread over the High Reach Range and went to T'kul. First! Once I'd roused the Weyr, I realized that there might have been Thread over Nabol so I went to check."

"And told Meron about the premature Threadfall?"

"Of course."

"Then?"

"I took the lizard back with me. I didn't want to lose her again." When F'lar ignored that jibe, she went on. "I picked up a flame thrower, so naturally I flew with Merika's wing. Scant thanks I got for my help from that Weyrwoman."

She was telling the truth, F'lar realized, for her emotions were very much in evidence.

"When my lizard saw Thread falling, she seemed to go mad. I couldn't control her. She flew right at a patch and—ate it."

"Did you give her firestone?" D'ram asked, his eyes keen with real interest.

"I didn't have any. Besides, I want her to mate," and Kylara's smile had a very odd twist to it as she stroked the lizard's back. "She'll burrow, too," she added, extolling her creature's abilities. "A ground crewman said he'd seen her enter one. Of course I didn't know that until later."

"Is the High Reaches Hold clear of Thread now?"

Kylara shrugged indifferently. "If they aren't, you'll hear."

"How long did Threadfall continue after you saw it? Were you able to determine the leading Edge when you flew over to Nabol?"

"It lasted about three hours. Under, I'd say. That is, from the time the wings *finally* got there." She gave a condescending smile. "As to the leading Edge, *I'd* say it must have been high up in the Range," and she dared them to dispute it, hurrying on when no one did. "It'd fall on bare rock and snow there. I did sweep the Nabol side but Prideth saw no sign."

"You did extremely well, Kylara, and we are exceedingly grateful to you," F'lar said, and the other Leaders endorsed his commendation so firmly that Kylara smiled expansively, turning from one man to another, her eyes glittering with self-appreciation.

"We've had five Falls now," F'lar went on gravely, glancing at the other Leaders, trying to see how far he could continue in his move to consolidate himself as their spokesman. T'kul's defection had shaken D'ram badly. What T'ron's reaction would be, F'lar didn't try to guess, but if the Fort Weyrleader found himself in a minority of one against the other four Leaders, would he decide to act against T'kul, even if it did mean siding with F'lar? "At Tillek Hold, eight days ago; Upper Crom Hold, five; high Lemos Hold north, three; Southern far west, two; and now High Reaches Hold. Undoubtedly Thread fell in the Western Sea but there is no question that Falls are more frequent and increasing in scope. No point on Pern is safe. No Weyr can afford to relax its vigil to a traditional six-day margin." He smiled grimly. "Tradition!"

D'ram looked about to argue, but F'lar caught and held his eyes until the man slowly nodded.

"That's easy to say, but what are you going to do about T'kul? Or T'ron?" Kylara had just realized no one was paying her any attention. "He's just as bad. He refuses to admit times have changed. Even when Mardra deliberately . . ."

There was a brisk knock on the door but it swung open instantly, to admit the giant frame of Fandarel.

"I was told you were here, F'lar, and we are ready."

F'lar scrubbed at his face, regretting the diversion.

"The Lord Holders are in Conclave," he began and the Smith grunted acknowledgment, "and there has been another unexpected development . . ."

Fandarel nodded toward the fire lizard on Kylara's arm. "I was told about them. There are many ways to fight Thread, of course, but not all are efficient. The merits of such creatures remain to be seen."

"The merits—" Kylara began, ready to explode with outrage.

Robinton the Harper was beside her, whispering in her ear.

Grateful to Robinton, F'lar turned to attend the Smith, who had stepped to the door, obviously wanting the dragonmen to accompany him. F'lar was reluctant to see the distance-writer. It wouldn't receive the attention it deserved from the Lords or the people or the riders. The distance-writer made so much more sense in this emergency than unreliable lizards. And yet, if they did eat Thread . . .

He paused on the threshold, looking back toward Kylara and the Harper. Robinton looked directly at him.

Almost as if the Harper read his mind, F'lar saw him smile winningly down at Kylara (though F'lar knew the man detested her).

"F'lar, do you think it's wise for Kylara to go out into that mob? They'll scare the lizard," said the Harper.

"But I'm hungry—" Kylara protested. "And there's music —" as the nearby thrum of a gitar was plainly audible.

"That sounds like Tagetarl," Robinton said, with a bright grin. "I'll call him in and send you choice victuals from the kitchen. Far better than struggling with that noisome rabble out there, I assure you." He handed her to a chair with great courtesy, motioning behind his back to F'lar to leave.

As they stepped out into the bright sunlight, the crowd swirling noisily around them, F'lar saw the merry-faced young man, gitar in hand, who had answered the Harper's whistle. Undoubtedly Robinton would be free to join them in a few moments if he read matters rightly. The young journeyman would definitely appeal to Kylara's—ah—nature.

Fandarel had set up his equipment in the far corner of the Court, where the outside wall abutted the cliff-Hold, a dragonlength from the stairs. Three men were perched atop the wall, carefully handing something down to the group working on the apparatus. As the Weyrleaders followed Fandarel's swath through the press of bodies (the fellis blossom fragrance had long since given way to other odors), F'lar was the object of many sidelong glances and broken conversations.

"You watch, you'll see," a young man in the colors of a minor Hold was saying in a carrying voice. "Those dragonmen won't let *us* near a clutch . . ."

"The Lord Holders, you mean," another said. "Fancy anything trusting that Nabolese. What? Oh. Great shells!"

Now, if everyone on Pern could possess a fire lizard, wondered F'lar, would that really solve the problem?

More dragons in the sky. He glanced up and recognized T'ron's Fidranth and Mardra's queen, Loranth. He sighed. He wanted to see what Fandarel planned with his distance-writer before he had to tackle T'ron.

"Mnementh, what is happening at the Conclave?"

Talk. They await the other two Lord Holders.

F'lar tried to see if the Fort Weyrleaders had brought the missing Lords Groghe of Fort and Sangel of South Boll. Those two wouldn't take kindly to a Conclave adjudicating without them. But if Lord Groghe had heard about High Reaches Hold . . .

F'lar suppressed a shudder, trying to smile with sincere

apologies as he edged past a group of small Holders who apparently couldn't see him. As if recognizing the smith-crafters as neutral, the Weyrwomen had gathered in a wary group to the right of the mass of equipment which Fandarel's people were setting up. They were pretending great interest, but even G'narish's pretty Weyrmate, Nadira, looked troubled and she was a sweet-tempered lady. Bedella, representing Telgar Weyr, looked completely confused but she wasn't bright.

Just then Mardra broke through the guests, demanding to know what was going on. Had T'kul and Merika arrived? Where were their Hosts? Modern Holds were certainly lacking in plain courtesy. She didn't expect traditional ceremonies any more but . . .

At that moment, F'lar heard the clang of steel against steel and saw Lord Groghe of Fort pounding the Hall door with his knife handle, his heavy featured face suffused with anger. The slighter, frosty Sangel, Lord of South Boll, was scowling darkly behind him. The door opened a slit, widened slightly to allow the two Lord Holders to enter. Judging by their expression, it would take time and more talk before these two were pacified.

"How much more needs to be done?" asked F'lar as he joined the Smith. He tried to remember how the distance-writer had looked in the Hall. This collection of tubes and wire seemed much too big.

"We need only attach this wire so," Fandarel replied, his huge fingers deftly fitting word to action, "and that one, here. Now. I place the arm in position over the roll and we shall send out a message to the Hall to be sure all is in order." Fandarel beamed down at his instrument as fondly as any queen over a golden egg.

F'lar felt someone rather too close behind him and looked irritably over his shoulder to see Robinton's intent face. The Harper gave him an abstracted smile and nodded for him to pay attention.

The Smith was delicately tapping out a code, the irregular lengths of red lines appearing on the gray paper as the needle moved.

" 'Hook-up completed,' " Robinton murmured in F'lar's ear. " 'Efficiently and on time.' " Robinton chuckled through that translation. " 'Stand by.' That's the long and the short of it."

The Smith turned the switch to the receive position and

looked expectantly at F'lar. At that moment, Mnementh gave a squall from the heights. He and all the dragons began to extend their wings. The mass movement blotted out the sun which was lowering over the Telgar Cliffs and sent shadows over the guests to still their chatter.

Groghe told the Lords that T'ron has found a distance-viewer at Fort. He has seen the Red Star through it. They are upset. Be warned, said Mnementh.

The doors of the Great Hall swung wide and the Lord Holders came striding out. One look at Lord Groghe's face confirmed Mnementh's report. The Lord Holders ranged themselves on the steps, in a solid front against the Dragonmen gathered in the corner. Lord Groghe had lifted his arm, pointed it accusingly at F'lar, when a disconcerting hiss split the pregnant silence.

"Look!" the Smith bellowed and all eyes followed his hand as the distance-writer began receiving a message.

" 'Igen Hold reports Thread falling. Transmission broken off midsentence.' "

Robinton reported the sounds as they were printed, his voice growing hoarser and less confident with each word.

"What nonsense is this?" Lord Groghe demanded, his florid face brick-red as attention was diverted from his proposed announcement. "Thread fell in the High Reaches at noon yesterday. How could it fall at Igen Hold this evening? What the Shells is that contraption?"

"I don't understand," G'narish protested loudly, staring up at Lord Laudey of Igen Hold who stood in stunned horror on the steps. "I've swepriders on constant patrol . . ."

The dragons bugled on the heights just as a green burst into the air over the court, causing the crowd to scream and duck, scurrying to the walls for safety.

Threads fall at Igen southwest, came the message loud and clear. To be echoed by the dragonriders in the court.

"Where are you going, F'lar?" bellowed Lord Groghe as the Benden Weyrleader followed G'narish's plunge to the Gate. The air was full of dragon wings now, the screams of frightened women counterpointing the curses of men.

"To fight Thread at Igen, of course," F'lar shouted back.

"Igen's my problem," G'narish cried, halting and wheeling toward F'lar, but there was gratitude, not rebuke in his surprised face.

"G'narish, wait! Where in Igen?" Lord Laudey was demanding. He pushed past the infuriated Lord Groghe to catch up with his Weyrleader.

"And Ista? Is the island in danger?" Lord Warbret wanted to know.

"We'll go and see," D'ram reassured him, taking his arm and urging him toward the Gate.

"Since when has Benden Weyr concerned itself with Igen and Ista?" T'ron planted himself squarely in F'lar's way. The menace in his voice carried to the steps of the Hall. His belligerent stance, obstructing the way to the Gate, halted them all. "And rushed to Nabol's aid?"

F'lar returned his scowl. "Thread falls, dragonman. Igen and Ista fly winglight, with riders helping at Telgar Weyr. Should we feast when others fight?"

"Let Ista and Igen fend for themselves!"

Ramoth screamed on high. The other queens answered her. What she challenged no one knew, but she suddenly winked out. F'lar had no attention to spare to wonder that she'd gone *between* without Lessa riding for he saw T'ron's hand on his belt knife.

"We can settle our difference of opinion later, T'ron. In private! Thread falls . . ."

The bronzes had begun to land outside the Gate, juggling to let as many land close as possible.

The green rider from Igen had directed his beast to perch on the Gate. He was repeatedly yelling his message to the static, tense group below.

T'ron would not stop. "Thread falls, huh, F'lar? Noble Benden to the rescue! And it's not *Benden's* concern." He let out a raucous shout of derisive contempt.

"Enough, man!" D'ram stepped up to pull T'ron aside. He gestured sharply at the silent spectators.

But T'ron ignored the warning and shook him off so violently that the heavy-set D'ram staggered.

"I've had enough of Benden! Benden's notions! Benden's superiority! Benden's altruism! *And* Benden's Weyrleader . . ."

With that last snarled insult, T'ron launched himself toward F'lar, his drawn knife raised for a slashing blow.

As the ragged gasp of fear swept through the ranks of spectators, F'lar held his ground until there was no chance

T'ron could change his direction. Then he ducked under the blade, yanking his own out of its ornamental sheath.

It was a new knife, a gift from Lessa. It had cut neither meat nor bread and must now be christened with the blood of a man. For this duel was to the death and its outcome could well decide the fate of Pern.

F'lar had sunk to a semicrouch, flexing his fingers around the hilt, testing its balance. Too much depended on a single belt knife, a half-hand shorter than the blade in his opponent's fingers. T'ron had the reach of him and the added advantage of being in wher-hide riding gear whereas F'lar wore flimsy cloth. His eyes never left T'ron as he faced the older man. F'lar was aware of the hot sun on the back of his neck, the hard stones under his feet, of the deathly hush of the great Court, of the smells of bruised fellis blooms, spilled wines and fried food, of sweat—and fear.

T'ron moved forward, amazingly light on his feet for a man of his size and age. F'lar let him come, pivoted as T'ron angled off to his left, a circling movement designed to place him off balance—a transparent maneuver. F'lar felt a quick surge of relief; if this were the measure of T'ron's combat strategy . . .

With a bound the Oldtimer was on him, knife miraculously transferred to his left hand with a motion too quick to follow, his right arm coming over and down in a blow that struck F'lar's wrist as he threw himself backward to avoid, by the thickness of a hair, the hissing stroke of the foot-long blade. He backed, his arm half-numbed, aware of the shock that coursed through him like a drenching of icy water.

For a man blind with anger, T'ron was a shade too controlled for F'lar's liking. What possessed the man to pick a quarrel—here and now? For T'ron had pushed this fight, deliberately baiting F'lar with that specious quibble. D'ram and G'narish had been relieved at his offer of help. So T'ron had *wanted* to fight. Why? Then suddenly, F'lar knew. T'ron had heard about T'kul's flagrant negligence and knew that the other Oldtimers could not ignore or obliquely condone it. Not with F'lar of Benden likely to insist that T'kul step aside as Weyrleader of High Reaches. If T'ron could kill F'lar, he could control the others. And F'lar's public death would leave the modern Lord Holders without a sympathetic Weyrleader. The domination of Weyrs over Hold and Craft would continue unchallenged, and unchanged.

T'ron moved in, pressing the attack. F'lar backed, watching the center of the Oldtimer's wher-hide-cased chest. Not the eyes, not the knife hand. The chest! That was the spot that telegraphed the next move most accurately. The words of old C'gan, the weyrling instructor, seven Turns dead, seemed to echo in F'lar's mind. Only C'gan had never thought his training would prevent one Weyrleader from killing another, to save Pern in a duel before half the world.

F'lar shook his head sharply, rejecting the angry line his thoughts were taking. This wasn't the way to survive, not with the odds against him.

He saw T'ron's arm move suddenly, swayed back in automatic evasion, saw the opening, lunged . . .

The watchers gasped as the sound of torn fabric was clearly heard. The pain at his waist had been such a quick stab that F'lar had all but decided T'ron's swipe was only a scratch when a wave of nausea swept him.

"Good try. But you're just not fast enough, Oldtimer!" F'lar heard himself saying; felt his lips stretch into a smile he was far from feeling. He kept to the crouch, the belt pressing against his waist, but the torn fabric dangled, jerking as he breathed.

T'ron threw him a half-puzzled look, his eyes raking him, pausing at the hanging rag, flicking to the knife blade in his hand. It was clean, unstained. A second realization crossed T'ron's face, even as he lunged again; F'lar knew that T'ron was shaken by the apparent failure of an attack he had counted on to injure badly.

F'lar pulled to one side, almost contemptuously avoiding the flashing blade, and then charged in with a series of lightning feints of his own, to test the Oldtimer's reflexes and agility. There was no doubt T'ron needed to finish him off quickly —and F'lar hadn't much time either, he knew, as he ignored the hot agony in his midriff.

"Yes, Oldtimer," he said, forcing himself to breathe easily, keeping his words light, mocking. "Benden Weyr concerns itself with Ista and Igen. And the Holds of Nabol, and Crom, and Telgar, because Benden dragonmen have not forgotten that Thread burns anything and anyone it touches, Weyr and commoner alike. And if Benden Weyr has to stand alone against the fall of Thread, it will."

He flung himself at T'ron, stabbing at the horny leather tunic, praying the knife was sharp enough to pierce it. He spun aside barely in time, the effort causing him to gasp in pain. Yet he made himself dance outside T'ron's reach, made himself grin at the other's sweaty, exertion-reddened face.

"Not fast enough, are you, T'ron? To kill Benden. *Or* muster for a Fall."

T'ron's breathing was ragged, a hoarse rasping. He came on, his knife arm lower. F'lar backed, keeping to a wary crouch, wondering if it was sweat he felt trickling down his belly, or blood. If T'ron noticed . . . .

"What's wrong, T'ron? All that rich food and easy living beginning to tell? Or is it age, T'ron? Age creeping up on you. You're four hundred and forty-five Turns old, you know. You can't move fast enough any more, with the times, or against me."

T'ron closed in, a guttural roar bursting from him. He sprang, with a semblance of his old vitality, aiming for the throat. F'lar's knife hand flashed up, struck the attacking wrist aside, slashed downward at the other's neck, where the wher-hide tunic had parted. A dragon screamed. T'ron's right fist caught him below the belt. Agony lashed through him. He doubled over the man's arm. Someone screamed a warning. With an unexpected reserve of energy, F'lar somehow managed to pull himself sharply up from that vulnerable position. His head rocked from the impact against T'ron's descending knife, but it was miraculously deflected. Both hands on the hilt of his decorative blade, F'lar rammed it through wher-hide until it grated against the man's ribs.

He staggered free, saw T'ron waver, his eyes bulging with shock, saw him step back, the jeweled hilt standing out beneath his ribs. T'ron's mouth worked soundlessly. He fell heavily to his knees, then sagged slowly sideways to the stones.

The tableau held for what seemed hours to F'lar, desperately sucking breath into his bruised body, forcing himself to keep to his feet for he could not, *could not* collapse.

"Benden's young, Fort. It's our Turn. Now!" he managed to say. "And there's Thread falling at Igen." He swung himself around, facing the staring mass of eyes and mouths. "There's Thread falling at Igen!"

He pivoted back, aware that he couldn't fight in a torn dress tunic. T'ron had on wher-hide. He let himself down heavily on one knee and began to tug at T'ron's belt, ignoring the blood that oozed out around the knife.

Someone screamed and beat at his hands. It was Mardra.

"You've killed him. Isn't that enough? Leave him alone!" F'lar stared up at her, frowning.

"He's not dead. Fidranth hasn't gone *between*." It made him feel stronger somehow to know he hadn't killed the man. "Get wine, someone. Call the physician!"

He got the belt loose and was pulling at the right sleeve when other hands began to help.

"I need it to fight in," he muttered. A clean cloth was waved in his direction. He grabbed it and, holding his breath, jerked loose the knife. He looked at it a second and then cast it from him. It skittered across the stone, everyone jumping from its path. Someone handed him the tunic. He got up, struggling into it. T'ron was a heavier man; the tunic was too big. He was belting it tightly to him when he became aware again of the hushed, awed audience. He looked at the blur of expectant faces.

"Well? Do you support Benden?" he cried.

There was a further moment of stunned silence. The crowd's multihead turned to the stairs where the Lord Holders stood.

"Those who don't had better hide deep in their Holds," cried Lord Larad of Telgar, stepping down on a level with Lord Groghe and Lord Sangel, his hand on his knife belt, his manner challenging.

"The Smiths support Benden Weyr!" Fandarel boomed out.

"The Harpers do!" Robinton's baritone was answered by Chad's tenor from the sentry walk.

"The Miners!"

"The Weavers!"

"The Tanners!"

The Lord Holders began to call out their names, loudly, as if by volume they could redeem themselves. A cheer rose from the guests to fall almost instantly to a hush as F'lar turned slowly to the other Weyrleaders.

"Ista!" D'ram's cry was a fierce, almost defiant hiss, overtaken by G'narish's exultant "Igen" and T'bor's enthusiastic "Southern!"

"What can we do?" cried Lord Asgenar, striding to F'lar. "Can Lemos runners and groundmen help Igen Hold now?"

F'lar lost his immobility, tightened the belt one further notch, hoping the stricture would dull the pain.

"It's your wedding day, man. Enjoy what you can of it. D'ram, we'll follow you. Ramoth's already called up the Benden wings. T'bor, bring up the Southern fighters. *Every* man and woman who can fit on the dragons!"

He was asking for more than complete mobilization of the fighters and T'bor hesitated.

"Lessa," for she had her arms around him now. He pushed them gently to one side. "Assist Mardra. Robinton, I need your help. Let it be known," and he raised his voice, harsh and steely enough to be heard throughout the listening Court. "Let it be known," and he stared down at Mardra, "that any of Fort Weyr who do not care to follow Benden's lead must go to Southern." He looked away before she could protest. "And that applies to any craftsman, Lord Holder or commoner, as well as dragonfolk. There isn't much Thread in Southern to worry you. And your indifference to a common menace will not endanger others."

Lessa was trying to undo his belt. He caught her hands tightly, ignoring her gasp as his grip hurt.

"Where was Thread seen?" he yelled up to the Igen rider still perched atop the Gate Wall.

"South!" The man's response was an anguished appeal. "Across the bay from Keroon Hold. Across the water."

"How *long* ago?"

"I'll take you there and then!"

The ripple of cheering grew as it spread back, as people were reminded that the Weyrs would go *between* time itself and catch Thread, erasing the interval of time lost in the duel.

Dragonriders were moving toward beasts who were impatiently keening outside the walls. Wher-hide tunics were being thrust at riders in dress clothes. Firestone sacks appeared and flame throwers were issued. Dragons ducked to accept riders, hopping awkwardly out of the way, to launch themselves skyward. The Igen green hovered aloft, joined by D'ram and his Weyrwoman Fanna, waiting for Mnementh.

"You can't come, love," F'lar told Lessa, confused that she

was following him out to Mnementh. She could handle Mardra. She'd have to. He couldn't be everywhere at once.

"Not till you've had this numbweed." She glared up at him as fiercely as Marda had and fumbled at his belt again. "You won't last if you don't. And Mnementh won't take you up until I do."

F'lar stared at her, saw Mnementh's great eye gleaming at him and knew she meant it.

"But—he wouldn't—" he stammered.

"Oh, wouldn't he?" flashed Lessa, but she had the belt loose, and he gasped as he felt the cold of the salve on the burning lips of the wound. "I can't keep you from going. You've got to, I know. But I can keep you from killing yourself with such heroics." He heard something rip, saw her tearing a sleeve from her new gown into bandage-length strips. "Well, I guess they're right when they say green is an unlucky color. You certainly don't get to wear it long."

She quickly pressed the material against him, his wound already numbing. Deftly overlapping the outsized tunic, she tightened the wide belt to hold the bandage securely in place.

"Now, go. It's shallow but long. Get the Threadfall under control and get back. I'll do my part here." She gave his hand a final grip and, picking up her skirts, half-ran up the ramp, as if she were too busy to watch him leave.

She's worried. She's proud. Let's go.

As Mnementh wheeled smartly upward, F'lar heard the sound of music, gitars accompanying a ragged chorus. How like the Harper to have the appropriate music for this occasion, he thought.

> Drummer, beat, and piper, blow.
> Harper, strike, and soldier, go.
> Free the flame and sear the grasses
> Till the dawning Red Star passes.

Odd, thought F'lar, four hours later, as he and Mnementh returned to Telgar with the wings from Igen, it was over Telgar, seven Turns ago, that the massed Weyrs flew against the second Fall of Thread.

He stifled keen regret at the recollection of that triumphant day when the six Weyrs had been solidly in accord. And yet, the duel at Telgar Hold today had been as inevitable as Lessa's flight backward in time to bring up the Oldtimers. There was a subtle symmetry, a balance of good and bad, a fateful compensation. (His side ached. He suppressed pain and fatigue. Mnementh would catch it and then he'd catch it from Lessa. Fine thing when a man's dragon acted nursy. But the effects of that half-kettle of numbweed Lessa'd slathered on him was wearing off.) He watched as the wings circled to land. All the riders had been bidden back to Telgar.

So many things were coming back to their starting point: from fire lizards to dragons, a circle encompassing who knows how many thousands of Turns, to the inner circle of the Old Weyrs and Benden's resurgence.

He hoped T'ron would live; he'd enough on his conscience. Though it might be better if T'ron . . . He refused to consider that, in spite of the fact that he knew it would avoid another problem. And yet, if Thread could fall in Southern to be eaten by those grubs . . .

He wanted very much to see that distance-viewer T'ron had discovered. He groaned with a mental distress. Fandarel! How could he face him? That distance-writer *had* worked. It had relayed a very crucial message—faster than dragon wings! No fault of the Smith's that his finely extruded wire could be severed by hot Thread. Undoubtedly he would overcome that flaw in an efficient way—unless he'd thrown up his hands at the idea, what with being presented with a powerful, fully operative distance-viewer to compound the day's insults. Of all the problems undoubtedly awaiting him, he dreaded Fandarel's reproach the most.

Below, dragonriders streamed into the Court illumined by hundreds of glow baskets, to be met and absorbed into the throng of guests. The aroma of roasted meats and succulent vegetables drifted to him on the night air, reminding him that hunger depresses any man's spirits. He could hear laughter, shouts, music. Lord Asgenar's wedding day would never be forgotten!

That Asgenar! Allied to Larad, a fosterling of Corman's, he'd be of enormous assistance in executing what F'lar saw must be done among the Holder Lords.

Then he spotted the tiny figure in the gateway. Lessa! He told Mnementh to land.

About time, the bronze grumbled.

F'lar slapped his neck affectionately. The beast had known perfectly well why they'd been hovering. A man needed a few minutes to digest chaos and restore order to his thinking before he plunged into more confusions.

Mnementh agreed as he landed smoothly. He craned his neck around, his great eyes gleaming affectionately at his rider.

"Don't worry about me, Mnementh!" F'lar murmured in gratitude and love, stroking the soft muzzle. There was a faint odor of firestone and smoke though they'd done little flaming. "Are you hungry?"

Not yet. Telgar feeds enough tonight. Mnementh launched himself toward the fire ridge above the Hold, where the perching dragons made black, regular crags against the darkening sky, their jeweled eyes gleaming down on the festal activities.

F'lar laughed aloud at Mnementh's consideration. It was true that Lord Larad was stinting nothing, though his guest list had multiplied four-fold. Supplies had been flown in but Telgar Hold bore the brunt of it.

Lessa approached him with such slow steps that he wondered if something else had happened. He couldn't see her face in the shadow but as she slipped into step beside him, he realized that she'd been respecting his mood. Her hand reached up to caress his cheek, lingering on the healing Thread score. She wouldn't let him bend to kiss her.

"Come, love, I've fresh clothes and bandages for you."

"Mnementh's been telling on me?"

She nodded, still unusually subdued for Lessa.

"What's wrong?"

"Nothing," she assured him hastily, smiling. "Ramoth said you were thinking hard."

He squeezed her and the gesture pulled the muscles, making him wince.

"You're a trial to me," she said with mock exasperation and led him into the tower room.

"Kylara came back, didn't she?"

"Oh, yes," and there was an edge to Lessa's voice as she added, "she and Meron are as inseparable as their lizards."

She'd had a standing tub brought in, the water steaming invitingly. She insisted on bathing him while she reported what had happened while he'd fought Thread. He didn't argue, it was too pleasant to relax under her ministrations, though her gentle hands sometimes reminded him of other occasions and . . .

T'ron had been taken directly to Southern, swathed in heavy felt. Mardra had contested F'lar's authority to exile them but her protests fell on the deaf and determined front of Robinton, Larad, Fandarel, Lords Sangel and Groghe. They'd all accompanied Lessa and Kylara when Mardra was escorted back to Fort. Mardra had been certain she'd only to appeal to her weyrfolk to ensure her position as Weyrwoman. When she discovered that her arrogance and shrewishness had robbed her of all but a few adherents, she'd retired meekly to Southern with them.

"We nearly had a fight between Kylara and Mardra but Robinton intervened. Kylara was proclaiming herself Fort Weyrwoman."

F'lar groaned.

"Don't worry," Lessa assured him, briskly kneading the tight muscles across his shoulders. "She changed her mind directly she learned that T'kul and his riders were leaving the High Reaches Weyr. It's more logical for T'bor and the Southerners to take over that Weyr than Fort since most of the Fort riders are staying."

"That puts Kylara too near Nabol for my peace of mind."

"Yes, but that leaves the way clear for P'zar, Roth's rider, to take over as Fort Weyrleader. He's not strong but he's well-liked and it won't upset the Fort people as much. They're relieved to be free of both T'ron and Mardra but we oughtn't to press our luck too far."

"N'ton'd be a good Wing-second there."

"I thought of him so I asked P'zar if he'd object and he didn't."

F'lar shook his head at her tactics, then hissed, because she was loosening the old, dried numbweed.

"I'm not so sure but what I'd prefer the physician—" she began.

"No!"

"He'd be discreet but I'll warn you, all the dragons know."

He stared at her in surprise. "I thought it odd there were so many dragons shadowing me and Mnementh. I don't think we went *between* more than twice."

"The dragons appreciate you, bronze rider," Lessa said tartly, encircling him with clean, soft bandages.

"The Oldtimers, too?"

"Most of them. And more of their riders than I'd estimated. Only twenty riders and women followed Mardra, you know, from Fort. Of course," and she grimaced, "most of T'kul's people went. The fourteen who stayed are young riders, Impressed since the Weyr came forward. So there'll be enough at Southern . . ."

"Southern is no longer our concern."

She was in the act of handing him the fresh tunic and hesitated, the fabric gathered up in her hands. He took it from her, pulling on the sleeves, ducking his head into the opening, giving her time to absorb his dictum.

She sat slowly down on the bench, her forehead creased with a slight, worried frown.

He took her hands and kissed them. When she still did not speak, he stroked the hair which had escaped the braids.

"We have to make the break clean, Lessa. They can do no harm there to any but themselves. Some may decide to come back."

"But they can perpetuate their grievances . . ."

"Lessa, how many queens went?"

"Loranth, the Weyr queen at High Reaches and the other two . . . Oh!"

"Yes. All old queens, well past their prime. I doubt Loranth will rise more than once. The clutches at High Reaches have produced only one queen since they came forward. And the young queen, Segrith, stayed, didn't she, with Pilgra?"

Lessa nodded and suddenly her face cleared. She eyed him with growing exasperation. "Anyone would think you've been planning this for Turns."

"Then anyone could call me a triple fool for underestimating T'ron, closing my mind to the facts in front of me and defying fortune. What's the mood among Holders and crafters?"

"Relief," she said, rolling her eyes. "I admit the laughter has a slightly hysterical tinge, but Lytol and Robinton were right. Pern will follow Benden . . ."

"Yes, until my first mistake!"

She grinned mischievously at him, waggling a finger under his nose. "Ah-ha, but you're not allowed to make mistakes, Benden. Not while . . ."

He caught her hand, pulling her into the crook of his arm, disregarding the stabbing pain at his waist for the triumph of her instant response, the surrender in her slender body. "Not while I have *you*." The words came out in a whisper, and because he couldn't express his gratitude to her, his pride in her, his joy of her any other way, he sought her lips, held them in a long, passionate kiss.

She gave a languorous sigh when he finally released her. He laughed down at her closed eyes, kissing them, too. She struggled to a sitting position and, with another reluctant sigh, rose determinedly to her feet.

"Yes, Pern will follow you, and your loyal advisers will keep you from making mistakes, but I do hope you've an answer for pop-eyed old Lord Groghe!"

"Answer for Groghe?"

"Yes," and she gave him a stern look, "though I'm not surprised you've forgotten. He was going to demand that the dragonmen of Pern go directly to the Red Star and put an end to Thread forever."

F'lar got slowly to his feet.

"I've always said that you solve one problem and five more appear from *between*."

"Well, I think we've contrived to keep Groghe away from you tonight, but we promised to have a joint meeting of Hold and Craft at Benden Weyr tomorrow morning."

"That's a blessing."

In the act of opening the door, he hesitated and groaned again.

"Isn't the numbweed helping?"

"Not me. It's Fandarel. Between fire lizards, Threads and T'ron, I can't face him."

"Oh, him!" Lessa pulled the door open, grinning up at her Weyrmate. "He's already deep in plans to bury, coat or thicken those ungrateful wires. He's planning installations with every Lord Holder and Craft. Wansor's dancing like a sun-crazed wherry to get his hands on the distance-viewer, all the time wailing that he needn't've dismantled the first apparatus." She tucked her arm in his, lengthening her stride to match his. "The man who's really put out is Robinton."

"Robinton?"

"Yes. He'd composed the most marvelous ballad and teaching songs and now there's no reason to play them."

Whether Lessa had deliberately saved that until now, F'lar didn't know, but they crossed the courtyard, laughing, though it hurt his side.

Their passage would have been noted anyhow, but their smiling faces subtly reassured the diners seated at the make-shift tables about the yard. And suddenly F'lar felt there was indeed something to celebrate.

CHAPTER XI

Early Morning at Benden Weyr

"I wish you'd give me fair warning the next time you rearrange the social and political structure of this planet," F'nor told his half-brother when he strode into the queen's weyr at Benden the next morning. There wasn't, of course, a trace of resentment on his tanned, grinning face. "Who's where now?"

"T'bor is Weyrleader at the High Reaches with Kylara as Weyrwoman . . ."

"Kylara at High Reaches?" F'nor looked dubious but F'lar waved aside his half-born protest.

"Yes, there are disadvantages to that, of course. All but fourteen of the folk at High Reaches Weyr went with T'kul and Merika. Most of the Fort Weyr people wanted to stay . . ."

F'nor chuckled nastily. "Bet that was hard for Mardra to swallow." He looked expectantly at Lessa, knowing how often his Weyrwoman had mastered resentment and indignation at Mardra's hands. Lessa returned his gaze with polite unconcern.

"So P'zar is acting Weyrleader until a queen rises . . ."

"Any chance of making that an open flight for any bronze?"

"That is my intention," F'lar replied. "However, I think the biggest of the modern bronzes had better be conspicuous by their absence."

"Then why have you assigned N'ton there as Wing-second?" demanded Lessa in surprise.

F'lar grinned at his Weyrmate. "Because by the time a Fort queen rises in flight, N'ton will be known and well-liked by the Fort Weyrfolk and they won't mind. He'll be considered a Fort rider, not a Benden replacement."

Lessa wrinkled her nose. *"He* doesn't have much choice at Fort Weyr."

"He is quite capable of taking care of himself," F'lar replied with a wicked grin.

"Well, you seem to have arranged everything to your satisfaction," F'nor remarked. "I, however, resent having been yanked out of Southern. I'd spotted a very promising clutch of fire-lizard eggs in a certain Southern cove. Not quite hard enough to move with impunity. If you had held off a few more days, I'd—" He broke off, sliding into the chair Lessa motioned him to. "Say, F'lar, what's the matter with you? You been time-*betweening* or something?"

"No, he's been knifed between his top and bottom," Lessa answered with a sour glance at her Weyrmate. "And it is with exceptional difficulty that I can keep him in a chair. He belongs in a bed."

F'lar waved her recriminations aside good-humoredly.

"If you're—" F'nor half-rose, his face concerned.

"If you're—" mocked F'lar, his look indicating a growing irritation with his disability and their protectiveness.

F'nor laughed, reseating himself. "And Brekke said I was a cantankerous patient. Ha! How bad is it? I heard various tales about that duel, well embroidered already, but not that you'd been clipped. Must it always be belt knives—for our Blood? And the other man armed with a wherry-skewer?"

"And dressed in wher-hide," Lessa added.

"Look, F'lar, Brekke has pronounced me fit to fly *between*," and F'nor flexed his arm, fully but carefully. "I can appreciate your wanting to keep quiet about your injury, so I'll do all your popping about."

F'lar chuckled at his half-brother's eagerness. "Back a-neck and ready to go, huh? Well, resume your responsibilities then. They've changed."

"Noticeably, o exalted one."

F'lar frowned at that and brushed his forelock back irritably.

"Not that much. Did you see T'kul when he arrived from High Reaches at Southern?"

"No, nor did I want to. I *heard* him." F'nor's right hand clenched. "The fighting wings had already gone to join you at Igen for the Threadfall. T'kul ordered everyone, including the wounded, out of Southern in an hour's time. What they couldn't pack and take, he confiscated. He made it clear that the southern continent was his to have and hold. That his sweepriders were challenging any dragon and would flame them down like Thread if they didn't get the proper response. Some of those Oldtimer dragons are stupid enough to do it, too." F'nor paused. "You know, I've been noticing lately . . ."

"Did the Fort Weyr people arrive?"

"Yes, and Brekke checked T'ron to be sure he'd survived the trip." F'nor scowled.

"He'll live?"

"Yes, but . . ."

"Good. Now, I rather suspected that T'kul would react in that fashion. To be sure we've all of Igen, Ista and Southern Boll as breeding ground for fire lizards, but I want you to get Manora to rig you something for those other lizard eggs you found and bring them back here. We need every one we can find. Where's your little queen? They go back to their first feeding place, you know . . ."

"Grall? She's with Canth, of course. She heard Ramoth grumbling on the Hatching Ground."

"Hmm, yes. Fortunately, those eggs'll hatch soon."

"Going to invite all Pern's notables as you did before the Oldtimers got stuffy?"

"Yes," F'lar replied so emphatically that F'nor pretended alarm. "That courtesy did more good than harm. It'll be standard procedure at all the Weyrs now."

"And you've talked the Leaders into assigning riders to Hold and Hall?" F'nor's eyes gleamed when F'lar nodded.

"Can you slip through whatever patrol T'kul has mounted in Southern?" F'lar asked.

"No problem. There isn't a bronze there that Canth can't outfly. Which reminds me . . ."

"Good. I've two errands for you. Pick up those fire-lizard eggs and, do you remember the coordinates for the Threadfall in the western swamp?"

"Of course, but I wanted to ask you . . ."

"You saw the grub life in the soil there?"

"Yes . . ."

"Ask Manora for a tightly covered pot. I want you to bring me back as many of those grubs as you can. Not a pleasant job, I know, but I can't go myself and I don't want this—ah—project discussed."

"Grubs? A project?"

Mnementh bellowed a welcome.

"I'll explain later," F'lar said, gesturing toward the weyr entrance.

F'nor shrugged as he rose. "I'll fly the hazard, o inscrutable one!" Then he laughed as F'lar glared at him in angry reproach. "Sorry. Like the rest of Pern—the north, that is—I trust you." He gave them both a jaunty salute and left.

"The day F'nor doesn't tease you I'll start to worry," Lessa said, encircling his neck with her arms. She laid her cheek against his for an instant. "It's T'bor," she added, moving away just as the new High Reaches Weyrleader strode in.

The man looked as if he hadn't slept enough but he carried his shoulders back and his head high which made the the Benden Weyrleader more aware of the worried and wary expression on his face.

"Kylara's—" F'lar began, remembering that she and Meron had been gabbling together all last night.

"Not Kylara. It's that T'kul who thought himself such a great Weyrleader," T'bor said with utter disgust. "As soon as we brought our people up from Southern, I had the wings do a sweep check, really more to familiarize themselves with the coordinates than anything else. By the first Egg, I don't like seeing anyone run from dragonmen. Run. And hide!" T'bor sat down, automatically taking the cup of *klah* Lessa handed him. "There wasn't a watch fire or a watchman. But plenty of burn sign. I don't see how that much Thread could have got through. Not even if smokeless weyrlings were riding the sweep. So I dropped down to Tillek Hold and asked to see Lord Oterel." T'bor gave a low whistle. "That was some greeting I got, I want to tell you. I nearly had an arrow through my belly before I convinced the guard captain that I wasn't T'kul. That I was T'bor and there'd been a change of Leaders at the Weyr."

T'bor took a deep breath. "It took time to calm Lord Holder Oterel down to the point where I could tell him what had happened. And it seemed to me," and the Southerner looked nervously first at Lessa and then at F'lar, "that the only way to restore his confidence was to leave him a dragon. So—I left him a bronze and stationed two greens in those minor Holds along the Bay. I also left weyrlings at vantage heights along the Tillek Hold range. Then I asked Lord Oterel to accompany me to Lord Bargen's Hold at High Reaches. I'd a good idea I might not get past *his* guard at all. Now, we'd six eggs left over from that clutch Toric of the Seahold unearthed and so—I gave two each to the Lords and two to the Master-fisherman. It seemed the only thing to do. They'd heard Lord Meron had one—at Nabol Hold." T'bor straightened his shoulders as if to endure F'lar's opprobrium.

"You did the right thing, T'bor," F'lar told him heartily. "You did exactly the right thing. You couldn't have done better!"

"To assign riders to a Hold and a Craft?"

"There'll be riders in all Holds and Crafts before the morning's over," F'lar grinned at him.

"And D'ram and G'narish haven't objected?" T'bor glanced at Lessa, incredulous.

"Well," Lessa began, and was saved from answering by the arrival of the other Weyrleaders.

D'ram, G'narish and the Wing-second from Telgar Weyr entered first, with P'zar, the acting Weyrleader from Fort, very close behind them. The Telgar Weyr Wing-second introduced himself as M'rek, Zigeth's rider. He was a lanky, mournful-looking man, with sandy hair, about F'lar's age. As they settled themselves at the big table, F'lar tried to read D'ram's mood. He was the crucial one still, the oldest of the remaining Oldtimers and, if he'd cooled down from the stimulus of yesterday's tumultous events and had changed his mind after sleeping, the proposal F'lar was about to suggest might die a-hatching. F'lar stretched his long legs under the table, trying to make himself comfortable.

"I asked you here early because we had little chance to talk last night. M'rek, how's R'mart?"

"He rests easily at Telgar Hold, thanks to the riders from Ista and Igen." M'rek nodded gravely to D'ram and K'dor.

"How many at Telgar Weyr wish to go south?"

"About ten, but they're old riders. Do more harm than good, feeding nonsense to the weyrlings. Speaking of nonsense, Bedella came back from Telgar Hold with some mighty confusing stories. About us going to the Red Star and fire lizards and talking wires. I told her to keep quiet. Telgar Weyr's in no shape to listen to that kind of rumor."

D'ram snorted and F'lar looked at him quickly, but the Istan leader's head was turned toward M'rek. F'lar caught Lessa's eye and nodded imperceptibly.

"There *was* talk about an expedition to the Red Star," F'lar replied in a casual tone. Apprehension made the Telgar Weyr man's face more mournful than ever. "But there're more immediate undertakings." F'lar straightened cautiously. He couldn't get comfortable. "And the Lord Holders and other craftsmen will be here soon to discuss them. D'ram, tell me frankly, do you object to placing riders in Holds and Crafthalls while we can't pattern Thread—that is, until we can find another reliable form of quick communication?"

"No, F'lar, I've no objections," the Istan Weyrleader replied, slowly, not looking at anyone. "After yesterday—" He stopped and, turning his head, looked at F'lar with troubled eyes. "Yesterday, I think I finally realized just how big Pern is and how narrow a man can get, worrying so much about what he ought to have, forgetting what he's got. And what he's got to do. Times have changed. I can't say I like it. Pern had got so big—and we Oldtimers kept trying to make it small again because, I guess, we were a little scared at all that had happened. Remember it took us just four days to come forward four hundred Turns. That's too much time—too much to sink into a man's thinking." D'ram was nodding his head in unconscious emphasis. "I think we've clung to the old ways because everything we saw, from those great, huge hour-long sweeps of forests to hundreds and hundreds of new Holds and Crafthalls was familiar and yet—so different. T'ron was a good man, F'lar. I don't say I knew him well. None of us ever really got to know each other, you know, keeping to our Weyrs mostly and resting between Threadfalls. But all dragonmen are—are dragonmen. For a dragonman to go to *kill* another one—" D'ram shook his head slowly from side to side. "You could've killed *him*." D'ram looked F'lar straight in the eye. "You didn't. You fought Thread over Igen Hold. And don't think I didn't know T'ron's knife got you."

F'lar began to relax.

"Nearly made two of me, in fact."

D'ram gave another one of his snorts but the slight smile on his face as he leaned back in his chair indicated his approval of F'lar.

Mnementh remarked to his rider that everyone was arriving at once. A bigger ledge was needed. F'lar swore softly to himself. He'd counted on more time. He couldn't jeopardize the fragile new accord with D'ram by springing distasteful innovations on the man.

"I don't believe the Weyrs can remain autonomous these days," F'lar said, discarding all the ringing, smooth words he'd been rehearsing. "We nearly lost Pern seven Turns ago because dragonmen lost touch with the rest of the world; we've seen what happens when dragonman loses touch with dragonman. We need open mating flights, the exchange of bronzes and queens between Weyrs to strengthen Blood and improve the breed. We need to rotate the wings so riders get to know each other's Weyrs and territories. A man grows stale, careless, riding over ground he knows too well. We need public Impressions . . ."

They could all hear the rumble of greetings and the scuffling of heavy boots in the corridor.

"Ista Weyr followed Benden Weyr yesterday," D'ram interrupted him, his slow smile reaching his dark eyes. "But have a care which traditions you overset. Some cannot be discarded with impunity . . ."

They rose then as Lord Holders and Craftmasters strode into the weyr. Lord Asgenar, Mastersmith Fandarel and his wood Craftmaster, Bendarek, were first; Lord Oterel of Tillek Hold and Meron, Lord Holder of Nabol, his fire lizard squawking on his arm, arrived together, but Lord Oterel immediately sought Fandarel. A restless, eager atmosphere began to build, palpable with questions unanswered the previous evening. As soon as most were assembled, F'lar led the way into the Council Room. No sooner had the Weyrleaders ranged themselves behind him, facing the gathering of Lords and Craftsmen, than Larad, Lord of Telgar Hold, rose.

"Weyrleader, have you established where the next Thread is likely to fall?"

"Where you've evidently placed it, Lord Larad, on the western plains of Telgar Hold and Ruatha Hold." F'lar nodded toward Lord Warder Lytol of Ruatha. "Probably later today. It's early hours now in that part of the country and we don't intend to hold you here long . . ."

"And how long will we have riders assigned us?" asked Lord Corman of Keroon, staring pointedly at D'ram on F'lar's left.

"Until every Hold and Craft has an efficient communications system."

"I'll need men," Mastersmith Fandarel rumbled from his cramped position in the far corner. "Do you all really want those flame throwers you've been plaguing me for?"

"Not if the dragonmen *come* when we call." It was Lord Sangel of Boll Hold who answered, his face grim, his voice bitter.

"Is Telgar Weyr prepared to ride today?" Lord Larad went on, still holding the floor.

M'rek, the Telgar Weyr Wing-second, rose, glanced hesitantly at F'lar, cleared his throat and then nodded.

"High Reaches Weyr will fly with Telgar riders!" T'bor said.

"And Ista!" D'ram added.

The unexpected unanimity sent a murmurous ripple through the meeting, as Lord Larad sat down.

"Will we have to burn the forests?" Lord Asgenar of Lemos rose to his feet. The quiet question was the plea of a proud man.

"Dragonriders burn Thread, not wood," F'lar replied calmly but there was a ring in his voice. "There are enough dragonriders," and he gestured to the Weyrleaders on either side of him, "to protect Pern's forests . . ."

"That's not what's needed most, Benden, and you know it," Lord Groghe of Fort shouted as he rose to his feet, his eyes bulging. "I say, go after Thread on the Red Star itself. Enough time's been wasted. You keep saying your dragons'll go anywhere, anywhen you tell 'em to."

"A dragon's got to know where he's going first, man," G'narish, the Igen Leader, protested, jumping up excitedly.

"Don't put me off, young man! You can *see* the Red Star,

plain as my fist," and Lord Groghe thrust out his closed hand
like a weapon, "in that distance-viewer! Go to the source. Go
to the source!"

D'ram was on his feet beside G'narish now, adding his
angry arguments to the confusion. A dragon roared so loudly
that all were deafened for a moment.

"If that is the desire of the Lords and Craftsmen," F'lar said,
"then we shall mount an expedition to fly on the morrow." He
knew D'ram and G'narish had turned to stare at him, dumb-
founded. He saw Lord Groghe bristle suspiciously, but he had
the attention of the entire room. He spoke quickly, clearly.
"You've seen the Red Star, Lord Groghe? Could you describe
the land masses to me? Would you estimate that we had to
clear as large an area as, say, the northern continent? D'ram,
would you agree that it takes about thirty-six hours to fly
straight across? More? Hmmm. Tip-to-tip sweeps would be
most effective since we couldn't count on ground-crew support.
That would mean dragonweights of firestone. Masterminer,
I'll need to know exactly what supplies you have processed
for use. Benden Weyr keeps about five dragonweights on hand
at all times, the other Weyrs about the same, so
we'd probably need all you've got. And every flame thrower
on the continent. Now, dragonmen, I admit we don't know
if we can traverse such a distance without harm to ourselves
and the dragons. I assume that since Thread survives on this
planet, we can exist on that one. However . . ."

"Enough!" Groghe of Fort Hold bellowed, his face flushed,
his eyes protruding from their sockets.

F'lar met Groghe's eyes steadily so that the choleric Lord
Holder would realize that he was not being mocked; that F'lar
was in earnest.

"To be at all effective, Lord Groghe, such an undertaking
would leave Pern totally unprotected. I could not in conscience
order such an expedition now that I see how much is involved.
I hope you will agree that it is far more important, at this
time, to secure what we have." Better to risk Groghe's pride if
necessary to defeat that premature ambition. He couldn't
afford to evade an issue that could become a convenient
rallying cry for the disaffected. "I'd want to get a good look
at the Red Star before I took such a leap, Lord Groghe.
And the other Leaders would too. I can promise you that
once we are able to distinguish some jumping coordinates

acceptable to the dragons, we can send a volunteer group to explore. I've often wondered why no one has gone before now. Or, if they have, what happened." He had dropped his voice on those last words and there wasn't a sound in the Chamber for a long moment.

The fire lizard on Lord Meron's arm squawked nervously, causing an instant, violent reaction from every man.

"Probably that Record deteriorated, too," F'lar said, raising his voice to a level audible above the restless scraping and throat-clearing. "Lord Groghe, Fort is the oldest of the Holds. Is there a chance that your back corridors, too, hide treasures we can use?"

Groghe's reply was a curt nod of his head. He seated himself abruptly, staring straight ahead. F'lar wondered if he had alienated the man beyond reconciliation.

"I don't think I'd ever fully appreciated the enormity of such a venture," Corman of Keroon Hold remarked in a thoughtful drawl.

"One jump ahead of us, again, Benden?" asked Larad of Telgar Hold with a rueful grin.

"I shouldn't say that, Lord Larad," F'lar replied. "The destruction of all Thread at its source has been a favorite preoccupation of dragonmen Turn after Turn. I know how much territory one Weyr can cover, for instance; how much firestone is used by a Weyr in a Fall's span. Naturally we," and he gestured to the other Leaders, "would have information unavailable to you just as you could tell *us* how many guests you can feed at a banquet." That elicited a chuckle from many.

"Seven Turns ago, I called you together to prepare to defend Pern against its ancient scourge. Desperate measures were in order if we were to survive. We are in nowhere as difficult a condition as we were seven Turns ago but we have all been guilty of misunderstandings which have deflected us from the important concern. We have no time to waste in assigning guilt or awarding compensation. We are still at the mercy of Thread though we are better equipped to deal with it.

"Once before we found answers in old Records, in the helpful recollections of Masterweaver Zurg, Masterfarmer Andemon, Masterharper Robinton, and the efficiencies of Mastersmith Fandarel. You know what we've found in abandoned rooms at Benden and Fort Weyrs—objects made long Turns ago when we had not lost certain skills and techniques.

"Frankly," and F'lar grinned suddenly, "I'd rather rely on skills and techniques we, in our Turn, right now, can develop."

There was an unexpected ripple of assent to that.

"I speak of the skill of working together, the technique of crossing the arbitrary lines of land, craft and status, because we must learn more from each other than the simple fact that none of us can stand alone and survive!"

He couldn't go on because half the men were on their feet, suddenly cheering. D'ram was pulling at his sleeve, G'narish was arguing with the Telgar Weyr Second, whose expression was grievously undecided. F'lar got a glimpse of Groghe's face before someone stood in the way. Fort's Lord, too, was plainly anxious but that was better than overt antagonism. Robinton caught his eye and smiled broad encouragement. So F'lar had no choice but to let them unwind. They might as well infect each other with enthusiasm—probably with more effect than his best-chosen arguments. He looked around for Lessa and saw her slipping toward the hallway where she stopped, evidently warned of a late arrival.

It was F'nor who appeared in the entrance.

"I've fire-lizard eggs," he shouted. "Fire-lizard eggs," and he pushed into the room, an aisle opening for him straight to the Council Table.

There was silence as he carefully placed his cumbersome felt-wrapped burden down and glanced triumphantly around the room.

"Stolen from under T'kul's nose. Thirty-two of them!"

"Well, Benden," Sangel of Southern Boll demanded in the taut hush, "who gets preference here?"

F'lar affected surprise. "Why, Lord Sangel, that is for you," and his gesture swept the room impartially, "to decide."

Clearly that had not been expected.

"We will, of course, teach you what we know of them, guide you in their training. They are more than pets or ornaments," and he nodded toward Meron who bristled, so suspicious of attention that his bronze hissed and restlessly fanned his wings. "Lord Asgenar, you've two lizard eggs already. I can trust you to be impartial. That is, if the Lords share my opinion."

As soon as they fell to arguing, F'lar left the Council Room. There was so much more to do this morning but he'd do it the better for a little break. And the eggs would occupy the Lords and Craftsmen. They wouldn't notice his absence.

CHAPTER XII

Morning at Benden Weyr
Predawn at High Reaches Weyr

As soon as he could, F'nor left the Council Room in
search of F'lar. He retrieved the pot of revolting grubs which
he'd left in a shadowed recess of the weyr corridor.

He's in his quarters, Canth told his rider.

"What does Mnementh say of F'lar?"

There was a pause and F'nor found himself wondering if
dragons spoke among themselves as men spoke to them.

Mnementh is not worried about him.

F'nor caught the faintest emphasis on the pronoun and was
about to question Canth further when little Grall swooped, on
whirring wings, to his shoulder. She wrapped her tail around
his neck and rubbed against his cheek adoringly.

"Getting braver, little one?" F'nor added approving thoughts
to the humor of his voice.

There was a suggestion of smug satisfaction about Grall
as she flipped her wings tightly to her back and sunk her

223

talons into the heavy padding Brekke had attached to the left tunic shoulder for that purpose. The lizards preferred a shoulder to a forearm perch.

F'lar emerged from the sleeping room, his face lighting with eagerness as he realized F'nor was alone and awaiting him.

"You've the grubs? Good. Come."

"Now, wait a minute," F'nor protested, catching F'lar by the shoulder as the Weyrleader began to move toward the outer ledge.

"Come! Before we're seen." They got down the stairs without being intercepted and F'lar directed F'nor toward the newly opened entrance by the Hatching Ground. "The lizards were parceled out fairly?" he asked, grinning as Grall tucked herself as close to F'nor's ear as she could when they passed the Ground entrance.

F'nor chuckled. "Groghe took over, as you probably guessed he would. The Lord Holders of Ista and Igen, Warbret and Laudey, magnanimously disqualified themselves on the grounds that their Holds were more likely to have eggs, but Lord Sangel of Boll took a pair. Lytol didn't!"

F'lar sighed, shaking his head regretfully.

"I didn't think he would but I'd hoped he'd try. Not a substitute for Larth, his dead brown, but—well . . ."

They were in the brightly lit, newly cleaned corridor now, which F'nor hadn't seen. Involuntarily he glanced to the right, grinning as he saw that any access to the old peephole on the Grounds had been blocked off.

"That's mean."

"Huh?" F'lar looked startled. "Oh, that. Yes. Lessa said it upset Ramoth too much. And Mnementh agreed." He gave his half-brother a bemused grin, half for Lessa's quirk, half for the mutual nostalgic memory of their own terror-ridden exploration of that passage, and a clandestine glimpse of Nemorth's eggs. "There's a chamber back here that suits my purpose . . ."

"Which is?"

F'lar hesitated, giving F'nor a long, thoughtful look.

"Since when have you found me a reluctant conspirator?" asked F'nor.

"It's asking more than . . ."

"Ask first!"

They had reached the first room of the complex discovered by Jaxom and Felessan. But the bronze rider did not give F'nor time to examine the fascinating design on the wall or the finely made cabinets and tables. He hurried him past the second room to the biggest chamber where a series of graduated, rectangular open stone troughs were set around the floor. Other equipment had obviously been removed at some ancient time, leaving puzzling holes and grooves in the walls, but F'nor was startled to see that the tubs were planted with shrubs, grasses, common field and crop seedlings. A few small hardwood trees were evident in the largest troughs.

F'lar gestured for the grub pot which F'nor willingly handed over.

"Now, I'm going to put some of these grubs in all but this container," F'lar said, indicating the medium-sized one. Then he started to distribute the squirming grubs.

"Proving what?"

F'lar gave him a long deep look so reminiscent of the days when they had dared each other as weyrlings that F'nor couldn't help grinning.

"Proving what?" he insisted.

"Proving first, that these southern grubs will prosper in northern soil among northern plants . . ."

"And . . ."

"That they will eliminate Thread here as they did in the western swamp."

They both watched, in a sort of revolted fascination, as the wriggling gray mass of grubs broke apart and separately burrowed into the loose dark soil of the biggest tub.

"What?"

F'nor experienced a devastating disorientation. He saw F'lar as a weyrling, challenging him to explore and find the legendary peekhole to the Ground. He saw F'lar again, older, in the Records Room, surrounded by moldering skins, suggesting that they jump *between* time itself to stop Thread at Nerat. And he imagined himself suggesting to F'lar to support *him* when he let Canth fly Brekke's Wirenth . . .

"But we didn't see Thread do anything," he said, getting a grip on perspective and time.

"What else could have happened to Thread in those swamps? You know as surely as we're standing here that it was a four-hour Fall. And we fought only two. You saw the scoring. You saw the activity of the grubs. And I'll bet you had a hard time finding enough to fill that pot because they only rise to the surface when Thread falls. In fact, you can go back in time and see it happen."

F'nor grimaced, remembering that it had taken a long time to find enough grubs. It'd been a strain, too, with every nerve of man, dragon and lizard alert for a sign of T'kul's patrols. "I should have thought of that myself. But—Thread's not going to fall over Benden . . ."

"You'll be at Telgar and Ruatha Holds this afternoon when the Fall starts. This time, you'll *catch* some Thread."

If there had not been an ironical, humorous gleam in his half-brother's eyes, F'nor would have thought him delirious.

"Doubtless," F'nor said acidly, "you've figured out exactly how I'm to achieve this."

F'lar brushed the hair back from his forehead.

"Well, I am open to suggestion . . ."

"That's considerate, since it's my hand that's to be scored . . ."

"You've got Canth, and Grall to help . . ."

"If they're mad enough . . ."

"Mnementh explained it all to Canth . . ."

"That's helpful . . ."

"I wouldn't ask you to do it if I could myself!" And F'lar's patience snapped.

"I know!" F'nor replied with equal force, and then grinned because he knew he'd do it.

"All right." F'lar grinned in acknowledgment. "Fly low altitude near the queens. Watch for a good thick patch. Follow it down. Canth's skillful enough to let you get close with one of those long-handled hearthpans. And Grall can wipe out any Thread which burrows. I can't think of any other way to get some. Unless, of course, we were flying over one of the stone plateaus, but even then . . ."

"All right, let us assume I can catch some live, viable Thread," and the brown rider could not suppress the tremor that shook him, "and let us assume that the grubs do—dispose of them. What then?"

With a ghost of a smile on his lips, F'lar spread his arms wide. "Why then, son of my father, we breed us hungry grubs by the tankful and spread them over Pern."

F'nor jammed both fists into his belt. The man was feverish.

"No, I'm not feverish, F'nor," the bronze rider replied, settling himself on the edge of the nearest tank. "But if we *could* have this kind of protection," and he picked up the now empty pot, turning it back and forth in his hand as if it held the sum of his theory, "Thread could fall when and where it wanted to without creating the kind of havoc and revolution we're going through.

"Mind you, there's nothing remotely hinting at such events in any of the Harper Records. Yet I've been asking myself *why* it has taken us so long to spread out across this continent. In the thousands of Turns, given the rate of increase in population over the last four hundred, *why* aren't there more people? And why, F'nor, has no one tried to reach that Red Star before, if it is only just another kind of jump for a dragon?"

"Lessa told me about Lord Groghe's demand," F'nor said, to give himself time to absorb his brother's remarkable and logical questions.

"It isn't just that we couldn't *see* the Star to find coordinates," F'lar went on urgently. "The Ancients had the equipment. They preserved it carefully, though not even Fandarel can guess how. They preserved it for us, perhaps? For a time when we'd know how to overcome the last obstacle?"

"Which is the last obstacle?" F'nor demanded, sarcastically, thinking of nine or ten offhand.

"There're enough, I know." And F'lar ticked them off on his fingers. "Protection of Pern while all the Weyrs are away —which might well mean the grubs on the land and a well-organized ground crew to take care of homes and people. Dragons big enough, intelligent enough to aid us. You've noticed yourself that our dragons are both bigger and smarter than those four hundred Turns older. If the dragons were bred for this purpose from creatures like Grall, they didn't grow to present size in the course of just a few Hatchings. Any more than the Masterherdsman could breed those long-staying long-legged runners he's *finally* developed; it's a project that I understand started about four hundred Turns ago. G'narish says they didn't have them in the Oldtime."

There was an undercurrent to F'lar's voice, F'nor suddenly realized. The man was not as certain of this outrageous notion as he sounded. And yet, wasn't the recognized goal of dragonmen the complete extermination of all Thread from the skies of Pern? Or was it? There wasn't a line of the Teaching Ballads and Sagas that even suggested more than that the dragonmen prepare and guard Pern when the Red Star passed. Nothing hinted at a time when there would *be* no Thread to fight.

"Isn't it just possible that we, now, are the culmination of thousands of Turns of careful planning and development?" F'lar was suggesting urgently. "Look, don't all the facts corroborate? The large population in support, the ingenuity of Fandarel, the discovery of those rooms and the devices, the grubs—everything . . ."

"Except one," F'nor said slowly, hating himself.

"Which?" All the warmth and fervor drained out of F'lar and that single word came in a cold, harsh voice.

"Son of my father," began F'nor, taking a deep breath, "if dragonmen clear the Star of Thread, what further purpose is there for them?"

F'lar, his face white and set with disappointment, drew himself to his feet.

"Well, I assume you've an answer to that, too," F'nor went on, unable to bear the disillusion in his half-brother's scornful regard. "Now where's that long-handled hearthpan I'm supposed to catch Thread in?"

When they had thoroughly discussed and rejected every other possible method of securing Thread, and how they were to keep this project a secret—only Lessa and Ramoth knew of it—they parted, both assuring the other that he'd eat and rest. Both certain that the other could not.

If F'nor appreciated the audacity of F'lar's project, he also counted up the flaws and the possible disasters. And then he realized that he still hadn't had a chance to broach the innovation he himself desired to make. Yet, for a brown dragon to fly a queen was far less revolutionary than F'lar wanting to terminate the Weyrs' duties. And, reinforced by one of F'lar's own theories, if the dragons were now big enough for their ultimate breeding purpose, then no harm was done the species if a brown, smaller than a bronze, was mated to a queen—just this once. Surely F'nor deserved that compensation. Comforted that it would be merely an exchange of favors, rather than the gross crime it might once have been considered, F'nor went to borrow the long-handled hearthpan from one of Manora's helpers.

Someone, probably Manora, had cleaned his weyr during his absence at Southern. F'nor was grateful for the fresh, supple skins on the bed, the clean, mended clothes in his chest, the waxed wood of table and chairs. Canth grumbled that someone had swept the sandy accumulation from his weyr-couch and he had nothing to scour his belly hide with now.

F'nor dutifully sympathized as he lay back on the silky furs of his bed. The scar on his arm itched a little and he rubbed it.

Oil is for itching skin, said Canth. *Imperfect hide cracks in* between.

"Be quiet, you. I've got skin, not hide."

Grall appeared in his room, hovering over his chest, her wings wafting cool air across his face. She was curious, a curiosity with slight overtones of alarm.

He smiled, generating reassurance and affection. The gyrations of her lovely jewel-faceted eyes slowed and she made a graceful survey of his quarters, humming when she discovered the bathing room. He could hear her splashing about in the water. He closed his eyes. He would need to rest. He did not look forward to the afternoon's endeavor.

If the grubs did live to eat Thread, and if F'lar could maneuver the scared Lords and Craftsmen into accepting this solution, what then? They weren't fools, those men. They'd see that Pern would no longer be dependent on dragonriders. Of course, that's what they wanted. And what under the sun did out-of-work dragonriders do? The Lords Holders Groghe, Sangel, Nessel, Meron and Vincet would immediately dispense with tithes. F'nor wouldn't object to learning another trade, but F'lar had relinquished their tentative hold on the southern continent to the Oldtimers, so where would dragonmen farm? What commodity would they barter for the products of the Crafthalls?

F'lar couldn't be under the impression that he could mend that breach with T'kul, could he? Or maybe—well, they didn't know how large the southern continent was. Past the deserts to the west or the unexplored sea to the east, maybe there were other, hospitable lands. Did F'lar know more than he said?

Grall chirruped piteously in his ear. She was clinging to the fur rug by his shoulder, her supple hide gleaming golden from her bath. He stroked her, wondering if she needed oil. She was growing, but not at the tremendous rate dragons did in the first few weeks after Hatching.

Well, his thoughts were disturbing her as well as himself. "Canth?"

The dragon was asleep. The fact was oddly consoling.

F'nor found a comfortable position and closed his eyes, determined to rest. Grall's soft stirrings ended and he felt her body resting against his neck, in the curve of his shoulder. He wondered how Brekke was doing at the High Reaches. And if her small bronze was as unsettled by weyrlife in a cliff as Grall. A memory of Brekke's face crossed his mind. Not as he had last seen her, anxious, worried, rapidly mobilizing her wits to cope with moving so precipitously after T'kul had swooped down on the unsuspecting settlement. But as loving had made her, soft, gentled. He'd have her soon to himself, all to himself, for he'd see that she didn't overextend herself, fighting everyone's battles except her own. She'd be asleep now, he realized, for it was still night at High Reaches . . .

Brekke was not asleep. She had awakened suddenly, as she was accustomed to doing in the morning, except that the dark stillness around her was not simply that of an inner room in the weyr cliff, but was full of the soft solitude of night. The fire lizard, Berd, roused too, his brilliant eyes the only light in the room. He crooned apprehensively. Brekke stroked him, listening for Wirenth, but the queen was sound asleep in her stony couch.

Brekke tried to compose herself back into sleep, but even as she made her body relax, she realized it was a useless attempt. It might be late watch here at High Reaches, but it was dawn in Southern, and that's the rhythm her body was still tuned to. With a sigh, she rose, reassuring Berd who rustled around anxiously. But he joined her in the pool-bath, splashing with small vehemence in the warm water, utilizing the superfluous suds from her cleansing sands to bathe himself. He preened on the bench, uttering those soft voluptuous croons that amused her.

In a way, it was good to be up and about with no one to

interrupt her for there was so much to be done to settle the weyrfolk in their new habitation. She'd have to plan around some of the most obvious problems. There was little fresh food. T'kul had gratuitously left behind the oldest, scrawniest bucks, the worst furnishings, had made off with most of the supplies of cloth, cured woods, leathers, all the wine, and managed to prevent the Southern folk from taking enough from their stores to make up the deficits. Oh, if she'd had even two hours, or any warning . . .

She sighed. Obviously Merika had been a worse Weyrwoman than Kylara, for High Reaches was in a bad state of disrepair. Those Holds which tithed to High Reaches Weyr would be in no mood to make up the differences now. Maybe a discreet word to F'nor would remedy the worst of the lacks . . . No, that would suggest incompetency. First, she'd inventory what they did have, discover the most pressing needs, see what they could manufacture themselves . . . Brekke stopped. She'd have to adjust her thinking to an entirely new way of life, a life dependent on the generosity of the Holds. In Southern, you had so much to work with. In her father's Crafthall, you always made what you could from things to hand—but there were always raw materials—or you grew it—or did without.

"One thing certain, Kylara will not do without!" Brekke muttered. She had dressed in riding gear which was warmer and less hampering if she was to delve into storage caves.

She didn't like the pinched-faced Meron Lord of Nabol Hold. To be indebted to him would be abhorrent. There must be an alternative.

Wirenth was twitching as Brekke passed her and the dragon's hide gleamed in the darkness. She was so deeply asleep that Brekke did not even stroke her muzzle in passing. The dragon had worked hard yesterday. Could it really have been only yesterday?

Berd chirped so smugly as he glided past the queen that Brekke smiled. He was a dear nuisance, as transparent as pool water—and she must check and see if Rannelly was right about the Weyr lake. The old woman had complained bitterly last evening that the water was fouled—deliberately; maliciously fouled by T'kul.

It was startling to come out into crisply cold air with the pinch of late frost in the early hour chill. Brekke glanced up at the watchrider by the Star stones and then hurried down the short flight of steps to the Lower Caverns. The fires had been banked but the water kettle was comfortingly hot. She made *klah,* found bread and fruit for herself and some meat for Berd. He was beginning to eat with less of the barbarous voracity, and no longer gorged himself into somnolence.

Taking a fresh basket of glows, Brekke went into the storage section to begin her investigations. Berd cheerfully accompanied her, perching where he could watch her industry.

By the time the Weyr began to stir, four hours later, Brekke was full of contempt for past domestic management and considerably relieved about the resources on hand. In fact, she suspected that the best fabrics and leathers, not to mention wines, had not gone south with the dissenters.

But the lake water was indisputably fouled by household garbage and would have to be dredged. It wouldn't be usable for several days at least. And there was nothing in which water could be transported in any quantity from the nearby mountain streams. It seemed silly to send a dragon out for a couple of bucketsful, she reported to T'bor and Kylara.

"I'll get kegs from Nabol," Kylara announced, once she had recovered from ranting about T'kul's pettiness.

While it was obvious to Brekke that T'bor was not pleased to hear her solution, he had too much else to occupy his time to protest. At least, Brekke thought, Kylara was taking an interest in the Weyr and some of the responsibility.

So Kylara circled out of the Bowl, Prideth shining golden in the early morning sun. And T'bor took off with several wings for low-altitude sweeps, to get familiar with the terrain and set up appropriate watch fires and patrol check points. Brekke and Vanira, with the help of Pilgra, the only High Reaches Weyrwoman to stay behind, settled who would supervise which neccessary duties. They set the weyrlings to dragging the lake, sent others for immediate supplies of fresh water.

Deeply occupied in counting sacks of flour, Brekke did not hear Wirenth's first cry. It was Berd who responded with a startled squawk, flying round Brekke's head to attract her attention.

As Brekke felt for Wirenth's mind, she was astonished at

the incoherence, at the rough, wild emotions. Wondering what could have happened to a queen who'd been so peacefully asleep, Brekke raced through the corridors, to be met in the Lower Cavern by Pilgra, wide-eyed with excitement.

"Wirenth's ready to rise, Brekke. I've called back the riders! She's on her way to the Feeding Ground. You know what to do, don't you?"

Brekke stared at the girl, stunned. In a daze she let Pilgra pull her toward the Bowl. Wirenth was screaming, as she glided into the Feeding Ground. The terrified herdbeasts stampeded, keening their distress, adding to the frightening tensions in the air.

"Go on, Brekke," Pilgra cried, pushing her. "Don't let her gorge. She won't fly well!"

"Help me!" Brekke pleaded.

Pilgra embraced her reassuringly, with an odd smile. "Don't be scared. It's wonderful."

"I—I can't . . ."

Pilgra gave Brekke a shake. "Of course you can. You must. I've got to scoot with Segrith. Vanira's already taken her queen away."

"Taken her away?"

"Of course. Don't be stupid. You can't have other queens around right now. Just be thankful Kylara's at Nabol Hold with Prideth. That one's too close to rising herself."

And Pilgra, with one last push at Brekke, ran toward her own queen.

Rannelly was at Brekke's elbow suddenly, batting at the excited fire lizard who darted above their heads.

"Get away! Get away!. You, girl, get to your queen or you're no Weyrwoman! Don't let her gorge!"

Suddenly the air was again full of dragon wings—the bronzes had returned. And the urgency of mating, the necessity of protecting Wirenth roused Brekke. She began to run toward the Feeding Ground, aware of the rising hum of the bronzes, the expectant sensuality of the browns and blues and greens who now perched on their ledges to watch the event. Weyrfolk crowded the Bowl.

"F'nor! F'nor! What shall I do?" Brekke moaned.

And then she was aware that Wirenth had come down on a buck, shrieking her defiance; an altered, unrecognizable Wirenth, voracious with more than a blood urge.

"She mustn't gorge!" someone shouted at Brekke. Someone gripped her arms to her sides, tightly. "Don't let her gorge, Brekke!"

But Brekke was with Wirenth now, was feeling the insatiable desire for raw, hot meat, for the taste of blood in her mouth, the warmth of it in her belly. Brekke was unaware of extraneous matters. Of anything but the fact that Wirenth was rising to mate and that she, Brekke, would be captive to those emotions, a victim of her dragon's lust, and that this was contrary to all she had been conditioned to believe and honor.

Wirenth had gutted the first buck by now and Brekke fought to keep her from eating the steaming entrails. Fought and won, controlling herself and her beast for the bond-love she had with the golden queen. When Wirenth rose from the blooded carcass, Brekke became momentarily aware of the heavy, hot, musty bodies crowding around her. Frantic, she glanced up at the circle of bronze riders, their faces intent on the scene on the Feeding Ground, intent and sensual, their expressions changing them from well-known features into strange parodies.

"Brekke! Control her!" Someone shouted hoarsely in her ear and her elbow was seized in a painful vise.

This was wrong! All wrong! Evil, she moaned, desperately crying with all her spirit for F'nor. He had said he'd come. He had promised that only Canth would fly Wirenth . . . *Canth! Canth!*

Wirenth was going for the throat of the buck, not to blood it, but to rend and eat the flesh.

Two disciplines warred with each other. Confused, distraught, torn as violently as the flesh of the dead buck, Brekke nevertheless forced Wirenth to obey her. And yet, which force would finally win? Weyr or Crafthall? Brekke clung to the hope that F'nor would come—the third alternate.

After the fourth buck, Wirenth seemed to glow. With an astonishing leap, she was suddenly aloft. Trumpeting roars reverberated painfully back and forth from the sides of the Weyr as the bronzes leaped after her, the wind from their wings sweeping dust and sand into the faces of the watching weyrfolk.

And Brekke was conscious of nothing but Wirenth. For she was suddenly Wirenth, contemptuous of the bronzes trying to catch her as she sped upward, eastward, high above the mountains, until the land below was hollow black and sand, the flash of blue lake in the sun blinding. Above the clouds, up where the air was thin but speed enhanced.

And then, out of the clouds below her, another dragon. A queen, as glowingly golden as herself. A queen? To lure her dragons from her?

Screaming in protest, Wirenth dove at the intruder, her talons extended, her body no longer exulting in flight but tensed for combat.

She dove and the intruder veered effortlessly, turning so swiftly to rake her talons down Wirenth's exposed flank that the young queen could not evade the strike. Injured, Wirenth fell, recovering valiantly and swooping into cloud cover. The bronzes had caught up and bugled their distress. They wanted to mate. They wanted to interfere. The other queen—it was Prideth—believing her rival vanquished, called enticingly to the bronzes.

Fury was added to the pain of Wirenth's humiliation. She exploded from the clouds, bellowing her challenge, her summons to the bronzes.

And her opponent was there! Beneath Wirenth. The young queen folded her wings and dove, her golden body dropping at a fearsome rate. And her dive was too unexpected, too fast. Prideth could not avoid the mid-air collision. Wirenth's claws sank into her back and Prideth writhed, her wings fouled by the talons which she could not disengage. Both queens fell like Thread, toward the mountains, escorted by the distraughtly bugling bronzes.

With the desperation born of frenzy, Prideth wrenched herself free, Wirenth's talons leaving gouges to the bone along her shoulders. But as she twisted free, beating for altitude, she slashed at Wirenth's unprotected head, across one gleaming eye.

Wirenth's tortured scream pierced the heavens just as other queens broke into the air around them; queens who instantly divided, one group flying for Prideth, the other for Wirenth.

Implacably they circled Wirenth, forcing her back, away from Prideth, their circles ever decreasing, a living net around the infuriated, pain-racked queen. Sensing only that she was being deprived of revenge on her foe, Wirenth saw the one escape route and folding her wings, dropped out the bottom of the net and darted toward the other group of queens.

Prideth's tail protruded, and on this Wirenth fastened her teeth, dragging the other from protective custody. No sooner were they clear than Wirenth bestrode the older queen's back, talons digging deeply into her wing muscles, her jaws sinking into the unprotected neck.

They fell, Wirenth making no attempt to stop their dangerous descent. She could see nothing from her damaged eye. She paid no attention to the screams of the other queens, the circling bronzes. Then something seized her body roughly from above, giving her a tremendous jerk.

Unable to see on the right, Wirenth was forced to relinquish her hold to contend with this new menace. But as she turned, she caught a glimpse of a great golden body directly below Prideth. Above her—Canth! Canth? Hissing at such treachery, she was unable to realize that he was actually trying to rescue her from sure death on the dangerously close mountain peaks. Ramoth, too, was attempting to stop their plunge, supporting Prideth with her body, her great wings straining with effort.

Suddenly teeth closed on Wirenth's neck, close to the major artery at the junction of the shoulder. Wirenth's mortal scream was cut off as she now struggled for breath itself. Wounded by foe, hampered by friends, Wirenth desperately transferred *between,* taking Prideth with her, jaws deathlocked on her life's blood.

The bronze fire lizard, Berd, found F'nor preparing to join the wings at the western meadows of Telgar Hold. The brown rider was so astonished at first to see the little bronze in Benden so far from his mistress that he didn't immediately grasp the frenzied creature's thoughts.

But Canth did.

Wirenth has risen!

All other considerations forgotten, F'nor ran with Canth to the ledge. Grall grabbed at her perch on his shoulder, wrapping her tail so tightly around F'nor's neck that he had to loosen it forcibly. Then Berd could not be brought to roost and precious moments were lost while Canth managed to calm the little bronze sufficiently to accept instruction. As Berd finally settled, Canth let out so mighty a bugle that Mnementh challenged from the ledge and Ramoth roared back from the Hatching Ground.

With no thought of the effect of their precipitous exit or Canth's exceptional behavior, F'nor urged his dragon upward. The small pulse of reason that remained untouched by emotion was trying to estimate how long it had taken the little bronze to reach him, how long Wirenth would blood before rising, which bronzes were at High Reaches. He was thankful that F'lar had not had time to throw mating flights open. There were some beasts against whom Canth stood no chance.

When they broke into the air again over High Reaches Weyr, F'nor's worst fears were realized. The Feeding Ground was a bloody sight and no queen fed there. Nor was there a bronze among the dragons who ringed the Weyr heights.

Without order, Canth wheeled sharply down at dizzying speed.

Berd knows where Wirenth is. He takes me.

The little bronze hopped down to Canth's neck, his little talons gripping the ridge tightly. F'nor slid from Canth's shoulder to the ground, staggering out of the way so the brown could spring back aloft.

Prideth also rises! The thought and the brown's scream of fear were simultaneous. From the heights the other dragons answered, extending their wings in alarm.

"Rouse Ramoth!" F'nor shouted, mind and voice, his body paralyzed with shock. "Rouse Ramouth! Bronze riders! Prideth also rises!"

Weyrfolk rushed from the Lower Cavern, riders appeared on their ledges around the Weyr face.

"Kylara! T'bor! Where's Pilgra? Kylara! Varena!" Shouting with a panic that threatened to choke him, F'nor raced for Brekke's weyr, shoving aside the people who crowded him, demanding explanations.

Prideth rising! How could that happen? Even the stupidest Weyrwoman knew you didn't keep a queen near her weyr during a mating flight—unless they were broody. How could Kylara . . .

"T'bor!"

F'nor raced up the short flight of steps, pounded down the corridor in strides that jolted his half-healed arm. But the pain cleared his head of panic just as he burst into the weyr cavern, Brekke's angry cry halted him. The bronze riders grouped around her were beginning to show the effects of the interrupted mating flight.

"What's she doing here? How dare she?" Brekke was shrieking in a voice shrill with lust as well as fury. "These are my dragons! How dare she! I'll kill her!" The litany broke into a piercing scream of agony as Brekke doubled up, right shoulder hunching as if to protect her head.

"My eye! My eye! My eye!" Brekke was covering her right eye, her body writhing in an uncontrollable, unconscious mimicry of the aerial battle to which she was tuned.

"Kill! I'll kill her! No! No! She cannot escape. Go away!" Suddenly Brekke's face turned crafty and her whole body writhed sensuously.

The bronze riders were changing now, no longer completely in the thrall of the strange mental rapport with their beasts. Fear, doubt, indecision, hopelessness registered on their faces. Some portion of the human awareness was returning, fighting with the dragon responsiveness and the interrupted mating flight. When T'bor reached for Brekke, human fear was reflected in his eyes.

But she was still totally committed to Wirenth, and the incredible triumph on her face registered Wirenth's success in evading capture, in dragging Prideth from the encircling queens.

"Prideth has risen, T'bor! The queens are fighting," F'nor shouted.

One rider began to scream and the sound broke the link of two others who stared, dazed, at Brekke's contorting body.

"Don't touch her!" F'nor cried, moving to fend off T'bor and another man. He moved as close to her as possible but her ranging eyes did not see him or anything in the weyr.

Then she seemed to spring, her left eye widening with an unholy joy, her lips bared as her teeth fastened on an imaginary target, her body arching with the empathic effort.

Suddenly she hissed, craning her head sideways, over her right shoulder, while her face reflected incredulity, horror, hatred. As suddenly, her body was seized with a massive convulsion. She screamed again, this time a mortal shriek of unbelievable terror and anguish. One hand went to her throat, the other batted at some unseen attacker. Her body, poised on her toes, strained in an agonized stretch. With a cry that was more gasp than scream, she whirled. In her eyes was Brekke's soul again, tortured, terrified. Then her eyes closed, her body sagged in such an alarming collapse that F'nor barely caught her in time.

The stones of the weyr itself seemed to reverberate with the mourning dirge of the dragons.

"T'bor, send someone for Manora," F'nor cried in a hoarse voice as he bore Brekke to her couch. Her body was so light in his arms—as if all substance had been drained from it. He held her tightly to his chest with one arm, fumbling to find the pulse in her neck with the free hand. It beat—faintly.

What had happened? How could Kylara have allowed Prideth near Wirenth?

"They're both gone," T'bor was saying as he stumbled into the sleeping room and sagged down on the clothes chest, trembling violently.

"Where's Kylara? Where is she?"

"Don't know. I left this morning to fly patrols." T'bor scrubbed at his face, shock bleaching the ruddy color from his skin. "The lake was polluted . . ."

F'nor piled furs around Brekke's motionless body. He held his hand against her chest, feeling its barely perceptible rise and fall.

F'nor?

It was Canth, his call so faint, so piteous that the man closed his eyes against the pain in his dragon's tone.

He felt someone grip his shoulder. He opened his eyes to see the pity, the understanding in T'bor's. "There's nothing more you can do for her right now, F'nor."

"She'll want to die. Don't let her!" he said. "Don't let Brekke die!"

Canth was on the ledge, his eyes glowing dully. He was swaying with exhaustion. F'nor encircled the bowed head with his arms, their mutual grief so intense they seemed afire with pain.

It was too late. Prideth had risen. Too close to Wirenth. Not even the queens could help. I tried, F'nor. I tried. She— she fell so fast. And she turned on me. Then went between. *I could not find her* between.

They stood together, immobile.

Lessa and Manora saw them as Ramoth circled into High Reaches Weyr. At Canth's bellow, Ramoth had come out of the Hatching Ground, loudly calling for her rider, demanding an explanation of such behavior.

But F'lar, believing he knew Canth's errand, had reassured her, until Ramoth had informed them that Wirenth was rising. And Ramoth knew instantly when Prideth rose, too, and had gone *between* to Nabol to stop the mortal combat if she could.

Once Wirenth had dragged Prideth *between*, Ramoth had returned to Benden Weyr for Lessa. The Benden dragons set up their keen so that the entire Weyr soon knew of the disaster. But Lessa waited only long enough for Manora to gather her medicines.

As she and the headwoman reached the ledge of Brekke's weyr and the motionless mourners, Lessa looked anxiously to Manora. There was something dangerous in such stillness.

"They will work this out together. They *are* together, more now than ever before," Manora said in a voice that was no more than a rough whisper. She passed them quietly, her head bent and her shoulders drooping as she hurried down the corridor to Brekke.

"Ramoth?" asked Lessa, looking down to where her queen had settled on the sands. It was not that she doubted Manora's wisdom, but to see F'nor so—so reduced—upset her. He was much like F'lar . . .

Ramoth gave a soft croon and folded her wings. On the ledges around the Bowl, the other dragons began to settle in uneasy vigil.

As Lessa entered the Cavern of the Weyr, she glanced away from the empty dragon couch and then halted mid-step. The tragedy was only minutes past so the nine bronze riders were still in severe shock.

As well they might be, Lessa realized with deep sympathy. To be roused to performance intensity and then be, not only disappointed, but disastrously deprived of two queens at once! Whether a bronze won the queen or not, there was a subtle, deep attachment between a queen and the bronzes of her Weyr . . .

However, Lessa concluded briskly, someone in this benighted Weyr ought to have sense enough to be constructive. Lessa broke this train of thought off abruptly. Brekke had been the responsible member.

She turned, about to go in search of some stimulant for

the dazed riders when she heard the uneven steps and stertorous breathing of someone in a hurry. Two green fire lizards darted into the weyr, hovering, chirping excitedly as a young girl came in at a half-run. She could barely manage the heavy tray she carried and she was weeping, her breath coming in ragged gasps.

"Oh!" she cried, seeing Lessa. She stifled her sobs, tried to bob a curtsey and blot her nose on her shoulder at one and the same time.

"Well, you're a child with wits about you," Lessa said briskly, but not without sympathy. She took one end of the tray and helped the girl deposit it on the table. "You brought strong spirits?" she asked, gesturing to the anonymous earthenware bottles.

"All I could find." And the consonant ended in a sob.

"Here," and Lessa held out a half-filled cup, nodding toward the nearest rider. But the child was motionless, staring at the curtain, her face twisted with grief, the tears flowing unnoticed down her cheeks. She was washing her hands together with such violent motions that the skin stretched white across her knuckles.

"You're Mirrim?"

The child nodded, her eyes not leaving the closed entrance. Above her the greens whirred, echoing her distress.

"Manora is with Brekke, Mirrim."

"But—but she'll die. She'll die. They say the rider dies, too, when the dragon is killed. They say . . ."

"*They* say entirely too much," Lessa began and then Manora stood in the doorway.

"She lives. Sleep is the kindest blessing now." She flipped the curtain shut and glanced at the men. "These could do with sleep. Have their dragons returned? Who's this?" Manora touched Mirrim's cheek, gently. "Mirrim? I'd heard you had green lizards."

"Mirrim had the sense to bring the tray," Lessa said, catching Manora's eye.

"Brekke—Brekke would expect—" and the girl could go no further.

"Brekke is a sensible person," Manora said briskly and folded Mirrim's fingers around a cup, giving her a shove toward a rider. "Help us now. These men need our help."

In a daze, Mirrim moved, rousing herself to help actively

when the bronze rider could not seem to get his fingers to the cup.

"My lady," murmured Manora, "we need the Weyrleader. Ista and Telgar Weyrs would be fighting Thread by now and . . ."

"I'm here," F'lar said from the weyr entrance. "And I'll take a shot of that, too. Cold *between* is in my bones."

"We've more fools than we need right now," Lessa exclaimed, but her face brightened to see him there.

"Where's T'bor?"

Manora indicated Brekke's room.

"All right. Then where's Kylara?"

And the cold of *between* was in his voice.

By evening some order had been restored to the badly demoralized High Reaches Weyr. The bronze dragons had all returned, been fed, and the bronze riders weyred with their beasts, sufficiently drugged to sleep.

Kylara had been found. Or, rather, returned, by the green rider assigned to Nabol Hold.

"Someone's got to be quartered there," the man said, his face grim, "but not me or my green."

"Please report, S'goral." F'lar nodded his appreciation of the rider's feelings.

"*She* arrived at the Hold this morning, with some tale about the lake here being fouled and no kegs to hold any supply of water. I remember thinking that Prideth looked too gold to be out. She's been off cycle, you know. But she settled down all right on the ridge with my green so I went about teaching those Holders how to manage their fire lizards." S'goral evidently did not have much use for his pupils. "*She* went in with the Nabolese Holder. Later I saw their lizards sunning on the ledge outside the Lord's sleeping room." He paused, glancing at his audience and looking grimmer still. "We were taking a breather when my green cried out. Sure enough, there were dragons, high up. *I* knew it was a mating flight. You can't mistake it. Then Prideth started to bugle. Next thing I knew, she was down among Nabol's prize breeding stock. I waited a bit, sure that *she'd* be aware of what was happening, but when there wasn't a sign of her, I went looking. Nabol's bodyguards were at the door. The Lord didn't want to be disturbed. Well, I disturbed him. I stopped him doing what he was doing. And that's what was doing it! Setting Prideth off. That and being so close to rising herself, and seeing a mating flight right over her, so to speak. You *don't* abuse your dragon that way." He shook his head then. "There wasn't anything me and my green could do there. So we took off for Fort Weyr, for their queens. But—" and he held out his hands, indicating his helplessness.

"You did as you should, S'goral," F'lar told him.

"There wasn't anything else I could do," the man insisted, as if he could not rid himself of some lingering feeling of guilt.

"We were lucky you were there at all," Lessa said. "We might never have known where Kylara was."

"What I want to know is what's going to happen to her—now?" A hard vindictiveness replaced the half-shame, half-guilt in the rider's face.

"Isn't loss of a dragon enough?" T'bor roused himself to ask.

"Brekke lost her dragon, too," S'goral retorted angrily, "and she was doing what she should!"

"Nothing can be decided in heat or hatred, S'goral," F'lar said, rising to his feet. "We've no precedents—" He broke off, turning to D'ram and G'narish. "Not in our time, at least."

"Nothing should be decided in heat or hatred," D'ram echoed, "but there were such incidents in our time." Unaccountably he flushed. "We'd better assign some bronzes here, F'lar. The High Reaches men and beasts may not be fit tomorrow. And with Thread falling every day, no Weyr can be allowed to relax its vigilance. For anything."

CHAPTER XIII

Night at Fort Weyr:
Six Days Later

Robinton was weary, with a fatigue of the heart and mind that did not lift to the thrill the Masterharper usually experienced on dragonback. In fact, he almost wished he'd not had to come to Fort Weyr tonight. These past six days, with everyone reacting in varying ways to the tragedy at High Reaches, had been very difficult. (Must the High Reaches always push the knottiest problems on Pern?) In a way, Robinton wished that they could have put off this Red Star viewing until minds and eyes had cleared and were ready for this challenge. And yet, perhaps the best solution was to press this proposed expedition to the Red Star as far and as fast as possible—as an anodyne to the depression that had followed the death of the two queens. Robinton knew that F'lar wanted to prove to the Lord Holders that the dragonmen were in earnest in their desire to clear the air of Thread, but for once, the Masterharper found himself without a private opinion. He did not know if F'lar was wise in pushing the issue, particularly now. Particularly when the Benden Weyrleader wasn't recovered from T'ron's slash. When no one was sure how T'kul was managing in Southern Weyr or if the man intended to *stay* there. When all Pern was staggered by the battle and deaths of the two queens. The people had enough to rationalize, had enough to do with the vagaries of Threadfall complicating the seasonal mechanics of plowing and seeding. Leave the attack of the Red Star until another time.

Other dragons were arriving at Fort Weyr and the brown on which Robinton rode took his place in the circling pattern. They'd be landing on the Star Stones where Wansor, Fandarel's glassman, had set up the distance-viewer.

"Have you had a chance to look through this device?" Robinton asked the brown's rider.

"Me? Hardly, Masterharper. Everyone else wants to. It'll stay there until I've had my turn, I daresay."

"Has Wansor mounted it permanently at Fort Weyr?"

"It was discovered at Fort Weyr," the rider replied, a little defensively. "Fort's the oldest Weyr, you know. P'zar feels it should stay at Fort. And the Mastersmith, he agrees. His man Wansor keeps saying that there may be good reason. Something to do with elevation and angles and the altitude of Fort Weyr mountains. I didn't understand."

No more do I, Robinton thought. But he intended to. He was in agreement with Fandarel and Terry that there should be an interchange of knowledge between Crafts. Indisputably, Pern had lost many of the bemoaned techniques due to Craft jealousy. Lose a Craftmaster early, before he had transmitted all the Craft secrets, and a vital piece of information was lost forever. Not that Robinton, nor his predecessor, had ever espoused that ridiculous prerogative. There were five senior harpers who knew everything that Robinton did and three promising journeymen studying diligently to increase the safety factor.

It was one matter to keep dangerous secrets privy, quite another to guard Craft skills to extinction.

The brown dragon landed on the ridge height of Fort Weyr and Robinton slid down the soft shoulder. He thanked the beast. The brown rose a half-length from the landing and then seemed to drop off the side of the cliff, down into the Bowl, making room for someone else to land.

Glows had been set on the narrow crown of the height, leading toward the massive Star Stones, their black bulk silhouetted against the lighter night sky. Among those gathered there, Robinton could distinguish the Mastersmith's huge figure, Wansor's pear-shaped and Lessa's slender one.

On the largest and flattest rock of the Star Stones, Robinton saw the tripod arrangement on which the long barrel of the distance-viewer had been mounted. At first glance he was disappointed by its simplicity, a fat, round cylinder, with a smaller pipe attached to its side. Then it amused him. The Smith must be tortured with the yearning to dismantle the instrument and examine the principles of its simple efficiency.

"Robinton, how are you this evening?" Lessa asked, coming toward him, one hand outstretched.

He gripped it, her soft skin smooth under the calluses of his fingers.

"Pondering the elements of efficiency," he countered, keeping his voice light. But he couldn't keep from asking after Brekke and he felt Lessa's fingers tremble in his.

"She does as well as can be expected. F'nor insisted that we bring her to his weyr. The man's emotionally attached to her—far more than gratitude for any nursing. Between him, Manora and Mirrim, she is never alone."

"And—Kylara?"

Lessa pulled her hand from his. "She lives!"

Robinton said nothing and, after a moment, Lessa went on.

"We don't like losing Brekke as a Weyrwoman—" She paused and added, her voice a little harsher, "And since it is now obvious that a person can Impress more than once, and more than one dragonkind, Brekke will be presented as a candidate when the Benden eggs Hatch. Which should be soon."

"I perceive," Robinton said, cautiously choosing his words, "that not everyone favors this departure from custom."

Although he couldn't see her face in the darkness, he felt her eyes on him.

"This time it's not the Oldtimers. I suppose they're so sure she can't re-Impress, they're indifferent."

"Who then?"

"F'nor and Manora oppose it violently."

"And Brekke?"

Lessa gave an impatient snort. "Brekke says nothing. She will not even open her eyes. She can't be sleeping all the time. The lizards and the dragons tell us she's awake. You see," and Lessa's exasperation showed through her tight control for she was more worried about Brekke than she'd admit even to herself, "Brekke can hear any dragon. Like me. She's the only other Weyrwoman who can. And all the dragons listen to her." Lessa moved restlessly and Robinton could see her slender white hands rubbing against her thighs in unconscious agitation.

"Surely that's an advantage if she's suicidal?"

"Brekke is not—not actively suicidal. She's craftbred, you know," Lessa said in a flat, disapproving tone of voice.

"No, I didn't know," Robinton murmured encouragingly after a pause. He was thinking that Lessa wouldn't ever contemplate suicide in a similar circumstance and wondered what Brekke's "breeding" had to do with a suicidal aptitude.

"That's her trouble. She can't actively seek death so she just lies there. I have this incredible urge," and Lessa bunched her fists, "to beat or pinch or slap her—anything to get some response from the girl. It's not the end of the world, after all. She *can* hear other dragons. She's not bereft of all contact with dragonkind, like Lytol."

"She must have time to recover from the shock . . ."

"I know, I know," Lessa said irritably, "but we don't *have* time. We can't get her to realize that it's better to *do* things . . ."

"Lessa . . ."

"Don't you 'Lessa' me too, Robinton." In the reflection of the glow lights, the Weyrwoman's eyes gleamed angrily. "F'nor's as daft as a weyrling, Manora's beside herself with worry for them both, Mirrim spends more of her time weeping which upsets the trio of lizards she's got and *that* sets off all the babes and the weyrlings. And, on top of everything else, F'lar . . ."

"F'lar?" Robinton had bent close to her so that no one else might hear her reply.

"He is feverish. He ought never to have come to High Reaches with that open wound. You know what cold *between* does to wounds!"

"I'd hoped he'd be here tonight."

Lessa's laugh was sour. "I dosed his *klah* when he wasn't looking."

Robinton chuckled. "And stuffed him with mosstea, I'll bet."

"Packed the wound with it, too."

"He's a strong man, Lessa. He'll be all right."

"He'd better be. If only F'nor—" and Lessa broke off. "I sound like a wherry, don't I?" She gave a sigh and smiled up at Robinton.

"Not a bit, my dear Lessa, I assure you. However, it's not as if Benden were inadequately represented," and he executed a little bow which, if she shrugged it off, at least made her laugh. "In fact," he went on, "I'm a trifle relieved that F'lar isn't here, railing at anything that keeps him from blotting out any Thread he happens to see in that contraption."

"True enough." And Robinton caught the edge to her voice. "I'm not sure . . ."

She didn't finish her sentence and turned so swiftly to mark the landing of another dragon that Robinton was certain she was at odds with F'lar's wishing to push a move against the Red Star.

Suddenly she stiffened, drawing in her breath sharply. "Meron! What does he think he's doing here?"

"Easy, Lessa. I don't like him around any better than you, but I'd rather keep him in sight, if you know what I mean."

"But he's got no influence on the other Lords . . ."

Robinton gave a harsh laugh. "My dear Weyrwoman, considering the influence he's been exerting in other areas, he doesn't need the Lords' support."

Robinton did wonder at the gall of the man, appearing in public anywhere a scant six days after he'd been involved in the deaths of two queen dragons.

The Lord Holder of Nabol strode insolently to the focal point of the gathering, his bronze fire lizard perched on his forearm, its wings extended as it fought to maintain its balance. The little creature began to hiss as it became aware of the antagonism directed at Meron.

"And this—this innocuous tube is the incredible instrument that will show us the Red Star?" Meron of Nabol asked scathingly.

"Don't touch it, I beg of you." Wansor jumped forward, intercepting Nabol's hand.

"What did you say?" The lizard's hiss was no less sibilantly menacing than Meron's tone. The Lord's thin features, contorted with indignation, took on an added malevolence from the glow lights.

Fandarel stepped out of the darkness to his craftsman's side. "The instrument is positioned for the viewing. To move it would destroy the careful work of some hours."

"If it is positioned for viewing, then let us view!" Nabol said and, after staring belligerently around the circle, stepped past Wansor. "Well? What do you do with this thing?"

Wansor glanced questioningly at the big Smith, who made a slight movement of his head, excusing him. Wansor gratefully stepped back and let Fandarel preside. With two gnarled fingers, the Smith delicately held the small round protruberance at the top of the smaller cylinder.

"This is the eyepiece. Put your best seeing eye to it," he told Meron.

The lack of any courteous title was not lost on the Nabolese. Plainly he wanted to reprimand the Smith. Had Wansor spoken so, he would not have hesitated a second, Robinton thought.

Meron's lips slid into a sneer and, with a bit of a swagger, he took the final step to the distance-viewer. Bending forward slightly, he laid his eye to the proper place. And jerked his body back hastily, his face wearing a fleeting expression of shock and terror. He laughed uneasily and then took a second, longer look. Far too long a look to Robinton's mind.

"If there is any lack of definition in the image, Lord Meron —" Wansor began tentatively.

"Shut up!" Gesturing him away impatiently, Meron continued his deliberate monopoly of the instrument.

"That will be enough, Meron," Groghe, Lord of Fort said as the others began to stir restlessly. "You've had more than your fair turn this round. Move away. Let others see."

Meron stared insolently at Groghe for a moment and then looked back into the eyepiece.

"Very interesting. Very interesting," he said, his tone oily with amusement.

"That is quite enough, Meron," Lessa said, striding to the instrument. The man could not be allowed any privilege.

He regarded her as he might a body insect, coldly and mockingly.

"Enough of what—Weyrwoman?" And his tone made the title a vulgar epithet. In fact, his pose exuded such a lewd familiarity that Robinton found he was clenching his fists. He had an insane desire to wipe that look from Meron's face and change the arrangement of the features in the process.

The Mastersmith, however, reacted more quickly. His two great hands secured Meron's arms to his sides and, in a fluid movement, Fandarel picked the Nabolese Lord up, the man's feet dangling a full dragonfoot above the rock, and carried him as far away from the Star Stones as the ledge permitted. Fandarel then set Meron down so hard that the man gave a startled exclamation of pain and staggered before he gained his balance. The little lizard screeched around his head.

"My lady," the Mastersmith inclined his upper body toward Lessa and gestured with great courtesy for her to take her place.

Lessa had to stand on tiptoe to reach the eyepiece, silently wishing someone had taken into account that not all the viewers this evening were tall. The instant the image of the Red Star reached her brain, such trivial annoyance evaporated. There was the Red Star, seemingly no farther away than her arm could reach. It swam, a many-hued globe, like a child's miggsy, in a lush black background. Odd whitish-pink masses must be clouds. Startling to think that the Red Star could possess clouds—like Pern. Where the cover was pierced, she could see grayish masses, a lively gray with glints and sparkles. The ends of the slightly ovoid planet were completely white, but devoid of the cloud cover. Like the great icecaps of northern regions of Pern. Darker masses punctuated the grays. Land? Or seas?

Involuntarily Lessa moved her head, to glance up at the round mark of redness in the night sky that was this child's toy through the magic of the distance-viewer. Then, before anyone might think she'd relinquished the instrument, she looked back through the eyepiece. Incredible. Unsettling. If the gray was land—how could they possibly rid it of Thread? If the darker masses were land . . .

Disturbed, and suddenly all too willing that someone else be exposed to their ancient enemy at such close range, she stepped back.

Lord Groghe stepped forward importantly. "Sangel, if you please?"

How like the Fort Lord, Lessa thought, to play host when P'zar who was, after all, acting Weyrleader at Fort Weyr, did not act quickly enough to exert his rights. Lessa wished fervently that F'lar had been able to attend this viewing. Well, perhaps P'zar was merely being diplomatic with the Fort Lord Holder. Still, Lord Groghe would need to be kept . . .

She retreated—and knew it for a retreat—to Robinton. The Harper's presence was always reassuring. He was eager to have his turn but resigned to waiting. Groghe naturally would give the other Lord Holders precedence over a harper, even the Masterharper of Pern.

"I wish he'd go," Lessa said, glancing sideways at Meron. The Nabolese had made no attempt to re-enter the group from which he had been so precipitously expelled. The offensive stubbornness of the man in remaining where he clearly was not welcome provided a counterirritant to worry and her renewed fear of the Red Star.

Why must it appear so—so innocent? Why did it have to have clouds? It ought to be different. How it ought to differ, Lessa couldn't guess, but it ought to look—to look sinister. And it didn't. That made it more fearful than ever.

"I don't *see* anything," Sangel of Boll was complaining.

"A moment, sir." Wansor came forward and began adjusting a small knob. "Tell me when the view clarifies for you."

"What am I supposed to be seeing?" Sangel demanded irritably. "Nothing there but a bright—ah! Oh!" Sangel backed away from the eyepiece as if Thread had burned him. But he was again in position before Groghe could call another Lord to his place.

Lessa felt somewhat relieved, and a little smug, at Sangel's reaction. If the fearless Lords also got a taste of honest dread, perhaps . . .

"Why does it glow? Where does it get light? It's dark here," the Lord Holder of Boll babbled.

"It is the light of the sun, my Lord," Fandarel replied, his deep, matter-of-fact voice reducing that miracle to common knowledge.

"How can that be?" Sangel protested. "The sun's on the other side of us now. Any child knows that."

"Of course, but we are not obstructing the Star from that

light. We are below it in the skies, if you will, so that the sun's light reaches it directly."

Sangel seemed likely to monopolize the viewer, too.

"That's enough, Sangel," Groghe said testily. "Let Oterel have a chance."

"But I've barely looked, and there was trouble adjusting the mechanism," Sangel complained. Between Oterel's glare and Groghe trying to shoulder him out of the way, Sangel reluctantly stepped aside.

"Let me adjust the focus for you, Lord Oterel," Wansor murmured politely.

"Yes, do. I'm not half blind like Sangel there," the Lord of Tillek said.

"Now, see here, Oterel . . ."

"Fascinating, isn't it, Lord Sangel?" said Lessa, wondering what reaction the man's blathering had concealed.

He harumphed irritably, but his eyes were restless and he frowned.

"Wouldn't call it fascinating, but then I had barely a moment's look."

"We've an entire night, Lord Sangel."

The man shivered, pulling his cloak around him though the night air was not more than mildly cool for spring.

"It's nothing more than a child's miggsy," exclaimed the Lord of Tillek. "Fuzzy. Or is it supposed to be?" He glanced away from the eyepiece at Lessa.

"No, my Lord," Wansor said. "It should be bright and clear, so you can see cloud formations."

"How would you know?" Sangel asked testily.

"Wansor set the instrument up for this evening's viewing," Fandarel pointed out.

"Clouds?" Tillek asked. "Yes, I see them. But what's the land? The dark stuff or the gray?"

"We don't know yet," Fandarel told him.

"Land masses don't look that way as high as dragons can fly a man," said P'zar the Fort Weyrleader, speaking for the first time.

"And objects seen at a far greater distance change even more," Wansor said in the dry tone of someone who does know what he's talking about. "For example, the very mountains of Fort which surround us change drastically if seen from Ruatha Heights or the plains of Crom."

"Then all that dark stuff is land?" Lord Oterel had difficulty not being impressed. And discouraged, Lessa thought. Tillek's Lord Holder must have been hoping to press the extermination of Thread on the Red Star.

"Of that we are not sure," replied Wansor with no lessening of the authority in his manner. Lessa approved more and more of Wansor. A man ought not be afraid to say he didn't know. Nor a woman.

The Lord of Tillek did not want to leave the instrument. Almost as if he hoped, Lessa thought, that if he looked long enough, he'd discover a good argument for mounting an expedition.

Tillek finally responded to Nessel of Crom's acid remarks and stepped aside.

"What do you think is the land, Sangel? Or did you really *see* anything?"

"Of course I did. Saw the clouds plain as I see you right now."

Oterel of Tillek snorted contemptuously. "Which doesn't say much, considering the darkness."

"I saw as much as you did, Oterel. Gray masses, and black masses and those clouds. A star having clouds! Doesn't make sense. Pern has clouds!"

Hastily Lessa changed her laugh at the man's indignation to a cough, but she caught the Harper's amused look and wondered what his reaction to the Red Star would be. Would he be for, or against this expedition? And which attitude did she want him to express?

"Yes, Pern has clouds," Oterel was saying, somewhat surprised at that observation. "And if Pern has clouds, and more water surface than land, then so does the Red Star . . ."

"You can't be sure of that," Sangel protested.

"And there'll be a way of distinguishing land from water, too," Oterel went on, ignoring the Boll Lord. "Let me have another look, there, Nessel," he said, pushing the Crom Lord out of the way.

"Now, wait a minute there, Tillek." And Nessel put a proprietary hand on the instrument. As Tillek jostled him, the tripod tottered and the distance-viewer, on its hastily rigged swivel, assumed a new direction.

"Now you've done it," Oterel cried. "I only wanted to see if you could distinguish the land from the water."

Wansor tried to get between the two Lords so that he could adjust his precious instrument.

"I didn't get my full turn," Nessel complained, trying to keep physical possession of the distance-viewer.

"You'll not see anything, Lord Nessel, if Wansor cannot have a chance to sight back on the Star," Fandarel said, politely gesturing the Crom Lord out of the way.

"You're a damned wherry fool, Nessel," Lord Groghe said, pulling him to one side and waving Wansor in.

"Tillek's the fool."

"I saw enough to know there's not as much dark as there is that gray," Oterel said, defensively. "Pern's more water than land. So's the Red Star."

"From one look you can tell so much, Oterel?" Meron's malicious drawl from the shadows distracted everyone.

Lessa moved pointedly aside as he strolled forward, stroking his bronze lizard possessively. It affronted Lessa that the little creature was humming with pleasure.

"It will take many observations, by many eyes," Fandarel said in his bass rumble, "before we will be able to say what the Red Star looks like with any certitude. One point of similarity is not enough. Not at all."

"Oh, indeed. Indeed." Wansor seconded his Craftmaster, his eyes glued to the piece as he slowly swung it across the night sky.

"What's taking you so long?" Nessel of Crom demanded irritably. "There's the Star. We can all see it with our naked eyes."

"And it is so easy to pick out the green pebble you drop on the sands of Igen at high noon?" asked Robinton.

"Ah. I've got it," Wansor cried. Nessel jumped forward, reaching for the tube. He jerked his hand back, remembering what an unwise movement could do. With both hands conspicuously behind him, he looked again at the Red Star.

Nessel, however, did not remain long at the distance-viewer. When Oterel stepped forward, the Masterharper moved quicker.

"My turn now, I believe, since all the Lord Holders have had one sighting."

"Only fair," Sangel said loudly, glaring at Oterel.

Lessa watched the Masterharper closely, saw the tightening of his broad shoulders as he, too, felt the impact of that first sight of their ancient enemy. He did not remain long, or perhaps she was deceived, but he straightened slowly from the eyepiece and looked thoughtfully toward the Red Star in the dark heavens above them.

"Well, Harper?" asked Meron superciliously. "You've a glib word for every occasion."

Robinton regarded the Nabolese for a longer moment then he had the Star.

"I think it wiser that we keep this distance between us."

"Ha! I thought as much." Meron was grinning with odious triumph.

"I wasn't aware you thought," Robinton remarked quietly.

"What do you mean, Meron?" Lessa asked in a dangerously edged voice, "you thought as much?"

"Why, it should be obvious," and the Lord of Nabol had not tempered his attitude toward her much since his first insult. "The Harper does as Benden Weyr decrees. And since Benden Weyr does not care to exterminate Thread at source . . ."

"And how do you know that?" Lessa demanded coldly.

"And, Lord Nabol, on what grounds do you base your allegation that the Harper of Pern does as Benden Weyr decrees? For I most urgently suggest that you either prove such an accusation instantly or retract it." Robinton's hand was on his belt knife.

The bronze lizard on Meron's arm began to hiss and extend his fragile wings in alarm. The Lord of Nabol contented himself with a knowing smirk as he made a show of soothing his lizard.

"Speak up, Meron," Oterel demanded.

"But it's so obvious. Surely you can all see that," Meron replied with malicious affability and a feigned surprise at the obtuseness of the others. "He has a hopeless passion for—the Benden Weyrwoman."

For a moment Lessa could only stare at the man in a stunned daze. It was true that she admired and respected Robinton. She was fond of him, she supposed. Always glad to see him and never bothering to disguise it but—Meron was mad. Trying to undermine the country's faith in dragonmen with absurd, vicious rumors. First Kylara and now . . . And yet Kylara's weakness, her promiscuity, the general attitude of the Hold and Craft toward the customs of the Weyrs made his accusation so plausible . . .

Robinton's hearty guffaw startled her. And wiped the smile from Nabol's face.

"Benden's Weyrwoman has not half the attraction for me that Benden's wine has!"

There was such intense relief in the faces around her that Lessa knew, in a sinking, sick way, that the Lord Holders had been halfway to believing Meron's invidious accusation. If Robinton had not responded just as he had, if she had started to protest the accusation . . . She grinned, too, managed to chuckle because the Masterharper's fondness for wine, for the Benden wines in particular, was such common knowledge, it was more plausible than Meron's slander. Ridicule was a better defense than truth.

"Furthermore," the Harper went on, "the Masterharper of Pern has no opinion, one way or another, about the Red Star—not even a verse. Because that—that—child's miggsy scares him juiceless and makes him yearn for some of that Benden wine, right now, in limitless quantity." Robinton had not the slightest trace of laughter in his voice now. "I'm too steeped in the history and lore of our beloved Pern, I've sung too many ballads about the evil of the Red Star to want to get any closer to it. Even that—" and he pointed to the distance-viewer, "brings it far too near me. But the men who have to fight Thread day after day, Turn after Turn, can look upon it with less fearfulness than the poor Harper. And, Meron, Lord Holder of Nabol, you can wager every field and cot and hall upon your lands that the dragonmen of every Weyr would like to be quit of any obligation to keep *your* hide Threadfree—even if it means wiping Thread from every squared length of that Star." The vehemence in the Harper's voice caused Meron to take a backward step, to clap a hand on the violently agitated fire lizard. "How can you, any of you," and the Harper's opprobrium fell equally now on the other four Lords, "doubt that the dragonriders wouldn't be as relieved as you to see the end of their centuries of dedication to your safety. They don't *have* to defend you from Thread. You, Groghe, Sangel, Nessel, Oterel, you all ought to realize that by now. You've had T'kul to deal with, and T'ron.

"You all know what Thread does to a man. And you know

what happens when a dragon dies. Or must I remind you of that, too? Do you honestly believe that the dragonriders wish to prolong such conditions, such occurrences? What do they get out of it? Not much! Not much! Are the scores they suffer worth a few bags of grain, or a blade from the Smith's? Is a dragon's death truly recompensed by a length of goods or a scrawny herdbeast?

"And if there have been instruments for man with his puny eyes to view that bauble in the sky, why do we still have Thread? If it's just a question of finding coordinates and taking that jump? Could it be that it has been tried by dragonriders before? And they failed because those gray masses we see so clearly are not water, or land, but uncountable Threads, seething and writhing, until the topmost can, by some mysterious agency, win free to plague us? Could it be because, although there are clouds, they do not consist of water vapor as Pern's clouds, but something deadly, far more inimical to us than Thread? How do we know we will not find the bones of long-lost dragons and riders in the dark blots of the planet? There is so much we do *not* know that, yes, I think it wiser that we keep this distance between us. But I think the time for wisdom is now past and we must rely on the folly of the brave and hope that it will suffice them and us. For I do believe," and the Harper turned slowly toward Lessa, "though my heart is heavy and I am scared soulless, that the dragonmen of Pern will go to the Red Star."

"That is F'lar's intention," Lessa said in a strong, ringing voice, her head high, her shoulders straight. Unlike the Harper, she could not admit her fear, even to herself.

"Aye," rumbled Fandarel, nodding his great head slowly up and down, "for he has enjoined me and Wansor to make many observations on the Red Star so that an expedition can be sent as soon as possible."

"And how long must we wait until this expedition takes place?" Meron asked, as if the Harper's words had never been spoken.

"Come now, man, how can you expect any one to give a date—a time?" asked Groghe.

"Ah, but Benden Weyr is so adept at giving times and dates and patterns, is it not?" Meron replied so unctuously that Lessa wanted to scratch his face.

"And they saved your profit, Nabol," Oterel put in.

"Have you any idea, Weyrwoman?" Sangel asked Lessa in an anxious tone.

"I must complete the observations," Wansor put in, nervously dithering. "It would be folly—madness—until we have seen the entire Red Star, and plot in the distinctive features of the various color masses. See how often the clouds cover it. Oh, there is much preliminary investigation to be done. And then, some kind of protective . . ."

"I see," Meron broke in.

Would the man never cease smiling? And yet, Lessa thought, his irony might work in their favor.

"It could be a lifelong project," he went on.

"Not if I know F'lar," the Harper said dryly. "I've recently entertained the notion that Benden's Weyrleader takes these latest vagaries of our ancient scourge as a personal insult, since we had rather thought we'd got them neatly slotted in time and place."

There was such good-humored raillery in the Harper's tone that Oterel of Tillek gave a snort. Lord Groghe looked more thoughtful, probably not quite recovered from F'lar's rebuttal the other day.

"An insult to Benden?" asked Sangel, baffled. "But his time-tables were accurate for Turns. Used them myself and never found them wrong until just recently."

Meron stamped his foot, his affected pose gone.

"You're all fools. Letting the Harper sweet-talk you into complacency. We'll never see the end of Thread. Not in his lifetime or ours. And we'll be paying tithes to shiftless Weyrs, deferring to dragonriders and their women as long as this planet circles the sun. And there's not one of you great Lords, not one, with the courage to force this issue. We don't need dragonriders. We don't need 'em. We've fire lizards which eat Thread . . ."

"Then shall I inform T'bor of the High Reaches Weyr that his wings need no longer patrol Nabol? I'm certain he would be relieved," Lessa asked in her lightest, sweetest voice.

The Nabolese Lord gave her a look of pure hatred. The fire lizard gathered itself into a hissing launch position. A single clear note from Ramoth all but deafened those on the heights. The fire lizard disappeared with a shriek. Strangling on his curses, Meron stamped down the lighted path to the landing, calling harshly for his dragon. The green appeared with such alacrity that Lessa was certain Ramoth had summoned him, even as she had warned the little lizard against attacking Lessa.

"You wouldn't order T'bor to stop patrolling Nabol, would you, Weyrwoman?" asked Nessel, Lord of Crom. "After all, my lands march with his . . ."

"Lord Nessel," Lessa began, intending to reassure him that she had no such authority in the first place and in the second . . . "Lord Nessel," she repeated instead, smiling at him, "you notice that the Lord of Nabol did *not* request it, after all. Though," and she sighed with dramatic dedication, "we have been sorely tempted to penalize him for his part in the death of the two dragon queens." She gave Nessel a wan, brave smile. "But there are hundreds of innocent people on his lands, and many more about him, who cannot be permitted to suffer because of his—his—how shall I phrase it—his irrational behavior."

"Which leads me to ask," Groghe said, hastily clearing his throat, "what is being done with that—that Kylara woman?"

"Nothing," Lessa said in a flat hard voice, trusting that would end the matter.

"Nothing?" Groghe was incensed. "She caused the deaths of two queens and you're doing nothing . . ."

"Are the Lord Holders doing anything about Meron?" she asked, glancing sternly at the four present. There was a long silence. "I must return to Benden Weyr. The dawn and another day's watch come all too soon there. We're keeping Wansor and Fandarel from the observations that will make it possible for us to go to that Star."

"Before they monopolize the thing, I'd like another look," Oterel of Tillek said loudly. "My eyes are keen . . ."

Lessa was tired as she called Ramoth to her. She wanted to go back to Benden Weyr, not so much to sleep as to reassure herself about F'lar. Mnementh was with him, true, and he'd have reported any change in his rider's condition . . .

And I'd've told you, Ramoth said, sounding a little hurt.

"Lessa," the Harper's low voice reached her, "are you in favor of that expedition?"

She looked up at him, his face lighted by the path glows. His expression was neutral and she wondered if he'd really meant what he'd said back at the Star Rocks. He dissembled so easily, and so often against his own inclination, that she sometimes wondered what his candid thoughts were.

"It scares me. It scares me because it seems so likely that someone must have tried. Sometime. It just doesn't seem logical . . ."

"Is there any record that anyone, besides yourself, ever jumped so far *between* times?"

"No." She had to admit it. "Not so far. But then, there hadn't been such need."

"And there's no need now to take this other kind of a jump?"

"Don't unsettle me more." Lessa was unsure of what she felt or thought, or what anyone felt or thought, should or shouldn't do. Then she saw the kind, worried expression of the Harper's eyes and impulsively gripped his arm. "How can we know? How can we be sure?"

"How were you sure that the Question Song could be answered—by you?"

"And you've a new Question Song for me?"

"Questions, yes." He gave her a smile as he covered her hand gently with his own. "Answer?" He shook his head and then stepped back as Ramoth alighted.

But his questions were as difficult to forget as the Question Song which had led her *between* time. When she returned to Benden, she found that F'lar's skin was hot to the touch; he slept restlessly. So much so that, although Lessa willed herself to sleep beside him on the wide couch, she couldn't succeed. Desperate for some surcease from her fears —for F'lar, of the intangible unknown ahead—she crept from their couch and into the weyr. Ramoth roused sleepily and arranged her front legs in a cradle. Lulled by the warm, musty comfort of her dragon, Lessa finally did sleep.

By the morning, F'lar was no better, querulous with his fever and worried about her report on the viewing.

"I can't imagine what you expected me to see," she said with some exasperation after she had patiently described for the fourth time what she had seen through the distance-viewer.

"I *expected*," and he paused significantly, "to find some—some characteristic for which the dragons could fly *between*." He plucked at the bed fur, then pulled the recalcitrant forelock back from his eyes. "We have *got* to keep that promise to the Lord Holders."

"Why? To prove Meron wrong?"

"No. To prove it is or is not possible to get rid of Thread permanently." He scowled at her as if she should have known the answer.

"I think someone else must have tried to discover that before," she said wearily. "And we still have Thread."

"That doesn't mean anything," he countered in such a savage tone that he began to cough, an exercise which painfully contracted the injured muscles across his waist.

Instantly Lessa was at his side, offering him distilled wine, sweetened and laced with fellis fruit juice.

"I want F'nor," he said petulantly.

Lessa looked down at him for the coughing spasm had left him limp.

"If we can pry him away from Brekke."

F'lar's lips set in a thin line.

"You mean, only you, F'lar, Benden Weyrleader, can flout tradition?" she asked.

"That isn't . . ."

"If it's your pet project you're worrying about, I had N'ton secure Thread . . ."

"N'ton?" F'lar's eyes flew open in surprise.

"Yes. He's a good lad and, from what I heard at Fort Weyr last night, very deft in being exactly where he is needed, unobtrusively."

"And . . . ?"

"And? Well, when the next queen at Fort Weyr rises, he'll undoubtedly take the Leadership. Which is what you intended, isn't it?"

"I don't mean that. I mean, the Thread."

Lessa felt her guts turn over at the memory. "As you thought, the grubs rose to the surface the instant we put the Thread in. Very shortly there was no more Thread."

F'lar's eyes shone and he parted his lips in a triumphant smile.

"Why didn't you tell me sooner?"

At that, Lessa jammed both fists against her waist and awarded him one of her sternest looks.

"Because there have been a few other things to occupy my

mind and time. This is not something we can discuss in open session, after all. Why, if even such loyal riders as . . ."

"What did N'ton say? Does he fully understand what I'm trying to do?"

Lessa eyed her Weyrmate thoughtfully. "Yes, he does, which is why I chose him to substitute for F'nor."

That seemed to relieve F'lar, for he leaned back against the pillows with a deep sigh and closed his eyes. "He's a good choice. For more than Fort Weyrleadership. He'd carry on. That's what we need the most, Lessa. Men who think, who can carry on. That's what happened before." His eyes flew open, shadowed with a vague fear and a definite worry. "What time is it at Fort Weyr now?"

Lessa made a rapid calculation. "Dawn's about four hours away."

"Oh. I want N'ton here as soon as possible."

"Now wait a minute, F'lar, he's a Fort rider . . ."

F'lar grabbed for her hand, pulling her down to him. "Don't you see," he demanded his voice hoarse, his urgency frightening, "he's got to know. Know everything I plan. Then, if something happens . . ."

Lessa stared at him, not comprehending. Then she was both furious with him for frightening her, irritated with his self-pity, and terrified that he might indeed be fatally ill.

"F'lar, get a grip on yourself, man," she said, half-angry, half-teasing; he felt so hot.

He flung himself back down on the bed, tossing his head from side to side.

"This is what happened before. I know it. I don't care what he says, get F'nor here."

Lioth is coming and a green from Telgar, Mnementh announced.

Lessa took consolation from the fact that Mnementh didn't seem the least bit distressed by F'lar's ravings.

F'lar gave a startled cry, glaring accusingly at Lessa.

"Don't look at me. I didn't send for N'ton. It isn't even dawn there yet."

The green is a messenger and the man he bears is very excited, Mnementh reported, and he sounded mildly curious.

Ramoth, who had taken herself to the Hatching Ground after Lessa awakened, rumbled a challenge to bronze Lioth.

N'ton came striding down the passageway, accompanied by

Wansor, certainly the last person Lessa expected to see. The rotund little man's face was flushed with excitement, his eyes sparkling despite red rims and bloodshot whites.

"Oh, Weyrlady, this is the most exciting news imaginable. Really exciting!" Wansor babbled, shaking the large leaf under her nose. She had an impression of circles. Then Wansor saw F'lar. All the excitment drained out of his face as he realized that the Weyrleader was a very sick man. "Sir, I had no idea—I wouldn't have presumed . . ."

"Nonsense, man," F'lar said irritably. "What brings you? What have you there? Let me see. You've found a coordinate for the dragons?"

Wansor seemed so uncertain about proceeding that Lessa took charge, guiding the man to the bed.

"What's this leaf mean? Ah, this is Pern, and that is the Red Star, but what are these other circles you've marked?"

"I'm not certain I know, my lady, but I discovered them while scanning the heavens last night—or this morning. The Red Star is not the only globe above us. There is this one, too, which became visible toward morning, didn't it, N'ton?" The young bronze rider nodded solemnly but there was a gleam of amusement in his blue eyes for the glassman's manner of exposition. "And very faintly, but still visible as a sphere, is this third heavenly neighbor, to our northeast, low on the horizon. Then, directly south—it was N'ton's notion to look all around—we found this larger globe with the most unusual cluster of objects moving with visible speed about it. Why, the skies around Pern are crowded!" Wansor's dismay was so ludicrous that Lessa had to stifle her giggle.

F'lar took the leaf from the glassman and began to study it while Lessa pushed Wansor onto the stool by the sick man. F'lar tapped the circles thoughtfully as though this tactile contact made them more real.

"And there are four stars in the skies?"

"Indeed there are many more, Weyrleader," Wansor replied. "But only these," and his stained forefinger pointed to the three newly discovered neighbors, "appear so far as globes in the distance-viewer. The others are merely bright points of light as stars have always been. One must assume, then, that these three are also controlled by our sun, and pass around it, even as we do. For I do not see how they could escape the force that tethers us and the Red Star to the sun—a force we know to be tremendous . . ."

F'lar looked up from the rude sketches, a terrible expression on his face.

"If these are so near, then does Thread really come from the Red Star?"

"Oh dear, oh dear," moaned Wansor softly and began caressing his fingertips with his thumbs in little fluttery gestures.

"Nonsense," said Lessa so confidently that the three men glanced at her in surprise. "Let's not make more complications than we already have. The ancients who knew enough to make that distance-viewer definitely stipulate the Red Star as the origin of Thread. If it were one of these others, they'd have said so. It is when the Red Star approaches Pern that we have Thread."

"In that drawing in the Council Room at Fort Weyr there is a diagram of globes on circular routes," N'ton said thoughtfully. "Only there are six circles and," his eyes widened suddenly; he glanced quickly down at the sheet in Wansor's hand, ". . . one of them, the next to the last, has clusters of smaller satellites."

"Well, then, except that we've seen it with our own eyes, what's all the worry?" demanded Lessa, grabbing up the *klah* pitcher and mugs to serve the newcomers. "We've only just discovered for ourselves what the ancients knew and inscribed on that wall."

"Only now," N'ton said softly, "we know what that design means."

Lessa shot him a long look and nearly flooded Wansor's cup.

"Indeed. The actual experience is the knowing, N'ton."

"I gather you have both spent the night at that distance-viewer?" asked F'lar. When they nodded, he asked, "What of the Red Star? Did you see anything that could guide us in?"

"As to that, sir," N'ton answered after a questioning glance at Wansor, "there is an odd-shaped protuberance which puts me in mind of the tip of Nerat, only pointed east instead of west—" His voice trailed off and he gave a diffident shrug of his shoulders.

F'lar sighed and leaned back again, all the eagerness gone from his face.

"Insufficient detail, huh?"

"Last night," N'ton added in hurried qualification.

"I doubt the following nights will alter the view."

"On the contrary, Weyrleader," said Wansor, his eyes wide, "the Red Star turns on its own axis much as Pern does."

"But it is still too far away to make out any details," Lessa said firmly.

F'lar shot her an annoyed look. "If I could only see for myself . . ."

Wansor looked up brightly. "Well, now, you know, I had about figured out how to utilize the lenses from the magnifier. Of course, there'd be no such maneuverability as one can achieve with the ancient device, but the advantage is that I could set up those lenses on your own Star Stones. It's rather interesting, too, because if I put one lens in the Eye rock and set the other on the Finger Rock, you will see—or, but then you won't see, will you?" And the little man seemed to deflate.

"Won't see what?"

"Well, those rocks are situated to catch the Red Star only at winter solstice, so of course the angles are wrong for any other time of year. But then, I could—no," Wansor's face was puckered with his intense frown. Only his eyes moved, restlessly, as the myriad thoughts he was undoubtedly sifting were reflected briefly. "I will think about it. But I am sure that I can devise a means of your seeing the Red Star, Weyrleader, without moving from Benden."

"You must be exhausted Wansor," Lessa said, before F'lar could ask another question.

"Oh, not to mention," Wansor replied, blinking hard to focus on her.

"Enough to mention," Lessa said firmly and took the cup from his hand, half-lifting him from the stool. "I think, Master Wansor, that you had better sleep here at Benden a little while."

"Oh, could I? I'd the most fearful notion that I might fall off the dragon *between*. But that couldn't happen, could it? Oh, I can't stay. I have the Craft's dragon. Really, perhaps I'd just better . . ."

His voice trailed off as Lessa led him down the corridor.

"He was up all last night too," N'ton said, grinning affectionately after Wansor.

"There is no way to go *between* to the Red Star?"

N'ton shook his head slowly. "Not that we could see tonight—last night. The same features of dark, reddish masses were turned toward us most of the time we watched. Just before we decided you should know about the other planets, I took a final look and that Nerat-like promontory had disappeared, leaving only the dullish gray-red coloration."

"There must be some way to get to the Red Star."

"I'm sure you'll find it, sir, when you're feeling better."

F'lar grimaced, thinking that "unobtrusive" was an apt description of this young man. He had deftly expressed confidence in his superior, that only ill-health prevented immediate action, and that the ill-health was a passing thing.

"Since that's the way matters stand in that direction, let us proceed in another. Lessa said that you procured Thread for us. Did you see how those swampgrubs dealt with Thread?"

N'ton nodded slowly, his eyes glittering.

"If we hadn't had to cede the dissidents the continent, I'd've had a straight-flown Search discover the boundaries of the southern lands. We still don't know its extent. Exploration was stopped on the west by the deserts, and on the east by the sea. But it can't be just the swampy area that is infested with these grubs." F'lar shook his head. He sounded querulous to himself. He took a breath, forcing himself to speak more slowly and therefore less emotionally. "There's been Threadfall in the Southern Weyr for seven Turns and not a single burrow. The ground crews have never had to flame out anything. Now, even with the most careful, most experienced, sharpest-eyed riders, some Thread gets to the ground. T'bor insists there were never any burrows to be found anywhere after a Threadfall." F'lar grimaced. "His wings are efficient and Threadfall is light in the south, but I wished I'd known."

"And what would you have thought?" asked Lessa with her usual asperity as she rejoined them. "Nothing. Because until Thread started falling out of phase, and you had been at the swampfall, you'd never have correlated the information."

She was right, of course, but N'ton didn't have to look so torn between agreement with her and sympathy for him. Silently F'lar railed at this infuriating debility. He ought to be up and around, not forced to rely on the observations of others at a crucial time like this.

"Sir, in the Turns I've been a dragonrider," said N'ton,

considering his words even as he spoke, "I've learned that nothing is done without purpose. I used to call my sire foolish to insist that one tanned leather in just one way, or stretched hide only a little at a time, well-soaked, but I've realized recently that there is an order, a reason, a rhyme for it." He paused, but F'lar urged him to go on. "I've been most interested in the methods of the Mastersmith. That man *thinks* constantly." The young man's eyes shone with such intense admiration that F'lar grinned. "I'm afraid I may be making a nuisance of myself but I learned so much from him. Enough to realize that there're gaps in the knowledge that's been transmitted down to us. Enough to understand that perhaps the southern continent was abandoned to let the grubs grow in strength there . . ."

"You mean, that if the ancients knew they couldn't get to the Red Star," Lessa exclaimed, "they developed the grubs to protect growing fields?"

"They developed the dragons from fire lizards, didn't they? Why not grubs as ground crews?" And N'ton grinned at the whimsy of his thesis.

"That makes sense," Lessa said, looking hopefully at F'lar. "Certainly that explains why the dragons haven't jumped *between* to the Red Star. They didn't need to. Protection was being provided."

"Then why don't we have grubs here in the north?" asked F'lar contentiously.

"Ha! Someone didn't live long enough to transmit the news, or sow the grubs, or cultivate them, or something. Who can tell?" Lessa threw wide her arms. It was obvious to F'lar that she preferred this theory, subtle as she may have been in trying to block his desire to go to the Red Star.

He was willing to believe that the grubs were the answer, but the Red Star had to be visited. If only to reassure the Lord Holders that the dragonmen were trustworthy.

"We still don't *know* if the grubs exist beyond the swamps," F'lar reminded her.

"I don't mind sneaking in and finding out," N'ton said. "I know Southern very well, sir. Probably as well as anyone, even F'nor. I'd like permission to go south and check." When N'ton saw F'lar hesitate and Lessa frown, he went on hurriedly. "I can evade T'kul. That man's so obvious, he's pathetic."

"All right, all right, N'ton. Go. It's the truth I've no one else to send," and F'lar tried not to feel bitter that F'nor was involved with a woman; he was a dragonrider first, wasn't he? Then F'lar suppressed such uncharitable thoughts. Brekke had been a Weyrwoman; through no fault of hers (and F'lar still berated himself that he had not thought of keeping a closer check on Kylara's activities—he'd been warned), Brekke was deprived of her dragon. If she found some comfort in F'nor's presence, it was unforgivable to deprive her of his company. "Go, N'ton. Spot-check. And bring back samples of those grubs from every location. I *wish* Wansor had not dismantled that other contraption. We could look closely at the grubs. That Masterherder was a fool. The grubs might not be the same in every spot."

"Grubs are grubs," Lessa mumbled.

"Landbeasts raised in the mountains are different from landbeasts raised on the plains," N'ton said. "Fellis trees grown south are larger with better fruit than Nerat's best."

"You know too much," Lessa replied, grinning to take the sting from her words.

N'ton grinned. "I'm a bronze rider, Weyrwoman."

"You'd best be off. No, wait. Are you sure Fort is not going to need you and Lioth for Thread?" F'lar asked, wanting to be rid of this very healthy youngster who only emphasized his illness.

"Not for a while, sir. It's full night there still."

That underscored his youthfulness and F'lar waved him out, trying to suppress jealousy with gratitude. The moment he'd gone, F'lar let out a sudden exasperated oath that brought Lessa, all consideration, to his side.

"I'll get well, I'll get well," he fumed. He held her hand against his cheek, grateful, too, for the cool of her fingers as they curved to fit against his face.

"Of course you'll get well. You're never sick," she murmured softly, stroking his forehead with her free hand. Then her voice took on a teasing note. "You're just stupid. Otherwise you wouldn't have gone *between*, let cold into a wound, and developed fever."

F'lar, reassured as much by her caustic jibe as her cool and loving caresses, lay back and willed himself to sleep, to health.

CHAPTER XIV

Early Morning at Ruatha Hold
Midday at Benden Weyr

When word came that the Hatching was likely to occur that bright spring day, Jaxom didn't know whether he was glad or not. Ever since the two queens had killed each other ten days before, Lytol had been sunk in such a deep gloom that Jaxom had tiptoed around the Hold. His guardian had always been a somber man, never given to joking or teasing, but this new silence unnerved the entire Hold. Even the new baby didn't cry.

It was bad, very bad, to lose one queen, Jaxom knew, but to lose two, in such a horrible way! It was almost as if *things* were pointing toward even direr events. Jaxom was scared, a deep voiceless feeling in his bones. He almost dreaded seeing Felessan. He had never shaken off his sense of blasphemy for invading the Hatching Ground, and wondered if this were his punishment. But he was a logical boy and the death of the two queens had not occurred at Ruatha, not over Fort Weyr to which Ruatha Hold was bound. He'd never met Kylara or Brekke. He did know F'nor and felt sorry for him if half what he'd heard was true—that F'nor had taken Brekke into his weyr and had abandoned his duties as a Wing-second to care for her. She was very sick. Funny, everyone was sorry for Brekke but no one mentioned Kylara, and she'd lost a queen, too.

Jaxom wondered about that but *knew* he couldn't ask. Just as he couldn't ask if he and Lytol were really going to the Hatching. Why else would the Weyrleader send them word? And wasn't Talina a Ruathan candidate for the queen egg? Ruatha ought to be represented at the Hatching. Benden Weyr always had open Impressions, even when the other Weyrs didn't. And he hadn't seen Felessan in ages. Not that anyone had done much more than Thread-watch since the wedding at Telgar.

Jaxom sighed. That had been some day. He shivered, remembered how sick, cold and—yes—how scared he'd been. (Lytol said a *man* wasn't afraid to admit to fear.) All the time he'd watched F'lar fighting T'ron, he'd been scared. He shuddered again, his spine rippling with reaction to that memory. Everything was going wrong on Pern. Dragon queens killing each other, Weyrleaders dueling in public, Thread falling here and there, with no rhyme or reason. Order had slipped away from life; the constants that made his routine were dissolving, and he was powerless to stop the inexorable slide. It wasn't fair. Everything had been going so well. Everyone had been saying how Ruatha Hold had improved. Now, this past six days, they'd lost that northeastern farmhold and, if things kept up, there wouldn't be much left of all Lytol's hard work. Maybe that's why he was acting so—so odd. But it wasn't fair. Lytol had worked so hard. And now, it looked as though Jaxom was going to miss the Hatching and see who Impressed that littlest egg. It wasn't at all fair.

"Lord Jaxom," gasped a breathless drudge from the doorway, "Lord Lytol said for you to change to your best. The Hatching's to start. Oh, sir, do you think Talina has a chance?"

"More than a chance," Jaxom said, rude with excitement. "She's Ruathan-bred after all. Now get out."

His fingers were clumsy with the fastenings of his trousers

and the tunic which had been new for the Telgar wedding. *He* hadn't spilled on the fine fabric, but you could still see the greasy fingerprints on the right shoulder where an excited guest had pulled him away from his vantage point on the Telgar Hold steps during the fight.

He shrugged into the cloak, found the second glove under the bed and raced down into the Great Court where the blue dragon waited.

Sight of the blue, however, inevitably reminded Jaxom that Groghe's eldest son had been given one of the fire-lizard eggs. Lytol had deliberately refused the pair to which Ruatha Hold was entitled. That, too, was a rankling injustice. Jaxom should have had a fire-lizard egg, even if Lytol couldn't bear to Impress one. Jaxom was Lord of Ruatha and an egg had been his due. Lytol had no right to refuse him that perquisite.

"Be a good day for Ruatha if your Talina Impresses, won't it?" D'wer, the blue's rider, greeted him.

"Yes," Jaxom replied, and he sounded sullen even to himself.

"Cheer up, lad," D'wer said. "Things could be worse."

"How?"

D'wer chuckled and, while it offended Jaxom, he couldn't very well call a dragonman to task.

"Good morning, Trebith," Jaxom said to the blue, who turned his head, the large eye whirling with color.

They both heard Lytol's voice, dull-toned but clear as he gave instructions for the day's work to the stewards.

"For every field that gets scored, we plant two more as long as we can get seed in the ground. There's plenty of fallow land in the northeast. Move the Holders."

"But, Lord Lytol . . ."

"Don't give me the old wail about temporary dwellings. There'll be temporary eating if we aren't farsighted, and that's harder to endure than a draught or two."

Lytol gave Jaxom a cursory inspection and an absent good morning. The tic started in the Lord Holder's face the moment he climbed up Trebith's shoulder to take his seat against the neck ridges. He motioned curtly to his ward to get in front of him and then nodded to D'wer.

The blue dragonman gave a slight smile of response, as if he expected no more notice from Lytol, and suddenly they were aloft. Aloft, with Ruatha's fire height dwindling below.

And *between* with Jaxom holding his breath against the frightening cold. Then above Benden's Star Stones, so close to other dragons also winging into the Weyr that Jaxom feared collision at any moment.

"How—how do they know where they are?" he asked D'wer.

The rider grinned at him. *"They* know. Dragons never collide." And a shadow of memory crossed D'wer's usually cheerful face.

Jaxom groaned. How stupid of him to make any reference to the queens' battle.

"Lad, everything reminds us of that," the blue rider said. "Even the dragons are off color. But," he continued more briskly, "the Impression will help."

Jaxom hoped so but, pessimistically, he was sure something would go wrong today, too. Then he clutched wildly at D'wer's riding tunic for it seemed as if they were flying straight into the rock face of the Weyr Bowl. Or worse, despite D'wer's reassurance, right into the green dragon also veering in that direction.

But suddenly they were inside the wide mouth of the upper entrance, a dark core that led into the immense Hatching Ground. The whirr of wings, a concentration of the musty scent of dragons, and then they were poised above the slightly steaming sands, in the great circle theatre with its tiers of perches for men and beasts.

Jaxom had a dizzying view of the eggs on the Hatching Ground, of the colored robes of those already assembled, and the array of dragon bodies, gleaming eyes and furled wings, the great, graceful, blue, green and brown hides. Where were the bronzes?

"They'll bring in the candidates, Lord Jaxom. Ah, there's the young scamp," D'wer said, and suddenly Jaxom's neck was jerked as Trebith backwinged to land neatly on a ledge. "Off you go."

"Jaxom! You did come!"

And Felessan was thumping him, his clothes so new they smelled of dye and were harsh against Jaxom's hands as he pounded his friend's back.

"Thanks so much for bringing him, D'wer. Good day to you, Lord Warder Lytol. The Weyrleader and the Weyrwoman said to give you their greetings and to ask you to stay to eat after Impression, if you would give them a moment of your time."

It all came out in such a rush that the blue rider grinned. Lytol bowed in such solemn acknowledgment that Jaxom felt a surge of irritation for his stuffy guardian.

Felessan was impervious to such nuances and pulled Jaxom eagerly away from the adults. Having achieved a certain physical distance, the boy chattered away in so loud a whisper that everyone two ledges up could hear him distinctly.

"I was sure you wouldn't be allowed to come. Everything's been so sour and horrible since the—you know—happened."

"Don't you *know* anything, Felessan?" Jaxom said in a rebuking hiss that startled his friend into wide-eyed silence.

"Huh? What'd I do wrong?" he demanded, this time in a more circumspect tone, glancing around him apprehensively. "Don't tell me something's gone wrong at Ruatha Hold?"

Jaxom pulled his friend as far from Lytol as they could go on that row of seats and then sat the younger boy down so hard that Felessan let out a yip of protest which he instantly muffled behind both hands. Jaxom glanced surreptitiously back at Lytol but the man was responding to the greetings of those in the level above. People were still arriving, both by dragonwing and by a climb up the flight of stairs from the hot sands. Felessan giggled suddenly, pointing toward a portly man and woman now crossing the Hatching Ground. They obviously wore thin-soled shoes for they kept picking their feet up and putting them down in a curious mincing motion, totally at variance with their physical appearance.

"Didn't think so many people would come what with all that's been happening," Felessan murmured excitedly, his eyes dancing. "Look at them!" and he pointed out three boys, all with the Nerat device on their chests. "They look as if they smelled something unpleasant. You don't think dragons smell, do you?"

"No, of course not. Only a little and it's pleasant. They aren't candidates, are they?" Jaxom asked, disgusted.

"Nooo. Candidates wear white." Felessan made a grimace for Jaxom's ignorance. "They don't come in till later. Ooops! And later may be sooner. Didja see that egg rock?"

The motion had been observed, for the dragons began to hum. There were excited cries from late arrivals who now scurried for places. And Jaxom could scarcely see the rest of

the eggs for the sudden flutter of dragon wings in the air.
Just as suddenly, there were no more impediments to vision
and all the eggs seemed to be rocking. Almost as if they
finally found the hot sands underneath too much. Only one
egg was motionless. The little one, still off by itself against
the far wall.

"What's wrong with that one?" Jaxom asked, pointing.

"That smallest one?" Felessan swallowed, keeping his face
averted.

"We didn't *do* anything to it."

"*I* didn't," Felessan said firmly, glaring at Jaxom. "You
touched it."

"I may have touched it but that doesn't mean I hurt it,"
the young Lord Holder begged for reassurance.

"No, touching 'em doesn't hurt 'em. The candidates've been
touching 'em for weeks and they're rocking."

"Why isn't that one then?"

Jaxom had difficulty making Felessan understand him for
the humming had increased until it was a constant, exciting
thrum reverberating back and forth across the Hatching
Ground.

"I dunno," Felessan shrugged diffidently. "It may not even
Hatch. That's what *they* say, at any rate."

"But I didn't *do* anything," Jaxom insisted, mostly for his
own comfort.

"I told you that! Look, here come the candidates." Then
Felessan leaned over, his lips right at Jaxom's ear, whispering
something so unintelligible that he had to repeat it three
times before Jaxom did hear him.

"Re-Impress Brekke?" Jaxom exclaimed, far louder than
he meant to, glancing toward Lytol.

"Deafwit!" Felessan hissed at him, jerking him back in his
seat. "You don't *know* what's been going on here. Let me tell
you, it's been something!" Felessan's eyes were wide with
suppressed knowledge.

"What? Tell me!"

Felessan glanced toward Lytol but the man seemed oblivious of them; his attention was on the young boys marching toward the rocking eggs, their faces white and purpose-
ful, their bodies in the white tunics taut with excitement and
anticipation.

"What do you mean about Brekke re-Impressing? Why?

How?" Jaxom demanded, his mind assaulted by simultaneous conflicts: Lytol astride a dragon all his own, Brekke re-Impressing, Talina left out and crying because she was Ruathan-bred and should be dragonwoman.

"Just that. She Impressed a dragon once, she's young. They said she was a far better Weyrwoman than that Kylara." Felessan's tone echoed the universally bad opinion of the Southern ex-Weyrwoman. "That way Brekke'd get well. You see," and Felessan lowered his voice again, "F'nor loves her! And I heard—" he paused dramatically and looked around (as if anyone could overhear them), "I heard that F'nor was going to let Canth fly her queen."

Jaxom stared at his friend, shocked. "You're crazy! Brown dragons don't fly queens."

"Well, F'nor was going to try it."

"But—but . . .

"Yes, it is!" Felessan agreed sagely. "You should've heard F'lar and F'nor." His eyes widened to double their normal size. "It was Lessa, my mother, who said what they ought to do. Make Brekke re-Impress. She was too good, Lessa said, to live half-dead."

Both boys glanced guiltily toward Lytol.

"Do they—do they think she can re-Impress?" asked Jaxom, staring at the stern profile of his guardian and wondering.

Felessan shrugged. "We'll know soon. Here they come."

And sure enough, out of the black maw of the upper tunnel, flew bronze dragons in such rapid succession that they seemed nose to tail.

"There's Talina!" Jaxom exclaimed, jumping to his feet. "There's Talina, Lytol," and he crossed to pull at his guardian's arm. Lytol wouldn't have noticed either Jaxom's importunities or Talina's entrance. The man had eyes only for the girl entering from the Ground level. Two figures, a man and a woman, stood by the wide opening, as if they could accompany her this far, no further.

"That's Brekke all right," Felessan said in a hushed tone as he slid beside Jaxom.

She stumbled slightly, halted, seemingly impervious to the uncomfortably hot sands. She straightened her shoulders and slowly walked across to join the five girls who waited near the golden egg. She stopped by Talina, who turned and gestured for the newcomer to take a place in the loose semi-circle about the queen egg.

The humming stopped. In the sudden, unquiet silence, the faint crack of a shell was clearly audible, followed by the pop and shatter of others.

The dragonets, glistening, awkward, ugly young things, began to flop from their casings, squawking, crooning, their wedge-shaped heads too big for the thin, sinuous necks. The young boys stood very still, their bodies tense with the mental efforts of attracting the dragonets to them.

The first was free of its encumbrance, staggering beyond the nearest boy who jumped adroitly out of its way. It fell, nose first at the feet of a tall black-haired lad. The boy knelt, helped the dragonet balance on his shaky feet, looked into the rainbow eyes. Jaxom saw Lytol close his, and saw the fact of Lytol's terrible loss engraved on the man's gray face, as much of a torture now as the day his Larth had died of phosphine burns.

"Look," Jaxom cried, "the queen egg. It's rocking. Oh, how I wish . . ."

Then he couldn't go on without compromising himself in his friend's good opinion. For much as he wanted Talina to Impress which would mean three living Ruathan-bred Weyr-women, he knew that Felessan was betting on Brekke.

Felessan was so intensely involved in the scene below that he hadn't been aware of Jaxom's unfinished phrase.

The golden shell cracked suddenly, right down the center, and its inmate, with a raucous protest, fell to the sand on her back. Talina and two others moved forward quickly, trying to help the little creature right herself. The queen was no sooner on all four legs than the girls stepped back, almost as if they could not press their claim, by mutual consent leaving the first opportunity to Brekke.

She was oblivious. To Jaxom, it seemed she didn't care. She seemed limp, broken, pathetic, listing to one side. A dragon crooned softly and she shook her head as if only then aware of her surroundings.

The queen's head turned to Brekke, the glistening eyes enormous in the outsized skull. The queen lurched forward a step.

At that moment a small blur of bronze streaked across the Hatching Ground. With defiant screams, a fire lizard hung just above the queen's head. So close, in fact, that the little queen reared back with a startled shriek and bit at the air, instinctively spreading her wings as protection for her vulnerable eyes.

Dragons protested from their ledges. Talina interposed her body between the queen and her small attacker.

"Berd! Don't!" Brekke moved forward, arm extended, to capture the irate bronze. The little queen cried out in protest, hiding her face in Talina's skirts. The two women faced one another, their bodies tense, wary.

Then Talina stretched her hand out to Brekke, smiling. Her pose lasted only a moment for the queen butted her legs peremptorily. Talina knelt, arms reassuringly about the dragonet. Brekke turned, no longer a statue immobilized by grief, and retraced her steps to the figures waiting at the entrance. All the time, the little bronze fire lizard whirred around her head, emitting sounds that ranged from scolding to entreaty. The racket sounded so like the cook at Ruatha Hold at dinnertime that Jaxom grinned.

"She didn't want the queen," Felessan said, stunned. "She didn't try!"

"That fire lizard wouldn't let her," Jaxom said, wondering why he was defending Brekke.

"It would be wrong, terribly wrong for her to succeed," Lytol said in a dead voice. He seemed to shrink in on himself, his shoulders sagging, his hands dangling limply between his knees.

Some of the newly Impressed boys were beginning to lead their beasts from the Ground. Jaxom turned back, afraid to miss anything. It was all happening much too quickly. It'd be over in a few minutes.

"Didja see, Jaxom?" Fellessan was saying, pulling at his sleeve. "Didja see? Birto got a bronze and Pellomar only Impressed a green. Dragons don't like bullies and Pellomar's been the biggest bully in the Weyr. Good for you, Birto!" Felessan cheered his friend.

"The littlest egg hasn't cracked yet," Jaxom said, nudging Felessan and pointing. "Shouldn't it be hatching?"

Lytol frowned, roused by the anxiety in his ward's voice.

"They were saying it probably wouldn't hatch," Felessan reminded Jaxom, far more interested in seeing what dragons his friends had Impressed.

"But what if it doesn't hatch? Can't someone break it and help the poor dragon out? The way a birthing woman does when the baby won't come?"

Lytol whirled on Jaxom, his face suffused with anger.

"What would a boy your age know of birthing?"

"I know about mine," Jaxom replied stoutly, jerking his chin up. "I nearly died. Lessa told me so and she was there. Can a dragonet die?"

"Yes," Lytol admitted heavily because he never lied to the boy. "They can die and better so if the embryo is misformed."

Jaxom looked at his body quickly although he knew perfectly well he was as he should be; in fact, more developed than some of the other Hold boys.

"I've seen eggs that never hatched. Who needs to live—crippled?"

"Well, that egg's alive," Jaxom said. "Look at it rocking right now."

"You're right. It's moving. But it isn't cracking," Felessan said.

"Then why is everyone leaving?" Jaxom demanded suddenly, jumping to his feet. For there was no one anywhere near the wobbling small egg.

The Ground was busy with riders urging their beasts down to help the weyrlings, or to escort guests of the Weyr back to their Holds. Most of the bronzes, of course, had gone with the new queen. Vast as the Hatching Ground was, its volume shrank with so many huge beasts around. Yet not even the disappointed candidates spared any interest for that one small remaining egg.

"There's F'lar. He ought to be told, Lytol. Please!"

"He knows," Lytol said, for F'lar had beckoned several of the brown riders to him and they were looking toward the little egg.

"Go, Lytol. Make them help it!"

"Small eggs can occur in any queen's laying life," Lytol said. "This is not my concern. Nor yours."

He turned and began to make his way toward the steps, plainly certain that the boys would follow.

"But they're not doing anything," Jaxom muttered, rebelliously.

Felessan gave him a helpless shrug. "C'mon. We'll be eating soon at this rate. And there's all kinds of special things tonight." He trotted after Lytol.

Jaxom looked back at the egg, now wildly rocking. "It just isn't fair! They don't care what happens to you. They care about that Brekke, but not you. Come on, egg. Crack your shell! Show 'em. One good crack and I'll bet they'll do something!"

Jaxom had edged along the tier until he was just over the little egg. It was rocking in time with his urgings now, but there was no one within a dragonlength. There was something frenzied about the way it rocked, too, that made Jaxom think the dragonet was desperate for help.

Without thinking, Jaxom swung over the wall and let himself drop to the sands. He could now see the minute striations on the shell, he could hear the frantic tapping within, observe the fissures spreading. As he touched the shell, it seemed like rock to him, it was so hard. No longer leathery as it had been the day of their escapade.

"No one else'll help you. I will!" he cried and kicked the shell.

A crack appeared. Two more stout blows and the crack widened. A piteous cry inside was followed by the bright tip of the dragonet's nose, which battered at the tough shell.

"You want to get born. Just like me. All you need is a little help, same as me," Jaxom was crying, pounding at the crack with his fists. Thick pieces fell off, far heavier than the discarded shells of the other hatchlings.

"Jaxom, what are you doing?" someone yelled at him but it was too late.

The thick inner membrane was visible now and this was what had been impeding the dragonet's emergence. Jaxom ripped the slippery stuff open with his belt knife and, from the sac, fell a tiny white body, not much larger than Jaxom's torso. Instinctively Jaxom reached out, helping the back-stranded creature to its feet.

Before F'lar or anyone could intervene, the white dragon had raised adoring eyes to the Lord of Ruatha Hold and Impression had been made.

Completely oblivious to the dilemma he had just originated, the incredulous Jaxom turned to the stunned observers.

"He says his name is Ruth!"

CHAPTER XV

Evening at Benden Weyr: Impression Banquet

It had been like coming up out of the very bowels of the deepest hold, thought Brekke. And Berd had shown her the way. She shuddered again at the horror of memory. If she slipped back down . . .

Instantly she felt F'nor's hand tighten on her arm, felt the touch of Canth's thoughts and heard the chitter of the two fire lizards.

Berd had led her out of the Ground to F'nor and Manora. She'd been surprised at how tired and sad they both looked. She'd tried to talk but they'd hushed her. F'nor had carried her up to his weyr. She smiled now, opening her eyes, to see him bending over her. Brekke put her hand up to the dear, worried face of her lover; she could say that now, her lover, her Weyrmate, for he was that, too. Deep lines from the high-bridged nose pulled F'nor's mouth down at the corners. His eyes were darkly smudged and bloodshot, his hair, usually combed in crisp clean waves back from his high forehead, was stringy, oily.

"You need cozening, love," she said in a low voice which cracked and didn't seem to be hers at all.

With a groan that was close to a sob, F'nor embraced her. At first as if he were afraid of hurting her. Then, when he felt her arms tightening around him—for it was good to feel his strong back under her seeking hands—he almost crushed her until she cried out gladly for him to be careful.

He buried his lips in her hair, against her throat, in a surfeit of loving relief.

"We thought we'd lost you, too, Brekke," he said over and over while Canth crooned an exuberant descant.

"It was in my mind," Brekke admitted in a tremulous voice, burrowing against his chest, as if she must get even closer to him. "I was trapped in my mind and didn't own my body. I think that's what was wrong with me. Oh, F'nor," and all the grief that she'd not been able to express before came bursting out of her, "I even hated Canth!"

The tears poured down her cheeks and shuddering sobs shook a body already weakened by fasting. F'nor held her to him, patting her shoulders, stroking her until he began to fear that the convulsions would tear her apart. He beckoned urgently to Manora.

"She's got to cry, F'nor. It'll be an easing for her."

Manora's anxious expression, the way she folded and unfolded her hands, was strangely reassuring to F'nor. She, too, cared about Brekke, cared enough to let concern pierce that imperturbable serenity. He'd been so grateful to Manora for opposing a re-Impression, though he doubted his blood mother knew why he'd be against it. Or perhaps she did. Manora in her calm detachment missed few nuances or evasions.

Brekke's frail body was trembling violently now, torn apart by the paroxysm of her grief. The fire lizards took to fluttering anxiously and Canth's croon held on a distressed note. Brekke's hands opened and closed pathetically on his shoulders but the tearing sobs did not permit her to speak.

"She can't stop, Manora. She can't."

"Slap her."

"Slap her?"

"Yes, slap her," and Manora suited actions to words, fetching Brekke several sharp blows before F'nor could shield her face. "Now into the bathing pool with her. The water's warm enough to relax those muscles."

"You didn't have to slap her," F'nor said, angrily.

"She did, she did," said Brekke in a ragged gasp, shuddering as they bundled her into the warm pool water. Then she felt the heat penetrate and relax muscles knotted by racking sobs. As soon as she felt Brekke's body easing, Manora dried her with warmed towels and gestured for F'nor to tuck her back under the furs.

"She needs feeding up now, F'nor. And so do you," she said, looking sternly at him. "And you are to kindly remember that you've duties to others tonight. It's Impression Day."

F'nor snorted at Manora's reminder and saw Brekke smiling wanly up at him.

"I don't think you've left me at all since . . ."

"Canth and I needed to be with you, Brekke," he cut in when she faltered. He smoothed her hair back from her forehead as if such an action were the most important occupation in the world. She caught his hand and he looked into her eyes.

"I felt you there, both of you, even when I wanted most to die." Then she felt anger in her guts. "But how you could force me onto the Hatching Ground, to face another queen?"

Canth grumbled a protest. She could see the dragon through the uncurtained archway, his head turned toward her, his eyes flashing a little. She was startled by the unhealthy green tinge to his color.

"We didn't want to. That was F'lar's idea. And Lessa's. They thought it might work and they were afraid we'd lose you."

The empty ache she tried not to remember threatened to become a hole down which she must go if only to end that tearing, burning pain of loss.

No, cried Canth.

Two warm lizard bodies pressed urgently against her neck and face, affection and worry so palpable in their thoughts it was like a physical touch.

"Brekke!" The terror, the yearning, the desperation in F'nor's cry were louder than the inner roaring and pushed it back, dispersed its threat.

"Never leave me! Never leave me alone. I can't stand being alone even for a second," Brekke cried.

I am here, said Canth, as F'nor's arms folded hard around her. The two lizards echoed the brown's words, the sound of their thoughts strengthening as their resolve grew. Brekke clung to the surprise of their maturity as a weapon against that other terrible pain.

"Why, Grall and Berd care," she said.

"Of course they care." F'nor seemed almost angry that she'd doubt it.

"No, I mean, they *say* they care."

F'nor looked into her eyes, his embrace less fiercely possessive. "Yes, they're learning because they love."

"Oh, F'nor, if I hadn't Impressed Berd that day, what would have happened to me?"

F'nor didn't answer. He held her against him in loving silence until Mirrim, her lizards flying in joyous circles around her, came briskly into the weyr, carrying a well-laden tray.

"Manora had to attend to the seasoning, Brekke," the girl said in a didactic tone. "You know how fussy she is. But you are to eat every bit of this broth, and you've a potion to drink for sleeping. A good night's rest and you'll be feeling more yourself."

Brekke stared at the young girl, watching in a sort of bemusement while Mirrim deftly pushed F'nor out of her way, settled pillows behind her patient, a napkin at her throat, and began to spoon the rich wherry broth to Brekke's unprotesting lips.

"You can stop staring at me, F'nor of Benden," Mirrim said, "and start eating the food I brought you before it gets cold. I carved you a portion of spiced wherry from the breast, so don't waste prime servings."

F'nor rose obediently, a smile on his face, recognizing the child's mannerisms as a blend of Manora and Brekke.

To her own surprise, Brekke found the broth delicious, warming her aching stomach and somehow satisfying a craving she hadn't recognized until now. Obediently she drank the sleeping potion, though the fellis juice did not entirely mask the bitter aftertaste.

"Now, F'nor, are you going to let poor Canth waste away to a watch-wher?" Mirrim asked as she began to settle Brekke for the night. "He's a sorry shade for a brown."

"He did eat—" F'nor began contritely.

"Ha!" Mirrim sounded like Lessa now.

I'll have to take that child in hand, Brekke thought idly, but an enervating lassitude had spread throughout her body and movement was impossible.

"You get that lazy lump of brown bones out of his couch and down to the Feeding Ground, F'nor. Hurry it up. They'll be out to feast soon and you know what a feeding dragon does to commoner appetites. C'mon now. You, Canth, get out of your weyr."

The last thing Brekke saw as F'nor obediently followed Mirrim out of the sleeping room was Canth's surprised look as she bore down on him, reached for his ear and began to tug.

They were leaving her, Brekke thought with sudden terror. Leaving her alone . . .

I am with you, was Canth's instant reassurance.

The two lizards, one on each side of her head, pressed lovingly against her.

And I, said Ramoth. *I, too,* said Mnementh and, mingled with those strong voices, were others, soft but present.

"There," said Mirrim with great satisfaction as she re-entered the sleeping room. "They'll eat and come right back." She moved quietly around the room, turning the shields on the glow baskets so that the room was dark enough for sleeping. "F'nor says you don't like to be left alone so I'll wait until he comes back."

But I'm not alone, Brekke wanted to tell her. Instead, her eyes closed and she fell into a deep sleep.

As Lessa looked around the Bowl, at the tables of celebrants lingering long past the end of the banquet, she experienced a wistful yearning to be as uninhibited as they. The laughter of the hold and craftbred parents of the new riders, the weyrlings themselves fondling their hatchlings, even the weyrfolk, was untinged by bitterness or sorrow. Yet she was aware of a nagging sadness, which she couldn't shake, and had no reason to feel.

Brekke was herself, weak but no longer lost to reason; F'nor had actually left the girl long enough to eat with the guests; F'lar was recovering his strength and had come to realize that he must delegate some of his new responsibilities. And Lytol, the most distressing problem since Jaxom had Impressed that little white dragon—how *could* that have happened?—had managed to get roaring drunk, thanks to the tender offices of Robinton who had matched him drink for drink.

The two were singing some utterly reprehensible song that only a Harper could know. The Lord Warder of Ruatha Hold kept falling out of tune, though the man had a surprisingly pleasant tenor voice. Somehow, she'd have thought him a bass; he had a gloomy nature and bass voices are dark.

She toyed with the remains of the sweet cake on her platter. Manora's women had outdone themselves: the fowls had been stuffed with fermented fruits and breads, and the result was a remission of the "gamy" taste that wherry often had. River grains had been steamed so that each individual morsel was separate and tender. The fresh herbs must have come from Southern. Lessa made a mental note to speak to Manora about sneaking down there. It simply wouldn't do to have an incident with T'kul. Maybe N'ton had gathered them when he went on his "grubbing" expeditions. She'd always liked the young bronze rider. Now that she'd got to know him better . . .

She wondered what he and F'lar were doing. They'd left the table and gone to the Rooms. They were always there these days, she thought irritably. They must be cleaning the grubs' orifices. Could she, too, slip away? No, she'd better stay here. It wasn't courteous for both Weyrleaders to absent themselves on such an auspicious occasion. And people ought to be leaving soon.

What were they going to do about young Jaxom? She looked around, locating Jaxom easily by the white hide of his dragon in the group of weyrlings watering their beasts by the lakeside. The beast had charm, true, but had he a future? And why Jaxom? She was glad that Lytol could get drunk tonight, but that wouldn't make tomorrow easier for the ex-dragonrider to endure. Maybe they ought to keep that pair here, until the beast died. The consensus was that Ruth would not mature.

At the other end of the long "high" table were Larad, Lord of Telgar, Sifer of Bitra, Raid of Benden Hold, and Asgenar of Lemos with Lady Famira (she really did blush all the time). The Lemos Hold pair had brought their fire lizards—fortunately a brown and a green—which had been the object of much overt interest by Lord Larad, who had a pair hardening on his hearth, and covert inspection by old Raid and Sifer of Bitra, who also had eggs from F'nor's last find. Neither older Lord Holder was entirely sure of the experiment with fire lizards but they had watched the Lemos pair all evening. Sifer had finally unfrosted enough to ask how to care for one. Would this influence their minds in the matter of Jaxom and his Ruth?

By the Egg, they couldn't want to disrupt the territorial balance because Jaxom had Impressed a sport dragon that hadn't a chance in Threadfall of surviving! How could you make an honorific out of Jaxom? J'om? J'xom? Most weyr-women chose names for their sons that could be contracted decently. Then Lessa was amused to be worrying over how to shorten a name, a trivial detail in this dilemma. No, Jaxom must remain at Ruatha Hold. She'd relinquished her Bloodright on Ruatha Hold to *him*, Gemma's son, because he *was* Gemma's son and had at least some minute quantity of Ruathan Blood. She certainly would contest the Hold going to any other Bloodline. Too bad Lytol had no sons. No, *Jaxom* must remain as Lord Holder at Ruatha. Just like men to make a piece of work over something so simple. The little beast would not survive. He was too small, his color—who ever heard of a white dragon?—indicated other abnormalities. Manora'd mentioned that white-skinned, pink-eyed child from Nerat Hold who hadn't been able to endure daylight. A nocturnal dragon?

Obviously Ruth would never grow to full size; new-hatched, he was more like a large fire lizard.

Ramoth rumbled from the heights, disturbed by her rider's thoughts, and Lessa sent a hundred apologies to her.

"It's no reflection on you, my darling," Lessa told her. "Why, you've spawned more queens than any other three. And the largest of their broods is no better than the smallest of yours, love."

Ruth will prosper, Ramoth said.

Mnementh crooned from the ledge and Lessa stared up at them, their eyes glowing in the shadows over the glow-lit Bowl.

Did the dragons know something she didn't? They often seemed to these days, and yet, how could they? They never cared about tomorrow, or yesterday, living for the moment.

Which was not a bad way to live, Lessa reflected, a trifle enviously. Her roving eyes fastened on the white blur of Ruth. Why had those two Impressed? Didn't she have troubles enough?

"Why should I mind? Why should I?" demanded Lytol suddenly in a loud, belligerent voice.

The Harper beamed up at him in an idiotish way. "Tha's what I say. Why should you?"

"I love the boy. I love him more than if he were flesh and blood of me, of me, Lytol of Ruatha Hold. Proved I love him, too. Proved I care for him. Ruatha's rich. Rich as when the Ruathan Bloodline ruled it. Undid all Fox's harm. And did it all, not for me. My life's spent. I've been everything. Been a dragonrider. Oh, Larth, my beautiful Larth. Been a weaver so I know the Crafts. Know the Holds now, too. Know everything. Know how to take care of a white runt. Why *shouldn't* the boy keep his dragon? By the First Shell, no one else wanted him. No one else wanted to Impress him. He's special, I tell you. Special!"

"Now, just a moment, Lord Lytol," Raid of Benden said, rising from his end of the table and stalking down to confront Lytol. "Boy's Impressed a dragon. That means he must stay in the Weyr."

"Ruth's not a proper dragon," Lytol said, neither speaking nor acting as drunk as he must be.

"Not a proper dragon?" Raid's expression showed his shock at such blasphemy.

"Never been a white dragon ever," Lytol said pontifically, drawing himself up to his full height. He wasn't much taller than the Lord Holder of Benden but he gave the impression of greater stature. "Never!" He appeared to feel that required a toast but found his cup empty. He managed to pour wine with creditable deftness for a man swaying on his feet. The Harper motioned wildly for his own glass to be filled but had trouble keeping it steady under the flow of wine.

"Never a whi' dragon," the Harper intoned and touched cups with Lytol.

"May not live," Lytol added, taking a long gulp.

"May not!"

"Therefore," and Lytol took a deep breath, "the boy must remain in his Hold. Ruatha Hold."

"Absolutely must!" Robinton held his cup high, more or less daring Raid to contradict him.

Raid favored him with a long inscrutable look.

"He must remain in the Weyr," he said finally, though he didn't sound as definite.

"No, he must come back to Ruatha Hold," said Lytol, steadying himself with a firm grip on the table edge. "When the dragon dies, the boy must be where obligations and responsibilities give him a hold on life. I know!"

To that Raid could give no answer, but he glowered in disapproval. Lessa held her breath and began to 'lean' a little on the old Lord Holder.

"I know how to help the boy," Lytol went on, sinking slowly back into his chair. "I know what is best for him. I know what it is to lose a dragon. The difference in this case is that we *know* Ruth's days are numbered."

"Days are numbered," echoed the Harper and put his head down on the table suddenly. Lytol bent toward the man, curiously, almost paternally. He drew back, startled when the Harper began to snore gently.

"Hey, don't go to sleep. We haven't finished this bottle." When Robinton made no response, Lytol shrugged and drained his own cup. Then he seemed to collapse slowly until his head was on the table, too, his snores filling the pause between Robinton's.

Raid regarded the pair with sour disgust. Then he turned on his heel and walked back to this end of the head table.

"I don't know but what there isn't truth in the wine," Larad of Telgar Hold commented as Raid reseated himself.

Lessa 'leaned' quickly against Larad. He was nowhere near as insensitive as Raid. When he shook his head, she desisted and turned her attentions to Sifer. If she could get two of them to agree . . .

"Dragon and his rider both belong in the Weyr," Raid said. "You don't change what's natural for man and beast."

"Well now, take these fire lizards," Sifer began, nodding toward the two across the table from him, in the arms of the Lord and Lady of Lemos Hold. "They're dragons of a sort, after all."

Raid snorted. "We saw today what happens when you go against natural courses. That girl—whatever her name is— lost her queen. Well, even the fire lizard warned her off

Impressing a new one. The creatures know more than we think they do. Look at all the years people've tried to catch 'em . . ."

"Catch 'em now, in nestsful," Sifer interrupted him. "Pretty things they are. Must say I look forward to mine hatching."

Somehow their quarreling reminded Lessa of old R'gul and S'lel, her first "teachers" in the Weyr, contradicting themselves endlessly as they purportedly taught her "all she'd need to know to become a Weyrwoman." It was F'lar who had done that.

"Boy has to stay here with that dragon."

"The boy in question is a Lord Holder, Raid," Larad of Telgar reminded him. "And the one thing we don't need is a contested Hold. It might be different if Lytol had male issue, or if he'd fostered long enough to have a promising candidate. No, Jaxom must remain Lord at Ruatha Hold," and the Telgar Lord scanned the Bowl in search of the boy. His eyes met Lessa's and he smiled in absent courtesy.

"I don't agree, I don't agree," Raid said, shaking his head emphatically. "It goes against all custom."

"Some customs need changing badly," said Larad, frowning.

"I wonder what the boy wants to do," interjected Asgenar in his bland way, catching Larad's eye.

The Telgar Lord threw back his head with a hearty laugh. "Don't complicate matters, brother. We've just decided his fate, will-he, won't-he."

"The boy should be asked," Asgenar said, no longer mild-spoken. His glance slid from Larad to the two older Lord Holders. "I saw his face when he came out of the Hatching Ground. He realized what he'd done. He was as white as the little dragon." Then Asgenar nodded in Lytol's direction. "Yes, Jaxom's all too aware of what he's done."

Raid harumphed irritably. "You don't *ask* youngsters anything. You tell 'em!"

Asgenar turned to his lady, touching her shoulder lightly, but there was no mistaking the warmth of his expression as he asked her to request young Jaxom's presence. Mindful of her sleepy green lizard, she rose and went on her errand.

"I've discovered recently that you find out a great deal by asking people," Asgenar said, looking after his wife with an odd smile on his face.

"People, yes, but not children!" Raid managed to get a lot of anger into that phrase.

Lessa "leaned" against him. He'd be more susceptible in this state of mind.

"Why doesn't he just pick the beast up?" the Benden Lord Holder demanded irritably as he watched the stately progress of the Lady of Lemos Hold, the young Lord of Ruatha and the newly hatched white dragon, Ruth.

"I'd say he was establishing the proper relationship," Asgenar remarked. "It would be easier and faster to carry the little beast, but not wiser. Even a dragon that small has dignity."

Raid of Benden Hold grunted, whether in acknowledgment or disagreement Lessa couldn't tell. He began to fidget, rub the back of his head with one hand, so she stopped her "pushing."

The whir of dragon wings back-beating to land caught her attention. She turned and saw the gleam of a bronze hide in the darkness by the new entrance to the Rooms.

Lioth brings the Masterfarmer, Ramoth told her rider.

Lessa couldn't imagine why Andemon would be required, nor why N'ton would be bringing him. The Masterfarmerhall had its own beast now. She started to rise.

"D'you realize the trouble you've caused, young man?" Raid was asking in a stiff voice.

Lessa swung round, torn between two curiosities. It wasn't as if Jaxom were without champions in Asgenar and Larad. But she did wonder how the boy would answer Raid.

Jaxom stood straight, his chin up, his eyes bright. Ruth's head was pressed to his thigh as if the dragonet were aware that they stood on trial.

"Yes, my good Lord Raid, I am fully aware of the consequences of my actions and there may now be a grave problem facing the other Lord Holders." Without a hint of apology or contrition, Jaxom obliquely reminded Raid that, for all his lack of years, he was a Lord Holder, too.

Old Raid sat straighter, pulling his shoulders back, as if . . . Lessa stepped past her chair.

"Don't . . ."

The whisper was so soft that at first Lessa thought she was mistaken. Then she saw the Harper looking at her, his eyes as keen as if he were cold sober. And he, the dissembler, probably was, for all that act he'd pulled earlier.

"Fully aware, are you?" Raid echoed, and suddenly launched himself to his feet. The old Lord Holder had lost inches as he gained Turns, his shoulders now rounding slightly, his belly no longer flat and his legs stringy in the tight hide of his trousers. He looked a caricature confronting the slim proud boy. "D'you know you've got to stay at Benden Weyr now you've Impressed a dragon? D'you realize that Ruatha's lordless?"

"With all due respect, sir, you and the other Lords present do not constitute a Conclave since you are not two-thirds of the resident Holders of Pern," replied Jaxom. "If necessary, I should be glad to come before a duly constituted Conclave and plead my case. It's obvious, I think, that Ruth is not a proper dragon. I am given to understand that his chances of maturing are slight. Therefore he is of no use to the Weyr which has no space for the useless. Even old dragons no longer able to chew firestone are retired to Southern Weyr—or were." His slight slip disconcerted Jaxom only until he saw Asgenar's approving grin. "It's wiser to consider Ruth more of an overgrown fire lizard than an undersized dragon." Jaxom smiled with loving apology down at Ruth and caressed the upturned head. It was an action so adult, so beautiful that Lessa felt her throat tightening. "My first obligation is to my Blood, to the Hold which cared for me. Ruth and I would be an embarrassment here in Benden Weyr. We can help Ruatha Hold just as the other fire lizards do."

"Well said, young Lord of Ruatha, well said," cried Asgenar of Lemos, and his applause started his lizard shrieking.

Larad of Telgar Hold nodded solemnly in accord.

"Humph. Shade too flip an answer for me," Raid grumbled. "All you youngsters act before you think these days."

"I'm certainly guilty of that, Lord Raid," Jaxom said candidly. "But I had to act fast today—to save the life of a dragon. We're taught to honor dragonkind, I more than most." Jaxom gestured toward Lytol. His hand remained poised and a look of profound sorrow came over his face.

Whether Jaxom's voice had roused him or the position of his head was too uncomfortable was debatable, but the Lord

Warder of Ruatha Hold was no longer asleep. He rose, gripping the table, then pushing himself away from its support. With slow steps, as if he were forced to concentrate on each movement, Lytol walked the length of the table until he reached his ward. Lytol placed an arm lightly across Jaxom's shoulders. As though he drew strength from that contact, he straightened and turned to Raid of Benden Hold. His expression was proud and his manner more haughty than Lord Groghe at his worst.

"Lord Jaxom of Ruatha Hold is not to blame for today's events. As his guardian, I am responsible—if it *is* an offense to save a life. If I chose to stress reverence for dragonkind in his education, I had good reason!"

Lord Raid looked uneasily away from Lytol's direct gaze.

"*If,*" and Lytol stressed the word as though he felt the possibility was remote, "the Lords decide to act in Conclave, I shall strongly urge that no man fault Lord Jaxom's conduct today. He acted in honor and at the promptings of his training. He best serves Pern, however, by returning to his Hold. At Ruatha, young Ruth will be cared for and honored —for as long as he is with us."

There was no doubt that Larad and Asgenar were of Lytol's mind. Old Sifer sat pulling at his lip, unwilling to look toward Raid.

"I still think dragonfolk belong in Weyrs!" Raid muttered, glum and resentful.

That problem apparently settled, Lessa turned to leave and nearly fell into F'nor's arms.

He steadied her. "A weyr is where a dragon is," he said in a low voice rippling with amusement. The strain of the past week still showed in his face but his eyes were clear and his lips no longer thin with tension. Brekke's resolution was evidently all in his favor.

"She's asleep," he said. "I told you she wouldn't Impress."

Lessa made an impatient gesture. "At least the experience snapped her out of that shock."

"Yes," and there was a wealth of relief in the man's soft affirmative.

"So, you'd better come with me to the Rooms. I want to find out why Masterfarmer Andemon has just flown in. And it's about time you got back to work!"

F'nor chuckled. "It is, if someone else has been doing *my*

work. Did anyone bring F'lar his Threads?" There was a note
in his voice that told Lessa he was concerned.

"N'ton did!"

"I thought he was riding Wing-second to P'zar at Fort
Weyr!"

"As you remarked the other morning, whenever you're
not here to keep him under control, F'lar rearranges matters."
She saw his stricken look and caught his arm, smiling up at
him reassuringly; he wasn't up to teasing yet. "No one could
take your place with F'lar—or me. Canth and Brekke needed
you more for a while." She gave his hand a squeeze. "But
that doesn't mean things haven't been happening and you'd
better catch up. N'ton's been included in our affairs because
F'lar had a sudden glimpse of his mortality when he was
sick and decided to stop being secretive. Or it might be
another four hundred Turns or so before we control Thread."
She gathered her skirt so she could move more rapidly
over the sandy floor.

"Can I come, too?" asked the Harper.

"You? Sober enough to walk that far?"

Robinton chuckled, smoothing his rumpled hair back into
place at his neck. "Lytol couldn't drink me drunk, my dear
Lady Lessa. Only the Smith has the—ah—capacity."

There was no doubt that he was steady on his feet as the
three walked toward the glow-marked entrance to the Rooms.
The stars were brilliant in the soft black spring sky, and the
glows on the lower levels threw bright circles of light on the
sands. Above, on weyr ledges, dragons watched with gleaming
opalescent eyes, occasionally humming with pleasure. High up,
Lessa saw three dragon silhouettes by the Star Stones: Ramoth and Mnementh were perched to the right of the watch-
dragon, their wings overlapping. They were both smug tonight; she'd heard Ramoth's tenor often that evening. It
was such a relief to have her in an agreeable mood for a
while. Lessa rather hoped there'd be a long interval before
the queen felt the urge to mate again.

When they entered the Rooms, the spare figure of the
Masterfarmer was bending over the largest of the tubs, turning the leaves of the fellis sapling. F'lar watched him with a
wary expression while N'ton was grinning, unable to observe the solemnity of the moment.

As soon as F'lar caught sight of F'nor, he smiled broadly

and quickly crossed the room to clasp his half-brother's arm.

"Manora said Brekke had snapped out of shock. It's twice a relief, believe me. I'd have been happier still if she'd brought herself to re-Impress . . ."

"That would have served no purpose," F'nor said, so flatly contradictory that F'lar's grin faded a little.

He recovered and drew F'nor to the tubs.

"N'ton was able to get Thread and we infected three of the big tubs," F'lar told him, speaking in a low undertone as if he didn't wish to disturb the Masterfarmer's investigations. "The grubs devoured every filament. And where the Thread pierced the leaves of that fellis tree, the char marks are already healing. I'm hoping Master Andemon can tell us how or why."

Andemon straightened his body but his lantern jaw remained sunk to his chest as he frowned at the tub. He blinked rapidly and pursed his thin lips, his heavy, thick-knuckled hands twitching slightly in the folds of a dirt-stained tunic. He had come as he was when the Weyr messenger summoned him from the fields.

"I don't know how or why, Good Weyrleader. And if what you have told me is the truth," he paused, finally raising his eyes to F'lar, "I am scared."

"Why, man?" And F'lar spoke on the end of a surprised laugh. "Don't you realize what this means? If the grubs can adapt to northern soil and climate, and perform as we—all of us here," his gesture took in the Harper and his Wingsecond as well as Lessa, "have seen them, Pern does not need to fear Thread ever again."

Andemon took a deep breath, throwing his shoulders back, but whether resisting the revolutionary concept or preparing to espouse it was not apparent. He looked toward the Harper as if he could trust this man's opinion above the others.

"You saw the Thread devoured by these grubs?"

The Harper nodded.

"And that was five days ago?"

The Harper confirmed this.

A shudder rippled the cloth of the Masterfarmer's tunic. He looked down at the tubs with the reluctance of fear. Stepping forward resolutely, he peered again at the young fellis tree. Inhaling and holding that deep breath, he poised one gnarled hand for a moment before plunging it into the dirt. His eyes were closed. He brought up a moist handful of earth and, opening his eyes, turned the glob over, exposing a cluster of wriggling grubs. His eyes widened and, with an exclamation of disgust, he flung the dirt from him as if he'd been burned. The grubs writhed impotently against the stone floor.

"What's the matter? There can't be Thread!"

"Those are parasites!" Andemon replied, glaring at F'lar, badly disillusioned and angry. "We've been trying to rid the southern parts of this peninsula of these larvae for centuries." He grimaced with distaste as he watched F'lar carefully pick up the grubs and deposit them back into the nearest tub. "They're as pernicious and indestructible as Igen sandworms and not half as useful. Why, let them get into a field and every plant begins to droop and die."

"There's not an unhealthy plant here," F'lar protested, gesturing at the burgeoning growths all around.

Andemon stared at him. F'lar moved, grabbing a handful of soil from each tub as he circled, showing the grubs as proof.

"It's impossible," Andemon insisted, the shadow of his earlier fear returning.

"Don't you recall, F'lar," Lessa said, "when we first brought the grubs here, the plants did seem to droop?"

"They recovered. All they needed was water!"

"They couldn't." Andemon forgot his revulsion enough to dig into another tub as if to prove to himself that F'lar was wrong. "There're no grubs in this one!" he said in triumph.

"That's never had any. I used it to check the others. And I must say, the plants don't look as green or healthy as the other tubs."

Andemon stared around. "Those grubs are pests. We've been trying to rid ourselves of them for hundreds of Turns."

"Then I suspect, good Master Andemon," F'lar said with a gentle, rueful smile, "that farmers have been working against Pern's best interests."

The Masterfarmer exploded into indignant denials of that charge. It took all Robinton's diplomacy to calm him down long enough for F'lar to explain.

"And you mean to tell me that those larvae, those grubs, were developed and spread on purpose?" Andemon demanded of the Harper who was the only one in the room he seemed inclined to trust now. "They were meant to spread, bred by the same ancestors who bred the dragons?"

"That's what we believe," Robinton said. "Oh, I can appreciate your incredulity. I had to sleep on the notion for several nights. However, if we check the Records, we find that, while there is no mention that *dragonmen* will attack the Red Star and clear it of Thread, there is the strong, recurring belief that Thread will one day not be the menace it is now. F'lar is reasonably . . . "

"Not reasonably, Robinton; completely sure," F'lar interrupted. "N'ton's been going back to Southern—jumping *between* time, as far back as seven Turns, to check on Threadfalls in the southern continent. Wherever he's probed, there're grubs in the soil which rise when Thread falls and devour it. That's why there have never been any burrows in Southern. The land itself is inimical to Thread."

In the silence, Andemon stared at the tips of his muddy boots.

"In the Farmercrafthall Records, they mention specifically that we are to watch for these grubs." He lifted troubled eyes to the others. "We always have. It was our plain duty. Plants wither wherever grub appears." He shrugged in helpless confusion. "We've always rooted them out, destroyed the larval sacks with—" and he sighed, "flame and angenothree. That's the only way to stop the infestations.

"Watch for the grubs, the Records say," Andemon repeated and then suddenly his shoulders began to shake, his whole torso became involved. Lessa caught F'lar's eyes, concerned for the man. But he was laughing, if only at the cruel irony. "Watch for the grubs, the Records say. They do not, they do not say *destroy* the grubs. They say most emphatically 'watch for the grubs.' So we watched. Aye, we have watched."

The Harper extended the wine bottle to Andemon.

"That's a help, Harper. My thanks," Andemon said, wiping his lips with the back of one hand after a long pull at the bottle.

"So someone forgot to mention why you were to watch the grubs, Andemon," F'lar said, his eyes compassionate for the man's distress. "If only Sograny'd been as reasonable. Once, so many men must have known why you were to watch for the grubs, they didn't see a need for further implicit instructions. Then the Holds started to grow and people drifted apart. Records got lost or destroyed, men died before they'd passed on the vital knowledge they possessed." He looked around at the tubs. "Maybe they developed those grubs right here in Benden Weyr. Maybe that's the meaning of the diagram on the wall. There's so much that has been lost."

"Which will never be lost again if the Harpercraft has any influence," said Robinton. "If *all* men, Hold, Craft, Weyr have full access to every skin—" he held up his hand as Andemon started to protest, "well, we've better than skin to keep Records on. Bendarek now has a reliable, tough sheet of his wood pulp that holds ink, stacks neatly and is impervious to anything except fire. We can combine knowledge and disseminate it."

Andemon looked at the Harper, his eyes puzzled. "Master Robinton, there are some matters within a Craft that must remain secret or . . ."

"Or we lose a world to the Thread, is that it, Andemon? Man, if the truth about those grubs hadn't been treated like a Craft secret, we'd have been hundreds of Turns free of Thread by now."

Andemon gasped suddenly, staring at F'lar. "And dragonmen—we wouldn't need dragonmen?"

"Well, if men kept to their Holds during Threadfall, and grubs devoured what fell to the ground, no, you wouldn't need dragonmen," F'lar replied with complete composure.

"But dragonmen are su-supposed to fight Thread—" the Farmer was stuttering with dismay.

"Oh, we'll be fighting Thread for a while yet, I assure you. We're not in any immediate danger of unemployment. There's a lot to be done. For instance, how long before an entire continent can be seeded with grubs?"

Andemon opened and closed his mouth futilely. Robinton indicated the bottle in his hand, pantomimed a long swig. Dazedly the Farmer complied. "I don't know. I just don't know. Why, for Turn upon Turn, we've watched for those grubs—exterminating them, razing an entire field if it got infected. Spring's when the larval sacks break and we'd be . . ."

He sat down suddenly, shaking his head from side to side.

"Get a grip on yourself, man," F'lar said, but it was his attitude which caused Andemon the most distress.

"What—what will dragonmen do?"

"Get rid of Thread, of course. Get rid of Thread."

Had F'lar been a feather less confident, F'nor would have had trouble maintaining his composure. But his half-brother *must* have some plan in mind. And Lessa looked as serene as —as Manora could.

Fortunately Andemon was not only an intelligent man, he was tenacious. He had been confronted with a series of disclosures that both confused and disturbed basic precepts. He must reverse a long-standing Craft practice. He must rid himself of an inborn, carefully instilled prejudice, and he must accept the eventual abdication of an authority which he had good reason to respect and more reason to wish to perpetuate.

He was determined to resolve these matters before he left the Weyr. He questioned F'lar, F'nor, the Harper, N'ton and Manora when he learned she'd been involved in the project. Andemon examined all the tubs, particularly the one which had been left alone. He conquered his revulsion and even examined the grubs carefully, patiently uncoiling a large specimen as if it were a new species entirely. In a certain respect, it was.

Andemon was very thoughtful as he watched the unharmed larva burrow quickly back into the tub dirt from which he'd extracted it.

"One wishes fervently," he said, "to find a release from our long domination by Thread. It is just—just that the agency which frees us is . . ."

"Revolting?" the Harper suggested obligingly.

Andemon regarded Robinton a moment. "Aye, you're the man with words, Master Robinton. It is rather leveling to think that one will have to be grateful to such a—such a lowly creature. I'd rather be grateful to dragons." He gave F'lar a rather abashed grin.

"You're not a Lord Holder!" said Lessa, wryly, drawing a chuckle from everyone.

"And yet," Andemon went on, letting a handful of soil dribble from his fist, "we have taken the bounties of this rich earth too much for granted. We are from it, part of it, sustained by it. I suppose it is only mete that we are protected by it. If all goes well."

He brushed his hand off on the wher-hide trousers and with an air of decision turned to F'lar. "I'd like to run a few experiments of my own, Weyrleader. We've tubs and all at the Farmercrafthall . . ."

"By all means," F'lar grinned with relief. "We'll cooperate in every way. Grubs, Threads on request. But you've solved the one big problem I'd foreseen."

Andemon raised his eyebrows in polite query.

"Whether or not the grubs were adaptable to northern conditions."

"They are, Weyrleader, they are." The Farmer was grimly sardonic.

"I shouldn't think that would be the major problem, F'lar," F'nor said.

"Oh?" The quiet syllable was almost a challenge to the brown rider. F'nor hesitated, wondering if F'lar had lost confidence in him, despite what Lessa had said earlier.

"I've been watching Master Andemon, and I remember my own reaction to the grubs. It's one thing to say, to know, that these are the answer to Thread. Another—quite another to get the average man to accept it. And the average dragonrider."

Andemon nodded agreement and, judging by the expression on the Harper's face, F'nor knew he was not the only one who anticipated resistance.

But F'lar began to grin as he settled himself on the edge of the nearest tub.

"That's why I brought Andemon here and explained the project. We need help which only he can give us, once he himself is sure of matters. How long, Masterfarmer, does it take grubs to infest a field?"

Andemon dropped his chin to his chest in thought. He shook his head and admitted he couldn't estimate. Once a field showed signs of infestation, the area was seared to prevent spreading.

"So, we must find out how long first!"

"You'll have to wait for next spring," the Farmer reminded him.

"Why? We can import grubs from Southern."

"And put them where?" the Harper asked, sardonically.

F'lar chuckled. "Lemos Hold."

"Lemos!"

"Where else?" and F'lar looked smug. "The forests are the hardest areas to protect. Asgenar and Bendarek are determined to preserve them. Asgenar and Bendarek are both flexible enough to accept such an innovation and carry it through. You, Masterfarmer, have the hardest task. To convince your crafters to leave off killing . . ."

Andemon raised a hand. "I have my own observations to make first."

"By all means, Master Andemon," and F'lar's grin broadened, "I'm confident of the outcome. I remind you of your first journey to the Southern Weyr. You commented on the luxuriant growths, the unusual size of the trees and bushes common to both continents, the spectacular crops, the sweetness of the fruits. That is not due to the temperate weather. We have similar zones here in the north. It is due," and F'lar pointed his finger first at Andemon and then toward the tubs, "to the stimulation, the protection of the grubs."

Andemon was not totally convinced but F'lar did not press the point.

"Now, Master Andemon, the Harper will assist you all he can. You know your people better than we—you'll know whom you can tell. I urge you to discuss it with your trusted Masters. The more the better. We can't lose this opportunity for lack of disciples. We might be forced to wait until your Oldtimers die off." F'lar laughed wryly. "I guess the Weyrs are not the only ones to contend with Oldtimers; we've all got re-education to do."

"Yes, there will be problems." The magnitude of the undertaking had suddenly burst on the Masterfarmer.

"Many," F'lar assured him blithely. "But the end result is freedom from Thread."

"It could take Turns and Turns," Andemon said, catching F'lar's glance and, as if that consoled him somehow, straightened his shoulders. He was committed to the project.

"And well may take Turns. First," and F'lar grinned with pure mischief in his eyes, "we've got to stop you farmers from exterminating our saviors."

An expression of pure shock and indignation passed across Andemon's weather-lined face. It was swiftly replaced by a tentative smile as the man realized that F'lar was ribbing him. Evidently an unusal experience for the Masterfarmer.

"Think of all the rewriting I have to do," complained the Harper. "I'm dry just considering it." He looked mournfully at the now empty wine bottle.

"This certainly calls for a drink," Lessa remarked with a sidelong glance at Robinton. She took Andemon's arm to guide him out.

"I'm honored, my lady, but I've work to oversee, and the investigations I ought to conduct." He pulled away from her.

"Surely one drink?" Lessa pleaded, smiling in her most winning way.

The Masterfarmer ran his hand through his hair, clearly reluctant to refuse.

"One drink then."

"To seal the bargain of Pern's fate," said the Harper, dropping his voice to a sepulchral bass and looking solemnly portentous and amazingly like Lord Groghe of Fort.

As they all trooped out of the Rooms, Andemon looked down at Lessa.

"If it isn't presumptuous of me, the young woman, Brekke, who lost her queen—how is she?"

Lessa hesitated only a second. "F'nor here can answer you better than I. They're Weyrmates."

F'nor was forced to step up. "She's been ill. Losing one's dragon is a tremendous shock. She has made the adjustment. She won't suicide now."

The Masterfarmer halted, staring at F'nor. "That would be unthinkable."

Lessa caught F'nor's eye and he remembered he was talking to a commoner.

"Yes, of course, but the loss is unsettling."

"Certainly. Ah, does she have any position at all now?" The words came slowly from the Farmer, then he added in a rush, "she is from my Crafthall you see, and we . . ."

"She is well loved and respected by all Weyrs," Lessa broke in when Andemon faltered. "Brekke is one of those rare people who can hear any dragon. She will always enjoy a unique and high position with dragonfolk. She may, if she chooses, return to her home . . ."

"No!" The Masterfarmer was definite about that.

"Brekke is weyrfolk now," F'nor said on the heels of that denial.

Lessa was a little surprised at such vehemence from both men. She'd had the notion from Andemon's attitude that perhaps her Craft wanted her back.

"My apologies for being so brusque, my lady. It would be hard for her to live simply again." His voice turned hard and lost all hesitancy. "What of that adulterous transgressor?"

"She—lives," and there was an uncompromising echo of the Farmer's coldness in Lessa's voice.

"She lives?" The Masterfarmer stopped again, dropping Lessa's arm and staring at her with anger. "She lives? Her throat should be cut, her body . . ."

"She lives, Masterfarmer, with no more mind or wit than a babe. She exists in the prison of her guilt! Dragonfolk take no lives!"

The Farmer stared hard at Lessa for a moment longer, then nodded slowly. With great courtesy he offered Lessa his arm when she indicated they should continue.

F'nor did not follow for the events of the day were taking a revenge of fatigue on him.

He watched as Andemon and Lessa joined the others at the main table, saw the Lemos and Telgar Lords come over. Lytol and young Jaxom with his white Ruth were nowhere to be seen. F'nor hoped Lytol had taken Jaxom back to Ruatha. He was more grateful to his discovery of fire lizards than at any other single time since Grall had first winked at him. He walked quickly toward the steep flight to his weyr, wanting to be with his own. Canth was in his weyr, all but one lid closed over his eyes. When F'nor entered, the final lids sagged shut. F'nor leaned his body against the dragon's neck, his hands seeking the pulsespots in the soft throat, warm and steadying. He could "hear" the soft loving thoughts of the two lizards curled by Brekke's head.

How long he stood there he couldn't gauge, his mind rehearsing the Impression, Brekke's release, Jaxom's performance, the dinner, everything that had jammed into one eventful afternoon.

There was much to be done, certainly, but he felt unable to move from the presence of Canth.

Most vividly he recalled Andemon's shock when the man

realized that F'lar had proposed the end of dragonmen. Yet —F'lar hadn't. He certainly had some alternate in mind.

Those grubs—yes, they devoured Thread before it could burrow and proliferate. But they were repulsive to look at and commanded neither respect nor gratitude. They weren't obvious, or awesome, like dragons. People wouldn't *see* grubs devouring Thread. They wouldn't have the satisfaction of watching dragons flame, sear, char, destroy Thread mid-air, *before* the vicious stuff got to earth. Surely F'lar realized this, knew that men must have the visible proof of Thread's defeat. Would dragonmen become tokens? No! That would make dragonfolk more parasitic than Thread. Such an expedient would be repugnant, insupportable to a man of F'lar's integrity. But what had he in mind?

The grubs might be the ultimate answer but not—particularly after thousands of Turns of conditioning—not an answer acceptable to Pernese, Holder, Crafter, commoner *and* dragonman.

CHAPTER XVI

Evening at Benden Weyr
Later Evening at Fort Weyr

For the next few days, F'nor was too busy to worry. Brekke was recovering her strength and insisted that he return to his duties. She prevailed on Manora to permit her to come down to the Lower Caverns and be of some use. So Manora put her to tying off the woof ends of some finished wall hangings where Brekke could also be part of the busy Cavern activities. The fire lizards rarely left her side. Grall twittered with conflicting wishes when F'nor went off on errands, so he would order her to stay with Brekke.

F'lar estimated correctly that Asgenar and Bendarek would accept any solution that might preserve the forests. But the incredulity and initial resistance he encountered showed him what a monumental task he had undertaken. Both Lord Holder and Craftmaster were frankly contemptuous of his claims until N'ton came in with a panful of live Thread—it could be heard hissing and steaming—and dumped it over a tub of verdant growths. Within a matter of moments, the tangle of Thread which they had seen poured over the fellis saplings had been completely consumed by grubs. Dazed, they even accepted F'lar's assertion that the pierced and smoking leaves would heal in a matter of days.

There were many things about grubs that the dragonmen did not know, as F'lar was careful to explain. How long it would take them to proliferate so that a given area could be considered "Threadproof"; the length of the grub life cycle, what density of grub life would be necessary to ensure the chain of protection.

But they did decide where to start in Lemos Hold: among the precious softwoods so in demand for furniture, so vulnerable to Thread incursion.

Since the former residents of the Southern Weyr had not been farmcraft trained, they had been oblivious to the significance of the larval sacks in the southern woods. It was fall now in the southern hemisphere but F'nor, N'ton and another rider had agreed to jump *between* to the previous spring. Brekke helped, too, knowing as she did so many facets of the Southern management that she was able to tell them where they would not collide with others in the past. Though farmcraftbred, Brekke had been occupied with nursing during her tenure at Southern, and had deliberately stayed away from the farming aspects of the Weyr to sever connections with her past life.

Although F'lar did not press Masterfarmer Andemon, he proceeded with his plans as if he had Farmcraft cooperation. Several times, Andemon requested Thread and grubs which would be rushed to him, but he issued no progress reports.

Mastersmith Fandarel and Terry had been informed of the project and a special demonstration arranged for them. Once he'd conquered the initial revulsion over the grubs and horror at being so close to live Thread, Terry had been as enthusiastic as anyone could wish. The performance of the grubs elicited only a deep grunt from the Mastersmith. He had limited his comments to a scornful criticism of the long-handled hearthpan in which the Thread was captured.

"Inefficient. Inefficient. You can only open it once to catch the things," and he had taken the pan, stalking off toward his waiting dragon-messenger.

Terry had been profuse in his assurances that the Mastersmith was undoubtedly impressed and would cooperate in every way. This was indeed a momentous day. His words were cut off by Fandarel's impatient bellow and he'd bowed his way out, still reassuring the somewhat disconcerted dragonriders.

"I'd've thought Fandarel would at least have found the grubs efficient," F'lar had remarked.

"He was struck dumb with amazement?" F'nor suggested.

"No," and Lessa grimaced, "he was infuriated by inefficiency!"

They'd laughed and gone on to the next job. That evening a messenger arrived from the Smithcrafthall with the purloined hearthpan and a truly remarkable contrivance. It was bulbous in shape, secured to a long handle from the end of which its lid could be opened, operated by a trigger inside the tubular handle. The lid was the truly ingenious part for it fanned open upward and outward so that Thread would be guided down into the vessel and could not escape if the lid was reopened.

The messenger also confided to F'lar that the Mastersmith was having difficulties with his distance-writer. All wire must be covered with a protective tubing or Thread cut right through the thinly extruded metal. The Smith had experimented with ceramic and metal casings but he could turn neither out in great or quick enough quantity. With Threadfall coming so frequently now, his halls were besieged with demands to fix flame throwers which clogged or burned out. Ground crews panicked when equipment failed them mid-Fall and it was impossible not to accede to every urgent request for repair. The Lord Holders, promised the distance-writers, as links between help and isolated Holds, began to press for solutions. And for the ultimate—to them—solution: the proposed expedition to the Red Star.

F'lar had begun to call a council of his intimate advisors and Wing-seconds daily so that no facet of the over-all plan could be lost. They also decided which Lords and Mastercraftsmen could accept the radical knowledge, but had moved cautiously.

Asgenar told them that Larad of Telgar Hold was far more conservative in his thinking than they'd supposed and that the limited demonstration in the Rooms would not be as powerful a persuader as a protected field under full attack by Thread.

Unfortunately, Asgenar's young bride, Famira, on a visit to her home, inadvertently made a reference to the project. She'd had the good sense to send her lizard for her Lord who had bodily forced his blood relative to Benden Weyr for a full explanation and demonstration. Larad had been unconvinced and furious with what he called "a cruel deception and treacherous breach of faith" by dragonmen. When Asgenar then insisted Larad come to the softwood tract that was being protected and had live Thread poured over a sapling, uprooting the young tree to prove that it had been adequately protected, the Telgar Lord Holder's rage began to subside.

Telgar's broad valleys had been hard hit by the almost constant Threadfalls. Telgar's ground crews were disheartened by the prospect of ceaseless vigilance.

"Time is what we haven't got," Larad of Telgar had cried when he heard that grub protection would be a long-term project. "We lose fields of grain and root every other day. The men are already weary of fighting Thread interminably, they've little energy for anything. At best we've only the prospect of a lean winter, and I fear for the worst if these past months are any indication."

"Yes, it's hard to see help so close—and as far away as the life cycle of an insect no larger than the tip of your finger," said Robinton, an integral part of any such confrontation. He was stroking the little bronze fire lizard which he had Impressed a few days earlier.

"Or the length of that distance-viewer," Larad said, his lips tight, his face lined with worry. "Has nothing been done about going to the Red Star?"

"Yes," F'lar replied, holding firmly to an attitude of patient reasonableness. "It's been viewed every clear night. Wansor has trained a wing of watchers and borrowed the most accurate draftsmen from Masterweaver Zurg and the Harper. They've made endless sketches of the masses on the planet. We know its faces now . . ."

"And . . ." Larad was adamant.

"We can see no feature distinct enough to guide the dragons."

The Lord of Telgar sighed with resignation.

"We do believe," and F'lar caught N'ton's eyes since the young bronze rider did as much of the investigating as Wansor, "that these frequent Falls will taper off in a few more months."

"Taper off? How can you tell that?" Hope conflicted with suspicion in the Telgar Lord's face.

"Wansor is of the opinion that the other planets in our sky have been affecting the Red Star's motion; slowing it, pulling it from several directions. We have near neighbors, you see; one is now slightly below the middle of our planet, two above and beyond the Red Star, a rare conjunction. Once the planets move away, Wansor believes the old routine of Threadfall will be established."

"In a few months? But that won't do us any good. And can you be sure?"

"No, we can't be sure—which is why we have not announced Wansor's theory. But we'll be certain in a few more weeks." F'lar held up his hand to interrupt Larad's protests. "You've surely noticed the brightest stars, which are our sister planets, move from west to east during the year. Look tonight, you'll see the blue one slightly above the green one, and very brilliant. And the Red Star below them. Now, remember the diagram in the Fort Weyr Council Room? We're positive that that is the diagram of skies around our sun. And you've watched your fosterlings play stringball. You've played it yourself. Substitute the planets for the balls, the sun for the swinger, and you get the general idea. Some balls swing more rapidly than others, depending on the speed of the swing, the length and tension of the cord. Basically, the principle of the stars around the sun is the same."

Robinton had been sketching on a leaf and passed the diagram over to Larad.

"I must see this in the skies for myself," the Telgar Lord replied, not giving an inch.

"It's a sight, I assure you," Asgenar said. "I've become fascinated with the study and *if*," he grinned, his thin face suddenly all creases and teeth, "Wansor ever has time to duplicate that distance-viewer, I want one on Lemos' fire height. We're at a good altitude to see the northern heavens. I'd like to see those showering stars we get every summer through a distance-viewer!"

Larad snorted at the notion.

"No, it's fascinating," Asgenar protested, his eyes dancing with enthusiasm. Then he added in a different tone, "Nor am

I the only one beguiled by such studies. Every time I go to Fort I'm contending with Meron of Nabol for a chance to use the viewer."

"Nabol?"

Asgenar was a little surprised at the impact of his casual remark.

"Yes, Nabol's forever at the viewer. Apparently *he's* more determined than any dragonrider to find coordinates." No one else shared his amusement.

F'lar looked inquiringly at N'ton.

"Yes, he's there all right. If he weren't a Lord Holder—" and N'ton shrugged.

"Why? Does he say why?"

N'ton shrugged again. "He says he's looking for coordinates. But so are we. There aren't any features distinct enough. Just shapeless masses of gray and dark gray-greens. They don't change and while it's obvious they're stable, are they land? Or sea?" N'ton began to feel the accusatory tension in the room and shifted his feet. "So often the face is obscured by those heavy clouds. Discouraging."

"Is Meron discouraged?" asked F'lar pointedly.

"I'm not sure I like your attitude, Benden," Larad said, his expression hard. "You don't appear eager to discover any coordinates."

F'lar looked Larad full in the eyes. "I thought we'd explained the problem involved. We have to *know* where we're going before we can send the dragons." He pointed to the green lizard perched on Larad's shoulder. "You've been trying to train your fire lizard. You can appreciate the difficulty." Larad stiffened defensively and his lizard hissed, its eyes rolling. F'lar was not put off. "The fact that no Records exist of any previous attempt to go there strongly indicates that the ancients—who built the distance-viewer, who knew enough to plot the neighbors in our sky—did not go. They must have had a reason, a valid reason. What would you have me do, Larad?" F'lar demanded, pacing in his agitation. "Ask for volunteers? You, you and you," F'lar whirled, jabbing a finger at an imaginary line of riders, "you go, jump *between* to the Red Star. Coordinates? Sorry, men, I have none. Tell your dragons to take a long look halfway there. If you don't come back, we'll keen to the Red Star for your deaths.

But men, you'll die knowing you've solved our problem. Men can't go to the Red Star."

Larad flushed under F'lar's sarcasm.

"If the ancients didn't record any intimate knowledge of the Red Star," said Robintin quietly into the charged silence, "they did provide domestic solutions. The dragons, and the grubs."

"Neither proves to be effective protection right now, when we *need* it," Larad replied in a bitter, discouraged voice. "Pern needs something more conclusive than promises—and insects!" He abruptly left the Rooms.

Asgenar, a protest on his lips, started to follow but F'lar stopped him.

"He's in no mood to be reasonable, Asgenar," F'lar said, his face strained with anxiety. "If he won't be reassured by today's demonstrations, I don't know what more we can do or say."

"It's the loss of the summer crops which bothers him," Asgenar said. "Telgar Hold has been spreading out, you know. Larad's attracted many of the small Holders who've been dissatisfied in Nerat, Crom and Nabol and switched their allegiances. If the crops fail, he's going to have more hungry people—and more trouble—than he can handle in the winter."

"But what more can we do?" demanded F'lar, a desperate note in his voice. He tired so easily. The fever had left him little reserve strength, a state he found more frustrating than any other problem. Larad's obduracy had been an unexpected disappointment. They'd been so lucky with every other man approached.

"*I* know you can't send men on a blind jump to the Red Star," Asgenar said, distressed by F'lar's anxiety. "I've tried to tell my Rial where I want him to go. He gets frantic at times because he can't see it clearly enough. Just wait until Larad starts sending his lizard about. He'll understand. You see, what bothers him most is the realization that you *can't* plan an attack on the Red Star."

"Your initial mistake, my dear F'lar," and the Harper's voice was at its drollest, "was in providing salvation from the last imminent disaster in a scant three days by bringing up the Five Lost Weyrs. The Lord Holders really expect you to provide a second miracle in similar short order."

The remark was so preposterous that F'nor laughed out loud before he could stop himself. But the tension and anxiety dissolved and the worried men regained some needed perspective.

"Time is all we need," F'lar insisted.

"Time is what we don't have," Asgenar said wearily.

"Then let's use what time we have to the best possible advantage," F'lar said decisively, his moment of doubt and disillusion behind him. "Let's work on Telgar. F'nor, how many riders can T'bor spare us to hunt larval sacks *between* time at Southern? You and N'ton can work out coordinates with them."

"Won't that weaken Southern's protection?" asked Robinton.

"No, because N'ton keeps his eyes open. He noticed that a lot of sacks started in the fall get blown down or devoured during the winter months. So we've altered our methods. We check an area in spring to place the sacks that survive, go back to the fall and take some of those which didn't last. There were a few wherries who missed a meal but I don't think we disturbed the balance much."

F'lar began to pace, one hand absently scratching his ribs where the scar tissues itched.

"I need someone to keep an eye on Nabol, too."

Robinton let out a snort of amusement. "We do seem beholden to the oddest agencies. Grub life. Meron. Oh yes," and he chuckled at their irritation. "He may yet prove to be an asset. Let him strain his eyes and crick his neck nightly watching the Red Star. As long as he is occupied that way, we'll know we have time. The eyes of a vengeful man miss few details he can turn to advantage."

"Good point, Robinton. N'ton," and F'lar turned to the young bronze rider. "I want to know every remark that man makes, which aspects of the Red Star he views, what he could possibly see, what his reactions are. We've ignored that man too often to our regret. We might even be grateful to him."

"I'd rather be grateful to grubs," N'ton replied with some fervor. "Frankly, sir," he added, hesitant for the first time about any assignment since he'd been included in the council, "I'd rather hunt grubs or catch Thread."

F'lar eyed the young rider thoughtfully for a moment.

"Think of this assignment then, N'ton, as the ultimate Thread catch."

Brekke had insisted on taking over the care of the plants in the Rooms once she was stronger. She argued that she was farmcraftbred and capable of such duties. She preferred not to be present during the demonstrations. In fact she went out of her way to avoid seeing anyone but weyrfolk. She could abide their sympathy but the pity of outsiders was repugnant to her.

This did not affect her curiosity and she would get F'nor to tell her every detail of what she termed the best-known Craft secret on Pern. When F'nor narrated the Telgar Lord's bitter repudiation of what the Weyrs were trying to accomplish, she was visibly disturbed.

"Larad's wrong," she said in the slow deliberate way she'd adopted lately. "The grubs are the solution, the right one. But it's true that the best solution is not always easy to accept. And an expedition to the Red Star is *not* a solution, even if it's the one Pernese instinctively crave. It's obvious. Just as two thousand dragons over Telgar Hold was rather obvious seven Turns ago." She surprised F'nor with a little smile, the first since Wirenth's death. "I myself, like Robinton, would prefer to rely on grubs. They present fewer problems. But then I'm craftbred."

"You use that phrase a lot lately," F'nor remarked, turning her face toward him, searching her green eyes. They were serious, as always, and clear in the candid gaze was the shadow of a sorrow that would never lift.

She locked her fingers in his and smiled gently, a smile which did not disperse the sorrow. "I *was* craftbred," she corrected herself. "I'm weyrfolk now." Berd crooned approvingly and Grall added a trill of her own.

"We could lose a few Holds this Turn around," F'nor said bitterly.

"That would solve nothing," she said. "I'm relieved that F'lar is going to watch that Nabolese. He has a warped mind."

Suddenly she gasped, gripping F'nor's fingers so tight that her fingernails broke the skin.

"What's the matter?" He put both arms around her protectively.

"He *has* a warped mind," Brekke said, staring at him with frightened eyes. "And he also has a fire lizard, a bronze, as old as Grall and Berd. Does anyone *know* if he's been training it? Training it to go *between?*"

"All the Lords have been shown how—" F'nor broke off as he realized the trend of her thought. Berd and Grall reacted to Brekke's fright with nervous squeals and fanning wings. "No, no, Brekke. He can't," F'nor reassured her. "Asgenar has one a week or so younger and he was saying how difficult he found it to send his Rial about in his own Hold."

"But Meron's had his longer. It could be further along . . ."

"Nabol?" F'nor was skeptical. "That man has no conception of how to handle a fire lizard."

"Then why is he so fascinated with the Red Star? What else could he have in mind but to send his bronze lizard there?"

"But he knows that dragonmen won't attempt to send dragons. How can he imagine that a fire lizard could go?"

"He doesn't *trust* dragonmen," Brekke pointed out, obviously obsesssed with the idea. "Why should he trust that statement? You've got to tell F'lar!"

He agreed to because it was the only way to reassure her. She was still so pathetically thin. Her eyelids looked transparent though there was soft flush of color in her lips and cheeks.

"Promise you'll tell F'lar."

"I'll tell him. I'll tell him, but not in the middle of the night."

With a wing of riders to direct *between* time for larval sacks the next day, his promise slipped F'nor's mind until late that evening. Rather than distress her with his forgetfulness, he asked Canth to bespeak N'ton's Lioth to pass the theory on to N'ton. If the Fort Weyr bronze rider saw anything that gave Brekke's premise substance, then they'd tell F'lar.

He had a chance to speak to N'ton the following day as they met in the isolated valley field which Larad of Telgar Hold had picked to be seeded by grubs. The field, F'nor noticed with some jaundice, was planted with a new hybrid vegetable, much in demand as a table luxury and grown successfully only in some upland areas of Telgar and the High Reaches Hold.

"Brekke may have something, F'nor," N'ton admitted. "The watchriders have mentioned that Nabol will stare for a long time into the distance-viewer and then suddenly stare into his fire lizard's eyes until the creature becomes frantic and tries to rise. In fact, last night the poor thing went *between* screaming. Nabol stalked off in a bad mood, cursing all dragonkind."

"Did you check what he'd been looking at?"

N'ton shrugged. "Wasn't too clear last night. Lots of clouds. Only thing visible was that one gray tail—the place that resembles Nerat but points east instead of west. It was visible only briefly."

F'nor remembered that feature well. A mass of grayness formed like a thick dragon tail, pointing in the opposite direction from the planet's rotation.

"Sometimes," N'ton chuckled, "the clouds above the star are clearer than anything we can see below. The other night, for instance, there was a cloud drift that looked like a girl," N'ton made passes with his hands to describe a head, and a few to one side of the air-drawn circle, "braiding her hair. I could see her head, tilted to the left, the half-finished braid and then the stream of free hair. Fascinating."

F'nor did not dismiss that conversation entirely for he'd noticed the variety of recognizable patterns in the clouds around the Red Star and often had been more absorbed in that show than in what he was supposed to be watching for.

N'ton's report of the fire lizard's behavior was very interesting. The little creatures were not as dependent on their handlers as dragons. They were quite apt to disappear *between* when bored or asked to do something they didn't feel like doing. They reappeared after an interlude, usually near dinnertime, evidently assuming people forgot quickly. Grall and Berd had apparently matured beyond such behavior. Certainly they had a nice sense of responsibility toward Brekke. One was always near her. F'nor was willing to wager that Grall and Berd were the most reliable pair of fire lizards on Pern.

Nevertheless, Meron would be watched closely. It was just possible that he could dominate his fire lizard. His mind, as Brekke said, was warped.

As F'nor entered the passageway to his weyr that evening, he heard a spirited conversation going on although he couldn't distinguish the words.

Lessa is worried, Canth told him, shaking his wings flat against his back as he followed his rider.

"When you've lived with a man for seven Turns, you *know* what's on his mind," Lessa was saying urgently as F'nor entered. She turned, an almost guilty expression on her face, replaced by relief when she recognized F'nor.

He looked past her to Brekke whose expression was suspiciously blank. She didn't summon even a welcoming smile for him.

"Know what's on whose mind, Lessa?" F'nor asked, unbelting his riding tunic. He tossed his gloves to the table and accepted the wine which Brekke poured him.

Lessa sank awkwardly into the chair beside her, her eyes darting everywhere but toward him.

"Lessa is afraid that F'lar may attempt to go to the Red Star himself," Brekke said, watching him.

F'nor considered that as he drank his wine. "F'lar's not a fool, my dear girls. A dragon has to know where he's going. And we don't know what to tell them. Mnementh's no fool either." But as F'nor passed his cup to Brekke to be refilled, he had a sudden flash of N'ton's hair-braiding cloud lady.

"He can't go," Lessa said, her voice harsh. "He's what holds Pern together. He's the only one who can consolidate the Lord Holders, the Craftmasters and the dragonriders. Even the Oldtimers trust him now. Him. No one else!"

Lessa was unusually upset, F'nor realized. Grall and Berd came gliding in to perch on the posts of Brekke's chair, chirping softly and preening their wings.

Lessa ignored their antics, leaning across the table, one hand on F'nor's to hold his attention. "I heard what the Harper said about miracles. Salvation in three days!" Her eyes were bitter.

"Going to the Red Star is salvation for no one, Lessa!"

"Yes, but we don't *know* that for certain. We've only assumed that *we* can't because the ancients didn't. And until we prove to the Lords what the actual conditions there are, they will not accept the alternative!"

"More trouble from Larad?" F'nor asked sympathetically,

rubbing the back of his neck. His muscles felt unaccountably tight.

"Larad is bad enough," she said bitterly, "but I'd rather him than Raid and Sifer. They've somehow got hold of rumors and they're demanding instant action."

"Show 'em the grubs!"

Lessa abruptly released F'nor's hand, pursing her lips with exasperation. "If grubs didn't reassure Larad of Telgar, they'll have less effect on those old blow-hards! No, *they*," and in emphasizing the pronoun she underscored her contempt for the old Lord Holders, "are of the opinion that Meron of Nabol *has* found coordinates after nights of watching and is maliciously withholding them from the rest of Pern."

F'nor grinned and shook his head. "N'ton is watching Meron of Nabol. The man has found nothing. He couldn't do anything without our knowledge. And he certainly isn't having any luck with his fire lizard."

Lessa blinked, looking at him without comprehension.

"With his fire lizard?"

"Brekke thinks Meron might attempt to send his fire lizard to the Red Star."

As if a string in her back had been pulled, Lessa jerked up in her chair, her eyes huge and black as she stared first at him, then at Brekke.

"Yes, that would be like him. He wouldn't mind sacrificing his fire lizard for that, would he? And it's as old as yours." Her hand flew to her mouth. "If he . . ."

F'nor laughed with an assurance he suddenly didn't honestly feel. Lessa had reacted far too positively to a notion he privately considered unlikely. Of course, she didn't have a fire lizard and might not appreciate their limitations. "He may be trying," he felt obliged to say. "N'ton's been watching him. But he's not succeeding. I don't think Meron can. He doesn't have the temperament to handle fire lizards. You simply can't order them about the way you do drudges."

Lessa clenched her fists in an excess of frustration.

"There's got to be something we can do. I tell you, F'nor, I *know* what F'lar has on his mind. I know he's trying to find some way to get to the Red Star if only to prove to the Lord Holders that there is no other alternative but the grubs!"

"He may be willing to risk his neck, my dear Lessa, but is Mnementh willing?"

Lessa flashed F'nor a look of pure dislike. "And put the notion in the poor beast's head that this is what F'lar wants? I could throttle Robinton. Him and his three-day salvation! F'lar can't stop thinking about that. But F'lar is not the one to go" and she broke off, biting her lip, her eyes sliding toward Brekke.

"I understand, Lessa," Brekke said very slowly, her eyes unwinking as she held Lessa's. "Yes, I understand you."

F'nor began to massage his right shoulder. He must have been *between* too much lately.

"Never mind," Lessa said suddenly, with unusual force. "I'm just overwrought with all this uncertainty. Forget what I said. I'm only imagining things. I'm as tired as—as we all are."

"You're right there, Lessa," F'nor agreed. "We're all seeing problems which don't exist. After all, no Lord Holder has come to Benden Weyr and thrown down any ultimatum. What could they do? F'lar certainly has been forthright, explained the project of grub protection so often I'll be ill if I have to listen to it once more. Certainly he's been open with the other Weyrleaders, the Craftmasters, being sure that everyone knows exactly what the over-all plan is. Nothing will go wrong this time. This is one Craft secret that won't get lost because someone can't read a Record skin!"

Lessa rose, her body taut. She licked her lips. "I think," she said in a low voice, "that's what scares me most. He's taking such precautions to be sure everyone knows. Just in case . . ."

She broke off and rushed out of the Weyr.

F'nor stared after her. That interpretation of F'lar's overtness began to assume frightening significance. Disturbed, he turned to Brekke, surprised to see tears in the girl's eyes. He took her in his arms.

"Look, I'll get some rest, we'll eat, and then I'll go to Fort Weyr. See Meron myself. Better still," and he hugged her reassuringly, "I'll bring Grall along. She's the oldest we've got. I'll see if *she'd* take the trip. If any of the fire lizards would go, she'd be the one. There now! How's that for a good idea?"

She clung to him, kissing him so urgently that he forgot

Lessa's disturbing idea, forgot he was hungry and tired, and responded with eager surprise to her ardent demands.

Grall hadn't wanted to leave Berd where the bronze fire lizard was cuddled on the cushion by Brekke's head. But then, F'nor didn't much want to leave Brekke. She'd reminded him, after they'd loved each other deeply, that they had obligations. If Lessa had been worried enough about F'lar to confide in Brekke and F'nor, she was more deeply concerned than she'd admit. Brekke and F'nor must assume such responsibility as they could.

Brekke was a great one for assuming responsibility, F'nor thought with affectionate tolerance as he roused Canth. Well, it wouldn't take long to check on Meron. Or to see if Grall would consider going to the Red Star. That certainly was a better alternative than F'lar making the trip. *If* the little queen lizard would consider it.

Canth was in high good humor as they wheeled first above Benden Weyr, then burst out of *between* above Fort Weyr's Star Stones. There were glows along the crown of the Weyr rim and, beyond the Star Stones, the silhouettes of several dragons.

Canth and F'nor of Benden Weyr, the brown dragon announced in answer to the watchrider's query. *Lioth is here and the green dragon who must stay at Nabol,* Canth added as he backwinged to a light landing. Grall swooped above F'nor's head, waiting until Canth had taken off to join the other beasts before she took her shoulder perch.

N'ton stepped out of the shadows, his welcoming grin distorted by the path glows. He jerked his head back, toward the distance-viewer.

"He's here and his lizard's in a fine state. Glad you came. I was about to ask Lioth to bespeak Canth."

The bronze Nabol lizard began to screech with a distress which Grall echoed nervously. Her wings extended. F'nor stroked them down to her back, emitting the human version of a lizard croon which usually calmed her. She tightened her wings but started to hop from one foot to the other, her eyes whirling restlessly.

"Who's that?" demanded Meron of Nabol peremptorily. Meron's shadow detached itself from the larger one of the rock on which the distance-viewer was mounted.

"F'nor, Wing-second of Benden Weyr," the brown rider answered coldly.

"You've no business in Fort Weyr," Meron said, his tone rasping. "Get out of here!"

"Lord Meron," N'ton said, stepping in front of F'nor. "F'nor of Benden has as much right in Fort Weyr as you."

"How dare you speak to a Lord Holder in that fashion?"

"Can he have found something?" F'nor asked N'ton in a low voice.

N'ton shrugged and moved toward the Nabolese. The little lizard began to shriek. Grall extended her wings again. Her thoughts were a combination of dislike and annoyance, tinged with fear.

"Lord Nabol, you have had the use of the distance-viewer since full dark."

"I'll have the use of the distance-viewer as long as I choose, dragonman. Go away. Leave me!"

Far too accustomed to instant compliance with his orders, Nabol turned back to the viewer. F'nor's eyes were used to the darkness by now and he could see the Lord Holder bend to place his eye to the viewer. He also saw that the man held tight to his fire lizard though the creature was twisting and writhing to escape. Its agitated screeching rose to a nerve-twitting pitch.

The little one is terrified, Canth told his rider.

"Grall terrified?" F'nor asked the brown dragon, startled. He could see that Grall was upset but he didn't read terror in her thoughts.

Not Grall. The little brother. He is terrified. The man is cruel.

F'nor had never heard such condemnation from his dragon.

Suddenly Canth let out an incredible bellow. It startled the riders, the other two dragons, and put Grall into flight. Before half the dragons of Fort Weyr roused to bugle a query, Canth's tactic had achieved the effect he'd wanted. Meron had lost his hold on the fire lizard and it had sprung free and gone *between.*

With a cry of rage for such interference, Meron sprang toward the dragonriders, to find his way blocked by the menacing obstacle of Canth's head.

"Your assigned rider will take you back to your Hold,

Lord Meron," N'ton informed the Lord Holder. "Do not return to Fort Weyr."

"You've no right! You can't deny me access to that distance-viewer. You're not the Weyrleader. I'll call a Conclave. I'll tell them what you're doing. You'll be forced to act. You can't fool me! You can't deceive Nabol with your evasions and temporizing. Cowards! You're cowards, the pack of you! Always knew it. Anyone can get to the Red Star. Anyone! I'll call your bluff, you neutered perverts!"

The green dragon, her eyes redly malevolent, dipped her shoulder to Meron. Without a break in his ranting denunciation, the Lord of Nabol climbed the riding straps and took his place on her neck. She had not cleared the Star Stones before F'nor was at the distance-viewer, peering at the Red Star.

What could Meron have seen? Or was he merely bellowing baseless accusations to unsettle them?

As often as he had seen the Red Star with its boiling cover of reddish-gray clouds, F'nor still experienced a primitive stab of fear. Tonight the fear was like an extra-cold spine from his balls to his throat. The distance-viewer revealed the westward-pointing tail of the gray mass which resembled a featureless, backward Nerat. The jutting edge of the swirling clouds obscured it. Clouds that swirled to form a pattern—no lady braiding her hair tonight. Rather, a massive fist, thumb of darker gray curling slowly, menacingly over the clenched fingers as if the clouds themselves were grabbing the tip of the gray mass. The fist closed and lost its definition, resembling now a single facet of a dragon's complex eye, half-lidded for sleep.

"What could he have seen?" N'ton demanded urgently, tapping F'nor's shoulder to get his attention.

"Clouds," F'nor said, stepping back to let N'ton in. "Like a fist. Which turned into a dragon's eye. Clouds, that's all he could have seen, over backward Nerat!"

N'ton looked up from the eyepiece, sighing with relief.

"Cloud formations won't get us anywhere!"

F'nor held his hand up for Grall. She came down obediently and when she started to hop to his shoulder, he forestalled her, gently stroking her head, smoothing her wings flat. He held her level with his eyes and, without stopping the gentle caresses, began to project the image of that fist, lazily forming over Nerat. He outlined color, grayish-red, and whitish where the top of the imagined fingers might be sun-struck. He visualized the fingers closing above the Neratian peninsula. Then he projected the image of Grall taking the long step *between* to the Red Star, into that cloud fist.

Terror, horror, a whirling many-faceted impression of heat, violent wind, burning breathlessness, sent him staggering against N'ton as Grall, with a fearful shriek, launched herself from his hand and disappeared.

"What happened to her?" N'ton demanded, steadying the brown rider.

"I asked her," and F'nor had to take a deep breath because her reaction had been rather shattering, "to go to the Red Star."

"Well, that takes care of Brekke's idea!"

"But why did she overreact that way? Canth?"

She was afraid, Canth replied didactically, although he sounded as surprised as F'nor. *You gave vivid coordinates.*

"I gave vivid coordinates?"

Yes.

"What terrified Grall? You aren't reacting the way she did and you heard the coordinates."

She is young and silly. Canth paused, considering something. *She remembered something that scared her.* The brown dragon sounded puzzled by that memory.

"What does Canth say?" N'ton asked, unable to pick up the quick exchange.

"He doesn't know what frightened her. Something she remembers, he says."

"Remembers? She's only been hatched a few weeks."

"A moment, N'ton." F'nor put his hand on the bronze rider's shoulder to silence him for a thought had suddenly struck him. "Canth," he said taking a deep breath, "You said the coordinates I gave her were vivid. Vivid enough—for *you* to take me to that fist I saw in the clouds?"

Yes, I can see where you want me to go, Canth replied so confidently that F'nor was taken aback. But this wasn't a time to think things out.

He buckled his tunic tightly and jammed the gloves up under the wristbands.

"You going back now?" N'ton asked.

"Fun's over here for the night," F'nor replied with a nonchalance that astonished him. "Want to make sure Grall got back safely to Brekke. Otherwise I'll have to sneak in to Southern to the cove where she hatched."

"Have a care then," N'ton advised. "At least we've solved one problem tonight. Meron can't make than fire lizard of his go to the Red Star ahead of us."

F'nor had mounted Canth. He tightened the fighting straps until they threatened to cut off circulation. He waved to N'ton and the watchrider, suppressing his rising level of excitement until Canth had taken him high above the Weyr. Then he stretched flat along Canth's neck and looped the hand straps double around his wrists. Wouldn't do to fall off during this jump *between*.

Canth beat steadily upward, directly toward the baleful Red Star, high in the dark heavens, almost as if the dragon proposed to fly there straight.

Clouds were formed by water vapors, F'nor knew. At least they were on Pern. But it took air to support clouds. Air of some kind. Air could contain various gases. Over the plains of Igen where the noxious vapors rose from the yellow mountains you could suffocate with the odor and the stuff in your lungs. Different gases issued from the young fire mountains that had risen in the shallow western seas to spout flame and boiling rock into the water. The miners told of other gases, trapped in tunnel hollows. But a dragon was fast. A second or two in the most deadly gas the Red Star possessed couldn't hurt. Canth would jump them *between* to safety.

They had only to get to that fist, close enough for Canth's long eyes to see to the surface, under the cloud cover. One look to settle the matter forever. One look that F'nor—not F'lar—would make.

He began to reconstruct that ethereal fist, its alien fingers closing over the westering tip of grayness on the Red Star's enigmatic surface. "Tell Ramoth. She'll broadcast what we see to everyone, dragon, rider, fire lizard. We'll have to go slightly *between* time, too, to the moment on the Red Star when I saw that fist. Tell Brekke." And he suddenly realized that Brekke already knew, had known when she'd seduced him so unexpectedly. For that was why Lessa had confided in them, in Brekke. He couldn't be angry with Lessa. She'd had the courage to take just such a risk seven Turns ago, when she'd seen a way back through time to bring up the five missing Weyrs.

Fill your lungs, Canth advised him and F'nor felt the dragon sucking air down his throat.

He didn't have time to consider Lessa's tactics because the cold of *between* enveloped them. He felt nothing, not the soft hide of the dragon against his cheek, nor the straps scoring his flesh. Only the cold. Black *between* had never existed so long.

Then they burst out of *between* into a heat that was suffocating. They dropped through the closing tunnel of cloud fingers toward the gray mass which suddenly was as close to them as Nerat's tip on a high-level Thread pass.

Canth started to open his wings and screamed in agony as they were wrenched back. The snapping of his strong forelimbs went unheard in the incredible roar of the furnace-hot tornadic winds that seized them from the relative calm of the downdraft. There was air enveloping the Red Star—a burning hot air, whipped to flame-heat by brutal turbulences. The helpless dragon and rider were like a feather, dropped hundreds of lengths only to be slammed upward, end over end, with hideous force. As they tumbled, their minds paralyzed by the holocaust they had entered, F'nor had a nightmare glimpse of the gray surfaces toward and away from which they were alternately thrown and removed: the Neratian tip was a wet, slick gray that writhed and bubbled and oozed. Then they were thrown into the reddish clouds that were shot with nauseating grays and whites, here and there torn by massive orange rivers of lightning. A thousand hot points burned the unprotected skin of F'nor's face, pitted Canth's hide, penetrating each lid over the dragon's eyes. The overwhelming, multileveled sound of the cyclonic atmosphere battered their minds ruthlessly to unconsciousness.

Then they were hurled into the awesome calm of a funnel of burning, sand-filled heat and fell toward the surface—crippled and impotent.

Painridden, F'nor had only one thought as his senses failed him. The Weyr! The Weyr must be warned!

Grall returned to Brekke, crying piteously, burrowing into Brekke's arm. She was trembling with fear but her thoughts made such chaotic nonsense that Brekke was unable to isolate the cause of her terror.

She stroked and soothed the little queen, tempting her with morsels of meat to no effect. The little lizard refused to be quieted. Then Berd caught Grall's anxiety and when Brekke scolded him, Grall's excitement and anguish intensified.

Suddenly Mirrim's two greens came swooping into the weyr, twittering and fluttering, also affected by the irrational behavior of the little queen. Mirrim came running in then, escorted by her bronze, bugling and fanning his gossamer wings into a blur.

"Whatever is the matter? Are you all right, Brekke?"

"I'm perfectly all right," Brekke assured her, pushing away the hand Mirrim extended to her forehead. "They're just excited, that's all. It's the middle of the night. Go back to bed."

"Just excited?" Mirrim pursed her lips the way Lessa did when she knew someone was evading her. "Where's Canth? Why ever did they leave you alone?"

"Mirrim!" Brekke's tone brought the girl up sharp. She flushed, looking down at her feet, hunching her shoulders in the self-effacing way Brekke deplored. Brekke closed her eyes, fighting to be calm although the distress of the five fire lizards was insidious. "Please get me some strong *klah*."

Brekke rose and began to dress in riding clothes. The five lizards started to keen now, flitting around the room, swooping in wild dives as if they wanted to escape some unseen danger.

"Get me some *klah*," she repeated, because Mirrim stood watching her like a numbwit.

Her trio of fire lizards had followed her out before Brekke realized her error. They'd probably rouse the lower Caverns with their distress. She called but Mirrim didn't hear her. Cold chills made her fingers awkward.

Canth wouldn't go if he felt it would endanger F'nor. Canth has sense, Brekke told herself trying to convince herself. He knows what he can and can't do. Canth is the biggest, fastest, strongest brown dragon on Pern. He's almost as large as Mnementh and nearly as smart.

Brekke heard Ramoth's brassy bugle of alarm just as she received the incredible message from Canth.

Going to the Red Star? On the coordinates of a cloud? She staggered against the table, her legs trembling. She managed to sit but her hands shook so, she couldn't pour the wine. Using both hands, she got the bottle to her lips and swallowed some that way. It helped.

She'd somehow not believed they'd see a way to go. Was that what had frightened Grall so?

Ramoth kept up her alarm and Brekke now heard the other dragons bellowing with worry.

She fumbled with the last closing of her tunic and forced herself to her feet, to walk to the ledge. The fire lizards kept darting and diving around her, keening wildly; a steady, nerve-jangling double trill of pure terror.

She halted at the top of the stairs, stunned by the confusion in the crepuscular gloom of the Weyr Bowl. There were dragons on ledges, fanning their wings with agitation. Other beasts were circling around at dangerous speeds. Some had riders, most were flying free. Ramoth and Mnementh were on the Stones, their wings outstretched, their tongues flicking angrily, their eyes bright orange as they bugled to their weyr-mates. Riders and weyrfolk were running back and forth, yelling, calling to their beasts, questioning each other for the source of this inexplicable demonstration.

Brekke futilely clapped her hands to her ears, searching the confusion for a sight of Lessa or F'lar. Suddenly they both appeared at the steps and came running up to her. F'lar reached Brekke first, for Lessa hung back, one hand steadying herself against the wall.

"Do you know what Canth and F'nor are doing?" the Weyr-leader cried. "Every beast in the Weyr is shrieking at the top of voice and mind!" He covered his own ears, glaring furiously at her, expecting an answer.

Brekke looked toward Lessa, saw the fear and the guilt in the Weyrwoman's eyes.

"Canth and F'nor are on their way to the Red Star."

F'lar stiffened and his eyes turned as orange as Mnementh's. He stared at her with a compound of fear and loathing that sent Brekke reeling back. As if her movement released him, F'lar looked toward the bronze dragon roaring stentoriously on the heights.

His shoulders jerked back and his hands clenched into fists so tight the bones showed yellow through the skin.

At that instant, every noise ceased in the Weyr as every mind felt the impact of the warning the fire lizards had been trying inchoately to project.

Turbulence, savage, ruthless, destructive; a pressure inexorable and deadly. Churning masses of slick, sickly gray surfaces that heaved and dipped. Heat as massive as a tidal wave. Fear! Terror! An inarticulate longing!

A scream was torn from a single throat, a scream like a knife upon raw nerves!

"Don't leave me alone!" The cry came from chords lacerated by the extreme of anguish; a command, an entreaty that seemed echoed by the black mouths of the weyrs, by dragon minds and human hearts.

Ramoth sprang aloft. Mnementh was instantly beside her. Then every dragon in the Weyr was a-wing, the fire lizards, too; the air groaned with the effort to support the migration.

Brekke could not see. Her eyes were filled with blood from vessels burst by the force of her cry. But she knew there was a speck in the sky, tumbling downward with a speed that increased with every length; a plunge as fatal as the one which Canth had tried to stop over the stony heights of the High Reaches range.

And there was no consciousness in that plummeting speck, no echo, however faint, to her despairing inquiry. The arrow of dragons ascended, great wings pumping. The arrow thickened, once, twice, three times as other dragons arrived, making a broad path in the sky, steadily striving for that falling mote.

It was as if the dragons became a ramp that received the unconscious body of their weyrmate, received and braked its fatal momentum with their own bodies, until the last segment of overlapping wings eased the broken-winged ball of the bloody brown dragon to the floor of the Weyr.

Half-blinded as she was, Brekke was the first person to reach Canth's bleeding body, F'nor still strapped to his burned neck. Her hands found F'nor's throat, her fingers the tendon where his pulse should beat. His flesh was cold and sticky to the touch and ice would be less hard.

"He isn't breathing," someone cried. "His lips are blue!"

"He's alive, he's alive," Brekke chanted. There, one faint shallow flutter against her seeking fingers. No, she didn't imagine it. Another.

"There wasn't any air on the Red Star. The blueness. He suffocated."

Some half-forgotten memory prompted Brekke to wrench F'nor's jaws apart. She covered his mouth with hers and exhaled deeply into his throat. She blew air into his lungs and sucked it out.

"That's right, Brekke," someone cried. "That may work. Slow and steady! Breathe for yourself or you'll pass out."

Someone grabbed her painfully around the waist. She clung to F'nor's limp body until she realized that they were both being lifted from the dragon's neck.

She heard someone talking urgently, encouragingly to Canth.

"Canth! Stay!"

The dragon's pain was like a cruel knot in Brekke's skull. She breathed in and out. Out and in. For F'nor, for herself, for Canth. She was conscious as never before of the simple mechanics of breathing; conscious of the muscles of her abdomen expanding and contracting around a column of air which she forced up and out, in and out.

"Brekke! Brekke!"

Hard hands pulled at her. She clutched the wher-hide tunic beneath her.

"Brekke! He's breathing for himself now. Brekke!"

They forced her away from him. She tried to resist but everything was a bloody blur. She staggered, her hand touching dragon hide.

Brekke. The pain-soaked tone was faint, as if from an incalculable distance, but it was Canth. *Brekke?*

"I am not alone!" And Brekke fainted, mind and body overtaxed by an effort which had saved two lives.

Spun out by ceaseless violence, the spores fell from the turbulent raw atmosphere of the thawing planet toward Pern, pushed and pulled by the gravitic forces of a triple conjunction of the system's other planets.

The spores dropped through the atmospheric envelope of Pern. Attenuated by the friction of entry, they fell in a rain of hot filaments on the surface of the planet.

Dragons rose, destroying them with flaming breath. What Thread eluded the airborne beasts was efficiently seared into harmless motes by ground crews, or burrowed after by sand-worm and fire lizard.

Except on the eastern slope of a northern mountain plantation of hardwood trees. There men had carefully drawn back from the leading Edge of the Fall. They watched, one with intent horror, as the silver rain scorched leaf and fell hissing into the soil. When the leading Edge had passed over the crest of the mountain, the men approached the points of impact cautiously, the nozzles of the flame throwers they carried a half-turn away from spouting flame.

The still smoking hole of the nearest Thread entry was prodded with a metal rod. A brown fire lizard darted from the shoulder of one man and, chirping to himself, waddled over to the hole. He poked an inquisitive half-inch of nose into the ground. Then he rose in a dizzying movement and resumed his perch on the specially padded shoulder of his handler and began to preen himself fastidiously.

His master grinned at the other men.

"No Thread, F'lar. No Thread, Corman!"

The Benden Weyrleader returned Asgenar's smile, hooking his thumbs in his broad riding belt.

"And this is the fourth Fall with no burrows and no protection, Lord Asgenar?"

The Lord of Lemos Hold nodded, his eyes sparkling. "No burrows on the entire slope." He turned in triumph to the one man who seemed dubious and said, "Can you doubt the evidence of your eyes, Lord Groghe?"

The ruddy-faced Lord of Fort Hold shook his head slowly.

"C'mon, man," said the white-haired man with the prominent, hooked nose. "What more proof do you need? You've seen the same thing on lower Keroon, you've seen it in Telgar Valley. Even that idiot Vincet of Nerat Hold has capitulated."

Groghe of Fort Hold shrugged, indicating a low opinion of Vincet, Lord Holder of Nerat.

"I just can't put any trust in a handful of squirming insects. Relying on dragons makes sense."

"But you've seen grubs devour Thread!" F'lar persisted. His patience with the man was wearing thin.

"It isn't right for a *man*," and Groghe drew himself up, "to be grateful to grubs!"

"I don't recall your being overgrateful to dragonkind either," Asgenar reminded him with pointed malice.

"I don't trust grubs!" Groghe repeated, jutting his chin out at a belligerent angle. The golden fire lizard on his shoulder crooned softly and rubbed her down-soft head against his cheek. The man's expression softened slightly. Then he recalled himself and glared at F'lar. "Spent my whole life trusting dragonkind. I'm too old to change. But you're running the planet now. Do as you will. You will anyhow!"

He stalked away, toward the waiting brown dragon who was Fort Hold's resident messenger. Groghe's fire lizard extended her golden wings, crooning as she balanced herself against his jolting strides.

Lord Corman of Keroon fingered his large nose and blew it out briskly. He had a disconcerting habit of unblocking his ears that way. "Old fool. He'll use grubs. He'll use them. Just can't get used to the idea that it's no good wanting to go to the Red Star and blasting Thread on its home ground. Groghe's a fighter. Doesn't sit well with him to barricade his Hold, as it were, and wait out the siege. He likes to charge into things, straighten them out *his* way."

"The Weyrs appreciate your help, Lord Corman," F'lar began.

Corman snorted, blew out his ears again before waving aside F'lar's gratitude. "Common sense. Protect the ground. Our ancestors were a lot smarter than we are."

"I don't know about that," Asgenar said, grinning.

"I do, young fellow," Corman retorted decisively. Then added hesitantly, "How's F'nor? And what's his name—Canth."

The days when F'lar evaded a direct answer were now past. He smiled reassuringly. "He's on his feet. Not much the worse for wear," although F'nor would never lose the scars on the cheek where particles had been forced into the bone. "Canth's wings are healing, though new membrane grows slowly. He looked like raw meat when they got back, you know. There wasn't a hand-span on his body, except where F'nor had lain, that hadn't been scoured bare. He has the entire Weyr hopping to when he itches and wants to be oiled. That's a lot of dragon to oil." F'lar chuckled as much to reassure Corman who looked uncomfortable hearing a list of Canth's injuries as in recollection of the sight of Canth dominating a Weyr's personnel.

"Then the beast will fly again."

"We believe so. And he'll fight Thread, too. With more reason than any of us."

Corman regarded F'lar levelly. "I can see it's going to take Turns and Turns to grub the continent thoroughly. This forest," and he gestured to the plantation of hardwood saplings, "my corner on Keroon plains, the one valley in Telgar, used all the grubs it's safe to take from Southern this Turn. I'll be dead, long since, before the job is finished. However, when the day comes that all land is protected, what do you dragonmen plan to do?"

F'lar looked steadily back at the Keroon Holder, then grinned at Asgenar who waited expectantly. The Weyrleader began to laugh softly.

"Craft secret," he said, watching Asgenar's face fold into disappointment. "Cheer up, man," he advised, giving the Lord of Lemos an affectionate clout on the shoulder. "Think about it. You ought to know by now what dragons do best."

Mnementh was settling carefully in the small clearing in response to his summons. F'lar closed his tunic, preparatory to flying.

"Dragons go places better than anything else on Pern, good Lord Holders. Faster, farther. We've all the southern continent to explore when this Pass is over and men have time to relax again. And there're other plancts in our skies to visit."

Shock and horror were mirrored in the faces of the two Lord Holders. Both had had lizards when F'nor and Canth had taken their jump *between* the planets; they'd known intimately what had happened.

"They can't all be as inhospitable as the Red Star," F'lar said.

"Dragons belong on Pern!" Corman said and honked his big nose for emphasis.

"Indeed they do, Lord Corman. Be assured that there'll always be dragons in the Weyrs of Pern. It is, after all, their home." F'lar raised his arm in greeting and farewell and bronze Mnementh lifted him skyward.